Hearts of Fire

Hearts of Fire

Julia Parker

PIATKUS

Copyright © 1995 by Julia Parker

First published in Great Britain in 1995 by
Judy Piatkus (Publishers) Ltd of
5 Windmill Street, London W1

**The moral right of the author
has been asserted**

*A catalogue record for this book is available
from the British Library*

ISBN 0–7499–0306–6

Set in 11/12 pt Times by Datix International
Printed and bound in Great Britain by
Biddles Ltd, Guildford & King's Lynn

To
Jacqueline Korn
with love and thanks

1892

Chapter One

'Emma? Em!'

Mrs Cooper took the dish of pig's trotters from the range where they'd been poaching.

'Come on, girl! Come *on*!' Having cut two thick slices of bread and spread them generously with dripping, she shouted again, under her breath accusing her daughter of daydreaming.

Emma, who was pulling up a few young weeds from the tiny plot in the front of their terraced cottage, didn't hear her mother's initial call, but made her way to the back kitchen as soon as she realised she was wanted.

''Ere you are at last. Take this down to Pa. It's nearly twelve already, and you know how angry he'll get if it's late.'

She tied the food into a piece of cloth along with a slice of cheese and a pickled onion, and handed it to Emma.

'And call in on Mrs Tyrrell to see if she wants any ironing done. Bring it back if she's got it. We can do it this afternoon.'

Her mother's abruptness and good organisation contrasted vividly with Emma's mood. Silently the girl took the dinner, left the cottage and made her way down to her father's boot-repairing shop in 52 Blythe Road, Hammersmith.

The shop seemed dark in spite of its large plate-glass window. Behind the counter facing the window worked Will Cooper, expertly tearing off old soles, replacing them with new leather or rubber, and strengthening many boys' and girls' and working men's boots with a multitude of hobnails. Everything was black. The tools were black and greasy, and the walls covered with peeling dark-brown paint. The shop smelled heavily of sweaty feet, boot polish, mastic, rubber and just a hint of new fresh leather. Today it was hot, so the sweat smell prevailed. When it was wet, the atmosphere was even thicker and danker.

Emma was a tall, slim girl, considered skinny by many, but she was very strong. She walked well and took a great pride in her appearance, which was always neat and clean, and as smart as it possibly could be when she had little or no money of her own to spend on clothes. She made most of them for herself, or altered garments she purchased for a penny or two at the church jumble sales.

She had a clear complexion and sensitive skin. She took care of her hands because she had once been told that they were a good shape. She hated to see her mother's rough and sore in winter from scrubbing and other household chores, so she treated her own with simple remedies – lemon and cucumber when she could get hold of them, and simple cold cream when she could afford to buy a tiny pot from the Blythe Road pharmacist.

She'd done this particular job since leaving school just after her fourteenth birthday, when the family had first come into the neighbourhood. Now it was summer, and she'd be eighteen on New Year's Day.

'Thanks, Em. Busy today. Put it over there.'

Silently Dmma did as she was bid, and managed half a smile at her thin, active father. From his attitude, she assumed he was in a good mood today – he usually was if trade was brisk.

Having been brought up in the Old Kent Road, where he had learned his trade from his father, Will Cooper was a hard, ambitious man. The fact that he had been able to move to west London some two and a half years ago was a considerable achievement, of which he was justifiably proud. He wanted to be respected, to be looked up to; but his harsh background had scarred his personality, and because he had a very volatile temper, the lives of his immediate family were far too often intolerable. But because neither he nor his long-suffering wife Susan wanted more children, he suffered sexual frustration, and in any case, even married intercourse left

4

him with feelings of guilt. This made him violent in anger, all his frustrations channelled into energetic sadism. To Will everything had to appear to be 'right and proper'. But where this mattered most, within the family, it seldom was.

'And how's my lovely sister this fair dinnertime?'

The nasal tones came from the back of the shop where George, Emma's elder brother, was sorting nails. He looked up from his hunched position and smiled sneakily as he spoke.

'None the better for your asking,' she pertly replied. 'Bye, Pa.'

'Thanks, girl!'

Glad to get out into the fresh air, she straightened the white apron which protected her gingham ankle-length skirt and ran her fingers through her Alice-length, fine, fair hair. She was relieved that her father hadn't been grumpy, and that George had been busy.

Now she could call in at the laundry.

Number 50, smaller than 52, had a totally contrasting atmosphere. Here everything was white: white walls and a scrubbed wooden floor, coppers from which huge jets and clouds of white steam rose, sinks piled with bubbles, washboards, and bars of white Sunlight soap. Here there was a clean antiseptic smell which very successfully disguised the body odours rising from the piles of dirty sheets and pillowcases, shirts and men's long underpants piled against the back wall of the laundry.

The boss, Mrs Tyrrell, a kind woman who would not in modesty have been able to cover herself with even the biggest bath sheet, gave Emma her usual beaming smile.

''Ello, love! Ma want some work? Katy! Kaaaateee!'

'Ma says she could do it this afternoon. I'll help too, of course.'

Katy appeared, unwrapping a block of Rickett's Blue for a final cold rinse.

'Get Mr Hughes's lot and Mr Cohen's, and – oh yes, then there's Mrs Piggot's. Mrs Cooper and Emma can do them for us. You help Em carry 'em, and you can go for your dinner after you've 'elped her.'

Katy was Emma's best friend. They'd become very close

5

over the last two and a half years, since Emma's family had moved from the Old Kent Road to 'better themselves', as her father had put it. And he had been right – they had bettered themselves.

Carrying the heavy, deep, square basket between them, the two girls left the laundry to make their way back to the Coopers' home. They were in no hurry.

Katy was a happy-go-lucky girl who had had fewer opportunities than Emma. Her guardian, Mrs Tyrrell – known as Aunty T – had looked after her since she was four years old, when her real parents had died in a cholera epidemic. She had unruly, dark, curly hair, the ends of which would insist on springing out between each twist of her long plait, so that it never looked sleek or tidy. She was prone to chubbiness, considered desirable in the 1890s, but she would, as she got older, become rotund. She loved her Aunty T dearly, and Aunty T loved her as if she were her own child (her husband had been lost at sea years ago). She always encouraged Katy and was proud of her and the fact that she always seemed so contented, which was more than could said of her best friend Emma, who, for all her good education, always looked very worried these days – not natural in a young gal, thought Aunty T.

'How's things, then?' asked Katy.

'Oh, Katy, it's horrible! Don't know what to do. I can't go on much longer, I really can't.'

'If I were you I'd leave 'ome. Go to one of them agencies and get a job. You'd do fine – soon be a parlour maid. After all, you speak proper – far better than me!'

It was true, Emma did 'speak proper'. The church school which she had attended had been strict, and she'd received a good education for one of her class.

'Pa won't hear of it. He says I must stay with Ma and help her, and deliver his dinner. Thinks about that a lot. Doesn't want his daughter in service – that hurts his sense of pride. Keeping me home to help out is important to him, even when trade's slack. I love Ma dearly, though she gets cross – more so lately. I don't think she's very well. But I want to do things, maybe even go places. A new family moved in next door, last week. There's a son – a chap about twenty. Ma's

6

started dropping hints – he's nice, he's so clean, handsome –
you know the sort of thing.'

Katy had been listening intently. 'Is he all those things?
Could you . . .? Do you?'

'Oh, shut up, Katy! No, I couldn't. I don't want anything
to do with men, and you know why. I can't. Oh, Gawd, it's
awful!'

In her stress, Emma lapsed momentarily into a hint of
cockney.

'Tell your ma – she'll understand. I really think she would,
honest.'

At that Katy gave out a squeal and dropped her handle of
the laundry basket. George had overtaken them, grinning all
over his face.

'Here, you . . . Don't you goose me like that again – I
won't have it! I'll clobber you, see if I won't!' Katy yelled for
all the street to hear.

'Cor, I'd like that. Whoopee!'

And he disappeared into the Havelock Arms for his
midday pint.

'Bloody cheek!' Katy cursed.

'I wish that was all he did – at least he did it to you in
broad daylight. You see, he's always so good to Ma and Pa:
"Yes, Ma, I'll do that . . . Of course, Pa." Treats me like a
lady if they're around – he'll even fetch and carry. Then, as
soon as Pa's snoring and I hear Ma's deep breathing, he's at
it. In he comes. Most nights he stinks of beer, and that's a
good sign. Oh, he's never really drunk, but if he's had a pint
or two he's . . . well, not so . . .'

'Excitable? Active? Big?' Katy, although uninhibited and
worldly, blushed a little at the last adjective.

'Yes, that's about it. I'm really quite thankful for the
Havelock Arms!' Emma gestured to the pub as she spoke.

'Has he actually, you know . . . done it? Got it in, down
there?'

At that, Emma burst into tears.

'Cor, as bad as that, eh?'

'Well, no, not quite – but last night his dirty fingers up my
. . . you know. And it really hurt, a sharp pain. And he tore
my nightdress. I'm strong, you know, and I managed to fight

him off. But he's so clever – he never makes a sound. One night last week I bit him. He didn't cry out, but he left me alone. And last night when ... when ...' She broke off. 'I pushed him right off the bed. Ma and Pa didn't hear – they were sound asleep.'

'If you don't move out soon he's going to spoil you. And then you'll have to face up to the shame of it all, and maybe even find yourself with a bun in the oven.'

'Don't, don't! You're right, I'll have to do something. But it's so difficult. How can I tell Ma? And I know she won't believe me – much less Pa. There'll be the most awful row, and George will deny everything. He's the son, the only son. He's in the business.'

Suddenly Emma stopped speaking. She remembered something else.

'While we were still down in the Old Kent Road, Katy, I remember being put into the back kitchen when there was an awful row going on between Ma, Pa and George and Sarah. And Sarah swept out. I wonder ... Sarah hasn't been home since.'

'You must go and talk to her. Where is she now – what theatre?'

'She's in George Edwardes's new show, *In Town*, at the Prince of Wales. Oh, Katy, she's doing ever so well! I think she'll be famous. But the family don't like me seeing her.'

'You must, you really must.' Katy was a quick thinker. 'Look, today's Thursday. Saturday afternoon we'll go up West and call at the stage door between the matinée and the evening performance. Can you get away?'

'It'll be difficult Saturday – Ma prepares –'

Ignoring Emma, Katy went on, 'We'll take a picnic into Kensington Gardens – your ma'll let you do that. Then we'll get the 'orse bus to Piccadilly and walk from there. Needn't say we're going to see Sarah ...'

They took the big basket of laundry into the kitchen, and ate bread and cheese and drank strong tea with Mrs Cooper, who was already heating up flatirons on the range for the afternoon's work.

Moving to 3 Craven Cottages had been the best, the most exciting thing that had ever happened to Mrs Cooper, who

8

had spent her life until then in the dreary atmosphere of Bermondsey, with its dirt and confined spaces. All her married years she had coped with the heavy round of fighting the dirt, and had done her best – with considerable success – to keep her home and the children, when they came along, clean and smart.

She admired her husband in many ways. He was hard-working and she had never known him get drunk, even if he did on the odd occasion have a pint or two. His associates were the few men in the district who were as ambitious as he, and as keen to move on and better themselves. All ardent church members, they kept their distance from those who drank their meagre earnings, leaving their wives to scrape a few coppers together – or get 'tick' – to feed their children.

The Coopers had worked hard and saved hard, and then the opportunity came for Will to take over a business and to rent the working man's cottage in Hammersmith, whose owner had died.

All their labours had not been in vain. When they first moved to Hammersmith, Mrs Cooper had missed her old friends, but soon discovered the area was quite as friendly as the Old Kent Road; she and the rest of the family had on the whole been welcomed to the district. Some of her neighbours, whose families had lived in the cottages since they had been built some fifty years previously, had been inclined to look down on the Coopers, calling them 'that family from the East End'; but the respect that they gained from their involvement in the local church helped to bring the neighbours round.

Here in Hammersmith the air was cleaner and her house-keeping duties were lighter. The house was neat and pretty. To Mrs Cooper it was a palace, and when rarely her old friends made the journey over from the Old Kent Road for a day's visit, they were very envious.

There was a sizeable front parlour, a dining room – used for Sunday dinner, Christmas and a few very special occasions – a kitchen, and an outside lavatory in a small back yard surrounded by a five-foot-high brick wall giving good privacy. Upstairs was the front bedroom, occupied by Mr and Mrs Cooper, and the two back bedrooms used by Emma and George. The upstairs walls were hung with pretty Victorian wallpaper covered in roses, while downstairs they were painted cream (and beginning to look rather the worse for wear). When they moved in, Mrs Cooper and Emma had made fresh white net curtains, which enhanced the small, neat windows and gave the cottage something of a country appearance.

The front garden was Emma's preserve. She had planted it with bulbs which flowered regularly in the spring, and they had inherited several healthy rose trees and a minute plot of grass that she was able to cut with an ancient pair of shears.

'Lovely up here, isn't it?'

Emma and Katy were walking under huge trees, the strong sunlight breaking the patterns of the leaves into several distinct shades of green. The dry summer grass was short and Katy could not resist falling down on it, stretching out her whole body and relaxing.

'Katy, it's not at all nice to do that. We are young women, and it's most unladylike. Let's sit over there and have our tea.'

Emma pointed to a wood and wrought-iron seat which had a good view of the Round Pond. In the distance they could see the roof of Kensington Palace.

'I don't want to get up – it's 'ot!'

'Maybe not, but your whites will get all marked with grass stains, and Mrs T'll scold you if you take too long over your own washing.'

Uncharacteristically meekly, Katy obeyed her friend.

Kensington Gardens were blissful. They reflected the opulence of the fashionable district of London in which they were set. Well-dressed couples paraded up and down the Broad Walk and nurses wheeled babies in bassinets and or walked slightly larger charges to feed the ducks and sail small boats on the Round Pond. The bandstand was the centre of attraction, with the band of the Grenadier Guards playing selections from *The Gondoliers*.

All this made for a pleasant break from the more mundane lives of the two friends who did not live a great distance away from this rich man's paradise, though they had had a long and hot enough walk to get there.

'You should sing that,' Katy remarked.

'What?'

'What the band's playing – "A Regular Royal Queen".'
Katy attempted to hit the right notes. Always ready with an
idea, she went on, 'You should ask Sarah if she could get
you on the stage, then all your problems would be solved.
You'd marry a rich man and be just like 'er over there.'

"Er over there' was a young woman of about twenty
walking past them with her smartly dressed young man. She
was wearing a beautiful cream tussore silk suit with a tight
bodice and sleeves, high neck and a little train which trailed
on the path. Her tiny hat sported some artificial daisies and a
group of brown feathers.

'She looks lovely. But all that's not for me, though I
would like it to be, I must admit . . . And I'd never ever have
the nerve to go on the stage like Sarah.'

'Just an idea – sorry. Look, let's eat.'

They unpacked their tea of bread and jam and currant
buns made by Mrs Cooper, who had surprised Emma by
being quite pleased to allow her daughter to go out for the
afternoon.

'The sunshine'll do you good – but you behave yourself,
my girl. Don't you let that Katy lead you astray.'

She thought that Katy was just a little too worldly and a
mite common for her Emma; but she was aware that Emma
needed cheering up. She had been noticeably moody in the
past few months. Her mother put that down to growing up,
and had decided that the sooner Emma met a nice young
man and got married, the better; then she'd have far too
much to think about to be moody. Mrs Copper never connected her younger daughter's moodiness to what had driven
her elder daughter Sarah out of the house four years ago.

'Cor, look over there!'

'What is it now?'

'Horton's Italian ice cream from Bayswater.'

'Look, I can afford a penny. I'll get us two ha'penny
cornets.' Katy was already racing over to the man with a cart
attached to a bicycle. A minute or two later and rather
breathless, she was back, her abundant dark curls, which today
she had tied back with a big, pink bow, more unruly than ever.

11

'I got 'im to put a dollop of cream on top for us – just smiled and fluttered me eyelashes a bit and blushed, and he didn't charge me for any of it!'

Soon both young women were lost in their enjoyment of the double luxury. For once they were away from the bustle of home, for once able to enjoy a summer's afternoon. Emma knew that soon she'd be seeing her glamorous sister. But what would she do if her father found out? And Katy was excited at the prospect of going backstage at the theatre and meeting, for the first time, a young woman who was not only talented and beautiful but by all accounts growing increasingly rich. Did she have lovers? Was she – wicked?

'You will tell her everything, won't you? From what you've told me, I bet she went through it with 'im too.'

'Yes, 'course I will, but it won't be easy. Hope she'll understand.'

'She will, and she'll make some suggestions, I bet.'

They finished their ice cream and packed away the remains of their picnic.

'Look, Katy! What's that over there in the grass?' Emma was pointing to something catching the light.

'Drop of water!'

'It hasn't rained for weeks, there's no dew, and we aren't that near to the Round Pond!'

'Dog's pee, then,' suggested her prosaic friend.

'Don't believe it.'

Emma got up and took the few steps over to what had caught her eye.

'Oh, I certainly don't believe it! Definitely not dog's piddle – look!'

'Oh, my Gawd! Em, we're rich! Let's go right back and take it to Uncle's, and get what we can for it.'

The ring had three large diamonds set in gold.

'I've never seen anything like it, ever – 'ave you?'

'No – must be worth a fortune. No wonder it was shining in the sun!'

'Oh, do let's sell it and have half each. Please! Think what we could do – be real toffs, buy clothes –.'

'Shut up, Katy! We must think. No, I'm not going to be dishonest about it, that'll do us no good in the long run. I'm

12

going to show it to Sarah. She'll tell us what to do. I think we should take it to the police station.'

'Oh, no – not the police! What a waste! Whoever owns a thing like that'll be stinking rich. They won't mind losing it one bit.'

Emma knew that Katy had a point. They were poor – not as poor as many an immigrant family down in the East End, but poor by the standards of anyone who could own such a thing.

'No, we can't keep it. I think it's special to the owner. I think it's a betrothal ring – see here, the initials RLA and there's a little heart.'

Emma was examining the inside of the ring.

'Oh, yes. Romantic, that! P'raps she threw it at him – they had a quarrel right here in the middle of Kensington Gardens. Best put it on for safety, and let's get on our way.'

The ring fitted quite comfortably on the third finger of Emma's right hand, but she clenched her fist for fear of it falling off, and decided that if Katy had asked to have a turn at wearing it, she'd say no. After all, it was she who'd found it!

'And what can I do for you two young ladies?'

'Please, sir, we want to see Miss Sarah Cooper. Which is her dressing room?'

'Now, not so fast! How do we know that Miss Sarah wants to see you? Is she expecting you?'

'Er, no . . .' Emma was starting to feel very nervous, but went on, 'I'm her sister, and this is my best friend Katy.'

The stage doorkeeper of the Prince of Wales Theatre had heard that one before. Young aspiring 'actresses' got up to all sorts of dodges to get backstage. He looked at the two girls over his steel-rimmed spectacles and hesitated.

'It's true,' Katy put in. 'She *is* 'er sister. Why don' you ask Sarah? *Go* on, *ask* 'er.'

Emma gave Katy a little kick. She thought that maybe she was being rather too aggressive, which would do no good at all.

'If it would be possible, please, sir – it's important.'

'Hang on, I'll see what I can do.' Then, in a loud voice, 'Jimmy! Come 'ere.'

Jimmy came, and after messages had been delivered and returned, it was, 'Step this way, young ladies. Jimmy'll take you up.'

Backstage had none of the glamour of the front of the house. There were stone steps and floors which looked grey and dingy, though they glittered here and there because of the particular mix of cement and sand; walls were painted in glossy cream paint with a dado of dark green some three feet six above the ground. The air was stuffy and dusty, with a smell of wood, glue and the occasional whiff of perfume, perspiration and greasepaint, topped up by an aroma of Havana cigars.

The girls had quite a long walk with Jimmy, who sped quickly ahead of them, in spite of a severe limp. People were everywhere – women carrying costumes and sewing things, carpenters with nails and hammers – and because it was between houses, minions were bustling to and fro carrying bottles of stout, pots of tea, sandwiches and cakes. It was a noisy place, this backstage. They climbed two flights of stairs.

''Ere you are. Number 16 – Miss Sarah Cooper.' And he was off.

The two friends hesitated at the door.

'Well, go on knock. She's your sister!'

'Come in!'

At once Emma recognised Sarah's voice. She was sitting at her dressing table with her back to them, but saw Emma's reflection in the mirror.

'My God, Emma! I can't believe it! How you've grown! How wonderful!'

She got up, and the sisters, who had not seen each other since a secret meeting some two years ago, hugged each other with warmth and enthusiasm. Despite their separation, there was a sympathetic and loving bond between them. As they embraced, Emma felt the smoothness of Sarah's expensive satin negligée, and when they broke away she noticed it was a delicate shade of pink, and heavily trimmed with frills of matching lace at the end of the three-quarter-length sleeves.

'What a surprise! How are you? How's Ma? And Pa, is he still as bad-tempered? Did you read about the show? It's a

14

great success – you must see it!' Then, with a smile at Katy, 'Introduce me to your friend and tell me how you got here. Something's up, that's for sure.'

They settled down. A bony elderly woman with a grim expression brought in Sarah's light tea.

'Sal, get another pot of tea and go over to the cake shop and get a nice Dundee cake. This is my sister and her friend. They must be hungry.'

The fact that Emma and Katy had had their picnic an hour or so earlier was neither here nor there.

Sal didn't say a word, only glared at the two girls, and left as quickly as she'd arrived.

'She's my dresser – hopeless! Her bony fingers nearly kill me.'

There was so much to take in. Running the whole length of the small room was a large built-in wardrobe rail on which hung ten heavy, lavish costumes. The table was cluttered with sticks of greasepaint, a large bowl of powder, hairpins, brushes, a comb and a tin of Crow's Cremine for the removal of theatrical make-up. A long blonde wig stood ready on a stand, and several vast hats, which matched the costumes, were lined up on the shelf above the wardrobe rail. The worn curtain, which was there to protect the costumes when they were not in use, was carelessly thrown back. The two girls sat side by side on a narrow and not very comfortable reclining couch.

'Now, what's it all about? It's not Ma, is it? She's not ill? Oh, Em, tell me she's not ill!'

'No, Sarah, it's not Ma. She's . . . all right.' The last words came out rather slowly and without much conviction.

Sarah wasn't satisfied. 'You sure?'

'Well, she's not been too well lately. Moody and grumpy – you know.'

'Oh, Em, that's the change – she's on the change. You must be patient with her. I'll be in touch, we'll work something out. I don't care about Pa, the old devil, he can take care of himself, but Ma – well, she's different. So what is it? You must have some news. How can I help?'

'Go on, go on, tell 'er – tell 'er what's bothering you!'

'Oh, no, not *that*! You're not p –'

15

Emma caught Sarah's drift at once. 'No, 'course not!' she replied quickly and indignantly.

'But she will be if she don't look out!'

'Shut up, Katy! Oh, Sarah, it's . . . it's . . .'

'Who is it – what is it?' Then, knowingly, 'Is it that George? Has he been messing you about?'

Emma nodded, head down, tears welling up in her eyes.

'I can't go on any longer, I really can't, Sarah. If only you knew! But of course you do know, don't you? That was why you got out, wasn't it? I realise that now. It only came to me a few days ago. I suddenly remembered that awful row before you left. Of course I was too young to understand then, and now . . .'

She stopped to blow her nose.

Sarah continued for her. 'And now it's happening to you. Blast him! He should be shot.'

'What can I do? I can't tell Ma, much less Pa. George is so good to them – he works hard – they'd never believe me. I can't go on the stage like you. And they won't hear of my going into service.'

'Em, dear Em! You must leave home, Ma or no Ma. I'll see to it that she's all right, trust me. But you must leave home, even if you have to run away. I'll give you some money – in fact, I think I could find you a job. I know quite a few people now – some of 'em real toffs. I've got to be a bit careful – a lot of "ladies" won't come near us actresses – but I might well be able to do something.'

She suddenly drew in a breath with a gasp. She had seen the ring on Emma's finger.

'What is that? Where did you get that?' The girls told her the happier half of their story. 'Are you sure you're telling me the whole story? I've only seen diamonds like that before once, and that was when Blanche Browne got herself hooked to Lord Derwentwater.'

'Maybe that's who it belongs to, then.'

'You'd better find out. You've really got to be honest about this. I know how you feel, Katy, but remember, there could well be quite a big reward. That ring's obviously important to the owner.'

'We hadn't thought of that,' said Katy, already in her

16

imagination starting to take some exotic trip on the proceeds.

'Half an hour, ladies and gentlemen! Half an hour!' a town-crier-like voice bawled down the passage outside.

'Oh, is that the time already?'

As Sarah spoke, Sal came back loaded with the tray of tea and a large Dundee cake.

'Could 'ardly get across Coventry Street! So many carriages and crowds of people – some say the Prince of Wales is in town tonight. Don't think he's coming 'ere, though. Here's your tea, ladies – and that'll be a shillin' for the cake.'

'Here you are!' Sarah reached for some change in an old make-up jar. 'Leave us for another ten minutes, Sal, would you?'

Sal grunted and left, closing the door noisily behind her.

'Now, there are two things you have to do. When you leave the theatre, take a hansom to Bow Street police station and pass in that ring. Then the pair of you go straight home. Tonight, Em, put the back of a chair under the handle of your bedroom door. Chances are you'll sleep in peace anyway – it being Saturday, George will have been drinking with his cronies. He'll stagger a bit, but he'll be canny enough not to want to disturb Pa – as well I know. Tomorrow I'm having lunch with Mr Edwardes and three of the girls at his place on the Thames. I'll ask around to see if anyone wants a lady's maid.'

'Sarah, I couldn't do that, I really couldn't. I can't dress hair, don't know very much about clothes –'

'She sews like an angel,' Katy interrupted. 'That's why she always looks so smart.'

'Emma, you'll hear from me on Monday. Take care of each other. I must get on. Here, have these. That'll be enough to get you to Bow Street and home – and more!'

She handed her sister two sovereigns. The three of them hugged each other, both the younger girls getting splodges of stage make-up on their cheeks. They left the theatre feeling a lot happier; holding their heads high, they hailed a cab and drove up to Bow Street police station in style.

The hansom drew to a halt just in front of the main entrance to the Royal Opera House.

17

'Here you are, ladies. Can't stop across the road – too much traffic. Just can't get through. Mind 'ow you go as you cross. Don't want you mown down by one of them fashionable 'orses – they're not all like my good old Bess 'ere. That'll be one and three, if you please.'

Emma handed him one of the sovereigns, butterflies jumping around her inside but outwardly calm and as if to the manner born. She had never paid a cabby before.

Waiting for the change, Katy whispered, 'A tip – don't you 'ave to give 'im a tip?'

'How much do you think? Sixpence?'

'Dunno ... no, too much. Give 'im a threepenny bit if there's one in your change.'

There was, and Emma gave the cabby back the tiny silver coin. He seemed pleased enough, and drove off into the throng of carriages and horses.

Fashionable people were arriving at the theatre in fabulous clothes. Pastel-coloured silk rustled, and one or two of the more daring women sported bright red. Many carried huge feather fans or wore feather boas. Gems glistened, pearls glowed from white necks, gloved wrists and expertly coiffed hair. The men's black tail coats and stiffly starched shirt fronts, collars and white bow ties made a distinctive contrast to the elaborate designs and extravagance of the women's attire. Educated voices guffawed. The mood was excited but with restraint – people were aware that they were there to be seen, as much as to experience the evening's entertainment ahead.

'It's all so beautiful! I've never seen folk like this, have you, Katy? Wonder what's happening tonight.'

'Look, there's a poster: "A Benefit Performance by Dame Nellie Melba in aid of St Bartholomew's 'Ospital". So that's what's going on.'

They were standing on the pavement, getting a glimpse of a life style they had only read about in magazines. Here it was in front of their eyes.

A bell was heard from inside the foyer, and gradually the smart audience moved away and into the auditorium.

'Oh, Em!' Katy gasped excitedly. 'Wasn't that beautiful?' Then she pointed across the street to the police station with

18

its blue gas lamp already lit, although it was by no means yet dark. 'Look, that's where we've got to go.'

The grim inside of Bow Street police station contrasted vividly with the richness of the building opposite, but as they approached the counter they were cheered by the appearance of a large, jovial policeman with a red face, huge moustache and deep voice.

'And what can I do for you two young ladies? Nothing wrong, I hope?'

'No, sergeant.'

Emma assumed he was a sergeant, and fortunately she was right.

'You see, Katy and me ... well, we had a picnic tea in Kensington Gardens this afternoon, and we were sitting on the grass and I saw this.' Reluctantly she took the ring off her finger and put it carefully on the high counter.

'We think it's valuable. And we went to see my sister – she's in the show at the Prince of Wales Theatre – and she said, like we thought, that it's valuable and that we ought to pass it in to you as someone's lost it.' Emma told her tale quickly and was breathless by now.

'Sister on the stage, eh?' The sergeant seemed more interested in that than the ring. 'I went to the Prince of Wales last week. Lovely show! Different from the rest, but lovely. I must 'ave seen her – what's 'er name?'

'Sarah Cooper.'

'Oh, you've got some sister! Plays Clara, doesn't she? Shan't forget her in a hurry. Now let's see, where did you say you found the ring?'

Emma repeated that part of her story and then, speaking slowly and carefully so that the sergeant could write it down, gave him her name and address.

'Well, thank you, Miss Cooper. This ring has indeed been reported missing. Go right home now. It's Saturday night, you know – no time for two young ladies to be out in these parts without your sweethearts so get home quick!'

'So that's that, I suppose,' Katy remarked with a bit of a sigh as they left the police station.

'But we've had a bit of fun, girl, haven't we?'

'And we're going home in style.'

19

Feeling like real toffs, they giggled to each other as they started their second cab ride that evening. They drove along Oxford Street, where rows of little shops were still open for business as housewives made last-minute purchases for Sunday dinner on the morrow; and then along the Bayswater Road – not so far from the spot where they'd found the ring – and down Holland Park Avenue beyond Notting Hill Gate, lined with strong young trees, its large, relatively new houses expressing the wealth and prosperity of the late Victorian age.

As the cab was about to cross a railway bridge a few minutes from home, Emma had a sudden thought and called out to the driver.

'Can you stop just the other side of the bridge, please?'

'Right you are, missie!'

The driver pulled his horse to a halt. Again Emma paid the fare – two shillings and sevenpence – and she gave the driver a sixpenny tip.

'Why've we got out here? Why didn't you let 'im take us right home?' Katy was really quite angry.

'How could we arrive home in a hansom? How would they think we paid for it? We'll have to keep really quiet about all this. And look, it's nearly nine o'clock! Ma'll be worried and Pa furious. How can we explain why we're late?'

'Tell 'em about the ring, and how we had to take it to the police station. We can say we had to wait while they locked up some drunks. Leave that to me, I'll make up something. You make sure you put the rest of that money away – you may well need it.'

Emma opened her mouth to speak, but Katy went on, 'I know what you're going to say. You want to give it to your ma and tell 'er you've seen Sarah. Don't. Leave it to Sarah, like she said.'

'Come on, come on. You're late! Where have you been? It's gone nine. You deserve a good thrashing, my girl.'

William Cooper glared at his daughter, his fury making him splutter, his lean body shaking with rage.

'And you, Katy – you get off home. Mrs Tyrrell'll throw you out if you've been misbehaving. Which you have – you can't tell me anything about girls of your age.'

20

He turned rapidly and grabbed a stick from the corner by the front door.

'Oh, Will, don' be so hard on her, let her speak!' Mrs Cooper pleaded with him.

But it was too late. He lifted the stick and brought it heavily down on Emma's left forearm. She shrieked with pain.

'Let her speak? She's spoke too much already tonight and to men, I bet. Go up to your room or I'll give you the real thrashing you deserve.' His eyes, wild with fury, had a sadistic gleam.

'Will, listen –'

Mrs Cooper protested again, and grabbed the strong, hairy arm which was tensely gripping the stick, ready to bring it down on his daughter for the second time. Emma was trying not to cry. The dull pain would soon turn to a nasty bruise.

Reluctantly he lowered his arm and listened sullenly as his wife gestured to the girls.

'Em, what have you been up to? Have you two been doing bad things?'

'No, Ma.'

'No, Mrs Cooper – good things, honest.'

And they explained, with Katy's vivid imagination doing them proud when it came to just how long they had to spend waiting at the police station to return the ring.

When Emma went to bed, she put the chair under the handle of the door of her room. Even so, she lay awake waiting to hear George come in. As the clock of St Matthew's struck two, she drifted off to sleep.

George didn't come home that night.

'Immortal, invisible God, only wise . . .'

Will Cooper was singing as he put that extra bit of spit and polish on his Sunday boots, ready for church. His wife would put the dinner in the oven just before they left, and Emma, still upstairs, was getting into her 'Sundays' – a neat muslin with little rosebuds embroidered in a spot pattern. She was brushing her hair before putting it into two plaits, and wondering just how soon her mother would let her put it up and wear a full-length dress . . .

21

'Are you ready, Em?'

'Nearly, Ma!'

She grabbed the second piece of well-ironed blue hair ribbon and hastily tied it in a bow on the unfinished plait, then rushed downstairs to her parents, in sober mood, smartly dressed, prayer books in hand. Why did they need them? she wondered. They knew all the responses, hymns and psalms by heart. No, it was just to let the neighbours know they were good churchgoing people.

'Where's George?' she asked.

'We, er . . . don't know. He didn't come home last night.'

Her mother was embarrassed.

Emma was furious. Why was he allowed out all night? Not that she minded, it was good riddance. Nevertheless, she had to bite her tongue to prevent another row flaring up.

Just then there was a sharp knock at the front door. Her father pushed in front of them to answer it. A man dressed in a morning suit stood there.

'Does Miss Emma Cooper live here, sir?'

'Yes. What do you want with her? What's she been up to?'

'Can I speak to her, if you please?'

'What's 'e want, Will?'

'He wants to see Emma!'

'I'm Emma Cooper.'

Emma had come up behind her father.

'Miss Cooper, I am requested by Lady Rosamund Alston to invite you to accompany me to her residence. She very much wants to meet you.'

Chapter Two

'I won't, I won't! It's too childish! I want to come with you.'

'That is not possible, Lizzie. I shall go to Admiralty House as I always do, and you and Joe will go to the Citadel with Aggie, and wave from there.'

'The whole idea is stupid! We might just as well watch from the garden – we'll see Papa far more clearly.'

'You know very well that you children always go to the Citadel, and Papa sees you through his telescope while I await his arrival with the Admiral.'

Mrs Caroline Newcombe was fast losing patience with her daughter.

'That was when we were little.' Lizzie straightened up as she spoke, flicking her thick chestnut curls in defiance.

'Neither you nor Joe has been invited to Admiralty House. You cannot possibly come with me.'

Lizzie tried another approach – anything to get out of standing in the wind and the rain, watching for HMS *Rameses* to creep over the horizon through the mist and into Plymouth Sound.

'We'll not get wet if we stay and wave from the garden – at least let us do that.'

'No. Papa will be worried if you aren't where he expects to see you. Find Joe now, and tell Aggie to get your thick coats and umbrellas. I shall leave for Admiralty House in half an hour.'

Lizzie stamped out of the drawing room.

'Horrid Citadel! It's always wet and cold, and what if my friends see me there waving and peering? It's stupid. When will Mama realise I'm a woman? I'm not a child, and neither is Joe – he's a man . . . well, almost, I suppose.'

In spite of her anger at the way she was to welcome her father home after two years at sea, Lizzie was delighted at the prospect of seeing him. Both she and her younger brother were devoted to him, although there had always been long periods of time when he was not around, and they sometimes had to wait for months before getting letters. That was part of their lives, they had always lived with it. And to that pattern Mrs Caroline Newcombe had had to become accustomed since her marriage some eighteen years previously.

Lizzie was now sixteen, going on seventeen – a lively, athletic girl with a great zest for life. She was considered by the older generation, especially some of her stricter teachers, to be tomboyish. Her warm complexion gave her a healthy glow and her bright-blue eyes missed nothing. She was of average height, but the strength of her personality somehow made her seem taller. Her natural sense of humour and easy smile, complemented by perfect teeth, endeared her to everyone – and helped her out of many tricky situations.

Fully aware of her well-formed body, she knew she was fast becoming very attractive to men. This presented her with certain apprehensions, but Lizzie was always ready to cope with difficult situations when they arose. Her quest for knowledge and adventure was at this point in her life far more important than young men.

She climbed the stairs of the large terraced house to find Aggie and Joe in their old nursery. Joe had his head in a book, as ever; Aggie was attempting to tidy the room.

'It's no good, Joe – we have to go up to the Citadel just as we always do.'

Her brother would be fourteen next birthday. His mop of blond hair had enough curl in it to make it seem continually untidy, and he sometimes looked a little pale, but when he went sailing or riding his skin took the sun well and he developed a healthy tan. He did well at school, he could swim and was keen to be strong and healthy, knowing that one day he would follow in his father's, his grandfather's and great-grandfather's footsteps and have a naval career. At present, when he looked in the mirror, he thought he was too

24

skinny, but in fact he was wiry and strong. A very caring boy, he was also extremely intuitive, and his family and old nanny always said that he had an old head on young shoulders.

'Why *is* Mama so illogical?' he asked rhetorically. 'Oh, yes, I know –'

'Tradition!' they chorused. Tradition was one of their parents' continual themes.

'Quite right too. Don't know where we'd be without it,' their old nurse chimed in. 'The Queen, God bless her, is all for tradition – that I do know – and don't you children forget it!'

'Come on, Lizzie. Let's make the best of it.' Joe could see that Lizzie's indignation was about to boil over yet again.

'Oh, I suppose you're right. But I'm really far too grown-up for all this. If we could go with friends, it would be more fun – or even alone. But always with Aggie, always watched . . . Mama doesn't trust us. When will we begin to live our own lives?'

Sighing and trying to calm herself a little – she knew full well there was no way of getting out of the silly ritual – she turned to her nurse.

'And she says we're to wear our thick coats, Aggie.'

'Quite right too, in this drizzle. I'll get 'em. And you mind your manners, my girl. Don't you speak of your mama like that. Most disrespectful, I call it. You be thankful you've got such a lovely home. And you, too!'

She prodded Joe in the back as he sat facing the window which looked over the narrow channel towards Drake's Island.

'Look at this room! It's a mess. And you two thinking you're both so grown-up – more like six-year-olds than sixteen!'

'Darling!'

'It's been far too long – especially this time.'

'I know. You really are wonderful to put up with it all.'

'I do my best – but the children . . .'

'Oh – the children! They couldn't be more fortunate, having such a perfect mother.'

25

'Peter, I know you always see a big difference in them every homecoming, but this time . . .'

Captain Peter Newcombe prevented his beautiful, elegantly dressed wife from uttering another word. He bent and passionately kissed her. As she responded to him she felt as if he'd never been away; the familiarity of his body close to her, the strength of his arms and the tenderness and warmth of his passion took her back two years, to their very last moments of farewell.

'You know, you don't age a bit. You're just as beautiful as that day when you walked down the aisle of St Andrew's.'

He was quite right. His wife had kept her figure, shown to advantage today in a gown of golden-brown taffeta. Her hat was decorated with gold feathers and a spray of miniature cream artificial roses. Lizzie had definitely inherited her mother's chestnut hair.

He caught her blushing; and said she was just like a girl. She accused him of teasing her, and got her own back when she noticed a white hair in his beautifully shaped beard.

They were riding in a hackney which made its way along Edgecumbe Street into Union Street and turned right at the Octagon, where lowlife and sailors joined in merrymaking, fights, too much drink and encounters with prostitutes. As it did so, Mrs Newcombe felt she should warn her husband that their children had changed a great deal.

'Peter . . . Peter?'

'I am here, you know,' he replied smilingly.

'I have to be serious for a moment.'

'What's wrong?'

'Well, nothing really, but . . .'

'But something is. Tell me, Caro.'

'Well, I think I can cope with Lizzie – but she's become so strong-willed'.

'She always has been.'

'Oh yes, I know, but now . . . well, she's grown up.'

'She's only sixteen.'

'Yes, but she's . . . well, you know, she's a woman, she's . . . developed.'

'I would hope so. And Joseph? Has his voice broken?'

'I think it's about to. Oh, dear! Can I cope with that?'

'Looks as though I've come home just in time. I have some ideas for young Joseph – and I don't think he'll mind them too much.'

'I suppose I'm more worried about Lizzie. She's so, so . . . *wild* I suppose is the only way to describe her.'

'Don't you worry, Caro. We'll sort it out.'

The cab drew up to the front door of number 6 West Hoe Terrace.

'Thank you, Laura. You may clear and bring in the dessert – and we'll have the best Madeira.'

Mrs Newcombe instructed the housekeeper as the family were finishing the main course of their celebratory dinner.

'You're right, Caro – we do have a grown-up pair here!' said Peter, smiling at Joe and Lizzie in turn and looking at them and his wife with considerable pride.

'Oh, Papa!'

Lizzie dashed from her chair to the head of the table, flung her arms around her father's neck and hugged him with spontaneous enthusiasm.

'Lizzie, we know you love Papa. We all do. But, dear, don't strangle him just as he's come home!' Then, a little more seriously, 'You know you should begin to show more restraint in the way you express yourself, now you're a young woman.'

'I know, I know – but it's so *good* to have Papa home again. And that fan, Papa – I've never *ever* seen anything so beautiful! Thank you again and again!'

'Oh, and the book you brought me . . . all those photographs of all those places, it's fantastic!' It was Joe's turn to add his appreciation of his present.

The Captain smiled at his offspring. 'Now, let's demolish this trifle and have a glass of Madeira.'

'Do you think they should, Peter? It is fortified wine, you know.'

'Just a little. Young Joe here ought really to be sampling Best Navy Rum. Seriously, it'll do them good – build 'em up! Then I want to hear Lizzie play her latest and most difficult piece, so I hope the piano's in tune!'

To get her fingers exercised, Lizzie began her programme

27

with 'Fur Elise', went on to Chopin's A Major Prelude, then gave her father a rip-roaring finale by rendering 'The Blue-bells of Scotland, with Variations'. As an encore she presented him with a selection from *The Gondoliers*.

'I'm impressed with Lizzie's playing. No, don't draw the curtains, leave them back – look, there's a full moon.'

The Captain tended to change subjects very quickly. Used to this, his wife replied, 'Yes, she enjoys her practice, and she wanted to impress you.'

Caroline left the curtains open so that they could see the moon over the water. The heavy mist and drizzle of earlier in the day had given way to a perfect summer's night. As she spoke, she turned from the first-floor window with its dramatic view of Plymouth Sound. The moonlight caught the transparency of her chiffon negligée and nightdress, and the light breeze from the open window caused it to float away from her slim body.

She made her way over to the large double bed which now, after twenty-four long, lonely months, was occupied by her adored husband.

'Come, my love! The sailor's returned from the sea.'

Whenever Caroline became bad-tempered or tense while her husband was away, she knew that it was due to the lack of sex. She did her best to express her energy in other ways, but so often when she felt the frustration she also felt guilty. Should she enjoy what most women thought of as a duty? She wondered if perhaps she was abnormal, even sinful . . . She could only get the drift of what other women felt from their reactions to even the slightest hint of their marital duty in polite conversation. She could not discuss it with anyone, and so of necessity had to keep her feelings to herself; and the longer she was parted from Peter, the more the problem bothered her.

But now all the apprehension, tension and guilt melted away. As she sank into her husband's arms and felt the familiar fire rise to a glorious climax, she was totally happy, fulfilled and at peace with the world.

'Wanton woman!' He was teasing her.

'Oh, Peter, do you really think so?'

28

His jokey remark brought all her fears flooding back to her. Was she . . . all those bad things?

'Darling, darling Caro! If you could hear the stories I hear from the other officers, the problems they have with inhibited wives – how they just "lie back and think of England" . . . It's not surprising they aren't exactly faithful to them while they're away – they have no enduring and loving passion to come home to. No, dearest, your beauty and the way you respond to me are perfect – well worth waiting for. And after, all the Bible doesn't say that man and woman shouldn't enjoy married love.'

His warm affection turned to renewed desire, and they once more expressed their pleasure in each other's bodies. The two-year separation now seemed even shorter than it had when they had enjoyed their first real kiss earlier that day.

Peter Newcombe had been brought up in an entirely naval atmosphere, and for generations the male members of his family had dedicated their lives to the senior service.

Now fifty, he had the bearing of a man of his rank. Fair, strict and just in his role as captain of his ship and leader of her crew, he carried his responsibilities brilliantly, taking harsh disciplinary action when and where it was needed – but only when it was needed.

Mrs Newcombe, thirteen years her husband's junior, was as proud of him as he was of her, his family and his ship, in that order; and on the occasions when she had been on board with him she had been both flattered and amused to see the other side of his character – the other Peter of whom she knew so little.

The hot summer sun flooded through the open French windows of the ground-floor drawing room. The crisp shadows of the potted palm and the aspidistra leaves moved slightly in the breeze across the patterns of the fashionable William Morris wallpaper, its dusky pink to maroon shades echoed in the damask-velvet sofa and winged armchair covers. Rich carpets covered the floor and the Collard and Collard grand piano carried a selection of family photographs by the side of a large bowl of roses and a candelabra which matched a similar pair on the ornate marble mantelpiece over the fireplace.

The ormolu clock struck eleven.

The Captain put down his copy of the *Western Daily Mercury*, got up from a slightly creaky rocking chair, and went over to one of the bell pulls by the side of the fireplace to call Aggie or Laura. It was Aggie who appeared.

'Tell Elizabeth and Joseph to come in here as soon as possible. Mrs Newcombe is on her way. And get Laura to serve the coffee. I think the children will like lemonade, as it's hot.'

'Right you are, sir. Lizzie! Joe!'

Her powerful, coarse voice was heard in the hall. Peter called her back.

'Aggie, now that Elizabeth and Joseph are growing up I'd – we'd – much prefer it if you didn't abbreviate their names. It was excusable when they were little, but now we prefer them to be called as they were christened – if you please.'

Acknowledging the rebuke in a disgruntled way, Aggie left to go in search of the children. She found them relaxing in the large garden overlooking the narrow channel which led from the Sound up the Hamoaze into the dockyard. Directly in front of the terrace, and perhaps a quarter of a mile away, was tiny Drake's Island and beyond it could be seen the lush, green grounds of the Mount Edgcumbe estate.

Mrs Newcombe poured the coffee, and the two young people sat down apprehensively side by side on the large sofa.

'Your mother and I have thought a great deal about your respective futures, and this is what we have in mind. You, Elizabeth, first. If I were a commodore or a rear admiral I could do a lot more for you, my dear. I'd like to send you to finishing school, perhaps in Switzerland.'

The merest suggestion of travel and Europe made Lizzie's pupils dilate.

'But,' her father went on, 'that's not possible. However, you've had a good education. You might even get to Cambridge a little later on, but you're too young to go away to college yet. What we feel you should do for the next two years is to become a pupil teacher. Miss Creeber and Miss

30

Young need someone, and they suggested you. You haven't been unhappy there, have you?'

For a moment Lizzie was confused. Her revulsion at the idea was such that her face rapidly darkened.

'Well, dear, what do you think? Would you like to do that? We think you would be rather good at it, especially with the very young children.'

Her mother tried to coax an answer out of her daughter.

'Go back to school? I couldn't bear it! I've *left* school. I want to do other things. And yes, I was *very* unhappy there.'

Lizzie was tense, her fists clenched; she thought of all the unpleasant scenes that had occurred during her school days, and none of the pleasant ones (of which in fact there had been a great many).

The school was small, and though the teachers taught well they could be unreasonably strict, and the whole atmosphere was claustrophobic. Her last report had described her as highly intelligent but equally high-spirited. It had gone on:

Elizabeth's wilful streak is unbecoming, but her enthusiasm is infectious. She has always contributed a very great deal in class and has been a source of inspiration to her fellow pupils. If she can learn to behave like a young lady, she should make a very supportive wife and, when the time comes, a caring mother.

It was this report that her father held in his hand as he spoke.

'I won't do it! I won't!'

She turned on a defiant heel and made a bolt for the door.

'Elizabeth! Come back *at once!*'

Her father assumed his most commanding voice. Lizzie tossed her head and returned to her place on the sofa, where she sat very upright, her face showing for once a hard, grim expression.

Narrowing her eyes, she cried, 'You really want me to go back to school? *They* want me back? I don't understand!'

Her mother broke in, 'My dear, do calm yourself. Of course you don't understand. You didn't really listen to what your father was saying, and I must say you're behaving abominably to him. You owe him an apology. There's no

31

idea of your returning as a pupil. You'll be a member of the staff – a very junior one, granted, but still a teacher. Surely that has some appeal for you?'

'Me, a teacher?'

The idea seemed as strange as going back as a pupil. But as she began to get the picture, it no longer seemed quite so unattractive.

'The Misses Creeber and Young said they would pay you two guineas a term. And if you wanted to prepare for the university entrance examination, they would be happy to give you extra coaching. What do you say to that?'

Lizzie's expression softened still further at the thought of earning two guineas a term, and after a pause her enthusiasm began to build.

'Shall I read stories to the children, and teach them poems and their tables, and tell them all about history and the far-away places Papa has seen?'

'I'm sure that's just what you would have to do, and perhaps give beginners' piano lessons.'

'Oh, that's easy.'

'You agree, then?'

'Yes, I think so. I suppose I'll start in September, with the new term? I'm sorry I was so rude, but I just hated the thought of going back to school – but it will be different, won't it? I'll have midday dinner with the other teachers, and not have to obey all those silly rules, and I'll put my hair up and wear a long skirt.'

'Oh, will you? Well, we'll have to see about that! You won't be eighteen for over a year, you know, and that's when hair goes up – during the day, anyway. Evening parties are different!'

Mrs Newcombe was not as keen as all that for her daughter to grow up before her time; but she knew in her heart just how advanced she was for her age – and admired her, in many ways. It was not the same world for young women as that in which she had grown up. Lizzie had none of the worries and inhibitions it had taken her years to shake off. In fact, she sometimes wondered if her daughter was a little too advanced, too modern. She was certainly ahead of her time, even if she was only sixteen.

She also felt, privately, that it might be to Lizzie's advantage not to go to college. Most people said that a university education hampered a young woman's chances of making a good marriage; and might it not be right that in the long run it was actually harmful?

'Papa, Mama, thank you for arranging all this for me. I am truly sorry for my temper – and for not listening to you properly in the first place, Papa. I will think about going to college in a year or so. You know, though I do look forward to going to dances, I don't know that I am very interested in young men. There's so much else to do. I want to be a better pianist, I want –'

'Yes, well, all in good time, Elizabeth. We accept your apology. But do try to listen to what people say and don't jump so quickly to conclusions in future. And now it's your turn, Joseph.'

'Yes, sir!' Joe stood up.

'Sit down, old chap. No need to be as formal as that – yet!' His father smiled. 'Now, you know already that I would very much like you to continue in the family tradition and go into the service.'

'Yes, sir, and that is what I would like to do. I want to see the world, I want to take command of a big ship like yours, and I think I could do it.'

'I'm sure you will, one day,' his mother put in gently. 'But success in the navy doesn't come easily, you know. First there must be training – quite a lot of training. When your Father was your age –'

'Allow me, Caroline. Yes, as your mother says, the training is hard – very hard, though it has much improved since my young day. Now, you're thirteen and a half – the age at which you can apply for a place on HMS *Britannia* at Dartmouth. You will be a cadet there until your training is completed; and sixteen months or two years from the time you join her, you can go to sea. And that is what I propose for you.'

'You mean I shall leave the grammar school? Leave home? Will it be like boarding school? When shall I go?'

Joe suddenly seemed much younger than his years. He wanted to go to sea, yes – but he had heard some dreadful stories, in the holidays, from friends who had been sent to

33

boarding school. One, at Blundell's, had been ... Biting his lower lip, he put the thought out of his mind.

'I can take it, Papa. I can cope with the discipline. I can even climb ropes if I have to, and get really strong muscles. When will I go?'

'There will be an interview and an entrance examination some time next month. With our family record you will receive sympathetic consideration.' The Captain glanced at the portrait of his father, the Admiral, hanging over the fireplace.

'You will start your course at about the same time as Elizabeth starts her teaching. Will you be ready?'

Joe stood up again, clicked his heels and saluted his father.

'Aye aye, sir!'

'My dear, what grown-up children we have! No longer babies – though of course they will always be *my* babies. But I know we're going to be so very, very proud of both of you.'

'And now for the next few weeks, until I have to go back to sea, we must enjoy each other's company,' her husband responded warmly.

'Good night, darling.'

Joe heard his mother's voice from the landing as she closed the door of Lizzie's room. It was now ten o'clock, her bedtime.

'Ninety-six, ninety-seven, ninety-eight, ninety-nine, one hundred – now that's done!'

In spite of the thick walls of the early Victorian house, he heard Lizzie count the hundred brush strokes which kept her hair shining and in good condition. Then her bed creaked and all was quiet. He got out of his own bed, silently opened his door, and timidly knocked on hers.

'Lizzie, can I come in?'

'Oh! Joe – yes, of course. What's wrong?'

Joe, in his dressing gown, slipped into his sister's room.

'Here, sit down.' Lizzie patted her colourful patchwork quilt.

'That scene with Papa this morning, it was awful.'

'Yes, I know. But I can't help it, sometimes I feel as if I can never ever be ... be ...' she hesitated. 'Be *me* – be myself!'

34

'I think I understand. You mean that everyone seems always to be telling you what to do and what not to do.'

'Yes, it really makes me very angry. I suppose in many ways I don't know what I actually want out of life, but I know what I *don't* want. I don't want a dreary routine; in fact, I don't really even know if I want to get married and have children.'

'Perhaps what you're trying to say is that you want adventure, that in some ways you'd like to be a boy. Then you could go to Dartmouth and join the navy.'

'And spend years and years travelling, seeing things – new lands, new people. Wouldn't it be marvellous? You are lucky!'

Lizzie's blue eyes were shining at the thought.

'Well, I don't expect life in the navy to be easy. I know it'll be jolly hard for me, but I really do want to go, Sis.' He was quiet and thoughtful for a while, then went on, 'I'm worried about you, though. Maybe you shouldn't go "pupil teaching" – is that what they called it? I can't see you spending hours telling little girls what's right and what's wrong.'

'Well, you know, since this morning I've been giving it a lot of thought. That's just what I *can* tell them. Oh, not all those snobbish things that Miss Young used to tell us, like not to talk to or mix with "poor children", but about consideration for others, helping people, being kind – oh yes, of course Miss Young wants us to be kind, but she's so . . . well, so out of touch. I actually feel that I can *do good*. I can make an impression on younger people, and that'll be a challenge in itself. Then there's the money; I'll earn quite a lot. I think I'll cope, once I get into the routine, and it'll surely be a lot different from just being a pupil. Bless you, dear Joe, for being so concerned. But I'm so happy for you – I really am!'

'Oh, Sis, I'll miss you so much.'

'You'll be too busy, and anyway Dartmouth is quite near, so there'll always be the holidays. We'll get together then. But you'd better get back to bed now, or Aggie'll sense we're up to something. Good night, sleep well.'

They gave each other a cuddly hug, and Joe returned to his room. His sister hadn't entirely reassured him, though he couldn't quite work out why. All that he did know for certain was that he and Lizzie were very close, and that he would stand by her if he was ever needed, even if it wasn't for ages and ages.

Lizzie and Joe had for several years been able to walk to school together, since the buildings were almost opposite each other in Lockyer Street. Joe was at the Hoe Grammar School for Boys, while the Plymouth Academy for Young Ladies occupied a large detached house in Windsor Terrace, on the east side of the street.

It was to the latter building that Mrs Newcombe and Lizzie made their way. As it was yet another lovely summer's day, they chose to take Lizzie and Joe's favourite route, turning right as they left the front door of number 6, and walking along Grand Parade Road with its view of the sound and the breakwater.

Soon they left the road and walked up the hilly grass slopes of the Hoe to cross the Grand Parade, known to locals as 'the Prom' – a wide stretch of tarmac, closed to traffic, a place to promenade, to meet friends and to flirt.

Walking in front of the two grandest rows of houses in the city – the Esplanade and Elliot Terrace – they eventually turned down into Lockyer Street itself, and were soon crossing the forecourt of the school. This area, when school was about to start or finish, was always a hive of activity, with nurses and maids and often parents having brought their young charges to school, or waiting for them to leave; then there were the older girls, comparing their recent lessons – or pretending to, while they actually discussed the boys just up and across the road. Here notes were exchanged, usually by someone who happened to have a brother at the boys' school. It was all great fun, but extremely risky, for if you were caught it meant some dreadfully frustrating punishment from the eagle-eyed Miss Creeber, who would dole out lines by the hundred, extra essays on the most boring of subjects, spelling lists, or French or Latin verbs – all to be learned or executed to perfection.

Today the forecourt was quiet – as uncharacteristically quiet as Lizzie had been on her walk there. The heavy, black front door, always open during school hours, was shut fast, and to announce their arrival they rang the bell, which clanged

36

noisily on a steel spring just inside the porch. The maid, in crisp afternoon uniform, showed them into the parlour.

A sort of holy of holies, it was the setting for serious meetings. A pupil summoned to it was either to be very specially praised, or to be so severely scolded that the sermon must be administered in private. It was here that expulsions were announced, or that a girl who unexpectedly discovered blood on her drawers would be privately reassured that she was not going to die.

This afternoon was quite different. The room seemed almost welcoming. There was a small table set with dainty cups and saucers, announcing the probability of tea. The lace curtains looked very fresh and – perhaps because of the good light – the room seemed, unusually and in its own grave way, to be smiling at her.

Lizzie and her mother had been sitting down for about a minute when the two ladies entered. Miss Creeber's brisk walk and the way she held her hands, fingers stiffly folded across her thin, tightly corseted stomach, indicated she was in a businesslike but not antagonistic mood. Miss Young, more gentle, followed behind, as she always seemed to. Her figure was rather rounder, and the full, soft muslin sleeves of her neat, tucked blouse, caught at the elbow and finishing in a deep frill, gave a much greater hint of tenderness than Lizzie was accustomed to.

'Mrs Newcombe, I'm so pleased we can have this meeting. How is the Captain? Enjoying his spell ashore, I assume?'

Mrs Newcombe made the appropriate reply.

Miss Creeber adjusted her pince-nez, its cord tangled in a huge cameo brooch which ornamented her scraggy bosom. Narrowing wrinkled eyes and lips, she smiled at Lizzie.

'Now, Elizabeth, I know your parents have informed you of our ideas for your future, and I also know that you are willing to come and work here. Of course you know precisely how we run the Academy. The teachings of the Bible, both Old and New Testaments, form an important part of our curriculum, and we will expect you to stand by them, always remembering that we are giving you a great opportunity to pass on to a younger generation – indeed, perhaps several generations – all the good things we have taught you here.'

Momentarily pausing to take breath, she continued, 'Remember, too, that you must always be grateful to the parents who gave you the opportunity to benefit from our high standards of education . . .'

She prattled on and on. So many of her phrases Lizzie had heard time and time again at assembly, when her headmistress was giving forth to the whole school about what she stood for, what the school stood for and indeed what she expected every pupil to stand for.

'We will pay you at the end of each term. We think that a salary of two guineas is generous. Many young pupil teachers only start at half a guinea a term, you know, but, well,' (here she gave a little girlish giggle) 'we think you are worth more than that; then, if you wish to be coached for Girton, I'm sure Miss Young will help you – won't you, Miss Young?'

'Oh yes, of course, Miss Creeber – if you think I'm capable.'

'Capable? Of *course* you are capable!' The head's tone was more than a little indignant.

'Will that suit you, Elizabeth?'

'Yes, Miss Creeber,' Lizzie replied with an element of resignation. How many times had she said 'Yes, Miss Creeber' over the years? But the money was good and she was bursting with ideas!

'Now to minor matters.'

'You will be expected to attend morning assembly, and I'm afraid I cannot release you for midday dinner, as when you were a pupil, for you will be needed to help with the girls. Incidentally, I believe your piano playing is making excellent progress. We are without a music teacher at present, and we shall expect you to play for the hymns and perhaps to give some private lessons, at least to the younger girls. I think that is about all. No! One more thing, Mrs Newcombe. Although Elizabeth is not yet eighteen, we would like her to appear – ah – rather more *mature*, especially since some of the girls will have known her as a pupil. By the by' – turning back to Elizabeth, – 'you will have to distance yourself from any friend you have made here, who still remains at the school. So, Mrs Newcombe, I think it would be wise if Elizabeth went into long skirts with a cotton blouse and tie – and corsets, of course. She must also wear her hair up, and learn to walk in a more ladylike fashion. Deportment is *not* one of her strong points.'

She picked up a small china bell and rang it. 'Shall we have tea?'

'How did you get on? Tell me everything!'

'I've never seen Miss Creeber in a better mood. Of course Mama was there, but do you know, Joe, she even smiled at me, once or twice! So did Miss Young, but that's not so hard for her, provided Miss Creeber doesn't see her do it. And I have to wear a long skirt and a tie, and something else too . . .'

'Can't say.' Lizzie, who wasn't given to blushing, felt her cheeks redden.

'Go on! what else have you got to wear? Tell me.'

'Corsets!'

'*Corsets*! But I thought that it was old ladies like Mama who –'

'You thought wrong. Young women have to wear corsets too. Mama says we've to go to Spooner's tomorrow for me to be measured, and then on to Lake's in Union Street to be measured for two or three tailored skirts – we can get the blouses at Spooner's.'

All that happened next day. After Lizzie had been measured for the corsets in the lush privacy of a changing room in Messrs Spooner, Drapers and Outfitters, mother and daughter proceeded to the tailors.

A few days later she was being fitted into the unfinished corsets by the elderly corsetière who went on a great deal about support and where it was most needed. She hated the feeling of restriction. Would she really have to imprison herself in something like this, every day?

'Now I would like you to sit down, please, miss.'

As Lizzie lowered herself to an elegant upright chair, bones from every seam in the corset sprang up in front of her face, just as though she were in a cage. Although it was something no lady should really discuss with a man – even with her brother – both she and Joe had a good laugh about it later. And perhaps the discomfort wouldn't be as great as she feared, after all.

39

Chapter Three

Mr and Mrs Cooper were momentarily speechless. But Emma, eyes darting from the rather grand messenger to a dogcart with its smart little pony pawing the ground, and a young footman sitting bolt upright holding the reins with great assurance, responded, 'Thank you, sir, of course I will come with you.'

Her quick brain realised that the *lady* he had mentioned was obviously the owner of the ring, and that maybe there was indeed a reward, as Sarah had suggested.

'You come 'ere, my girl! You're not going off to meet strangers with a strange man, and in that contraption.'

Her father's scrawny hand gripped her wrist.

'I assure you, sir, everything is quite in order. The request does come, as I said, from Lady Alston.'

'That don' mean she's respectable – 'ow do I know what'll 'appen to my girl once you've drove off?'

'Nothing untoward will happen to her, sir. Lady Alston wants to see your daughter on a most important matter.'

'Oh, let her go, Will – she'll be all right!' Mrs Cooper put in, digging her husband in the ribs.

Emma was furious. She managed to free herself from her father's hard grip, and said to the man under her breath, 'Quickly – let's get away.'

She jumped up into the dogcart, the butler (for that was what he seemed to be) mounted rather more slowly, the footman whipped up the pony, and off they trotted.

'I do apologise for my father's reaction – he's very possessive.'

40

'I quite understand, Miss.'

They made their way towards Kensington High Street. It was almost free of traffic, but the further east they travelled, the more people they saw, all in their Sunday clothes, walking to St Mary Abbot's, Kensington's large parish church, where an impressive peal of bells welcomed the worshippers to matins.

Emma realised how fortunate it was that the messenger had arrived when he did. A few minutes later, she and her parents would have been on their walk to church, and if he'd called the following morning or afternoon, she would have been in scruffy working clothes and he might not have wanted to wait around while she changed.

They were passing Kensington Gardens on their left when suddenly the footman lifted his whip and extended it in his right hand. The horse pulled them round into Queen's Gate – a beautiful, wide boulevard with trees and rows of very grand five-floored terraced houses. The young footman drew the horse to a halt outside number 1.

'Here we are, miss.'

The butler opened the door with his own key. Just inside, a smartly dressed young parlour maid was coming out of a side door with a tray of tea things. She surreptitiously eyed Emma up and down. Emma, who had a warm smile, coaxed one out of her.

The hall was wide and the wooden parquet floor highly polished. There was an ornate hall stand and on the walls hung large paintings of ladies and gentlemen who looked as though they were in fancy dress.

'This way, please, miss.'

The man led the way up the wide staircase, carpeted in deep pile with an oriental pattern in shades of red and brown. Brightly shining brass stair rods glinted up at her.

Emma was awe-stricken. She suddenly felt hot and shakily nervous and hoped she wouldn't break out in perspiration, which would soil her pretty dress.

At the top of the stairs, her guide led her towards a pair of double doors, opened one almost silently, and ushered her into what seemed an enormous drawing room. She was dimly conscious of a great number of ornaments, statuettes,

41

more paintings – and of an old lady sitting bolt upright in an elaborate wing chair, her feet resting on a low stool. She was thin and pale, dressed in grey silk, her hair thick and white and her expression alert but gentle.

'Miss Cooper, my lady,' said the man, bowing his head slightly.

'Thank you, Stratton. That will be all for now. Tell Toby he must wait while I talk to this young lady. I shall want him to drive her home.'

'Very good, my lady.' Stratton withdrew.

'I think we'd better introduce ourselves, don't you, my dear?'

The lady's kind, faded blue eyes lit up, and she smiled warmly at Emma.

Emma responded with a very quiet, 'Yes, madam.'

The lady went on, 'You will have gathered that I'm Lady Alston. And you are Emma Cooper?'

'Yes, my lady.'

'Do sit down. That chair is quite comfortable.'

She pointed to a charming little padded chair with an elaborately upholstered back, so shaped that Emma's full skirt was able to spread itself out gracefully as she accepted Lady Alston's invitation.

'My dear, I so wanted to meet you personally. A young girl who goes at once to the police station to return a very valuable ring must be extremely honest – a quality I very much admire in these days, when everyone is out for himself.'

'Thank you, my lady.'

Emma didn't quite know what else to say. She was dying to look round the big room but she felt it wasn't the thing to do, so she sat and listened.

'I expect you would like to know how I lost the ring. It was my betrothal ring. Lord Alston gave it to me when our engagement was announced. Until quite recently I wore it with my wedding ring.'

She pointed to the third finger of her left hand.

'But you see, now I'm old I have arthritis in my hands, and my joints are swollen, so I have been wearing both rings on my little finger.'

She smiled, but sadly. 'I had to use some butter to get them off.'

Emma made a sympathetic noise.

'On Saturday morning I was walking in Kensington Gardens – I must keep moving, you know, even if I am old and stiff in my joints – and my ring slipped off my little finger, and, well, you know the rest.'

'Oh, my lady, I am so glad we found it.'

'We? I didn't know you were with someone. Who was it, was it your young man?'

Emma blushed. 'Oh, no I don't have one. I was with my friend Katy.'

'Ah, well, she is obviously a good girl, too. Now, my dear, we must see to a reward for you, and your friend – Kate? – should have one too. Will you give it to her from me?'

'Of course, Lady Alston.'

'And my dear, what a pretty dress! Where did you get it? At Whiteley's?'

That made Emma smile. Whiteley's – what people called a department store – was just across the park from where they were; everything there was terribly expensive.

'No, my lady. I made it.'

'I can hardly believe you! It's perfect. Where did you learn to sew like that?'

'At school, and there's a dressmaker near my father's shop. She helps me with the cutting-out and fitting.'

'Turn around. I want to see the back.'

As she spoke, Lady Alston gently took Emma's left arm. Emma flinched. Lady Alston had caught the new, highly coloured and very sore bruise her father had given her the night before. The sleeves of her dress were somewhat transparent, but she'd been hoping that the bruise wouldn't show.

'Oh, my dear!' Lady Alston lowered her eyes and looked closely at the bruise. 'How did you get that?'

She noticed Emma's expression change at once from a sweet, happy girl to a very frightened, nervous one.

'I . . . I don't like to say . . .'

'That sounds ominous.'

Emma didn't quite know what ominous meant, and the older woman sensed it.

43

'Did you fall or . . . did someone hit you?'

Tears clouded Emma's blue eyes.

'Oh, you are upset. My dear, have confidence – you can tell me about it if you would like to.'

She took Emma's left hand in both her old ones.

How much could she tell? And dared she say from whom she had got the bruise? She decided she must.

Lady Alston listened intently.

'And your father was very angry because you were late home. He'd thought you had been, er, naughty? Does he often hit you?'

'From time to time – and he hits my mother too. Oh, he doesn't drink or anything like that, but he is very strict and very bad-tempered.'

'Does he go to church? Are you a Methodist, or perhaps Jewish? But no, you don't look Jewish.'

'We all go to St Matthew's Church near where we live. We were just leaving for matins when . . . when Mr . . .'

'Mr Stratton, my butler.'

'Yes, when he arrived.' Then she added, 'He – my father's – a sidesman.'

Lady Alston got the picture. Here was a man all too typical of his class, who presented an upright figure to the world, supported the church, did all the right things at the right time – then came home and assaulted his family.

'My dear, I am concerned for you. I dislike hearing stories like yours.' Then, after a little pause, 'Now you really must excuse me – I must rest before lunch.'

Holding two envelopes and her hat in her left hand, Emma made a little curtsy and thanked her benefactress, who summoned Stratton; and he in turn arranged for Toby, the young footman, to drive Emma home to Hammersmith.

Several local children crowded around the dogcart as Toby helped her down. At the same time her parents appeared round the corner, their service having ended a few minutes earlier.

'You were missed, my girl. It was a very impressive sermon, very impressive.'

Holding on to his coat lapels in one of his most common, self-important gestures, her father greeted her grumpily.

44

'Come on in. Take off that hat and help yer ma with the dinner.' Emma did as she was bid, but first rushed up the stairs to her room to tear open her envelope and find unbelievable riches: a large, crinkly, white five-pound note. She couldn't believe her eyes. Her sensible, immediate reaction was to stuff it back into the envelope and put it at the back of her underwear drawer. She decided to tell no one until she had consulted Katy. Did her friend's envelope contain the same? She thought it might, so she put it with her own.

'Come on, Emma! What you doing up there, girl? I want yer to dish the potatoes and greens, and your pa's waitin' with the carvin' knife.'

'I'm just putting my hat away,' she called back to her mother, and braced herself for the confrontation ahead.

'Well, 'ow much you get?'

Mr Cooper slammed down his knife and fork and rubbed his mouth with the back of his hand. Dinner had been eaten in total silence. Letting out a loud, contented belch, he repeated his question.

Emma had been waiting for this, knowing full well that her father would want to know, and would make suggestions about what she should do with her reward.

'How much reward, Pa?' she questioned, feigning a certain innocence.

''Ow much – that's what I said.'

'Well, no matter how big or how little, it's Em's to keep,' her mother interjected, trying to be firm with her domineering husband.

George, who was slumped over the table, still bleary-eyed from his night out, put on the charm. 'Emma's in the money. Better hand it over – I'll make it grow for you, sister dear.'

Mr Cooper was going red in the face. His question had not been answered. Leaning across the table and glaring at Emma, he shouted, ''Ow much?'

'P'raps she didn't get nothing,' suggested her peace-loving mother.

This interchange had given Emma more time to think.

'I got a sovereign, and Lady Alston gave me a half sovereign for Katy. She was so pleased we'd been honest and

45

she'd got her ring back. It was her betrothal ring. Oh, Ma, you should have seen it – it was beautiful. Big, big diamonds and it had –'

'Give me that money.'

'I won't! It's mine to do what I like with. I've never had so much, and Katy'll be glad to have hers too.'

'You'll do as I say! Give it to me – *now*!'

'You'd better, Em.'

'Why should I? It's mine.'

'While you're in my 'ouse you'll do as I say!'

The times Emma had heard that line! It made her very angry. But for her mother's sake she decided she must do as she was told. She had been very clever indeed.

She went upstairs to get the second of the two sovereigns Sarah had given her. Yes! She had been very clever, but all the time 'While you're in my 'ouse, you'll do as I say' rang in her ears. She was not happy. She wanted to escape, and it helped to know that her reward money was safe.

Meekly she gave her father the sovereign. He didn't bother to thank her, but simply put it in one of the pockets of his waistcoat. Yawning and stretching, he took off his starched collar and Sunday tie.

'Come on, Ma, time for our Sunday after-dinner nap. You, Emma, do the washing-up, then off to Bible class. Make sure they all see you. We don't want them thinkin' you've gone 'eathen.'

George slouched from the table to the armchair by the fireplace and soon started snoring. Emma went to the sink and made order out of chaos.

The last chorus of 'All Things Bright and Beautiful' died away and the younger children started to file out of the church schoolroom. Bible class was ending in the committee room next door.

'Thank you, girls, and may the love of Jesus protect you during the coming week.'

The dowdy young curate released his charges.

'Let's go for a walk, Katy. I've lots to tell you – and something to give you.'

'What's 'appened?'

46

Emma told her story. Opening her envelope, Katy couldn't believe her good fortune.

'Oh, Em! There's so much I want to do with this . . . Think of the clothes we could 'ave.'

'I know. But let's try hard to be sensible. We'll never get another five pounds without lots of hard work. We must put it away for when . . .'

She paused.

Katy went on for her. 'When we gets married?'

'*If* we get married,' Emma corrected her friend. 'But here's more for you – you'd better have the half sovereign too. Please take it.'

'No, I couldn', I really couldn' – no, honest!'

'You must, otherwise Pa'll find it. Look, you hate sewing – I know you do. So why don't you go to Whiteley's and buy one of those half-guinea costumes they advertised in the *Acton Gazette and Post*? You'll be a proper toff.'

'Oh, what a lark! Whiteley's! Never been in there. Could I, d'you think? "This way, modom. Would modom like to see anything else!" I can't wait to get 'ome! Aunty T'll be so 'appy for me – I know she will.'

Katy dearly loved the huge kindly guardian who had looked after her for so many years now. She knew that her news would be greeted with excitement and cuddles.

Emma read and reread the letter, written on thick notepaper heavily embossed with a family crest

> The Lady Rosamund Alston
> 1 Queen's Gate, Kensington, W.
> 15 August 1892

My dear Miss Cooper,

    There is something I wish to discuss with you. As it will also concern your parents, I suggest that all of you come to see me at three on Thursday afternoon.

    R.L.A.

'Well, how about that? Of course we can't go. How can we? Your pa never shuts the shop in the week – only for funerals.'

'But Ma, if you spoke really nice to him, perhaps he

47

might. If not –' she hesitated – 'then you and I must go without him.'

'Oh, he'd never let us do that.'

'Please, you must speak to him, you really must.'

'I'll see what I can do, but Em, I don't hold out much hope, I really don't. You know what he's like.'

Their conversation ended with Emma feeling totally frustrated and hopeless. Already she was working out in her mind how to reply regretfully to Lady Alston's letter.

Will Cooper's reaction had greatly surprised his wife and daughter, although on thinking about it Emma realised that the invitation appealed to his pretentiousness. The vicar and church council would be told, and while he could easily have left the shop in George's care, his snobbishness encouraged him to shut it, so that the neighbourhood would notice and gossip spread the word even more.

Wearing their Sunday clothes, the Coopers walked part of the way, to the end of Kensington High Street, then took a horse bus to Hyde Park Gate, from which it was only a short walk to Lady Alston's house.

'I'm so pleased to meet you, Mr Cooper – Mrs Cooper – and of course Emma, once again. Thank you for taking the time to come and see me. I won't keep you too long. Please sit down.'

Emma felt quite at home on the chair she'd occupied on her previous visit, while her parents perched uncomfortably on the edge of a sofa.

'We're truly *honoured* to be 'ere,' Will Cooper replied.

'Oh, yes, we *are*,' his wife put in very meekly, but in the 'smart' voice that she always adopted when speaking to the vicar, the doctor, or anyone she considered above her station.

'Now, this is what I propose. I believe that you have a very special daughter. Although I don't yet know her at all well, she has fine qualities and is very talented. I've seen her sewing, and I like her manners and the way she speaks.'

'It was her school what done that. She talks proper – went to a church school, you know.'

Mrs Cooper let her grammar slip in her enthusiasm to support what Lady Alston had said.

48

'As I was saying –' Lady Alston did not altogether care to be interrupted by a member of the lower class – 'she has fine qualities, and I am sure you must be very proud of her.'

'Oh, we are, we are, me lady,' both parents agreed.

If only he'd show it to me, thought Emma.

'For many years I had a loyal lady's companion, but sadly she has had for family reasons to leave me. Now, Mr and Mrs Cooper, I like young people. They stimulate me, they make me feel less old, and I find that I feel less pain when they are around. I have given the matter a lot of thought, and I would very much like to offer Emma the post of personal companion. Her duties would be interesting rather than heavy. She will accompany me when I go out in the carriage, or if I feel like taking a short walk. She will help with arranging seating when I give a dinner party – not too often these days.'

'Won't hear of it, y'ladyship. No. I says no. I won't 'ave my daughter becoming a servant.'

Emma was deeply shocked. Her first reaction to Lady Alston's suggestion was sheer joy. She liked the woman and the woman liked her – and it would be a marvellous opportunity.

'But Mr Cooper, I am not asking your daughter to be a servant. The post offers far more opportunities than even a head parlour maid could ever hope for. She would be my *companion*. And of course she would receive an appropriate wage.'

'How much?'

Lady Alston drew herself up. The question was so abrupt!

'Shall we say forty pound a year? With, of course, a clothes allowance. Needless to say she would live in – though with plenty of time to visit you on Sunday afternoons.'

'Forty pound a year!' Mr Cooper looked a little more thoughtful.

'Oh, Pa, please let me try! I'll never get another opportunity like this. It's more like being a lady-in-waiting. I won't be eating below stairs with the servants, will I, my lady?'

'My dear, the whole point is that you will be keeping me company. Of course you will liaise with the staff, but your role will be entirely different, and you will have a very pretty suite – two rooms all to yourself.'

49

Emma's eyes were a study.

'Lady Alston.'

Will Cooper stood up, stretching himself to his full height.

'You must *h*understand that I want the best for my daughter. I want to see that she is not only well looked after but well protected. I don' want her hurt or . . . or spoiled in any way, begging your pardon, my lady, if you gets my meaning.'

Mother and daughter exchanged wry glances.

'I quite understand your concern, Mr Cooper; but I do assure you that you will have no cause for worry on that score. My staff are impeccably behaved and carefully chosen. My people have been with me for years, and I can vouch for them.'

'I'll have to think about it. Emma's always just helped her mother an' me at home, since we moved – and that's what we've always wanted; no need for her to go out to work like a lot of girls. What we got to decide is if we can do without her.'

'Please, Mr Cooper, don't delay for too long. I will send Stratton round tomorrow evening to know your answer. If you will allow your daughter to join me, we will work out when she is to start. Would that suit you, Emma? Mrs Cooper?'

The wallpaper with its design of tiny rosebuds, the softness of the bed, the window with its curved head, heavy Venetian blinds and pure white lace curtains, all seemed to welcome Emma with a big, warm smile.

She sat on the bed and looked at her new surroundings in a daze. Her small trunk was a few feet away, where young Toby, the footman, had left it a few minutes earlier. This was the first time in several days that she had had a moment to herself, to think, to reflect . . . The changes that had come about in her life had seemed to tumble towards her like huge waves breaking at the tide line.

Here she was, only two or three miles away from her home, but in a totally different world. She could hear birdsong in the trees outside and the clip-clopping of horses' hooves as they trotted smartly along the broad carriageway of Queen's Gate.

50

Lady Alston had given her the afternoon to unpack and to get to know the staff. At four o'clock she was to join her in the drawing room for afternoon tea.

The bedroom's huge wardrobe would dwarf Emma's meagre collection of clothes. There was also a chest of drawers for her few undergarments, and a pretty dressing table occupied the place between the two windows. To get to the bedroom, she must walk through a sitting room with two elderly but comfortable chairs, a desk and a little worktable. There, as in the bedroom, the highly polished floor was liberally scattered with a variety of rugs.

In the corner of the bedroom was a small door. Apprehensively, Emma opened it.

'Oh – ooh!'

She cupped both hands over her mouth to stifle her astonished cry. It took her a moment or two to realise the function of the tiny room, since she had never seen one like it before. There was only a very small window, but her eyes soon became accustomed to the subdued light, and she saw a white washbasin, decorated with blue flowers, and two huge brass taps. The main feature was a large, deep bath with a curved panel of porcelain at the far end, various knobs, and a thing like the rose of a watering can fixed high above it.

By the side of the bath was a lavatory basin. Emma stepped up to it, and was even more amazed than at the bath and washbasin. It was not simply a dark, smelly pit above which was a piece of wood with an oval hole in it, like the one 'down the back' at home. This was quite different. The china bowl had flowers printed on it which matched the washbasin, and the words 'Crapper. London Patented.' Nearly touching the ceiling was a cistern from which hung a chain with a china handle, the word 'pull' emblazoned on it in an authoritative style.

She could have done with using the lavatory, but wondered if she dared do so. This might well be Lady Alston's private bathroom. But then she thought again. Lady Alston's bedroom suite was on the second floor. She was on the third. If Emma's suite had such a modern luxury, and she was only the companion, surely Lady Alston would have something even grander adjoining her bedroom. But if she used the lavatory, would the chain work, or should she get a bucket of water to throw down the pan? Would the thing make a lot of noise and disturb everyone else in the house? The more she thought about it, the more she wanted to pee.

Her discomfort grew. Eventually she turned around, closed the door, and noticed there was a key in the lock. She turned the key . . . and relieved herself. There was quite a noisy, gurgling rush of water as she pulled the chain, but she hoped for the best. Fancy being able to wash your hands so easily after, she thought to herself and turned the tap – and the water came out so hot that it made her flinch. White Castile soap was there ready for her, and a huckaback towel on which she dried her hands. She hoped she'd not acted out of turn in using the bathroom – she'd have to pluck up courage and tell her employer.

Ever since Will Cooper had opened his boot-repairing business in Hammersmith, he had made it his routine to visit the tanner on the first Monday of the month to order supplies of leather, and then to see an old ironmonger who provided him with nails and all the other requirements for the continuation of his steady business.

This early September day was no exception to the rule. It was the one day in the month when he left George in charge of the business. He opened the shop as usual, then, having given a great many instructions to George, he set off on his journey, right back to his roots in the Old Kent Road.

Mrs Cooper, in addition to coping with the general depression caused by her age, was feeling very lonely and sad, but at the same time very proud of her daughter's good fortune. She took the midday dinner down to George, who, on these particular days, was not allowed to go to the pub for a break – her husband would not allow the shop to be shut for even half an hour at any time during the working day.

As she arrived back at the cottage, she noticed a hansom cab turning the corner into Hofland Road. Don' see many of them round 'ere, she thought to herself. As she reached her garden gate, she recognised her elder daughter waiting at the front door.

'Hello, Ma!'

'Sarah! Oh, Sarah, my darlin'!'

'Ma – where's Pa?'

'He's – you know. First Monday.'

'Good. That's why I came. No matinée today. And George – is he out of the way?'

'Down at the shop. He won' be back till eight, I reckon. Let's go in the parlour, love. It is good to see yer.'

Then, noticing Sarah's fashionable pale-blue silk suit, its straight line showing off her tiny waist and elegant figure, she remarked, 'Ooh, you are a toff! Wish Pa would let me come and see yer show. And of course you don' know about our Em! She's –'

'Yes, Ma, I do know all about Emma.'

Mrs Cooper was very surprised to hear that Emma and Katy had visited Sarah at the theatre.

Sarah went on, 'Emma is a good, honest girl – that's the way you and Pa, for all his strictness and cruelty, have brought her up. She wrote to me to tell me all about Lady Alston and her new position.'

'Oh, Sarah, I do miss her, even though we'll see her every Sunday. Like I still misses you, too, you know. But what do you want with me, now you're famous? And clever too – I knows that.' The poor woman burst into tears. 'Oh, you don' know what it's like! I know I'm on the change, but all this makes me so miserable. I just wish I was feeling me old self, if you gets my meanin'.'

Sarah comforted her distraught mother, and tried to prepare her for what she'd come to tell her.

'Ma, I owe everything to you. Allowing me to go to that fancy dancing class – scraping the couple of pennies a week to pay for it, and then not letting Pa know what was going on. But but then there was that day . . .'

Sarah took a deep breath and paused. With her mother so upset, should she go on? Eventually Mrs Cooper, blowing her nose and drying her eyes, broke in.

'Go on. You was sayin'? Oh yes, that day . . . that terrible day four years ago – I remembers that allright. I'll never forget that day.'

'Ma – dear, dear Ma!' Sarah took her mother's rough hands into her own beautifully smooth ones. 'There's a lot you don't know, in spite of all those cruel words that me and Pa exchanged. There was far more to the quarrel than just Pa finding out about my dancing classes.'

'He said it was sinful – it was the devil in you.'

'Ma, there was no devil in *me*.'

'I don' understand.'

'Ma, I *allowed* Pa to find my dancing pumps and dress. I *wanted* him to know I was dancing.'

'But why? Why? You knew all along that if he found out that would be the end of everything for you.'

'I had my reasons.'

Mrs Cooper gazed absently at the sunlight shining through Sarah's abundant blonde hair. 'Still don' understand – what reasons?'

Sarah, hesitating, swallowed hard but managed to go on.

'I'm telling you this now because of what has been happening to Emma for well over a year now. I know that Emma isn't at home any more, but I think you should know the real reason why she came to see me at the theatre the other week. What was happening then to Emma had happened to me.'

Mrs Cooper was confused but listened intently.

'Ma, dear Ma, this is hard for me to say, but the real reason why I wanted to leave home – why I let Pa find my dancing pumps and dress – was because of George.'

'George? What can he have to do with anything? He don't do nothing but work 'ard – he's such a good son!'

Mrs Cooper was beginning to get angry with her daughter. She would never hear a word against George. Oh yes, she'd watched and listened with amusement when he and Emma sniped at each other, but that was surely just a strange expression of brotherly and sisterly love.

'Ma, you are going to find this hard to believe, but what I'm about to tell you is true. George is not the good son you think. Oh yes, he works hard, and in your eyes and Pa's he's faultless. When we were very little, I suppose it was all harmless – after we'd gone to bed we'd creep into each others beds and play . . . play mas and pas. Then he grew up. I was still a child, but I began to realise that he was more than just playing the games we'd always played – pretending to get married, to be ill and so on. That he wanted to touch me, well

54

. . . all over. That he wanted to feel me. And in time, when *my* body began to change, I knew that I didn't like what he was doing.'

Her mother was listening, stunned at what her daughter was telling her.

'George? Did George do things like that? No, surely? No, I can't believe it! Sarah, you and your stories – you know how you used to make them up when you was little. Are you *sure* you're tellin' the truth?'

'Yes, Ma, truly. Do you remember I kept asking for my own room? Well, I knew that was impossible, but I did get you to persuade Pa to put up that partition so that I could have my own tiny space.'

Mrs Cooper nodded.

'I suppose it was then that the trouble really began. The partition baffled any noise which you and Pa might have heard, and from then on George would all too often come to my part of the room and get into bed with me. He threatened me, saying that if I told you or Pa he'd deny it and that he'd tell Pa about my dancing classes – which really meant so much to me. "Besides," he used to say, "I'm the son, the only son – you're only a girl. They won't believe you because I'm such a good boy and I'll carry on the business and look after Ma and Pa when Pa's too old to work." Things like that he used to tell me every time he came to my room, and I believed him. Then I started to . . . to come on every month. I felt even more like a woman and he was even more persistent. He'd always manage somehow to keep me quiet – by his threats mostly, saying Pa would turn me out if he knew and that he would beat us – you and me, Ma – for deceiving him.'

At this point the older woman started violently to shake her head and put her hands over her ears.

'Sarah, Sarah, don't go on! I can't bear it. It can't be true. But you wouldn' make up something like that, would you?'

Sarah took her mother's hands again.

'It is true, Ma. You must listen to me. One night, he got hold of me and he pushed his big fingers right up . . . right up inside me – down there. Then . . . Oh, God! How can I go on? The memory's so awful . . .'

Sarah started to sob. It was her mother's turn to comfort her.

'He was holding me so tight, and then he did it. He raped me. I felt as if he was killing me. The pain was awful. I was torn apart up inside. You may not remember, Ma, but I stayed in bed next day, saying I had a guts-ache.'

'George! I simply can't believe that he could do such a thing to his own sister. George is such a good boy.'

'He did, Ma, it's God's truth. And as I lay in bed that day I realised I had to do something. Then I remembered his words: "If Pa finds out about the dancing, he'll throw you out!" I knew he was right. Pa with his church and respectability ... I knew you'd suffer, but I was frantic and I realised that if Pa did find out – sooner rather than later – yes, there would be a row, yes, he'd throw me out; but I also knew that I was the best in the class at dancing, even if I had nowhere to go.

'The next day I took my dancing dress and my pumps and left them on his chair in the kitchen. The rest you know – well, not quite all. When I walked out that evening – oh, Ma, how I hated leaving you to cope with him! – I went to Madame Binny and told her some of my story. She put me up for a week or two. Then I saw an advertisement in the *Era* saying that Mr George Edwardes wanted to audition young ladies. Madame Binny said I should go along. Well, that led to my first job.

'But now you can see why Emma came to see me the other day. The same thing was happening to her, though thank goodness George didn't actually rape her. If it hadn't been for Katy's good sense and worldliness, who knows what might have happened? Well, I can make a pretty good guess. You see, Ma, Emma's not as forthcoming or as confident as me, so Katy's really been a good friend to her. And now things have worked out so well. You have two very successful daughters – even if you will be lonely.'

'But Sarah, what can I do about George?'

'Nothing. Now that Emma's out of the way he'll not be tempted, and he'll either have to find himself a wife or have his fun with prost –'

'Sarah! None 'o that theatre talk 'ere, my girl!'

'Sorry, Ma, but you know what I mean. Chances are he'll settle down. You need him to work more and more as Pa gets older, so I don't think I'd upset the applecart. However, if ever he did anything dreadful you hold a trump card. He would deny everything, but he'd know that you knew.'

Chapter Four

As Laura was rather stiffly bending down to pick up the copy of the *Western Daily Mercury* to put in its usual place on the tray with the morning tea for her master and mistress, Joe thundered down the stairs, practically knocking the poor woman over, and grabbed the paper from her.

Eagerly he opened the pages. Just below the court circular was the message he was so keen to read.

'Candidates accepted for Her Majesty's training ship *Britannia* at Dartmouth for the new term are as follows,' he read aloud, 'Alcock, J., Beamish, A., Blackhorse, R., Coulman, M., . . . Oh, why is N such a long way down the alphabet?'

But then his eyes fell on his name. Grabbing the paper so tightly that it crumpled, he dashed up the stairs.

'Mama, Papa, Lizzie! I've got it! I've passed!'

He burst into his parents' bedroom without bothering to knock.

'Look, Papa – here's my name. I'm to go to Dartmouth!'

'But darling, of course you are. We know you're exactly what the navy requires, don't we, Peter?'

'Very proud of you, son. You'll carry on the Newcombe tradition in fine style!'

'Come and give me a big hug, darling.'

Joe slipped onto his parents' huge bed to be warmly cuddled by his mother, the lace of her nightgown tickling his face and her long chestnut hair covering his neatly cropped fair head as she pressed him to her breast.

'Now, go and tell Lizzie,' his mother suggested as she released her young son. But Lizzie was already standing at the door, and it was her turn to congratulate her brother, who had never been more excited in his life.

Joe wondered about his new life a very great deal, but he was excited rather than nervous, and his high-pitched, excited state added light and colour to the Newcombe household. Even Mrs Newcombe, who was more than a little upset at the sacrifice of her young son to the Royal Navy, could not but be encouraged by his enthusiasm, exuberance and keenness. Aggie sympathised with her mistress.

'I remember when the Captain went off to sea, madam. There 'e was in 'is uniform – every inch the man, the naval officer, just like our young Joe will be!'

Sentimental tears clouded her old eyes, and it was no bad thing that the Captain was out of the room, since she was finding it difficult to refer to the boy as 'Master Joseph'.

She had first joined the Newcombe family when she was a thirteen-year-old trainee nursemaid, so she had known Peter Newcombe since he was born; and though from time to time he and his wife had considered dismissing her, they realised that she would have nowhere to go but the workhouse. She appreciated the kindness and generosity the family was showing her, and they accepted her as the real family friend she was, even if she could be extremely irritating at times – all too inclined to express her opinion when she was very definitely not required to do so.

'Aggie? *Aggie!* Help! I need more pins!'

'You've got lots. You don' need any more!'

'I do, *really*. Look, all this won't stay in place unless I have at least three or four more. Please go and get some from Mama, otherwise they'll all be waiting for me.'

'Right y'are, Miss Elizabeth!'

It was easier for Aggie to remember Lizzie's new title now that she was in her heavy, long skirt and Spooner's cotton blouse. Lizzie was struggling to get her abundant chestnut locks piled on top of her head in something that she hoped would resemble a neat cottage loaf. Aggie eventually toddled back into her bedroom with the extra hairpins.

'They're all down there waiting for you in the drawing room. Don' be long. Your papa'll get cross, that he will.'

'Tell them I'll only be a moment.'

59

In sheer desperation she fixed a long, strong hairpin into the last section of hair and admitted that her efforts and her new outfit looked quite dashing. She walked downstairs with extreme care in case her hair should collapse – it felt most insecure – and joined her parents and Joe, who was equally resplendent in his cadet's uniform. Their father was in his full captain's rig, and their mother in an autumn costume that had just arrived by special carrier from Whiteley's in London. The rose-pink jacket and skirt, with its long, tapering line, suited her above-average height, and her new hat had been matched exactly by the clever milliner at Popham's of Bedford Street.

'Ah, here you are at last!' But before the Captain could praise his daughter, Laura entered to say that the carriage was waiting for them.

Major and Darker's impressive photographic studio was situated at 152 Union Street. There was a collection of cameras, several pieces of fashionable furniture and a variety of drapes, painted backgrounds and potted palms. On a small, round table with a plush tablecloth edged with fringe and bobbles were piled some leather-bound books.

'I thought that the two ladies could sit here.' Mr Darker pulled up a settee with curved legs and dainty arms. 'And the Captain could stand behind Mrs Newcombe, with the young officer leaning on the table with a book in his hand. Just here, young sir, if you please.'

Joe was about to pick up one of the books when the photographer had a sudden inspiration.

'No – why not a telescope? That would be more suitable. Here, try holding this one.' He handed Joe a rather cumbersome naval instrument.

'Joe dear, I know you love books, but I do think that the telescope would be most impressive.' His mother backed up Mr Darker's recommendation.

The daylight in the studio was glaring, and through it Lizzie could see galaxies of dust particles, the number of which increased noticeably as Mr Darker fussily arranged the heavy velvet drapes behind the family group, partly revealing a painted backcloth of a garden scene.

The ladies had their skirts expertly arranged; the Captain

60

stood bolt upright. The photographer hid under his black cloth. Everything was set for the necessary long exposure.

'You know, of course, that you must sit very still indeed. Please do not move, and try not to blink.'

They were all quite still, the lens cover was removed – but after a second or so Lizzie sneezed violently, and as she did so she jerked her head forward. To her dismay her hair fell down, right over her face. Joe collapsed in laughter and though their parents tried hard to look stern, it was not with great success.

'Mr Darker, I am so very sorry.'

'It won't happen again,' the Captain reassured him.

Joe's face was a study. The sight of Lizzie with all her hair falling right over her face made him laugh and laugh until he ached, and the more he tried to keep a straight face, the more he laughed. This set Lizzie off, though she really did her best to be ladylike.

Mr Darker was not at all amused. Mrs Newcombe saw his annoyance but also appreciated the funny side of the situation. She looked at the Captain, who was trying hard to keep an unruffled calm.

'I'm so sorry, Mr Darker, but I'm sure my daughter really couldn't help sneezing. It is a pity you've wasted a photographic plate, but of course we will reimburse you.'

Mr Darker relaxed a little in the knowledge he was not losing an expensive 'full plate'.

'Perhaps the young lady would like to go and fix her hair in the changing room? If madam would like to go and assist her? She obviously needs some help.'

The photographer gestured to the right, and mother and daughter beat a fast retreat.

'When the ladies return, perhaps we can have a little more decorum. The right atmosphere is absolutely essential if we are to produce the high-quality family group for which this studio is renowned. Captain, can you take your son in hand, please?'

'Joseph, do calm down.'

'Yes, Papa, I'll try.' And he spluttered into another paroxysm of laughter.

The group, and a series of *cartes de visite* for which each of

61

them sat individually, turned out quite beautifully, though Joe was sucking in his cheeks rather noticeably, in order to prevent another explosion of laughter.

The summer could not have been happier for Mrs Newcombe. She had had her darlings around her, and had been in her element. There had been pleasant afternoon picnics, a day's outing with the Admiral and his family on his impressive yacht, evening walks on the Hoe, and some excursions – to Exeter, to look once more at the cathedral and have tea at the Royal Clarence Hotel; to Torquay, where the four of them had stayed overnight at the Imperial, and had enjoyed dinner in the palatial dining room. How proud she had been of Lizzie and Joe, now so grown up – even more so during these last few weeks.

She was musing on this while her husband was at luncheon at Admiralty House. She knew that the Admiral of the Port would have news for him. Naval officer's wife that she was, she had lived through this experience many times over the years. There was always the great sadness of farewells and long partings – but this time their time together had been so special, with their plans for Lizzie and Joe cohering so well. The family had reached a crossroads, and its younger members were setting out on their respective journeys towards their future lives and into adulthood.

When the Captain came home, she was sitting on a wicker lounger on the tiled terrace which led to the lawn. The sun was warm and mellow, the sea breeze pleasantly cool.

She was jolted back into the immediate present by his footstep on the paving. Kissing his wife lightly on the forehead, he said, 'Not much time left, I'm afraid. Got to be off next week.'

'Oh, no! So soon! What ship? For how long?'

'The *Rameses* again – I'm pleased about that. It's a happy ship, as you know.'

'That's good, my dear. But will we be parted for yet another two years? Quite honestly, Peter, it gets harder and harder every time, now. Oh, I know it shouldn't, and in many ways I am used to it, but –'

'But listen. I dropped a few hints to the old man, reminded him of how long I'd been away last time. He likes you, by the way – fair blushed when I mentioned you, so you're scoring high with him!'

'You're teasing me. Go on, what else did he say?'

'Well, he suggested that perhaps later on you might like to join me on some overseas station, and we could be together for the last few months or so of the tour. Said he'd see what he could do, if you'd like that.'

'To travel and see the world! Oh, Peter, that would be marvellous! But I couldn't leave the children.'

'We'll see. There would only be one holiday period for both of them, after all – and Lizzie is no longer five years old. Do think about it. I have to sail on the evening tide on Thursday, by the way.'

He tried to sound as casual as possible by throwing away the last statement, but she caught at it. 'But my dear – it's Friday now. Oh no, I can't believe it! Absolutely everything is happening at once. Joe leaves for Dartmouth on Wednesday, and Lizzie starts teaching on Monday. So much upheaval in such a short space of time!'

'I say, there's Milly Luscumbe over there!'

Annie Midgley was addressing Elsie Penhaligan in the courtyard in front of Miss Creeber's Academy. It was the first day of term, and the young teenagers had a lot to talk about after the long summer holidays. There was the excitement of seeing friends again, but at the same time there was the thought of the boring weeks of hard work ahead, and of even stricter discipline than most of the girls endured at home to blanket the liveliness of the atmosphere.

'Milly, *Milly*! We're over here.'

Milly heard her friend from across the yard and made her way between a score of much younger children, including a group of tiny five-year-olds waiting with nurses and parents to be let in before the older pupils.

'Hello, and what have you two been up to? As if I didn't know.'

'We don't know what you're talking about – do we, Elsie? Just 'cos we've got brothers, and we all play together.'

Before Milly could reply to Elsie's pretended innocent coyness, Annie gave a gasp.

'Look, over there! A new teacher!'

'Where? Where?'

'No, it's not, it's that little girl's mama!'

'*Stupid*! She's no mother – whoever's seen a mother with a waist like that?'

'And what do you know about these things, pray?' Milly asked.

'Quite a lot, actually. She looks familiar ... I say – it's Lizzie!'

'*Lizzie*? But she left in July. What's she doing coming back dressed up like that? Look at her hair!'

'It's divine,' Milly cooed.

'Lizzie, Lizzie! What are you doing here? Thought you'd left!'

Annie shouted right across the yard, where Lizzie was starting to check off the names of the new five-year-olds from a list.

At this point Miss Young appeared from nowhere and aggressively prodded the noisy Annie in the back.

'Annie Midgley, this is no way to start the new term. Your behaviour is most unladylike. You do not shout in that street-urchin manner. You should have a hundred lines for such appalling behaviour, but as it's the first day of term I'll let you off with a caution. Do not interrupt Miss Elizabeth, you can see she is busy doing important work for the Academy. Be quiet at once!'

Miss Young scurried away to organise the eight-year-olds, who were about to become the new standard-three girls.

'Did you hear what she said? "*Miss* Elizabeth!" Hoity-toity!' As she spoke, Annie took a short, mock sophisticated walk.

'Oh, Annie, be careful! We don't want Miss Young to come back again,' Elsie cautioned.

'But why *Miss* Elizabeth? She's just Lizzie. It's stupid – after all, she's only a little bit older than us, and we're her friends.'

By now the new babies' class was in its place, and mothers and nurses were departing with some apprehension, leaving their small charges at school for the first time.

The bell clanged and the rest of the girls lined up, each in

64

her own standard, walking with almost military precision into the large schoolhouse.

Lizzie, who had heard Annie's call, wanted to go over and explain what had happened, but she knew she must ignore her friends.

The morning already seemed to have lasted for ages. She had been wakened by Laura with a cup of tea – the first time this had happened. It made her feel very grown up indeed. After enjoying the adult luxury, she had washed, laced herself into her restricting corsets and dealt with her hair. Then there was a nervously hurried breakfast – though she wasn't late – followed by reassurance from her parents and Joe, and she had taken the familiar brisk walk over the Hoe to Lockyer Street and the beginning of her working life.

Just before the majority of the pupils filed into the largest room in the house, once a ballroom but now an assembly hall, she took her place at the ancient piano to play for the girls to take their places at assembly for the morning hymn. She began a Schubert march and the pupils started to walk in, in reasonable time to the music. But some of the notes made no sound at all as Lizzie struck the uneven, worn keys – there was a totally dead E flat just above middle C. It sounded as though she were making mistakes – not at all like the beautiful grand piano at home.

She glanced at Miss Creeber, sitting majestically in her huge, carved oak chair in front of her lectern, expecting her to be glowering bad-temperedly. But no – for once she was smiling, tapping her fingers almost in time with the music. Miss Young was also looking happy. This reassured the suffering Lizzie, who assumed that they were so used to the awful sound of the geriatric piano that they simply didn't notice how dreadful it was. Indeed, Lizzie herself, though she had cringed from time to time when she had heard it in the past, was only now wholly aware that the neglected instrument should have long since been taken away by the rag-and-bone man.

By now the girls were in their places, standing in neat rows and not daring to make a sound. Lizzie struck a final chord which would have made Schubert turn in his grave, and all but laughed; but the solemnity of Miss Creeber's face when she stood up was such that any outburst was smothered. Nevertheless, Lizzie was glad that Joe wasn't there.

'We will sing hymn 576 – five, seven, six,' said Miss Creeber. 'The first and last verses only. Are you ready, Miss Elizabeth?'

Elizabeth nodded, and started another battle with the piano.

> 'Lord behold us with Thy blessing
> Once again assembled here . . .'

The girls were not terribly sure of the hymn or its tune, since they only sang it (and 'Lord, dismiss us with Thy blessing') at the beginning and end of term. But they struggled on until the final 'Amen'.

Miss Creeber, still standing, put down her hymn book, and in her most solemn voice began the first of the term's daily sermons. The older girls gritted their teeth and tried to look interested, though they had heard it all time and time again.

'"The fear of the Lord is the beginning of wisdom, and to depart from evil – that is understanding." We come now to the beginning of a new term – indeed, a new school year – and these words should always be uppermost in your minds as you proceed with your studies. If you remember them, the Lord will help you. Now, let us pray . . .'

They recited the Lord's Prayer and the Collect – about being good, well-behaved and studious – and asked for forgiveness for the sinful behaviour into which the evils of sloth and pride would most certainly lead them.

Then Miss Creeber addressed them yet again.

'Apart from the five-year-olds,' she said, screwing up her eyes and narrowing her lips, 'you will all by now have realised that Elizabeth Newcombe has joined Miss Young, myself and the other teachers on the staff. She has been your fellow pupil; now she has a different role to play – and so have you. You are no longer her friends, but her pupils. You will address her as Miss Elizabeth, and must at no time have any social commerce with her especially you older girls who were Miss Elizabeth's classmates. You must take special care to remember these new rules, which I shall not repeat; I shall be extremely strict with anyone who breaks them.

'Go now to your classrooms, where those members of staff who have been organising your books and adjusting the timetables for the coming term, are awaiting you. Now, Miss Elizabeth – some more music, if you please.'

Lizzie struck up the pretty coda to the march, which was quicker in tempo; the girls marched briskly out of the hall.

Her first day was busy, and she got through it with an element of satisfaction, some amusement, and a certain amount of horror. From an anthology called *Eighty Poems and Sacred Verses for Our Little Ones*, she had to choose a poem to teach the new five-year-olds, with whom she was to spend the whole day. Their first lesson was 'numbers', and she succeeded in getting them to count up to ten, in unison. Later she would have to discover just how many of them could manage the task individually, without the help of classmates or herself. Then she started to teach them their ABC – some knew it already. But it was the poems that made her angry. They were awful, and it was very difficult to find one in the book that was less awful than the rest. She chose the least sickly and obnoxious, but hated having to ram it down their little throats.

Frustrated, and having taught them the first two verses – she didn't dare do otherwise – she decided to teach them a nursery rhyme. When she recited it to them, the roomful of children exploded into happy, carefree laughter. Miss Young burst into the room.

'Miss Elizabeth, your class is making far too much noise. The children are thoroughly disturbing my senior girls' Latin, next door – do keep them quiet, please.'

And she swept out without another word.

Lizzie got up from her desk, put her fingers to her lips, and said, 'Shshh! Now we must all be very quiet – but let's see if we can say our funny poem in a whisper.'

They did so, and the bell went for the end of afternoon school. Lizzie's first day's work was over.

She managed to slip out of school a little before the senior girls, who had some extra clearing-up to do, and was well on her way across the Hoe Promenade when she heard Annie calling after her. She, Elsie and Milly were running to catch Lizzie up, satchels flying in the wind, hats all askew.

'How *awful* for you – we're not supposed to see you or anything. I hate school. I can't see why you took this job.' Annie was the spokeswoman of the trio.

'I simply don't care about those silly rules. We're all friends, and I don't see why we shouldn't continue to be so, especially at weekends and during holidays. But Annie, the job isn't *that* bad. I *am* getting paid, and they said they want me to go to Girton in a year or two.'

'Oh, you'll be a regular bluestocking then. We don't want that, do we, girls? We want to have beaux and get married and make our men look after us and –'

'Spend their money!' the three girls chorused.

'Yes, I know – but look, I must get home. Mama and Papa will be anxious to know how I've got on. I'll see you three on the pier on Saturday at half past two – we can have fun then. But even if we don't keep the sillier rules, let's at least try not to make each other laugh – especially when I'm trying to play that *dreadful* piano!'

'We'll try!'

They went their separate ways.

It had been the poems that had upset her most, and the awful food she had to swallow at the one-o'clock dinner. The greasy mutton stew with its half-cooked potatoes, and the watery tapioca pudding, had made her feel sick but, having to set an example to the pupils, she knew she must leave nothing on her plate. However, she was delighted by the way the little girls responded to her.

Having told her parents and Joe about her day, Lizzie slipped up to her room, tore off her corsets, put on one of her more comfortable dresses, and let her hair down, tying it with a piece of pale green ribbon just to keep it off her face.

Full of excitement, Joe rushed up the stairs to the top floor and his room. There was his trunk. It was huge about four feet long and two feet wide and deep. There was a great deal of room in its base for clothes and books, and a shelf near the top which on the right had a compartment containing an enamel bowl and a soap dish, both emblazoned with the words 'J. Gieves and Sons, Portsmouth and Devonport'. A mirror was fixed to the inside of the lid, and to the left the shelf supported a large black tin box – a special container for smaller and more valuable items such as pens and pencils and important notebooks. Just below it was another semi-secret place, where the aspiring naval officer could keep that specially rich fruitcake, chocolate or any other delicious consumable meant to supplement the notoriously dreary and often not very nutritious food. On the outside of the lid was a brass plate with Joe's name on it, glinting in the morning sun as it shone into his bright bedroom. Joe gazed at it in amazement.

'Is this really mine?'

'Yes, my dear, but remember this is your only space, and you do have your uniform and underclothes to pack into it, and of course those regulation things like toothbrush and - powder, things of that sort. Now look,' his mother went on, 'Aggie and I will pack your clothes – you sort out what else you want. But remember, there won't be that much space.'

Joe spent the morning selecting a small pile of his favourite books. *Treasure Island* was one he'd read and reread but never tired of, but, most importantly, he decided to take the huge book of photographs called *Round the World*. It was looking at this and reading the short descriptions of places he knew one day he'd visit that would be a real source of inspiration. A school atlas and, of course, his hymn and prayer books and his Bible, a notebook and a packet of stationery that Lizzie had bought him, and a very smart pen-and-pencil set from his parents were also carefully stowed away in the trunk. He then fixed to the inside of the lid, alongside the mirror, one of the photographs of the family taken at Mr Darker's studio, two silhouettes that he and Lizzie had had cut by the man on the pier, and a photograph of himself and his old classmates from Hoe Grammar School.

By early afternoon the trunk was packed and ready. Pickford's men called with a pantechnicon drawn by two heavy horses, and took it to Millbay Station to be sent by goods train to Dartmouth, where it would arrive at about the same time as he, the next day.

The last evening the four of them would be together was going to be very special, so that each member of the family would remember it during the long months ahead.

69

Laura had been busily cooking two ducks with an orange sauce, and had made a charlotte russe for dessert, and the very best china and glass was set out on the dining-room table, which was also decorated with some pretty small flower arrangements that Lizzie had organised after her arduous second day at school.

Mrs Newcombe was in a pensive mood. Tonight would mark the beginning of an exciting time for Joe in particular, and a challenging time for Lizzie, but it was a sad experience for herself. She felt her family was being wrenched apart. However, she knew she must not only catch Joe's excitement and encourage Lizzie but also recognise Peter's renewed energy and enthusiasm for the tasks ahead of him. The navy was his life, and she would not want in any way to encroach upon his second love – the command of his ship and the call of the sea. At least they were living through a period of relative calm – in wartime his role would have been considerably more dangerous.

Before dinner the family assembled in the drawing room, where the Captain opened a bottle of Moët et Chandon.

'We must have a champagne toast. To us – the Newcombe family. May we prosper and be successful!'

'To us,' they all chorused.

Joe hadn't tasted champagne before, and wasn't prepared for the bubbles, which at once went right up his nose. He didn't actually like it at first, and while the amount his father gave him was minimal, Mrs Newcombe wasn't at all sure whether he should have had any at all – especially as he had to travel early next morning. Lizzie had tasted it twice – once at a cousin's wedding and once the previous Christmas – but only a sip.

The atmosphere in the drawing room, as the sun was setting beyond the mouth of the Tamar, was one of a united family.

'We've all had a wonderful summer, haven't we?' The proud father smiled. 'And we've a lot of happy memories to see us through the coming months.'

His wife took his hand and gripped it hard, gazing at him in sad admiration. He knew what she was thinking.

'My love, we won't be parted for nearly as long. I'm quite

certain you'll be able to join me on the ship in about ten months' time.'

'I don't think I could leave Lizzie, even if Joe is at Dartmouth.'

'Mama, you really must. You must trust me. Besides, I'll have a lot of work to do by then; I'll be well into my extra studies for the entrance exam to Girton, so I won't be very good company, anyway. Aggie'll look after me, and who knows –' here Lizzie did some quick thinking – 'perhaps I'll persuade Laura to cook me the odd duck and, well . . . find another bottle of champagne in the cellar!'

'Lizzie, you're impossible! We'll see. I would like to travel . . .'

'There should be no problem. After all, it was the old man who suggested it.'

Captain Newcombe paused, then turned to Joe. 'Now, young Joseph, remember the navy today wants students – young men who are thinkers as well as men of action. You are a very thoughtful boy, and that's excellent; I'm sure you'll find your niche in one of the many branches of modern seacraft. You're about to set out on a great adventure, one from which you'll reap great rewards. And, of course, you'll be carrying on the family tradition for yet another generation.'

Joe, who had listened intently and seriously, replied with a simple 'Yes, Papa.'

The Captain sensed that the atmosphere was getting rather heavy – and if that went on too long, his wife might well succumb to tears.

'Lizzie,' he said, 'nip down to the kitchen and ask Laura and Aggie to come up. Tell Laura to bring another bottle of champagne – we must give Joe a special toast. They are part of the family too – they must join in wishing him well.'

'My dear, I really don't think Joe should have any more,' Mrs Newcombe protested.

'He won't. The rest of us will, though! Go, Lizzie.'

The two servants came in and, slightly confused, took their glasses. Everyone stood up.

'To Joe, God bless him,' the Captain toasted.

The rest of the household responded. Joe said a quiet thank you, and blushed to the roots of his blond curls.

'Joe, you'll be perfectly all right. And you look wonderful in your uniform – a real naval officer!'

'Thanks, Lizzie. But I'm going to miss you so much.'

'You'll make new friends, and I expect you just won't have time. I'll miss you too, of course, probably more than you'll miss me. But I really must go off to school now – otherwise I'll be too late to play for assembly.'

'What a pity if you missed the opportunity to play that beautiful piano!'

Even at a time like this, Joe managed to turn the attention away from himself to his sister. That piano had become a real family joke in the last couple of days.

'Shall I give it your love? Oh, Joe!'

Brother and sister came back to the reality of their farewells and hugged each other hard.

'Joe, write to me. I'll write to you.'

'Of course I will. This is it, isn't it?'

''Fraid so. Goodbye, Joe. Work hard – have fun, too.'

'I will, Lizzie – I'll try, anyway.'

They gave each other another big hug, and Lizzie, choking on a sob, rushed out of the front door to make her way to school.

'Do you really think Joe will manage on his own? He looked so young and vulnerable when he left.'

Mrs Newcombe was toying with a portion of smoked salmon served on a gold-rimmed plate displaying the Grand Hotel's monogram.

'My dear, of course he will. And so will Lizzie. You've done such a good job in bringing them up and have always so made them aware of their faults that they can only do well – and be happy.'

'That's the most important of all.' She managed a warm smile, which soon was clouded again as she went on, 'Peter, I do think we should have brought Lizzie with us tonight, to share our last dinner.'

'Darling, she understands. I told her I wanted to be alone with you. Besides, we had our family dinner last evening. Lizzie appreciates romance now she's growing up – just as I do. So forget you're the mother of two well-balanced, poten-

72

tially very successful children. Pretend to be twenty-one again, and that this is our wedding night!'

His loving wife blushed. 'Oh, really, Peter! How can you?'

Rolling his glass of claret in his hands, he looked seductively right into her eyes and replied, 'I can – surprisingly easily.'

She was wearing a pale-green pure-silk dinner gown and the triple-row pearl choker that her husband had given her when Lizzie was born. Matching it on her left wrist was a pearl bracelet he'd presented to her on the birth of their son. This quiet dinner in the subdued, elegant dining room of the Grand Hotel was something he'd been planning as a surprise since he knew that this particular week in September was going to be disruptive for his wife. He wanted to reassure her of his support and love – not that she needed any reassurance – and give her yet another happy memory.

The meal was perfect, and the relaxed atmosphere struck precisely the right chord for both of them. Soon they would have to face up to the reality of the morrow; but for now the devoted couple would enjoy each other's familiar company and deep affection, and would, a little later on, express their feelings through their warm, passionate love making.

Once more the moon shone brightly through the lace curtains and was reflected on the calm sea, as they slipped into bed and each other's arms.

Chapter Five

'My dear Rosa, how could you do such a thing? Taking a girl into your home, giving her all sorts of privileges she's never encountered before, and not even as a head parlour maid, but as a sort of friend. You know nothing of her – her background. She might even have . . . Well . . .'

'A disease? An inherited disease? Is that what you were about to say?'

'Oh, you *know* what I mean.'

The elderly Lady Cricklewood shifted uncomfortably in her chair and tried discreetly to rearrange her ample body inside her stays, which had suddenly become very tight, hot and uncomfortable on this sunny September afternoon.

Although they had been friends since their debutante days, they were very different people. However, it was Rosamund Alston who had lived life to the full. She had travelled with her husband, and together they had mixed with the famous writers and artists of their day. She was broad-minded and always open to new ideas. Hester Cricklewood was old-fashioned and conventional, and never put one foot out of line. Lady Alston found this amusing and infuriating; and if she had been asked, she would have said that it was these lively, conflicting ideas and attitudes that kept them together. While secretly wishing she could be as forward-looking and outspoken as Lady Alston, Lady Cricklewood had lent her respectability and good advice in support of her friend when she had been ostracised by society.

'I know I'm impulsive, but I'm not stupid. From the start the girl had everything in her favour. How many poor working-class girls these days would take something as valuable as that –' Lady Alston pointed to her ring – 'to the police station, when they know it would set them up for life? No, my dear, I thought of you and your reaction, but you have not met the girl. Of course, I'd planned to give a generous reward for the return of the ring. Then this dear, sweet, pretty creature turns up.'

She paused, and decided not to mention the heavy bruising on Emma's arm.

'So I gave her a reward.'

'Dear, sweet, innocent creature indeed! How much?'

'Does that matter?'

'*How much*?'

'Five pound.'

'You gave a stranger five pound? You really are mad. I've thought it for some time now. Rosa – you gave that child *five pound*? I can't believe it.' Lady Cricklewood could hardly contain her spluttering anger.

'I have money; I shall do as I like with it.' As she spoke, Lady Alston glanced across the room at a photograph in a heavy silver frame of a small girl of about four.

'Yes, I gave her five pound – and another five for her friend, who was with her at the time.'

'I suppose that was some worthless youth.'

'On the contrary, it was her girl friend. She's a laundress.'

'A laundress? My dear Rosa, pull yourself together – I think I'll have to talk to the vicar about you. He'll make you realise how foolishly you have behaved. How do we know that this . . . this *laundress* really exists? Your young friend may simply have made her up, to get more money out of you.'

'Calm down, Hester! You'll fall into a swoon if you go on like this. Here, take this fan.'

Lady Cricklewood took a black lace fan which her hostess handed her from a nearby whatnot, and started agitatedly to cool herself, the strands of her black and purple feather boa fluttering.

To break the tension, Lady Alston rang for tea.

Sybil, the experienced parlour maid, brought in a heavy tray loaded with an elaborate silver service and dainty Sèvres

75

china, and reappeared with a salver of minute sandwiches, bread and butter and Fortnum and Mason fruitcake. She glanced at the two old women and, as she closed the double doors of the drawing room, tutted to herself.

'Those two at it again. Not surprising, with all that's been going on in this household lately.'

She was tempted to listen at the keyhole, but resisted when she heard Stratton's soft footsteps on the thick stair carpet.

Meanwhile Lady Alston handed her old friend a cup of tea.

'So you think I simply met the girl, gave her ten pound, then asked her to be my companion – is that it?'

'Yes. It's typical of what you would do!'

'You are quite wrong. In the first instance, the next day I received these.'

She handed Lady Cricklewood two letters. One was beautifully written in the neatest copperplate handwriting, the other was poorly spelled and looked rather as if a spider had crawled over the lined exercise-book paper.

Hester Cricklewood fumbled in the depths of her ample bosom for her lorgnette, and took the letters from her friend, handling them gingerly, as if they had been dropped in farmyard dung. She sniggered as she tried to read the scrawl in which Katy's exuberance and overwhelming gratitude was so evident. When she turned to Emma's letter, her expression changed.

'Well, yes, very neat. Not a spelling mistake anywhere, and she addresses you properly. Very impressive, I'm sure. She must have been brought up decently.'

'She told me she went to a church school. I made enquiries. There was only one in her area, and I contacted the headmaster, who gave me an excellent report on her. She left two years ago. Then – I'd kept her from church, by the way, on that Sunday morning – I also contacted the vicar of St Matthew's in Hammersmith, and he too knew her and her parents well. Her father is a sidesman – a very upright, honest working man, though . . .'

Lady Alston again decided not to tell her friend of the man's violence towards his daughter.

'The vicar said Emma was honest, talented and very intelligent. Indeed, he was planning to ask her to take over the Bible class from his curate, who is overworked. So you see, my dear Hester, I did a lot of detective work before asking her and her parents round to see me again.'

'Quite the Sherlock Holmes, I must say! And what were they like – her parents?'

'The mother is a dear, sweet, simple soul, but I'm afraid I could hardly understand a word she said. She sounded like poor Lottie, my latest kitchen maid. The father, um ... pompous. Very strict with the girl and his wife. He is a bootmender.'

'A necessary trade for the lower classes. Well, I *suppose* you know your own mind. Can I meet this paragon of a protégée of yours?'

'Of course.'

Lady Alston rang for Sybil, who was instructed to call Emma.

'They want you in the drawing room.'

'Oh, thank you, Sybil.'

'Better be on your best behaviour – *miss*.'

Emma made her way to the drawing room.

Lady Alston introduced her. Emma tried to disguise her immediate reaction to Lady Cricklewood, who reminded her of a picture of the mythological Greek Gorgon she'd seen in a story book in Fulham Public Library. She bobbed a steady curtsy and muttered a polite 'M'Lady'.

'Come closer, child. I want to look at you.'

Emma did as she was bid.

'Nice hair but it's terribly fine. She's very thin. A pretty dress. Not fashionable, of course.'

Emma looked at Lady Alston, who nodded.

'If you please, your ladyship – I made it.'

'Talented with your needle! Umm. Tell me, do you like poetry? The work of dear Lord Tennyson?'

Emma was surprised at the question, but, having licked her lips, replied, 'Well, your ladyship, we all had to learn "The Revenge" at school – but it's very long, and I preferred "The Lady of Shalott".'

'"The Revenge" is majestic and heroic; but I think "The Lady of Shalott" somewhat outrageous, not to speak of that repulsive "Maud"! And do you play the piano and sing?'

'I can't play the piano, although I would so like to learn, but I often – I used often to – sing solos at church.'

'Um? That will be all. Run along now.'

Again Emma turned to her employer – she was inclined to think she ought not to take orders from strangers.

'Yes, my dear, run along. I will want you to help me change for dinner at the usual time.'

'Very good, my lady.'

'Well, Rosa, I suppose she has some good qualities, though she is totally lacking in class. You might have advertised in *The Lady* for a parson's daughter, or perhaps a country squire's girl, someone who –'

'Don't go on about it, Hester. Emma is very young, and I can train her. She will soon gain confidence. She learns quickly, and her education is not lacking – as you have already seen. She appreciates everything. She is living in Hannah's old suite, which, as you know, I had refurbished two or three years ago. Hannah was marvellous – but she too was getting old, like us, dear. Besides, I like young people.'

'*I* do *not* like the unknown. I don't know what I'd do if Bertha left me.'

'Neither do I,' replied Lady Alston.

Emma was settling into her new life at number 1 Queen's Gate. She was on good terms with Mrs Green, the cook, and on distant but polite terms with Stratton, the butler – whom she, like the other members of the staff, must call *Mr* Stratton. She had not had much contact with the kitchen maid Lottie – the poor child always seemed to be busy scrubbing and trying to satisfy Mrs Green, who incessantly explained to her the right way to hold her knife and apply it to the vegetable or fruit she was preparing in order to waste as little as possible in the peeling. Poor Lottie had a great deal to learn, and, like Emma, was just beginning.

Sybil held strong opinions about Emma, who as far as she was concerned was an intruder who had taken over Miss Hannah's rooms and acquired all her privileges. She was younger than Sybil, and of no better background. Yes, the new 'companion' could write very well, but Sybil was an experienced, smart head parlour maid and knew what she was about. Her jealousy of Emma contributed nothing towards the building of a happy relationship between them.

This was the only thing that marred Emma's happiness. She enjoyed reading to Lady Alston, and loved carrying out minor repairs to her employer's beautiful gowns. She was in her element working with the beautiful, rich fabrics and attempting, usually very successfully, to match the quality of the workmanship. Sometimes she acted as a secretary, writing little thank-you letters for Lady Alston, whose sight was not very good.

Nearly every day the old lady and the young girl would take short walks just across the road in Kensington Gardens or the western reaches of Hyde Park. On one of their first walks she was able to show Lady Alston where she and Katy has found her ring. All that seemed an age ago.

Another of the duties that she really enjoyed was a thrice-weekly visit to the florist, Arthur Larke, who was as cheerful as his lovely flowers were bright, always pleased to see her, and she him.

'Please, miss, may I dust and sweep the carpet?'

Emma looked up from the desk in her sitting room, where she was writing a letter for Lady Alston, to see Sybil in her morning print dress and large apron carrying her cleaning things.

'Yes, of course, Sybil.'

Sybil got busy, and so aggressively brushed a large rug that it slipped and became thoroughly rucked on the polished wood floor. Emma could feel her bad temper.

'Is anything wrong?'

'No, miss, nothing's wrong.'

'Can I help? Has her ladyship been getting at you?'

'Me? Oh, no, miss, not me.'

'Good. But by the way you hit out at that poor old rug, something's wrong.'

Sybil tossed her head and grudgingly straightened the rug.

'Sybil, do let's be friends. We both have her ladyship's interests at heart, and I believe you're fond of her, too. But, well, we have our different duties and we must work as a team, you know. Is there anything I can do for you?'

'Oh, miss!'

'Let's drop the "miss", please. Look, I know you don't like sewing. Can I make you a new dress for days off, or perhaps a new afternoon uniform?'

Emma could see the idea appealed to Sybil.

'That would be nice – er, Emma. But miss – oh, sorry – it's just that you have this nice room and that bathroom, and I only see it when I clean it. My room's at the top of the house and it's not like this.'

'Well, there's not much I can do about that. But I don't see why you shouldn't have a bath in my bathroom once a week. Would you like me to ask her ladyship?'

'She'd never allow it.'

'Well, we can but ask – though perhaps not yet for a while. But please, please, Sybil, don't let's quarrel. And don't think I've had an easy life, either.'

Since Emma had been with Lady Alston, there was one time of the day when she felt really nervous. This was at dinner. She had never seen so many shining pieces of cutlery laid on such superb table linen. She told herself to keep calm, and not to pick up a knife or fork until her employer had done so. Lady Alston always discreetly watched Emma's every move, and decided that until the time was right, she would do nothing to correct or instruct her young friend. Being a sympathetic person, she would make sure that the conversation was light-hearted and distracting for Emma, to help her relax and forget the nerve-racking experience.

What Emma dreaded most was having to pick up her cut-crystal glass of aerated water. She needed water to help her food down, but each evening the gleaming glass with its pompous gold rim seemed to glower at her more and more.

There were always small bowls of flowers on the dinner table – she herself arranged these – but Stratton, on this particular evening, had placed one of her little posies rather too near the dreaded glass.

What if I knock it over, what if I spill it? The thought went through her mind as, very tentatively, with shaking hand, she reached for the monster. As she did so, the frilled cuff of her sleeve caught a tiny thorn on one of the rosebuds in the flower arrangement. She misjudged her grasp. The glass toppled over, spilling its contents on the cloth, its stem snapping as it fell against the rose bowl.

Terrified, she burst into tears and rushed out of the dining room.

Very concerned, Lady Alston followed her and found her sitting on the stairs in the hall. Tearfully, she looked up at her employer.

'I'm so dreadfully sorry, Lady Alston, I . . . I don't know what to say. That glass . . . it must have been very valuable. I will pay for it. I'm so clumsy! All those knives and forks – it's so strange, I don't think I'll ever get used to them.'

The old lady put her arm around her and guided her back into the dining room, where Stratton had mopped up the water and removed the broken glass.

'My dear, I knew all this would be difficult for you, and I have been watching you these last few weeks. Believe me, you're coping extremely well – because you are so observant. I noticed that from the very first dinner we had together. Please don't worry about the glass! We must have about fifty more. Come now, dry your tears and eat up your chicken.'

Emma drew a deep breath, much relieved, but still felt awful inside. The meal proceeded.

After a while Lady Alston spoke again.

'Because you are now living in a very different society, you do, of course, have a lot to learn. I've been so surprised that you know so much – about fashion, who are the most important jewellers in London and who is who in society. How did that come about, my dear?'

Emma explained that she and Katy were friendly with a newsagent who would give them unsold copies of the *Illustrated London News* and other society newspapers.

Laughing, Lady Alston replied, 'So that's why you are so well informed. Excellent! However, from now on, we will have some lessons and I will teach you just a few little things that will make you feel more confident when we visit, or when Lady Cricklewood comes – we don't want her criticising you.'

And Emma learned a great deal. She learned that veils on hats were never worn before lunch, and hats were never worn after six o'clock. She learned how to open and eat a lobster – not that she liked it much – and that fish knives and forks were used only in lower-class establishments, as were napkin rings: a table napkin should definitely *not* be used more than once. She soon began to realise that there was a lot to becoming an acceptable member of society.

The first dry autumn leaves danced along the pavement as Emma boarded the horse bus to take her west along Kensington High Street to a point where she could turn right to walk along the west side of the Metropolitan and District Railway towards Sinclair Road. She was soon within sight of her old home. As she approached Craven Cottages, she saw Katy just about to go into her parents' house with a load of ironing.

'Katy! Katy!'

'Emma! Oh, 'ow wonderful to see yer!' Katy dropped her basket and kissed her friend. 'What a surprise! But it's Thursday – we don' see you round these parts on a Thursday.'

'No, I know. Let's go in and see Ma.'

Instinctively Emma picked up one of the handles of Katy's basket and the two girls burst excitedly into the Coopers' cottage.

'Em, what a surprise! I didn't expect this – all on a Thursday afternoon. Now don't say you've lost your job!'

'No, Ma, of course not. Her ladyship just gave me the afternoon off. Said she had some business to attend to, and I needn't get back till six.'

'Well, that's so nice, dear. Have a cup of tea and a bun, I've just made them. Still hot, like you always used to have one. And you, Katy, too.'

'But Ma, you're not looking very well.'

'To speak truth, Em, I've been very tired lately, and, well, I don't know . . . a bit miserable too. I've been worrying about you and missing you. Our Katy here cheers me up, but I seems to cry – well, for nothing really.'

'Ma, try not to be sad. I'm only up the road – really. And I am doing ever so well. Be pleased about that. I expect you'll feel better again soon.'

82

The three women caught up on their news. George, it seemed, was just the same, and Emma promised to go down and see her father on her way back.

'Now, Katy, what about you?'

'Tell her, Katy.'

'Oh, Emma – I'm courtin'! He's real lovely, an' he works so 'ard!'

Emma suddenly realised she hadn't felt really excited about anything since she started to work for Lady Alston. The rarefied atmosphere of Queen's Gate didn't lend itself to girlish exuberance.

'Tell me more. Who is he?'

'He lives next door with 'is old ma.'

'She's a nice old thing,' Mrs Cooper put in.

'You know, Emma – it's Jim Cook! He's twenty, and he's opened that fruit and vegetable shop next the laundry. It's ever so nice, an' he gets up at four every morning to go to Covent Garden to buy the stuff. Of course nothin's 'appened yet –'

'I should hope *not*, indeed,' said Mrs Cooper sharply.

'But 'e *is* nice and, well, I think I might love 'im later on.'

The three women spent a wonderful couple of hours together, Emma once more falling into the familiar ironing routine with her mother and Katy. Life at the laundry was busy enough, and now with the new attraction of her developing relationship with Jim, Katy's days were very full and very happy. Emma was delighted for her friend.

Later that afternoon, as it was just beginning to get dark, the two young women made their way down Masbro Road, Katy to return to the laundry with the neat piles of ironing, and Emma to see her father.

'Oh, Em, she's not 'er old self at all. Worries about you all the time. I finds 'er crying, sitting in 'er chair rocking to and fro, moaning that you ain't there to 'elp 'er. It's awful! You should be doing your duty like a good daughter.'

'But Pa, surely you feel just a bit proud of me? I know Ma is, even if she's not her old self at present.'

'I suppose so, but you're not doing what a good Christian girl should be doing.' He raised his voice threateningly. 'Go on then, get back to your Lady Alston. I suppose we can do

83

without you. We don't want you – and you don't want us. Thank the good Lord that Katy comes and helps out – now there's a good Christian girl for you.'

Emma arrived back at Queen's Gate just before six. As she approached the house, she saw two elderly men wearing black overcoats and top hats getting into a hansom cab immediately outside the house.

Stratton held the front door open for her – she had appeared on the doorstep before he had closed it after the two men.

'Miss Emma, her ladyship wants to see you at once in the drawing room.'

'My dear, shut the door. I've something to tell you. The other morning Dr Minton advised me that I should leave London as soon as possible, to avoid the unhealthy effect of the fog on my chest. Last year, you know, I was quite ill. I don't want to take his advice, but I realise I must do so. He allows me to spend the summer months here in London, but for about eight months of the year we will be living out of London. I'm not sure where yet, but it will be somewhere with a mild climate, and where the air is cleaner.'

'Move away from London? From this lovely house?'

It wasn't Emma's place to protest, but she couldn't help herself.

'I will certainly wish you to come with me, if you will consent to do so. Of course, you won't be near your family – but there will be the summers, as I said.'

'I just can't imagine living anywhere else but London!'

Lady Alston recognised Emma's dismay.

'Well, my dear, if you really don't want to come with me, then of course you and I must go our separate ways, though that would distress me, as we are getting on so well. Naturally you must think of your family. But none of them is sick or particularly old, so there's surely no really serious problem?'

Gradually Lady Alston's news started to sink in. Her father's comments ringing in her ears brought a surge of guilty emotion. Could she possibly put miles between herself and her mother? Of course she wanted to go with Lady Alston, but her duty to her mother and her duty to her employer were now decidedly at odds. Besides, she'd only ever travelled as far as Kent; she knew nothing of the rest of the British Isles. A lot would depend on where Lady Alston decided to live.

'Now, my dear, my two men of business have been with me all afternoon. They have suggested – and I agree – that quite a large estate I own in Yorkshire shall be sold as soon as possible; they will look out for a house as much like this one as possible, in some provincial town – somewhere where you and I can make new friends and take a small part in the local cultural and social life.'

'Can I think about it until tomorrow, perhaps, Lady Alston? It isn't an easy thing to decide at once.'

'Of course, but I shall be very disappointed if you decide not to make the move.'

'Do the others know about your plans yet?'

'No, dear, you're the first. I will tell them before dinner. We'll summon the staff when you have helped me to change.'

Later, Emma sat on her bed in deep thought. She knew she would never get another job like this one, but her divided loyalties were tearing her apart.

'What shall I do, what shall I do?' she cried aloud, as tears gushed down her cheeks.

Of course you must go,' said Sarah decisively as she applied her make-up. 'Look at it like this. Ma will get over her problems. They don't go on for ever, believe me. I know Pa upset you – that was typical of him. He made you feel guilty with all that talk about duty. But you have to make your own life, Emma, just like me. You go, girl. Besides, the summer's the best and most interesting time to be in London – it's easier to get around, and there's so much more going on. It's far dirtier and more unhealthy in the winter, what with the fogs. Go, Emma, that's my advice. Go! If I were you, I'd wait to tell them until you know precisely where you're going to be living. Then, to keep Pa quiet, I suggest you find out the name of the nearest church and tell him – that should help to keep him happy! Besides, if you make sure you tell them you'll be back in the summer, what more can they expect? I dare say Pa swanks about you to all his cronies!'

Here Sarah got up, thrust her thumbs under imaginary lapels, and imitated her father's voice: 'Oh yes, my gal – my Emma – lives with the haristocracy, you know. Done very well fer 'erself, 'as our Emma!'

'Overture and beginners, please!' A voice that could have filled the Albert Hall boomed out in the corridor. The sisters kissed each other. Sarah rushed out of the dressing room ahead of Emma, her opening-number costume floating out behind her, down the flights of stairs to the stage. Emma made her way back to Kensington.

'My dear, I cannot tell you how happy you have made an old woman. I am so pleased that you feel you can leave London to live with me. Now, we'll have a great deal to do before we – leave which will be as soon as Stillwall, Stillwall and Keen have found us a suitable house. We will leave most of the furniture here and close the house up; then, when summer comes, I will send the staff ahead to open it up ready for the London season.'

Another house! Would she have such pretty rooms? Emma wondered. More to the point, would she have another bathroom to herself, and to lend to Sybil on Saturday nights?

'I do hope Mr Stillwall will find something suitable. Will you be furnishing the new house?'

'There are some things on the Yorkshire estate – some very nice paintings, and one or two pieces of furniture from the last century. These will be sent to the new house. But Mr Stillwall is hoping to find a fully furnished place for us – we can always get rid of anything we don't like.

'Now, my dear, this afternoon you must go off to Whiteley's to choose one or two new outfits. Take a hansom, it will be quicker than getting Toby to drive you. Charge the clothes to my account – I'll write you an authority. You need a winter costume and a heavy winter coat, at least two afternoon dresses and an evening dress.'

'But I could make the dresses.'

'Yes, and very well, too; but you will simply not have the time.'

Emma got up. So did Lady Alston.

'On second thoughts, get my coat and hat. I feel energetic. Let us both go to Whiteley's.'

In addition to Lady Alston's original suggestion, she helped Emma to choose nightdresses, all manner of pretty yet practical underwear, a dressing gown, a hat with winter berries and pheasant feathers – which matched her new winter costume and coat – and a lovely black velvet beret which beautifully complemented her fine blonde hair.

'Emma, I have news. Mr Stillwall and Mr Keen have found what they think might be a most suitable house. The price is right and the transaction should go through quickly and smoothly. They have been to view it, and tell me the furnishings are excellent. It has the same number of rooms as this, but there are three bathrooms rather than only two. The previous owner died two months ago, and the family wants to sell both house and contents. Sensibly they have sent me this.'

Lady Alston handed Emma a box, the lid of which was highly decorated with cherubs taking photographs of each other and looking at and processing photographic prints. Among all this activity was a name: Major and Darker, Photographers, 152 Union Street, Plymouth.

Chapter Six

'Here she comes! Yes, that's her. And look, Mama, there *he* is – there's Papa! Look, he's waving. Oh, Papa! Papa!' Lizzie called at the top of her voice.

'Don't, my dear – I'm quite sure he can't hear us. But look, he's seen us, hasn't he!'

'Oh, yes! Doesn't he look magnificent?

Mrs Newcombe hastily brushed a tear from her eye. The ship moving through the deep but narrow channel was passing very close to the water's edge, just beyond the wall at the end of their garden. It was the last glimpse that she would have of her husband for many months.

Mother and daughter, arms wrapped round each other, watched the ship making her way past the breakwater, then receding into the distance until, some seventeen miles from shore, just beyond the Eddystone lighthouse, she disappeared below the horizon with the setting sun.

Mrs Newcombe folded her son's letter and replaced it in its envelope. Her lovely dark eyes clouded with tears.

'Darling, what a dear letter! I shall treasure it always. Oh, Lizzie, I do worry about him, you know.'

'Of course you do, Mama.' Putting her arm round her mother to comfort her, she went on, 'You know Joe wouldn't want to do anything else. He really *is* keen, and there's so much he says he enjoys, and he's obviously doing so well with all his studies and making new friends . . . I'm quite sure he'll be all right.'

'I know you're right . . .'

'But you're his mother, and you'll always think of him as your baby! Do try hard not to worry too much. Look, I'll write to him tonight and say you'll write at the weekend. By that time Laura and Aggie will have made a cake and some biscuits and you can send your letter with the parcel.'

Drying her eyes, her mother agreed.

'Lizzie, what *is* the matter?'

Pushing past her mother and an astounded Aggie in the hall, Lizzie rushed into the lounge, opened the piano and very carelessly banged off the opening bars of Chopin's Revolutionary Study.

'What has got into the girl?' Mrs Newcombe wondered aloud.

Aggie shrugged her shoulders and shuffled off to the kitchen to fill Laura in on the latest piece of family gossip.

'Darling, do stop, please. You're making a dreadful noise!'

Lizzie thumped on. It wasn't a piece she had thoroughly mastered yet. She played fast, but very inaccurately. About halfway through she suddenly stopped, crashed the keyboard cover down, took a deep breath and told her mother about the awful day she had had at school. She had taught some of her girls a poem that described Gypsy life. Miss Creeber had thought it most unsuitable and heathen, and had thoroughly scolded her.

'Oh, my dear, I am sorry. But you know, you will have to conform, I'm afraid – after all, they taught you well, and it's as a result of your education that you are so forward-thinking. You have them to thank for that.'

'Not really, Mama. The clever way you and Papa always questioned me about what I thought was much more important. I was always aware that there were things they told me at school that I didn't agree with.'

'Well, Lizzie dear, I know it's hard. But they are going to help you to get into Girton, and they *are* paying you, so . . .'

Mrs Newcombe drew a breath to give herself time to think what to say next. She change the subject. 'While we're talking like this, Lizzie, there is one thing I want to ask you.'

Lizzie looked a little surprised. 'Go on.'

'Now, dear, do you really and truly want to go to Cambridge?

You know it's not exactly – well, feminine. It could spoil your chances of getting married. I was talking things over with Mrs Norris – Captain Norris's wife – yesterday afternoon, and she begged me to make quite sure you knew your own mind on the subject. She said it could be quite devastating for a girl to go to college. You know, a good married life is the best security for a woman, and you must be quite, quite sure that you don't waste your youth and beauty on study. Then there's the influence of other advanced young women. Mrs Norris went so far as to tell me that Papa and I and should forbid you to go – she was really most horrified.'

'Dearest Mama,' said Lizzie, after a moment, 'please don't take any notice of ladies like Mrs Norris. Yes, I do want to go to college, more than anything else in the world.'

She was shaking with apprehension as she went on, 'There's so much to learn and so much to do. People – women in particular – must have richer and fuller lives, and I don't just mean more money. I want them to appreciate art and music, pictures and books and to speak the languages of other nations and to take their places beside men – not simply behind them. And I mean to help them do it.'

'Yes, dearest, that is what I've believed to be your view all along – but I do have to be sure in my own mind. For the time being, at least try not to upset Miss Creeber too much!'

Smiling weakly, Lizzie said she'd do her best.

'Now, dear, soon it'll be your birthday and I think we should make plans. It falls on a Saturday this year and so I thought I'd book a box for you and Elsie, Annie and Milly for the matinée at the Theatre Royal – I hear the show that's on at present is very pretty and quite suitable. Then you can all come back here and we'll have a huge high tea, all together. Would you like that?'

Lizzie was delighted, and went on to do some music practice to be ready for her regular Saturday-morning piano lesson with old Professor Rowe. She was keen to tidy up the Revolutionary Study, for more reasons than one – it was a simply marvellous piece to play when the frustration of the school day became too much for her.

*

90

'Wasn't it beautiful? Oh, those dresses!'

'Yes, of course, Milly, we knew *you'd* like the dresses best. What did you like best, Elsie?'

'The leading man, he was sooo handsome . . . And the songs.'

Elsie was in a dream world of her own, and tending to lag behind the other three as they made their way from the theatre to the Newcombe home at around six o'clock on Lizzie's birthday.

'Oh, come *on*, Elsie, we don't want to lose you. It's really dark now.' Lizzie was attempting to keep them all together.

'Yes, the songs were pretty, but what about –'

'Ta-ra-ra-boom-de-ay!' they all chorused together.

'I wish I could sing and dance like that Lottie Collins,' said Annie, the boldest of the four, and in a hearty voice right in the middle of the Promenade on Plymouth Hoe, she skipped round in a ring and sang at the top of her voice:

> 'Ta-ra-ra-boom-de-ay,
> Ta-ra-ra-boom-de-ay . . .'

and the others joined in for the sheer fun of it.

'What a simply marvellous birthday I'm having! I really can't remember a better one. It was so nice of the three of you to buy me the selection for piano from *Cinder–Ellen-up-too-Late* – I'm so glad that Mama suggested we should see it together. We'll have fun after tea – I'll try to play some of it to you! And – oh yes – I must show you what Joe sent me!'

'What is it?' they all asked at once.

'Well, you know he can't get out to the shops very easily, and so he sent me . . .' Here Lizzie paused and grinned mysteriously, her eyes flashing at each of her friends in turn.

'What *did* he send you? Oh, come *on*, Lizzie, tell us! I bet it was something beautiful.'

'Oh, shut up, Milly, let Lizzie tell us.'

'He sent me . . . a piece of rope.'

'A piece of rope! What ever for?'

'Well, it's special – to him – and so, of course, he thought I would like to have it. You see, it was the first piece of rope that he spliced himself.'

'Spliced? What does that mean?' asked Elsie.

'Joined together, one piece to another.' Annie's father had a small sailing boat, so she knew about these things.

'Ahh, that was nice.'

'Yes, I'll always treasure it, and when we are both really old I'll show it to him – he'll have forgotten about it by then.'

'Come on, it's getting very cold. Race you down the steps!'

Annie ran on ahead and the others followed. Breathless, excited, the sea wind hitting their faces and singing at the tops of their voices as they ran, they were in no way the demure young ladies that they had been taught to be. Happy and laughing, Elsie complaining of stitch, they were making quite a lot of noise as they reached the end house of West Hoe Terrace.

'Look, Lizzie, Milly, what's that?'

Observant Annie could see a vehicle with two horses. When they snorted, the steam coming out of their noses caught a shaft of light from a nearby gas streetlamp.

The four girls stopped dead in their tracks and were suddenly quiet.

'What does it say on the side? I can't see from here.'

Milly screwed up her eyes in the darkness. Annie cautiously took a step nearer to look more closely.

'It says ... "Ambulance, Royal Naval Hospital, Devonport".'

Lizzie stood stock still, unable to move.

'Isn't it near your house, Lizzie?'

She nodded a silent reply, then, struck by grim realisation, rushed towards the front door of her house.

'Look, there's Mrs Newcombe,' cried Annie, pointing to a lady who was being helped down from the ambulance. Two men followed her, carrying a stretcher.

'Who is it? Who's ill?'

'Oh, I expect it's one of their servants who's been knocked over by a horse bus, or something like that. I shouldn't worry,' Milly suggested.

'No, don't go over. We must wait here. Let's see what Lizzie's going to do.' Annie pulled at Elsie's sleeve, jerking her back a step.

'Mama! What is it? What's happened?'

'Oh, darling, it's Joe . . . He had an accident.'

The stretcher was just passing them to go into the house where a devastated Aggie and Laura were standing in the hall.

'But Mama, I don't understand.'

'I'll explain later. Let's get him in.' Mrs Newcombe was white with shock.

Joe, covered by red blankets and heavily sedated, was asleep.

'Oh, no! I can't believe it! It's . . . it's not serious, is it?'

'Yes, Lizzie, it is. Very serious indeed.'

Chapter Seven

Emma gingerly opened the box. Inside was a number of photographs of the exterior and interior of a large terraced house.

'Well, what do you think? Doesn't it look nice?'

Examining a photograph of a row of nine huge houses, Emma was impressed, and said so.

'But where is it, Lady Alston?'

'It's in Plymouth, right on the top of the Hoe. It's number 5 Elliot Terrace. The houses were built some thirty years ago, and from the beginning they have had their very own generator and are fully equipped with electric lighting – the first in the city to have it. So modern, my dear!'

'How exciting – no gas mantles to worry about! But . . . the Hoe?' That rang a distant bell in Emma's mind.

'Yes, you know, it's where Drake played bowls before the Armada.'

'Oh, of course. And right by the sea?'

Taking out another photograph, which showed the terrace from an angle, with a wide road above some cliffs leading down towards the sea, Emma began to get an idea of the position of the house.

'Look, it's the house which they've marked with a cross. That wide road must be the Promenade. It's where everyone walks, enjoys the sea air, the view, and yes, listens to the band.

'Mr Keen tells me there is the same number of rooms as here, but there is an additional bathroom at the top of the house, so the staff can have that for themselves. There's stabling at the back, too. Here's a photograph of the ground-floor dining room and the first-floor drawing room, which looks right over the sea. We have a balcony, as well, and a better view than here!'

Lady Alston's enthusiasm brought a gleam into her old eyes. Emma hadn't been aware of this light-hearted side to her employer's personality before. She could now see what the old woman must have been like when she was young, carefree and beautiful.

'It's obviously a lovely house, but the furniture looks . . . well . . .'

'You have reservations about the furniture?'

'It looks a little heavy. But then, of course, the photographs are rather dark, so it's difficult to tell.'

The furniture looked foreboding, Emma thought, and for a moment felt she would much rather sit on one of her parents' old chairs with the broken springs.

'We'll make any changes we think necessary. I am very pleased. I believe Plymouth has many amenities – a fine theatre, a beautiful church and some very good shops which we will explore.'

'My lady, do you know anyone who lives there?'

'No, not a soul, but that's perhaps no bad thing.' Seeing that her words had puzzled Emma, she went on, 'We'll make new friends. We'll ask the vicar round to tea. Who knows what will happen? I think all will be well. Now, I want you to take the photographs downstairs to show the staff. The deal on the Plymouth house is finalised, and my estate in Yorkshire is on the market. I'm going to spend some time referring to the inventory of paintings and antique furniture there. The tenants will be moving out quite soon, and we can then have my treasures from the north transported to Plymouth.'

Lady Alston's huge bedroom was cluttered with six travel-scarred and much-labelled Louis Vuitton wardrobe trunks and suitcases of various sizes. A middle-aged woman was using acres of tissue paper in the difficult task of packing numerous gowns.

Emma was in attendance, nervously helping by steadying sleeves while the expert padded them with tissue, and standing on a chair holding elaborate ball gowns high above her head so that the packer could make quite certain the dresses were hanging in their natural folds before carefully introducing them into the trunks. Costumes, skirts and accessories all had their right place. Hats were packed in large, round hat boxes, blouses neatly folded. The rustle of silk and tissue paper contrasted with the harsh voice of Miss Smeed, the professional packer, who barked her instructions to Emma. Fortunately, Emma soon realised that Miss Smeed's bark was worse than her bite and all the time was making mental notes of what was going on, so that when summer came she could cope with any packing that would have to be done in Plymouth for the return to London. After all, she thought to herself, Plymouth is provincial, and there may well not be the equivalent of a Miss Smeed so far from London.

Meanwhile, below stairs Sybil was packing favourite dinner and tea services, and Mrs Green had been informed that there was no need to take anything from the kitchen, for the Plymouth one was up to date and well equipped.

'Well, I don't know, I'm sure, Mr Stratton. I wants to take me knives. I can't use any old knife – I wants me own.'

'Mrs Green, I am quite sure that what Mr Stillwall said is correct. There will be fine knives in the Plymouth kitchen.'

He left to go about his own business.

The impatient cook looked round her kitchen and found an old apron. Wrapping three of her favourite knives carefully in it, she put them in her copious black handbag, which was never far away.

'Well, yes, the house does look quite nice, dear, but I do hope it won't be damp. Very wet, Plymouth, you know.'

'Yes, but very clean.'

Lady Alston slipped the photograph back into its box.

'I suppose you *will* get used to being so very far away from us all. It will seem terribly . . . terribly –' here Hester Cricklewood took a long, slow deep breath 'county, somehow. Certainly we all have our country estates, but we only visit them when we must – of course, you've never bothered much about yours, have you, Rosa?'

'I'm selling it, Hester.'

'Well, I can't say I blame you. After all, it wasn't family, was it? Just a reward for . . . services rendered, shall we say?'

'As you know, I'm taking Augustus's advice. You see, I've no intention of dying just yet. Besides, I'm ready for a little adventure. How's your digestion, by the way?'

Ignoring her old friend's question, Lady Cricklewood went on, 'A little adventure! I call it a major upheaval. But then, dear, you *are* used to that sort of thing, aren't you? Oh! The changes you've made! Some, of course, forced upon you – just like this one – if for rather different reasons.'

'I have heard that there's interesting and good society in Plymouth.'

'Well, yes, dear, there are the Mount Edgcumbes, but they're across the water. So difficult to cope with neighbours who live across water, don't you think? Then there's Saltram – who *is* at Saltram these days? An elegant house, but so cold and draughty, I thought, when I was there in '52. Then there are the Mildmays at Flete – not too far away, I suppose.'

'Hester, stop it. You know full well that I always fall on my feet when I have to move on.'

'Yes, dear, and it's not always been just your feet you've fallen on, has it? But let's order tea.'

The Albemarle tea salon was abuzz with polite society as the two old women smiled, looked pleasantly at each other, and exchanged barbed words.

They were having a wonderful afternoon tea party to say goodbye to Emma, who was very soon due to leave for Plymouth. Excitement was high because Emma had just presented her mother with a beautiful brown winter coat with a little fur collar. Mrs Cooper at first felt she could not accept it; coming from Whiteley's as it did, it was 'far too good for her'. The lovers Katy and Jim were unwrapping some quality linen sheets for their 'bottom drawer' and Aunty Tyrrell was liberally splashing herself with Yardley's Lavender Water. Emma, knowing she would not be with her family for Christmas, had decided to give them their presents well in advance.

During the middle of the jollifications, Will Cooper and

97

George arrived. Will Cooper, partly to show off to the neighbours, closed the shop early so that they could attend the tea party. As they entered, the atmosphere changed.

Emma was wearing her new winter costume from Whiteley's. Her father at once noticed.

'Quite the lady now, I see. 'Ow did you afford that, even on your grand wages? Don' you be so wasteful, my girl. You count your pennies.'

'Lady Alston provided me with it, and lots more like it too. Says I wear my clothes well. But here's a present for you, Pa – which I did pay for myself, so there.'

Her father undid what turned out to be a briar pipe, and managed one of his inverted smiles.

'Good for you! You stand up for yourself, Em!' Katy muttered under her breath.

'Oh yes, and George too – your present is down the back.'

George snorted, Emma glared at her brother knowingly, Katy nudged her encouragingly. George strode, hands deep in trouser pockets, into the back yard to find a crate of twelve bottles of porter.

That'll keep him quiet, she had thought as she made her choice.

There was so much to talk about over the tea of sausages, mashed potatoes and dried peas – well soaked before cooking. Then came spotted dick, trifle, strong cheddar cheese and home-baked bread. Gallons of tea flowed from the largest pot in the Cooper household.

'So when do you go, girl?' asked her father.

'On Monday morning, on the ten-thirty from Paddington. It'll take nearly six hours. Mr Stratton and Toby left yesterday – and Beauty went on the same train in a special truck they use for horses. They'll open up the house and get the fires lit. Mrs Green, Sybil and little Lottie go today. The solicitor's locking up Queen's Gate about now.'

George interrupted. 'So where's our Emma going to sleep over the weekend? Is she coming back to her old homestead – or is she too grand for that?'

Mrs Cooper glanced anxiously from George to Emma.

'Well, no, I can't do that. When I leave here I've to go to the hotel and join Lady Alston there.'

'I don' agree with hotels. Sin and wickedry goes on in hotels. Can't 'ave you staying in hotels. You'll stay 'ere, safe an' sound with me an' George to look after you.'

'I'm sorry, Pa, but I can't – I have to be with Lady Alston.'

'Bugger Lady Alston! I'm not 'aving you in a hotel.'

'You can't stop me.'

'Yes, I can. You're not twenty-one yet, you know. You should be 'ome 'ere helping to look after your ma. Selfish, that's what you are, girl, selfish! I don't approve of all this gallivanting all over the country. And there's another thing about this Plymouth lark. It's a naval town, sailors everywhere. You watch it! No goin' out with 'em or flirtin', or writin' tellin us you're courtin' one of 'em. He'll have other wives – all over the place, more than like. Em, I'll 'ave nothing more to do with you if that 'appens. Bring disgrace to the family, that would – just like that sinful sister of yours, kickin' up 'er legs in public and paintin' 'er face. Less said about 'er, the better. I won' warn you again, mind, so that's final.'

'Will, for God's sake let her alone. You should be proud of her. I can cope, I don' need any extra help.'

'Don' you blaspheme in this 'ouse, Susan – that's sinful too.'

'Well, I think Emma should stay 'ere for the weekend, then we can all say "bye-bye, Emma", proper like!'

George lifted his hand and wiggled his fingers up and down in a mocking parody; his eyes were rolling and he licked his lips at the prospect.

'Pa, George, I'm staying with Lady Alston. She has a large suite at the Albemarle, and I have an adjoining bedroom – she needs the company. So that's final too.'

Emma narrowed her eyes with firm determination.

'No, I'm not twenty-one, but remember, Pa, you gave Lady Alston your word that I could live and work with her. A true Christian never goes back on his word – that's what you always say, isn't it, Pa?'

Will snorted in disgust, frowned and folded his arms resignedly, knowing full well that Emma had cornered him with his own philosophies.

'Cor, the Albemarle! My girl at the Albemarle! Good on you. I'm proud of you. You go and enjoy yourself!' Her mother was at once sticking up for her.

'Thanks, Ma.'

It was getting dark as Emma took leave of her beloved mother and dear friends. But first she said goodbye to her pa, who had lost another battle with his successful and ambitious daughter. Her ambition she had directly inherited from him, but he failed to recognise this and was scorched with jealousy at her progress.

The autumn morning was sunny and the view of the fashionable Albemarle Street from her room looked particularly beautiful to Emma as she gathered up her things to escort Lady Alston down to the foyer where Mr Stillwall the younger was waiting with a carriage to take the two women to Paddington. For a brief moment Emma gazed out of the window. This was the last view of London she'd have for many months.

How can one be sad and happy, apprehensive and excited all at the same time? she wondered. Then, with a hard blink and something of a sniff, she turned her attention to practical matters, picked up her hat and, with the arrival of the porter to take her case, she joined Lady Alston.

Paddington Station was disconcertingly busy. Emma was glad to be following Mr Stillwall, since the experience of boarding a long-distance train was totally new to her. It was enough for her to be lightly holding Lady Alston's arm, both their handbags and a large plaid travelling rug.

Their first-class compartment was near the front of the train so there was no great distance to push themselves along the crowded platform.

The guard, standing to attention, saluted the elderly and distinguished lady when Mr Stillwall presented him with their tickets and seat reservations. Next to the guard was a man wearing a green baize apron and carrying a large wicker basket.

'Lady Alston, miss?' he enquired of Emma.

On being assured that it was he went to hand Emma the basket, but she was too heavily encumbered to take it.

100

'From Fortnum's, my man?'

'Yes, your ladyship.'

'Well, you should know better than to hand such a heavy basket to my companion. Put it at once in our compartment. Give him a penny for his trouble, Mr Stillwall, he's not worth more!'

They settled themselves into the very comfortable compartment, and Stillwall took his leave.

The six-hour journey from Paddington to Plymouth, and beyond as far as Penzance, was the premier run of the Great Western Railway – a speedy, smooth journey. The first-class carriages had no corridors, but a door in each lead to a toilet and washbasin for the exclusive use of the passengers in the compartment.

'Now, my dear, we are due into Plymouth Millbay Station at two forty-five. Stratton will meet us there. I suggest we lunch at one o'clock as usual. There should be a bottle of sherry in the hamper; you will pour us a glass each at about half past twelve.'

'May I look out of the window, Lady Alston?'

'Of course, but don't open it – we'll catch our deaths. Besides, it's dreadfully easy to get smuts in one's eyes.'

The train gathered speed past Wormwood Scrubs, not far from Emma's home. She recognised the foreboding prison. Later Reading, Swindon. She tried to read Louisa May Alcott's *Jo's Boys* – she was so enjoying it, but was far too excited and unsettled to concentrate.

Lunch was delicious. She hadn't had a picnic with Lady Alston before. It was quite different from picnics with her family, which had usually consisted of bread and cheese, or, on a day out to Southend, fish and chips while sitting on the beach, her hands getting greasy and smeared with print from the newspaper wrapping.

She often had a glass of sherry with her employer before dinner. This one was sweet – easy to drink and more of a comfort for midday, especially when one's travelling, she was told. There was cold chicken and tiny bread rolls, some perfect green seedless grapes, and exquisite slices of shortbread.

A thermos contained black coffee, and there was a tiny

sealed bottle of cream to accompany it. To finish the meal, a selection of crystallised fruits – peaches, pieces of pineapple and miniature oranges – and sugared almonds, pink, green and white, some wrapped in silver foil. The hamper also provided elegant white plates edged with gold, matching dishes, cups and saucers, along with all the necessary cutlery and huge damask napkins.

After their lunch, both Emma and Lady Alston felt very relaxed. They dozed, sinking back into the comfort of the well-sprung seats upholstered in deep-brown plush.

Emma woke with a start. Everywhere around her was dark. They were in a tunnel, but soon the daylight struck her eyes again. Glancing out of the window, she saw huge breakers. The train was now passing the dramatic Teignmouth and Dawlish coast. She was exhilarated but frightened at the sight. This was the real sea, and in an angry mood. Instead of the acres of flat mud that she had seen at Southend when the tide was out, this was quite different. This was a real coast with the waves crashing and breaking against the sand, the sort of coast she'd read about in adventure stories. Red cliffs hove into sight from time to time as the train clattered on.

If it is as rough as this here, she thought, what must it be like out at sea? Quite terrifying, I should think. After all, this is only the English Channel.

The beautiful view gave the Plymouth house its character. The balcony stretched the whole length of the front of the house, and was discreetly partitioned off from numbers 4 and 6. The panoramic outlook took Emma's breath away.

The light was beginning to fade as she seized her first opportunity to look around the house. It was impressive but, as she had seen from the photographs, the furniture was rather heavy. It was more fashionable than the pieces that graced Queen's Gate, and had obviously all been purchased within the last ten years. Dark-green plush and white lace curtains decorated and protected the windows of both the ground-floor dining room and the first-floor drawing room; the morning room, which faced the back of the house and looked out on a small courtyard where clusters of hydrangea bushes would flower in summer, was also somewhat dark and gloomy.

The wallpaper was extremely decorative with a large floral and leaf design in shades of dark green and brown. There were several little footstools decorated with garlands of roses on a black background and worked in the fashionable embroidery of the time, which she knew to be Berlin woolwork. A large marble fireplace supported a huge mirror surrounded with bronze figures – one looked like a picture in a library book Emma had seen of the Roman god Mercury. There were prints on the walls of exotic flowers – orchids, roses and lilies, and some she did not recognise. Not having learned Latin, she couldn't identify them from the copperplate inscriptions. There was no lack of Venetian glass and Chinese porcelain vases; in her mind's eye she saw them filled with flowers.

Overall, the room was extremely comfortable, with several sofas, easy chairs and small low chairs of a sort she had not seen before – she assumed that they had been made for young children. At the far end in a corner near the long stretch of windows there was a boudoir grand piano, and resting on it a rather oddly shaped wooden box. Opening some little brass clips, she lifted the lid: there, cushioned by bluish-green woollen material, was a guitar. Emma gingerly took it from its case and ran her fingers over the strings. The sound was unpleasing – she realised it was very much out of tune. Replacing it, and wondering why anyone should leave such an instrument in a house to be sold with the furniture, she closed the lid of the box.

She continued her exploration. Lady Alston's bedroom and bathroom were on the next floor, and towards the back of the house on that floor was a small sitting room or a study, along with two more spacious bedrooms. Lady Alston was sleeping after the long journey. Emma crept past her closed door and quietly ascended the stairs to what was to be her part of the house.

Both her sitting room and her bedroom had sea views, and the windows were of a good size. They too had heavy curtains, but their dark-red colour lacked the warm glow that usually accompanies red velvet. Her bed, though, was beautiful with its brass and black-lacquered head and foot. It was far bigger than the one she had at Queen's Gate – easily as big as, if not bigger than, the one her parents slept in. Looking at it, George came into her mind. She went hot and cold all over, but managed to dismiss him from her thoughts, suppressing the brief and frightening vision of how he would have lusted after her, had he had the opportunity to fall into the huge bed.

Emma unpacked her clothes: now she had much more to unpack and to hang in the impressive wardrobe than the last time she undertook such a task.

One evening, just after Sybil had brought in the decanter of sherry and two cut glasses on a silver tray, Lady Alston asked Emma to close the drawing-room curtains and switch on the electric light. Standing at the window, Emma noticed four young women of about her age dancing round each other and playing a sort of silly game. Briefly she slipped out on the balcony.

> 'Ta-ra-ra-*boom*-de-ay,
> Ta-ra-ra-*boom*-de-ay!'

Their young, excited voices rang out loud and clear.

Seeing these friends enjoying themselves suddenly made Emma miss Katy very much.

Chapter Eight

'Bring him in here, please.'

Mrs Newcombe, red-eyed and weak with grief, instructed the ambulance men, who carefully carried Joe on his stretcher into the small back sitting room on the ground floor. Lizzie, dazed and in a state of shock, followed her mother with Aggie and Laura behind her.

She glanced around the room. Joe's bookshelf, his little dressing table and the bedside table had been brought down, and after a few moments Lizzie registered the fact that their 'quiet room', as they called it, had been transformed into Joe's bedroom. Still speechless, she gazed down at the sleeping Joe, her mind befuddled. A few minutes ago she'd been with her friends, happy, carefree and enjoying the best birthday of her life. Suddenly it had become the worst.

The ambulance men retreated, leaving the women of the family with their frail charge. Mrs Newcombe stroked Joe's curly head. Joe slept peacefully, deeply. Aggie was crying, and Laura, her arm around her for comfort, quietly led the old family retainer out of the room.

After a while Lizzie simply had to speak. She tried hard not to let her words tumble out. To hold back when her powerful emotions surfaced was simply not in her nature, but now some deep instinct forced her into an uneasy calm, for which her mother was extremely grateful. Taking a deep breath, Lizzie simply said, 'Mama?'

She leaned over and warmly caressed her mother's shoulders while they both looked down at Joe.

Mrs Newcombe turned to her daughter. 'My darling, we'll

have to be very brave. It all happened yesterday morning.'
Tears welled up in her eyes yet again.

'Go on, Mama.' Lizzie was trying to be as patient as possible.

'Well, darling, it was frosty and it appears that Joe was climbing the rigging with his fellow cadets. He was chosen to go first and so reach the crow's-nest before the others. They said he was climbing very quickly and fearlessly. As he neared the top, he missed his footing – there was ice on the ropes – and . . . and . . .' She broke down completely.

'Oh no! I can't believe it!'

'Yes, he fell right down on *Britannia*'s deck.'

'But how badly is he injured? Surely he'll get well and be able to go back to Dartmouth soon?'

'That seems unlikely. The hospital at the college was marvellous, but they felt that a second opinion was needed. I had the telegram just after you went out this afternoon – oh, my darling, everything happened so quickly. The authorities sent him by train to North Road, where the ambulance picked him up and took him to the Naval Hospital at Devonport. They decided to re-set his hips and leg.'

'His hips and leg?' Lizzie couldn't believe what she was hearing, 'Are they . . .?'

'Both hips have what they call compound fractures, and his right leg is broken in two places. He is fortunate to be alive, Lizzie.'

'The telegram told me to go to Devonport at once, and it was a dreadful shock. I got a cab there immediately, and there was Joe in a private room with a lieutenant, who had accompanied him and gave me the details. They had expected to call us to Dartmouth, but decided that the Naval Hospital, then home, was the best plan. Oh, Lizzie, I'm so glad that he's home with us! I'm sure he'll get better far quicker with us than if he was just in hospital at *Britannia*.'

'Of course he will, Mama. I expect he'll be all right in a few months' time.'

'Well, the surgeon, Mr Blunsdon from the hospital, has conferred with our Dr Higgins, who will see Joe regularly. And what he said right away was that while young people's bones knit together far more easily than older people's, when

106

the breaks are very bad there can be deformities. Thank goodness they can now set broken limbs in plaster – poor Joe's hips and his leg are covered in it. It's all so heavy, and it will be on for ages, but it'll keep the leg completely still, which is much better for it, and Mr Blunsdon reassured me that his spinal cord is undamaged – which is something of a miracle.'

Lizzie suddenly thought about her father, somewhere in the Mediterranean. 'Does Papa know yet?'

'Dartmouth said they were contacting him for us, which was kind. He should have heard by now, but I very much doubt if he'll be allowed home. That would only happen if . . . if . . .' Mrs Newcombe could go no further.

Bravely Lizzie finished the sentence for her. 'If Joe had been killed, you mean?'

Her mother nodded. 'We'll have to carry on as best we may without him. This is going to be a very difficult winter for us, Lizzie, and an even harder one for Joe when he realises what's happened to him. We'll just have to wait and see how he progresses, and if it turns out that he can't go back to Dartmouth, we'll have to be as evasive as possible until he can cope with what I know would be the biggest disappointment of his life – such a turnabout, such a disaster! He's so set on his career – well, we all are, aren't we?'

'But, Mama, it may still be possible.'

'Darling, you know I'm no pessimist any more than you are, but I do very much doubt it. Heaven knows what Joe will do with his life if he can't carry on. He may just have to be an invalid in a wheelchair.'

'Mama, Joe is a very determined person. I can't see him allowing himself to sit around for the whole of his life. I'm sure it won't come to that, however serious his injuries. Look, let's leave him to sleep. Has he had a sedative?'

'Yes, and some strong painkillers.'

'Come, let's go into the drawing room.'

They passed the open door of the dining room as they made their way. It revealed the beautifully set-out birthday tea, now totally forgotten and to remain so until Laura could bring herself to clear it away.

*

The next day, after Dr Higgins and Mr Blunsdon's visit, Mrs Newcombe came into the drawing room to find her daughter sitting on the sofa, tears streaming down her young face. She was holding the piece of rope that Joe had so thoughtfully sent her for her birthday.

'Oh, Mama!' she cried. 'He'll never do any more lovely work like this, will he?'

Mrs Newcombe woke with a start. She heard screams coming from downstairs. Grabbing her dressing gown, she stumbled across the bedroom in the complete darkness of the cold, wet pre-dawn. Joe's agonising cries were splitting her eardrums. By the time she reached the stairs, Lizzie had joined her from the second floor, and there were footsteps coming from the attic rooms where Aggie and Laura slept.

'Has he fallen out of bed, Mama?'

'I don't know, but he sounds in dreadful pain.'

They rushed into Joe's room expecting the worst.

'Joe, darling, what's wrong? Are you in pain? Is your plaster hurting you?'

Joe, clinging to his mother with a powerful grip that made her flinch, cried pitifully, 'Mama, it's awful – oh, so awful! Take them away, take them away!'

'Darling, there's no one here, only me and Lizzie and – oh, and Aggie and Laura. We're all here to help you.'

For quite a while Joe was unconvinced. Then Lizzie very sensibly asked, 'Joe, who do you want us to take away? Look, there's no one here!'

Joe, his pillows, plumped up, his mother wiping his nose and cooling his forehead with a cold, damp cloth provided by Aggie, began to surface.

'Mama, Joe's had a nightmare.' Lizzie turned back to her brother. 'Tell us about it.' Joe started to shake with fear again, and to sob. 'It was dreadful! There were lots of nasty men all pushing and pulling me down into some filthy black mud. I couldn't get up. They were gripping my legs – they were so heavy. I think I was drowning. I couldn't breathe.'

Cuddling her injured son, Mrs Newcombe comforted him and reassured him it was only a dream.

Laura went to get Joe some warm milk, and as he drank

it, Lizzie went on, 'It *is* horrible – but try not to be too frightened by those nasty men. They've gone away now.'

They had, for the time.

Mrs Newcombe kissed her son, and reassuring Lizzie that he was settled she left the little room, leaving the door slightly open. Dawn was breaking. She knew she wouldn't sleep again. She made her way into the drawing room. Heavy rain was battering the large French windows, blurring the view of a dark-grey sea and sky. Bursting into tears, she cried, 'Peter, oh, Peter, I need you so very much! If only you could come home!'

But she knew that was impossible.

The nightmares continued so regularly that the women hardly ever managed to get a complete night's sleep. Joe's pitiful crying was always disturbing and distressing them, and their nerves were beginning to fray. Sometimes he would dream he was drowning, sometimes he would wake up quite convinced that someone had cut his leg off. At other times in his dream life, he was captain of his ship, rounding the Horn in a gale or winning some great sea battle. He would wake from these dreams in a euphoric state, which would immediately fade once he felt the weight of his plaster casts dashing the hopes raised in his unconscious. These dreams were quite as difficult for him to cope with as the nightmares.

Meanwhile, the Plymouth Academy for Young Ladies was beginning to prepare for Christmas. Lizzie was taking regular carol rehearsals ready for the service on the last day of term, when parents and friends were to be invited to hear the singing and readings from the Gospels.

But she was far from happy. Apart from the stress at home, Miss Creeber's restrictions and backward-looking attitudes were wearing her down, and the tension between them was growing. It was quite difficult for her to control her hot temper. The more she saw, the less she liked the school. She felt that she could be a far better teacher than she was allowed to be there; that the domination of young minds by worn-out attitudes rather than their stimulation was quite wrong.

All these pressures were building up, and making Lizzie

far less carefree and happy than usual. In fact, at times she felt really quite depressed; and to make matters worse she knew she had to hide her feelings from Joe and her mother. What kept her going was the result of a late-afternoon cup of tea and chat with Miss Young while they discussed a timetable of studies to begin in the new year, which would prepare Lizzie for the entrance exam to Girton. She would have tutorials twice a week after school with her old teacher, who would mark her essays and take her through the subjects – Latin and Greek among them – that she would be tested on when the time came for her to sit the examination. She was not daunted by the prospect. She looked forward to her new study regime, and the fact that Miss Young had mentioned 'tutorials' made her feel that Girton was not as remote as it had seemed when the scheme was first mooted. It was this and her beloved music that made life worthwhile.

Mrs Newcombe sat reading and rereading her husband's letter. It gave her a great deal of strength and support to know that she and their children were constantly in his thoughts; although distance and duty were keeping them apart, they were united in grief. She understood when he said he found it difficult to express his feelings – not only for Joe's distress but for the heavy burden placed upon her and Lizzie – and his warm words gave her courage at a time when she needed it most.

Chapter Nine

Lizzie, glad to be alone for a while, was sitting on a seat on the Promenade and gazing out to sea. The afternoon had gone well. She'd played the piano for carols, the older girls had read the Christmas story and the tiny five-year-olds had enacted a tableau of the birth of Christ while the rest of the school sang 'Away in a Manger'. The parents had loved it.

She had now completed a term as pupil teacher, and Miss Creeber had presented her with a discreet envelope which she knew contained her pay of two guineas. She would do some Christmas shopping tomorrow. Nevertheless, she was in a sad, contemplative mood.

Her thoughts centred on Joe, his disappointment and the pain he was suffering. In the last few days she believed he was beginning to realise he might never return to Dartmouth – although the surgeon had made no final pronouncement yet. But she knew her brother so well that his every expression, and the odd little phrases that slipped out, meant something to her. She felt that when the time came for her mother to tell him the whole truth, her task would be less difficult than she imagined; Joe had the inner strength of someone twice his age.

Nevertheless, Lizzie's feelings were difficult to cope with. She had been trying hard to be cheerful over the last few weeks, but now her sadness was getting the better of her.

On top of all this she was tired and had that end-of-term feeling of which all teachers speak. And this was mixed with a great deal of anger at the backward and repressive atmosphere of the school and the attitude of its headmistress in

111

particular. It was the negative snobbishness, the silly rules, the time wasted on 'lines' – doled out by the hundred for the tiniest misdemeanour – that she hated so much. There was very little emphasis on the essence of real goodness, and in Scripture lessons it was always 'thou shalt not' rather than 'love thy neighbour'. Lizzie had taken risks, and had done her best to awaken in her pupils a sense of greater kindness, of sharing with those less fortunate, rather than adopting the condescending attitude of Miss Creeber, when for instance she mentioned giving to the 'poor children'.

Lizzie felt as if she was being crushed. She wanted to feel free, but on the other hand she knew she would have to be very patient and work really hard in the new year if she was going to gain her place at Girton.

As the watery winter sun began to set over the Cornish side of the Hamoaze, where the river Tamar met the sea, her depression deepened. The last few weeks had been too much for her. She burst in to audible sobs.

'Er, excuse me, I don't want to intrude . . . but can I help you in any way?'

On hearing a rather shy and nervous voice, Lizzie looked up and through her flood of tears she saw another girl looking down at her. Brushing a few straggling hairs back from her face, she managed to give the vestige of a smile to the stranger, whose face seemed to show kind and very genuine concern.

'That's really nice of you, thank you. I am feeling very miserable at present.'

'Would you like to tell me all about it?'

'Oh, dear! It's dreadfully complicated.'

'Never mind. I know all too well how good it is to talk if one is worried or unhappy.'

The young woman's soft voice gave Lizzie the impression of immediate and natural sympathy.

'I don't think I've seen you before? I know most people who live round here – we've always lived nearby. I'm Lizzie Newcombe.'

'Emma Cooper.'

With a certain reserved formality the two young women shook hands and Emma sat down beside Lizzie.

112

'You can tell me what's upsetting you so much – that is, if you'd like to.'

Remembering her own unhappiness and homesickness, in spite of the family problems of a few months ago, Emma was ready to listen, just as Katy and then Sarah had listened to her. At first she wondered if her new friend was in trouble with a young man.

Lizzie told her about Joe.

'How dreadful for all of you! I suppose your pa can't come home. Your ma must be so worried.'

'We've had letters from Papa. He's dreadfully upset. So is Mama, of course. We don't think Joe will ever be able to join the navy now.'

'It's all so sad. I can see why you were crying. But still, it must be wonderful to have a brother you love and who is so fond of you.'

'Do you have brothers and sisters?'

'One brother, but he's . . . he's quite horrible – I hate him.' Suddenly there was a lot of aggression and tension in Emma's voice.

'That's a pity. Why?'

'I don't want to talk about it. But I've a sister. She's on the stage, in the West End – in London, I mean.'

'On the stage! I've never met anyone who's on the stage, though we go to the theatre from time to time.'

Emma was surprised and delighted at Lizzie's reaction.

'Yes, she's in a big show called *In Town*. She dances and sings and acts and has the most beautiful dresses to wear. I think she's going to be quite famous.'

Already Lizzie was beginning to be cheered by the lighter turn in the conversation. But it was her turn to be curious.

'But if your sister's on the stage in London, what are you doing all this distance away from her – and your mama and papa?'

It was Emma's turn to tell her tale.

An hour slipped by. Suddenly the two young women realised it was almost dark.

'Lady Alston will be wondering where I've got to. I only went out to post some letters I'd written for her.'

'And Mama will be anxious about me. Look, if you can,

perhaps you would like to come and met her and maybe Joe, tomorrow?'

'Well, I have to go and buy flowers and make some calls for Lady Alston.'

'I've just had my wages. I want to do some Christmas shopping. I could perhaps call for you? Where do you live?'

'Over there, at number 5.' Emma turned and pointed to the terrace just behind her.

'In Elliot Terrace? That's really grand! Those are the biggest houses in the centre of Plymouth. We live down there, look – right by the sea, just opposite Drake's Island.'

A distinct feeling of pride swept over Emma. For the first time in her life she realised that she wasn't a mere lower-working-class girl. Her new friend's house was smaller than Lady Alston's West Country home.

Apologising for her lateness, Lizzie – her spirits much restored – was eager to tell her mother about the new friend she'd made.

'My dear, what an interesting thing to happen to a young girl! But what is she like? Does she speak with a cockney accent?'

'I don't think so, Mama – though I don't think I know what a cockney accent sounds like. But she spoke like, well – like you and me, I would say.'

'She must have been to a good school then. And her father?'

'A boot repairer in London. But Mama, what was odd was that she said she had a brother she hates and wouldn't talk about him. I can't understand that.'

'Well, Lizzie, all families aren't like us, you know. There can be awful jealousy and rivalry. And she lives with whom?'

'A Lady Alston. She told me the most fantastic tale of how she was asked to be her . . . companion, I suppose you'd call her.'

And Lizzie told her mother about Emma and the ring and how she came to be living in Plymouth.

'It's all most interesting. Do you think Lady Alston would like to come to tea? She sounds nice. She mayn't know many people down here.'

Lizzie went on to tell her mother of the tentative arrangements she and Emma had made for the following day. Then Mrs Newcombe remembered that her daughter had other news too.

'Oh, Lizzie, have you been paid? How did the carol service go? You must have heaps more to tell me. Let's go in to Joe, and you can tell him all about your new friend and the celebrations at school.'

'Emma, here you are at last! Her ladyship's in a right old mood. You'd better go straight up to the drawing room,' Sybil greeted Emma as she burst into the front hall.

'I'm so sorry I'm late, Lady Alston.'

'Where *have* you been? I've been very worried about you. You went out at half past three and it's now well after five. You must not be so tardy, Emma. This is a naval town and a lot of harm could come to a young girl like you.' Lady Alston's tone of voice was severe.

'I'm so sorry, Lady Alston – but I've made a new friend.'

'Not a sailor, I hope.'

'Oh, no, Lady Alston! A girl of about my own age. She's very nice. I found her sitting on that seat we both like, over there on the Promenade. She was crying, and I asked her what was wrong. She's got a brother who's been injured and . . . and . . .'

'Emma!'

Lady Alston's usual good humour was beginning to return as she realised that there was a very plausible reason for Emma's lateness.

'Calm down, and tell me all about her.'

Emma collected her thoughts and became more coherent.

'Well, my dear, it will be a good thing for you to have some company of your own age. I've thought that from time to time you've been looking a little sad yourself, and I put it down to the fact that you were missing Kate and your mother. I think it will be very pleasant if you see this Lizzie – Elizabeth, I assume – again.'

'Now, darling, let me look at you. Yes, very smart. I don't think you've met a member of the aristocracy before, have you?'

'Yes, Mama, there was that old lady – you remember, she was terribly fat – at Cousin Bella's wedding. You told me to curtsy.'

'Yes, of course, and you will to Lady Alston.'

'I suppose I must.'

Lizzie's radical inclination was to think the idea silly – unless one was about to meet Queen Victoria herself, or the Prince of Wales, of course.

'I really think you should – just a little one. You don't want to let us down. We have a certain standing in the community too, you know.'

'Yes, Mama.'

Adjusting her brown velvet beret, Lizzie kissed her mother goodbye and set off up the familiar route to the Promenade and 5 Elliot Terrace.

'Come this way, miss. Her ladyship and Miss Emma are expecting you.'

Stratton led the way from the hall up to the first-floor drawing room.

Emma, sitting ready to go out, was wearing her Whiteley's costume and black velvet beret which was almost identical to Lizzie's. She introduced her to Lady Alston. Dutifully Lizzie bobbed a curtsy as the elderly lady shook her hand.

'I am pleased to meet you. Emma has told me all about you. How is your brother today, Miss Newcombe?'

'He slept much better, thank you, my lady. Sometimes he has dreadful nightmares.'

'That I can understand, after such a devastating experience.'

The conversation went on for a few minutes. Then Lady Alston noticed Lizzie glancing across to the piano, which had been the first object Lizzie had noticed in the large, very grand room.

'My dear, are you interested in music? Do you play the piano?'

'Oh yes, as much as I can.'

'Will you play something for me now? We've not heard the instrument since we've been here, have we, Emma? Go and open it up for Elizabeth.'

Lizzie joined Emma at the piano.

116

A little surprised at the sudden unexpected turn of events, she sat for a moment at the stool, rubbed her slightly chilly hands and decided on Chopin's A Major Prelude.

The short piece was well received by her small audience.

'That was quite beautiful. I shall want to hear much more, another time. Thank you, my dear. Now, you two, run along and let's see what nice flowers Elizabeth will help you find, Emma. Be back just before one, for luncheon – and don't be late.'

Emma promised.

Both young women enjoyed their outing, looking at the fashions in Spooner's and Popham's windows. Feeling prosperous and very grown-up, Lizzie treated Emma to coffee and biscuits in Spooner's Tea Rooms. They thoroughly did the town, but because they were talking so much, Lizzie found it difficult to concentrate on buying her Christmas presents. She did, however, take Emma into the market, to the stall where her mother always bought her flowers, fresh from Cornwall every morning.

Emma left the market loaded with chrysanthemums and greenery. A great deal of the afternoon would be spent arranging them.

So far, their conversation had been light-hearted, in pleasant contrast to the tone of their previous meeting, but now, as they walked up Lockyer Street and Lizzie showed Emma the Academy, Emma asked her just how much she enjoyed her work.

'Some of it's marvellous – the children respond well to me, and we have a lot of fun – but, Emma, there's a lot wrong with the place.'

Lizzie went on to explain to Emma what she thought was wrong.

'But you are aware of all these things. You're surely beginning to put them right?'

'No, I can't – not really. If I get caught trying, then I get into trouble. Miss Creeber is a snob – the worst kind of snob. She looks down her nose like this when she mentions the "poor children".'

And Lizzie gave a good impersonation of her headmistress's expression and tone of voice.

117

'Good morning, Miss Elizabeth. Enjoying yourself?'

Emma saw Lizzie turn white as a sheet as a gaunt, bad-tempered-looking woman overtook them.

'Oh y-yes, thank you, Miss Creeber!'

Miss Creeber with an imperious step strode ahead of the two friends and turned in to the forecourt of the school, nose in air.

'That was awful, awful! She must have heard every word I said and seen the face I pulled.'

'That was her? Miss Creeber? Lizzie, how dreadful! But you know she couldn't have seen your face – she was behind us.'

'I feel as if I want to dig a hole and crawl into it.'

'It was horrible – but you know what my friend Katy would say?'

'No.'

'Well, she'd say, "Them as listens don't never 'ear any good of themselves – and don' you forget it, my girl!"'

This appealed to Lizzie's sense of humour. She'd never heard anyone speak in broad cockney before. Both girls laughed, and Lizzie replied, 'Well, my handsome, I suppose you'm right!'

She had to translate the broad Devonshire for her new friend – it had been just as strange to her as the cockney had been to Lizzie.

Joe shifted about uncomfortably in his heavy plaster.

'Oh, Lizzie, I shouldn't worry too much about it. Miss Creeber's jolly old, and I dare say she's a bit deaf – she probably didn't hear a word you said. But then, who knows, p'raps she did hear you, and she'll take notice. You might see things getting a bit better next term.'

He was, as usual, flat on his back with just three pillows supporting him so that he could read and at least see around the room.

'It's possible. But I think she must have heard.'

'Well, at least, as Emma said, she couldn't have seen your face. Are you going to tell Mama?'

'I don't think so. I don't want to give her anything else to worry about.'

'No, you mustn't.' He paused. 'Lizzie . . . do you think I'll ever get back to Dartmouth? Be honest.'

'We just don't know, Joe. Young bones do mend well and quickly, as Mr Blunsdon says; we'll just have to wait and see.'

'Wait and see, always wait and see.' There was desperation in her brother's voice.

'I know, but that really is it for a few weeks, I'm afraid.'

'But if I can't go back, I've got to think what I'm going to do – when I'm grown-up. Will I go back to the Hoe Grammar School?' His white knuckles gripped the bed linen.

'That wouldn't be so awful, would it? You were happy there, weren't you?'

'Yes, but then I knew I'd eventually go to Dartmouth. But now, what?'

'Well, it still may be Dartmouth, for all we know. But you're good at all sorts of things – mathematics, science, and then there's your drawing, you like that, too. All these could be useful to you when . . . if you have to think about a different career.'

'Yes – technical drawing, that's best of all. We have such a good teacher in Mr –'

Joe was about to go on about his lively technical-drawing teacher at Dartmouth, when the accident and all its implications flooded back to him. He unsuccessfully tried to stifle a sob, then gave way to a flood of tears.

'Joe, dear, don't be so downhearted. You really are clever! I'm sure you're bound to be successful at something – you're brave and determined, and once you've decided what you want to do, you'll be just fine. And remember, we don't know yet that it won't be the navy.'

Had she comforted him or not? Lizzie wasn't sure. At this point their mother came in holding a letter.

'I've just had this from Mr Blunsdon. He says it's time your plaster was changed. It'll have to be done every month, and at the same time he can examine the breaks in your leg and hips and see how they're getting on. Then they'll put on the new plaster. So, next Monday morning the ambulance will take you to Devonport and he will see you there.'

'Perhaps Mr Blunsdon will be able to tell me if I can go

119

back to Dartmouth after Christmas,' said Joe, blowing his nose. 'D'you think so, Mama?'

'We may hear some news but, well, we'll just have to see.'

'The same old story,' Joe groaned to himself, and attempted to make himself more comfortable – that plaster was very itchy.

'Let's play chess,' Lizzie suggested.

He cheered up a little at the prospect.

Mr Blunsdon led Mrs Newcombe into a small, comfortable office.

'There's good news and there's bad. The good news is that the compound fractures in Joe's hips are healing remarkably well. I couldn't be more pleased with his progress. But I fear the leg is not so good. While it is still – even after several weeks – fairly early days, and the bones are certainly knitting together, the way they are joining causes me to think that he could have a problem. Now, very often these things sort themselves out, but I must warn you not to be too sanguine. By the end of January, when you come again, we will hope to see another improvement. As it is, the fragments of bone – some of which were very small – are not behaving in the way I would hope. But I can at least certainly say that it seems unlikely that Joe will have to spend the rest of his life in a wheelchair – which could have been the case if his hips were not mending properly. This surely will be a great relief to you.'

Mrs Newcombe took the mixed news with resolution. 'Can I at least tell him the good news?'

'Certainly, and gently warn him that we will have to continue to be patient about his leg.'

Back home Laura had a tray of coffee waiting for them, and they took it into Joe's room. Mrs Newcombe told him the good news about his hips.

'Then I will walk again, won't I? It's so good to know that's going to happen.' He paused, then went on, 'And what about my leg, Mama? Is that better too?'

She had been working out what to say to him all the way home in the ambulance.

'Darling, we don't know yet. It is getting better, and Mr

Blunsdon is quite pleased, but he'll want to see you again next month. Then he'll be able to tell us more.'

'It's not so good, is it, Mama? Tell me, Mama, please tell me. Don't hold back, I'd really rather know.'

'Joe – dear Joe! To be honest, it isn't quite such good news, but – and I am being really and truly honest, dear – Mr Blunsdon can't be sure about anything yet. He says your leg is not making quite such good progress as your hips, but there could still be good news next month. That really is the truth.'

Joe's face darkened. Suddenly he looked tired.

'But at least I'll be able to walk again, and that's good.'

Sensitive to his mother's concern, he was now trying to cheer her.

They hugged each other. Lizzie sat on his bed and joined in.

Lady Alston spent an afternoon planning her Christmas shopping with Emma. This resulted in long lists of presents and addresses sent to Fortnum and Mason's and Hatchard's bookshop, both in Piccadilly. While they were discussing who should have what, Emma arranged to have presents of food and flowers sent to her family and friends in Hammersmith. Although she would be using her employer's account, she at once said that she would pay Lady Alston for her part of the long and complicated order. Lady Alston respected Emma's honest streak where money was concerned. Such an attitude would be useful to her later in life. She also realised that Lizzie was already having a pleasant influence on Emma, and noticed with amusement that Emma, when speaking of her mother, now referred to her as 'Mama' rather than the somewhat coarser 'Ma'.

Emma had learned far more than Lady Alston realised, since they had been together. Her strict schooling and the discipline that had been dinned into her by her parents were standing her in good stead now that she was mixing in a totally different social circle. Her good deportment and gentle good looks were also greatly in her favour. What Lady Alston knew she must do was constantly to develop Emma's self-confidence, which was increasing daily; if it took a knock, Emma would suffer.

121

She also wondered how Emma would react to a lover. She herself had had lovers as well as a husband, and hoped that some day, even if she had to lose Emma as a result, the girl would fall in love and respond well. But she had an intuition that this would not come naturally to her companion. She had observed her become tense, gripping her hands and blinking if the conversation turned towards love and the opposite sex. Of course this was a prudent age, and her background would have been repressive. The attitude of her father would not have helped, either – of that Lady Alston was quite sure.

It was no bad thing that she and Emma had these months away from London, during which she could continue to train and mould the girl. By next summer, she would be able to take her anywhere. All this would bring great pleasure to Lady Alston in her fading years. She was very happy – and delighted that Emma had found a very suitable young friend. Lady Alston now resolved to get to know Lizzie's family, possibly during the coming holiday.

During the weeks that the old lady had been living in Plymouth, she had established accounts with the more important shops, and every so often parcels would arrive from Popham's, Spooner's and the well-known West Country jewellers Page, Keen and Page. Often Emma was requested to help her decide on her purchases. Sometimes she preferred to choose alone, because she wanted to find suitable surprises for Emma for Christmas or for her eighteenth birthday on New Year's Day.

Lady Alston mentioned to Emma how much she liked holly at Christmas and always decorated her home with garlands of it. Emma was about to order some from her market florist when, a few days before Christmas, one of the Newcombe family's Christmas traditions solved the problem.

'Miss Elizabeth, Lady Alston's carriage has arrived.'

Laura was calling her from the porch.

As Lizzie closed the front door of their house, Toby, in his smart footman's uniform, stepped down, opened the carriage door for her and gallantly helped her to step into the carriage. Emma was waiting inside.

Lizzie had only been in a private carriage once before, and was excited at the prospect.

She greeted Emma, who had a travelling rug over her knees.

'We'll go to Bluebell Woods and Linkety Lane – we're sure to find nice holly there.'

'Is it far? You'll have to direct Toby, give him plenty of time if we have to make a turning.'

They made their way north and slightly east, into the suburbs, where several large, impressive houses were being built. Eventually, after ascending and descending some characteristic Plymouth hills, Lizzie shouted to Toby to stop. They were at the entrance to a narrow and very steep lane.

'We have to go that way.'

'Miss, I can't take Beauty down there, it's far too steep.'

Emma and Lizzie got out of the carriage.

'I understand, Toby,' replied Lizzie. Taking hold of Beauty's bridle, she gave the mare a lump of sugar she'd brought for the purpose.

'I love horses. I ride quite well. Of course you mustn't take such a risk. Miss Emma and I can walk. We won't be long.'

The horse nuzzled Lizzie as she spoke.

About half an hour later the girls, having enjoyed the fresh country air and loaded up with armfuls of holly, agreed that the afternoon had been a great success.

'He's handsome!' said Lizzie.

'Who?'

'Toby – and look how well he handles Beauty and the carriage.'

'Is he? I hadn't noticed.'

'Oh, yes! I know several of my friends would think so too; in fact, Elsie.'

'Sorry, Lizzie, but I'm not interested – just *not* interested – do you hear me?'

Emma interrupted angrily and Lizzie saw her gripping her hands tightly together.

'Well, neither am I – like that . . . but still, he *is* handsome.'

Preparations for Christmas in both households began in earnest.

Chapter Ten

'Mrs Cooper?'

'Yes?'

'This is for you. The hamper is very heavy – may I put it on your kitchen table for you madam?'

'Thanks very much, I'm sure.'

A surprised Mrs Cooper opened her front door wider to allow Fortnum's delivery man into the passage and through to the back kitchen.

'Thank you, sir. You're sure it's for me?'

'Yes, madam.'

She was about to close the door when he announced, 'Just a moment, madam, there's something else for you.'

He went back to the impeccably clean, shining van with its two equally shining black horses and returned with a large cardboard box.

'This as well, sir?'

'Yes, madam. Thank you, and may I wish you the compliments of the season?'

'Oh yes, please, and merry Christmas to you, sir, thank you.'

Dazed, Mrs Cooper went back to the kitchen. She didn't know what to open first – the huge wicker basket or the large cardboard box, on which was printed, *Fortnum and Mason. Grocers and Florists. Piccadilly, W. Open at once – perishable.*

'Per-ish-a-ble.'

She read the word slowly before lifting the lid. Inside was a little card with the message, in Emma's handwriting, 'To dear Mama, with my love for Christmas. Emma.'

There was a selection of chrysanthemum blooms of various colours, as well as carnations and red roses. Mrs Cooper felt almost dizzy with delight, but at the same time realised just how much she was missing Emma. She got a bucket of water from the yard and placed all the flowers in it, with a view to putting them in every vase she could find later on. She'd never before seen roses and carnations at Christmas.

She turned her attention to the wicker hamper. Packed in clean, fresh straw and greaseproof paper was a beautiful goose, all prepared for the oven. Below it a full-sized ham, a Christmas cake and a Christmas pudding. There was a box of liqueur chocolates, a pot of mincemeat, a jar of brandy butter and a bottle of tawny port. Another card, also in Emma's handwriting, explained whom the gift was from.

'What a Christmas we'll have! We can eat our leg of pork on Boxing Day – that'll get George away from the pub come dinnertime – an' we'll have the goose tomorrow. I wonder what the pudding'll be like? Well, we have to see – but we'll have mine tomorrow, anyway.'

But in her burst of joy Emma's mother realised she might have a problem. How would Will react to such a present? They always had leg of pork on Christmas Day. Now he would have to adjust to something different.

'Mrs Cooper, are you there, dearie? Oh, what lovely flowers! And look at that goose, *well* . . . You *are* a lucky one!'

Mrs Tyrrell never bothered to knock.

'Thought you'd like to know Katy and me have had a surprise – and so have you, I see! Bless her 'eart, she does want to share her good fortune with us, don' she, the darling? Katy's some thrilled with her chocolates, and we've got a duck. I call that real that nice, don't you?'

The women gossiped and drank tea. And Mrs Cooper continued her preparations.

Will Cooper closed up the shop at five thirty. It was raining hard and a cold wind was blowing as he made his way home. The atmosphere of Christmas was filling the house. His wife was making stuffing for the goose when he appeared. She'd told him nothing of their good fortune at dinnertime, when she took him a cold meat pie and a hard-boiled egg.

Heavy-footed he stomped into the kitchen. The smell of the food crept up his nostrils, and even though it warmed him, it didn't prevent precisely the reaction Mrs Cooper had feared. She showed him Lady Alston's generous gifts and told him about Emma's beautiful flowers, now resplendent in the front parlour.

'What? Food from *her*? All this food from *her*? I warn you, Susan, don' you touch it! It's going straight back to Fortunes and Majors. I won't 'ave it in the 'ouse! I won't 'ave 'er charity. Yes, that's what it is – charity! Who do she think she is? Her, with her airs and graces? We don't want this stuff. Send it back.'

He clenched both fists aggressively. His face was dark with anger so that the stubble looked white against his skin, and his steely eyes flashed in the lamplight.

'We'll 'ave our pork as usual. Fancy stuff! Don' you touch it, Susan – I'm warnin' you, I'll belt you if you do!'

With that he flung his arm out and knocked the bowl of stuffing from where Mrs Cooper had it crooked in her arm to steady it while mixing it. It went crashing to the floor. The mixing bowl exploded into hundreds of pieces and the stuffing slopped all over the floor with the fragments of china.

It was her turn to be angry.

'Now look what you've done with all your ranting and raving! Look at the mess I'll have to clean up. Will, say you're sorry. That was my only mixing bowl. Go down to the corner shop and buy me another.'

'Not likely – I can't be seen buying women's things. Go down yourself.'

He paused for a moment, grunted several times, then went on with an air of pomposity, 'The best thing to do is to give all this stuff to the church – someone'll be glad of it. Yes, all those people who live over Shepherd's Bush Common. *They'll* be glad of it. *We* don't need it.'

She at once saw what he was getting at. She knew her old man like the back of her hand.

Ha! she fumed to herself. Give it to charity. Yes, and be careful to tell the vicar first, then he'll know how generous we've been. Just like Will, that.

126

But aloud, she replied, 'All right, Will, I'll go to the vicar this minute and bring him round so he can see what we have for the poor of the parish.'

'And what have we got for the poor of the parish?' George lolloped in.

His mother explained the situation as his father continued to grunt and occasionally muttered, 'It's got to go – I'm not having her charity. Let them have it as needs it.'

She left to fetch the vicar. She knew that if she explained the situation, he would recognise just how kind Lady Alston had been and how she was, in reality, saying thank you to Mr and Mrs Cooper for allowing their daughter to go with her. In matters like this Susan was intuitive and shrewd. She also realised that the vicar – who must be aware that Will was often very pretentious and snobbish – could easily make her husband feel silly and ungrateful.

Meanwhile George, who was delighted at the idea of having such a feast, confronted his father, who fiercely stood his ground. He thought he could increase his public standing in the church if he sent the food hamper from 'Fortunes and Majors' to the vicarage.

'Don't be bloody daft, Pa! You don' know your luck. Besides, no one would believe you could 'ave afforded to buy all this stuff – you don' even know where F –' he looked at the label – 'Fortnum and Mason's is. And if you did, they wouldn't allow you inside a shop like that. Everyone at the church, and the vicar, would know it come either from Emma or Lady Alston. If you hadn't been swanking so much about Emma and her job, you might've got away with it; but you wouldn' now – and that's a fact. There again, if they didn't know, they'd all say, "What a fool he is! If he can afford all this lot, what's he doing mendin' our boots?" You're caught either way, Father.'

George always called his Pa 'Father' when he realised he'd won an argument by using his quicker and craftier mind.

'I don't want charity, that's all.'

'Goose, Pa! Think of goose: that lovely, rich gravy . . . the crunchy skin! And think of how Ma'll be able to do the spuds. Then there's that puddin' –'

'Your mother's pudding's far better – we don' know where that thing was made.'

127

Sly George picked up the bottle of port and cracked open the seal.

'Smell this, Pa – it's the very best. You know how you likes a drop of the real stuff at Christmas.'

Will Cooper's nose twitched as George held the bottle under it, then filled a large glass tumbler and gave it to his reluctant father. It did the trick. He downed the port as if it were a glass of water. He had had a hard day and he was tired. The strong port went straight to his head. He staggered a bit, then passed out in the kitchen armchair.

Mrs Cooper came back looking very anxious.

'I couldn't find the vicar, George.' Seeing Will snoring in the chair, 'What have you done, George?'

'Nothing much, Ma – just encouraged Pa to fall into temptation. He's changed his mind.'

George explained what he had said – and what he had done.

'Don't worry, it'll be all right. So where's the vicar?'

'He'd been called out – old Mrs Barkworth's dying of the pneumonia. But *will* it be all right, George?'

'Trust me, Ma.'

'No, George, not usually,' she replied knowingly.

'What's that mean?' George asked quickly.

'Never you mind, my son – but yes, this time I think you probably have done a good job.'

George went to the sink and roughly washed his hands and face, spluttering loudly as he did so.

'I'm off now.'

'Where're you going, then?'

'Nowhere special – just with me mates.'

'Wish you'd find yourself a good woman, George.'

'One day, Ma, one day . . .'

Off he went round the corner to the Havelock Arms.

''Ello, Georgie Porgie! Gonna wish me a 'appy Christmas then?'

Lil Barrett sidled up to George, thrusting her ample bosom to his chest and making sure that her half-open blouse parted seductively as she spoke.

Pulling the older woman closer to him, he pushed his

128

mouth onto hers, roughly parted her lips, grabbing her behind and lifting her skirt as he did so.

'Oh, like that, is it? Well, we'll 'ave to see. I could get better offers tonight. A lot depends on what Santa Claus is bringin' me.'

'I'll Santa Claus you all right.'

And he thrust his tongue down her throat for the second time – to the cheers of all assembled in the noisy bar.

'Well, I'll 'ave a port an' lemon first, if you please, sir.'

Annoyed to be kept waiting, he shouted his order and downed his pint of favourite porter while the ageing Lil, acting ladylike, sipped her drink.

George's foot crept up her leg under the little bar table.

'Give over.' Lil pretended to be shocked.

'How much, then? All night, eh?'

'Five bob to you.'

Ten minutes later George left the bar for a night of debauchery with the worn-out prostitute. He could afford it because his pa had just doled out his Christmas bonus.

A couple of streets away they turned into a dirty mews. Lil lived in a room over some stables where a carrier kept his horse and cart, and as long as the one and sixpence a week rent turned up on time he asked no questions. To him Lil was 'quite the lady'.

The staircase was dark and dank, and on this squally Christmas night, wet footsteps made earlier that evening made the torn lino very slippery – and was proof that Lil had entertained other gentlemen before her foray to the Havelock Arms.

George took no notice of this. Once on the first floor and in her dreary room, with its damp-stained walls and threadbare rug, Lil pulled the curtain across the window. Lighting an oil lamp covered by a red glass shade, she moved it from the sill, putting it on the table beside the large, untidy bed.

George grabbed her and started to tear at her blouse. Lil, used to this rough approach, stepped back.

'Not yet, dearie. Wash first – you know where.'

She pointed to a small curtained-off portion of the room, which contained a washstand, jug of water, basin and under the stand a slop bucket.

'No need. I'm clean as a whistle – I've just 'ad one.'

Lil wasn't having any.

'Pull the other leg – it's got bells on! You might have washed your hands in the kitchen – but your prick? In front of your ma? Never! I knows your sort. Wash.'

George meekly obeyed. Hurriedly throwing off his trousers and his long wool underpants, he splashed his privates. The cold water began to make him lose his eager erection, so his ablutions were not as thorough as Lil would have wished. Having wiped himself on a soggy and not very clean towel, he came out of the cubicle to find Lil naked but for her black stockings and garters, ready for him on the bed. Starting to throw off his jacket and shirt, he was about to fall on her when she put up her hand.

'Cash first! Over there on the table, Georgie Porgie – then we'll 'ave a 'appy Christmas. But don' you try nothing fancy, d'ya 'ear? I may be feelin' generous, and if I give you a few extras – seeing as 'ow it's Christmas – that's up to me. Understand?'

He threw himself on her and immediately grabbed her full, drooping breasts, scrunching them in his rough, podgy hands. He bit her nipples hard so that she – even she with all her experience – let out a cry, which he took to be one of pleasure. He entered her, and after about five seconds and three harsh thrusts he broke away from her and ejaculated into a chamberpot at his side of the bed.

The first rush of passion over, he lay by her side.

''Ow was that, dearie? 'Ave I been nice to you?'

Bleary-eyed, George gawked at her and nodded. He went to grab her again.

'Georgie, the night's young. Let's take our time. We don't want to tire ourselves too soon, do we? Let me do some nice things to you.'

She was being generous to her client. George was young, and young clients in particular were getting increasingly difficult to get now that her age was against her; and it wasn't that often she had a booking for all night.

Most men, preferring something younger, went 'up West' to find the 'gay girls' who had their pitches in smarter bars, music halls and the streets around Piccadilly and Mayfair.

130

The older you got, the further out you moved. Lil was now the local tart for this little area of Hammersmith; being nearer forty than thirty she realised how fortunate she was to have such a good pitch. After all, she might be down in the docks, where the chances of getting murdered or done over were far greater. So Lil would stay as long as she could and try to put a bit of money by for when the worst happened and she was either too old or too sick to work.

'Do you like me legs?'

She thrust a flabby leg into the air, encouraging George to reach up and denude it of its black stocking, which up to now he'd ignored.

'Lie back, dearie, you'll like this too.'

She proceeded methodically to lick him all over. To Lil, George was a fine young man with a strong body – she wanted to make him one of her dwindling few 'regulars', so she was putting on a big show. He'd certainly get value for money.

'Cor! Cor, Lil!'

Ready for action once more, almost as roughly as the first time, he entered her.

He was moaning with pleasure and, in his ecstasy, he started to speak names.

'Sarah – oh, Sarah!'

He gorged himself on Lil, biting her shoulder, twisting her and gripping her so tight that she felt her ribs give way under the strain.

'Sarah!' he cried again.

Then, as he began to near his climax, he shouted out, 'Em, my Em!'

Lil didn't find this unusual – men often yelled out the names of their wives or other women. But, although she was ostracised by the good, hard-working, Christian wives and women of the neighbourhood, these two names made her think.

Meanwhile, George in his passion broke the rule. He came inside her.

'You bastard! You wen' off inside me. You shit! Why d'ya do that? You know I don' allow that, an' let me tell you, most of the likes of me don' allow kissin' and all the trimmin's that you've 'ad tonight. Get out! Go on, get out! And before you go – them names – I knows who they are. They belongs to your sisters. Had it off with them, eh? Is that why that Emma left 'ome? I bet you got 'er a bun in the oven. I hates the likes of you – now I can tell a tale or two! You watch it.'

She got up from the bed, rushed to the washstand and started scrubbing herself, while George, thoroughly chastened, sat dejectedly on the edge of the bed.

'Go on, get out! Take your bloody trousers, you're not staying here. Sister molester, that's what you are.'

George fumbled into his long underpants, trousers and shirt and threw on his jacket, rushed to the door and sped down the stairs. As he rushed out of the front door into the mews, Lil from her window on the first floor threw an old pair of boots after him and yelled out at the top of her voice for all the neighbours to hear:

'Fuck off! I'll tell 'em all you've 'ad it off with your sisters, you see if I don'! Go on, get the bloody 'ell out of 'ere!'

One of the boots caught his left ear. He yelled in pain, and soon realised that it was bleeding heavily. Although Lil knew that what she had said and done was bad for her ailing trade, she loathed incest. She'd been a victim of it from the time she was four years old, and was turned out by her parents when she became pregnant by her father at thirteen. The baby had died. She'd been on the streets ever since.

George staggered disconsolately over the cobbles in the cold, wet, unwelcoming Christmas night. Blindly, he turned out of the mews, which was on the borders of Hammersmith and Kensington, into Elsham Road. To him it was like crossing into another country. He never walked in this direction; but now, in spite of the heavy, beating rain, he ambled on. The gas lamps guttered, and dark shadows fell beneath the young trees in the gardens of the large houses. His mind was blank – as blank as his steps and the direction he was taking. At the end of the long, straight street he turned left and soon found himself in Holland Road.

Iron manhole covers were dotted at regular intervals along the pavement, giving into underground coal houses.

He came to a particularly dark patch of the road, as far

132

away from a streetlamp as it could be. Suddenly he hit something hard and tripped right into it. The occupiers of the house had had a late delivery of coal, and the merchant – presumably anxious to get home to his family on Christmas Eve – had not bothered to shovel the several hundred-weight down the hole. Most of it was still piled some four feet high in the middle of the pavement. George tripped so heavily that he fell face first. It was almost as if he was drunk, but he'd only had a pint, and that a couple of hours ago now. Somehow he managed to roll over on his back. He was not physically hurt but found himself lying on top of what he thought was a pile of stones or stony earth.

There he lay, sprawled facing the sky, his legs and arms at the four points of the compass. He'd lost his cap – probably left it at Lil's. His hair was streaming wet and the icy rain was beating down on his face and mixing with the blood which was still dripping from his ear. Although it was extremely cold, George, who had been sweating heavily, found the wetness and the temperature refreshing. Lifting a heavy arm, he attempted to wipe some of the rain out of his eyes and off his face. By this time his hands had been in contact with the wet, filthy coal. The back of his jacket and trousers were thick with black coal dust, but he wasn't aware of that either.

The evening's event had been a shock, but was also having a very sobering effect on him.

Lil's words rang in his ears. George was out for what he could get – sexually and in every other way. It hadn't seemed at all out of the way when, as his sisters became attractive young women, he lusted after them, and got what he wanted from Sarah (though not for long), and he'd almost made it with Emma. He felt no guilt – he'd enjoyed the underhanded secrecy of it all, and had liked having such a strong hold over Sarah. His father had always ruled the women of the household with a rod of iron, and George emulated him, in his own way. Power over the women was vital. Lust, and their simple availability, joined with excitement – the excitement of his sisters' attempts at fighting him off, the excitement of danger and of knowing that he was engaged in something that mustn't be found

133

out. Sex was, in all respects, totally taboo – never mentioned. He'd learned everything he knew from his basic instincts and by sacrificing his sisters.

He had been with Lil a few times before, and felt smug and very mature when he was with her. It was a different kind of smugness than he had felt with Sarah – besides, with Lil he had no physical battles to fight and that was something he'd had to get used to. He liked his women to put up a bit of a struggle, and while he was even rougher with Lil than he had been with Emma or Sarah, he never had the nerve to say, 'Fight me – I like it!' to Lil. Up to tonight, his visits had been twenty-minute affairs – occasionally during the dinnertime. This was the first time he'd planned a full night with the woman. It was to have been his Christmas present to himself. His much anticipated night of gratification had gone seriously wrong.

Still he lay there. Still the rain poured down on him. Still his ear bled.

He realised he had problems. Sisters now were out of the question. His tart had turned him out, and she was in a powerful position over him. If she cared to be vindictive, she could blackmail him or nurture suspicion and gossip which would eventually get round the district and reach his parents, who, he was sure, knew absolutely nothing of his activities. He must not devalue himself in their eyes. But it was a risky business. He was vulnerable.

'Wish you'd find yerself a good woman, George.'

His mother's words came back to him as he lay there on his back, getting wetter and wetter.

Well Georgie Porgie, it's up to you, he told himself. Your sisters are gone, you're on your own. 'A good woman,' that's what she said. Then, speaking aloud, he said, 'No, Ma, I don' want a good woman, I wants one with spirit, one I can – Katy, that's my gal! I'll 'ave Katy. Bugger that milksop of a bloke she's courtin'! I'll ... I'll ... yes, I'll kill him if necessary. Katy'll be my woman. Right, Ma, you wants it – so do I.'

Decisions having been made, he sat up on the coal and rather unsteadily got to his feet. With restored confidence, at least on some counts, he made his way back to Craven

134

Cottages. He fumbled for his key and pushed open the neat white front door with his left hand. He staggered upstairs to his room, threw his wet jacket and trousers to the floor, and fell into bed in his shirt and underpants.

On Christmas morning, Will Cooper got up to make his wife an early-morning cup of tea. As he descended the stairs, he noticed a series of black hand prints and smudges of blood on the wall and the inside of the front door. He was puzzled. It wasn't like Susan to leave mucky marks anywhere – especially at this time, the season of Christ's birth. He was on the point of calling her downstairs to show her, but as it was Christmas, he felt he wouldn't disturb her, knowing that very soon she would have a great deal of cooking to do. This was the one morning in the year when he condescended to spoil his long-suffering wife.

He lit the range and boiled up a kettle for the tea. As he was making it, George came through the kitchen on his way out to the lavatory.

'Merry Christmas, Pa' he yawned at his father, who looked up and stared hard at him, scarcely recognising his son.

'Heaven help us, George, what have you been up to, lad? Where've you been? May the good Lord forgive you, you're covered in evil – all black and bloody. Evil it must be – no one in your state could have been doin' good. Who've you been in a fight with?'

George thought his pa had gone mad. He didn't know what the old man was talking about.

'Filth, that's what it is, *filth*! The filth of the Devil. Oh, my son, my son! That you should be like this, today of all days! I will pray for you. May the good Lord in His wisdom forgive you for your sinful actions – whatever it is you've been up to. Oh, my! Oh, dear God, help us!'

And he sank to his knees, put his elbows on the edge of kitchen table and prayed in earnest – eyes hard shut, hands tightly clasped together.

George, still mystified, happened to catch a glance of himself in a tiny mirror that hung over the sink, and saw his black, bloodstained face for the first time. Then he looked down – even his underpants were covered in black stains, and so were the sleeves of his shirt, his arms and hands. He

135

now understood why his father had reacted so strangely. He left his father still kneeling in prayer, went down the back, and returned to discover the muck on the walls, the even more dreadful state of his outer clothing and the bed linen. He realised he would have some pretty serious explaining to do.

And it was Christmas Day.

Chapter Eleven

Archdeacon Wilkinson gave the blessing, and concluded the first service of Christmas Day with 'And may I wish you all a very happy and peaceful Christmas.'

The organist struck up a Bach partita, and the congregation started to file out of St Andrew's Church.

Mrs Newcombe and Lizzie looked at each other and smiled sadly.

'This would have been Joe's first Christmas communion, Lizzie.'

'I thought that, Mama. It would have been nice if he could have been here with us. But he is alive, I'm sure he's going to make the most of Christmas, and when he sees his presents I'm sure we'll see him smiling – smiling as he's not smiled since . . . since . . .' Lizzie hesitated. 'Since you know when.' She squeezed her mother's hand reassuringly.

Mother and daughter had reached the north door and were making their way out into the dark, damp night. It was just past one in the morning.

Suddenly Lizzie brightened. She had been keeping her eyes open because Emma had told her that if Lady Alston was feeling well enough they too would go to the midnight service.

'Look, Mama, there's Emma and Lady Alston. Now I can introduce you.'

Trying to be reasonably polite, she pushed through the crowd of people and attracted her two friends' attention. Soon introductions were being made.

'I hope you enjoyed our service. We're proud of our church, and think it very beautiful.'

137

'It is, Mrs Newcombe. So much older than Kensington's parish church – which is quite modern, you know.'

'Mrs Newcombe, would you and Elizabeth like to join Emma and me for tea and Christmas cake tomorrow – I mean this – afternoon? It would be charming if you could, and I so want to hear Elizabeth play the piano some more. Would it be possible?'

'Lady Alston, thank you so very much. Normally, yes, we'd love to, but I don't think we can leave Joe on Christmas Day.'

'I quite understand. Later, perhaps?'

'Lady Alston . . .'

'Elizabeth?'

'Would *you* like to join *us*? Laura's Christmas cake is very nice, and I know Joe would like to meet you.'

Emma was delighted. She waited rather apprehensively for her employer's response.

There was a pause.

'Thank you, Elizabeth – but what does your mama say to that? Has your daughter spoken somewhat impulsively, Mrs Newcombe? If she has, I will quite understand.'

'Lady Alston, that's typical of Elizabeth – but yes, of course we would be delighted to entertain you. Shall we say four o'clock?'

Lady Alston gave a warm smile and a gracious nod.

'And now to our carriages, before we get wet. It's beginning to drizzle.'

Mrs Newcombe crossed the bedroom and gazed out over the wide bay.

The misty drizzle of the last few days had given way to a clear, sparkling, frosty night. The moon was almost full and galaxies of stars punctured the sky over the calm sea. She knew every mood of sea and sky. She had seen them in summer's shimmering heat, and when angry waves broke over the strong wall at the end of the garden, and blotted out by fog.

Now, on this perfect Christmas night, she thought of her Peter and how much she wished he'd been able to spend the day with them. They had had so few Christmases together

138

since they'd been married. It was one of the many sacrifices she had to endure as a naval wife. She pictured him as he travelled further and further away from her, somewhere in the Suez Canal. She assumed he'd be sleeping. Would he have looked up at the moon, at the constellations? She knew he'd have been thinking of them, and trying to imagine the details of their day. She would write to him tomorrow.

She moved away from the window to sit by the fireside. The fading light of the fire deepened her pensive mood. Her thoughts drifted back over the past hours. There had been the sound of Emma's sweet, light voice – so unexpected. Lizzie had done well to persuade her to sing. The warmth of the music and the significance of the words had meant a lot to all of them. She hummed to herself:

> 'Oh, holy night, the stars are brightly shining:
> This is the night of the dear Saviour's birth . . .'

Then she thought of Joe smiling and exclaiming, 'Jolly good, Emma!' and the young woman's blushes. And of Lady Alston's reaction. 'Quite beautiful, my dear – the best present you could have given me.'

Yes, the day had been a success – as happy and as rewarding as it could possibly have been. The Berliner gramophone they had given Joe had been played time and time again, and his record collection had grown to two items. 'The Lost Chord', which had come with the machine, had been joined by 'A Regular Royal Queen' – the result of Emma's thoughtfulness.

She leaned over and with the fire tongs encouraged a few more flames to start from the dying embers in her bedroom grate. She wasn't yet quite ready for bed or for sleep. She thought on, turning her attention to Lizzie and Emma's friendship. The two young women could hardly have had more different backgrounds, and it was unusual that they should have come together. While the young people had been playing the gramophone and examining their other gifts, Lady Alston had taken Mrs Newcombe into her confidence, telling her of Emma's cruel father and the scars she'd seen on the young girl's arm. This came as a shock to Mrs Newcombe and revolted her. Of course, she knew that there

139

were cruel parents in all strata of society, but it had never been brought home to her so vividly before. Her eyes misted with tears at the thought. How could a father so ill-treat such a beautiful young girl – and his wife too, it seemed?

Obviously Emma's mother loved her; but there must surely always be present the dread of the fearful, egotistical father. Her education had been good – as good as Lizzie's, if without the refinements. There was practically no sign of a cockney accent. Emma had perhaps had less to kick against at school. It had been Lizzie's experience of a formal and very strict school that had ignited her spirit, as a match to a firework. Lizzie's exuberance and love of life contrasted vividly with Emma's quiet, apprehensive approach and reactions.

But Mrs Newcombe, like Lady Alston, had at once recognised that Emma had some fine qualities. She was certainly practical – far more practical than ever Lizzie would be. She was cautious – no bad thing, for Lizzie really could be very wild at times. She thought that perhaps Emma would tame Lizzie a little, though Mrs Newcombe would never want Lizzie to lose her spirit, her vivacity. But that couldn't possibly happen – it had, after all, been put pretty severely to the test in recent weeks – and it was Lizzie who had kept them all thinking positively, yet not with blind optimism.

The two girls were obviously cementing a very important friendship, and one that seemed very different from the more boisterous relationship Lizzie had with her lively, flighty school friends. She hoped that the two girls would grow yet closer together, and, like Lady Alston, felt that their ideas and talents would develop and blossom as the nineteenth century rolled on towards the twentieth.

Mrs Newcombe got up from the fireside, stretched and made her way to bed. As she did so, the faint strains of music wafted up to her – 'A Regular Royal Queen'. She decided not to go down to Joe, who wasn't stressed at the moment. In fact, the music acted as a lullaby, and she was asleep as the record came to an end.

A few days later, having answered the front door, Laura brought in a privately delivered letter.

'Madam, a young man's just brought this for you and Miss Elizabeth.'

Mrs Newcombe opened the thick envelope lined with purple tissue paper and extracted a gilt-edged card. In superb copperplate handwriting the message said:

The Lady Rosamund Alston requests the company of Mrs Caroline Newcombe and Miss Elizabeth Newcombe on Saturday the 31st of December at a performance of the Christmas Pantomime at the Theatre Royal, Plymouth, preceded by Dinner at 6.30 p.m. and followed by Supper, in celebration of Miss Emma Cooper's eighteenth birthday, and of the New Year.

R.S.V.P.

From his bed in the quiet room Joe saw his mother reading the card in the hall.

'What's that letter, Mama?'

'Oh, darling, it's nothing.'

'Mama, that's not fair – you're fibbing. You would scold me if I told a fib. It *is* something, I can see it's something, and it looks jolly grand!'

Joe's mother simply didn't want him to feel left out. They had always gone to the pantomime as a family, and she knew – as of course did Lady Alston when she instructed Emma to write the invitation – that Joe wouldn't be able to go.

She had to show him the card.

'You must go, Mama. I'll be all right, I really will. Lizzie would want you to go, and besides, you know you'll have lots to talk about to Lady Alston. She's a nice old duck.'

'Joe! How could you say such a thing? That's dreadfully disrespectful. She's . . . she's a lovely lady.'

'Oh yes, Mama, she is, but she really is an old duck, too. I like her. I want to talk to her about her travels – she told me she'd been abroad. But I didn't like to ask too much.'

'Quite right. It's rude to ask too many questions. I'm glad you weren't rude to her face. Old duck, indeed! Don't you dare . . . well, never mind!'

'You must go, Mama. Please accept. Emma's nice, too, I like Emma. I want to buy her a birthday present. Don't know what . . . I wouldn't want to give Lizzie's school

141

friends a birthday present, but I do want to give Emma one. The others have lots, after all. Emma may not have many presents since her parents are poor.'

'Now, Joe! Yes, her parents are poor, but they work hard, and you're not to talk about them to Emma or ask her questions about them. If she mentions them, well, that's different.'

Rather mystified, Joe agreed.

So Mrs Newcombe sent her reply to Lady Alston. Aggie delivered it.

Later that day Mrs Newcombe said, 'Darling, I think you should have a new evening dress.'

Lizzie was delighted. There was no time to have one made, so they went to Popham's and together chose a green velvet one which beautifully set off Lizzie's chestnut hair and warm skin tones. It was the most sophisticated dress she had yet had, and she really looked the young woman of fashion, with a heavy black velvet cape and hood to wear over it. Mrs Newcombe wished that her husband could see her.

As Toby carefully took Emma's hand to help her down from the carriage outside the Theatre Royal, her thoughts drifted back to that summer night, not so long ago, when she and Katy had stood watching the audience arrive at Covent Garden. Her heartbeat increased as she realised that here she was, in a beautiful pale-mauve evening dress and cape, being helped down from a carriage and about to go into a big theatre and she, Emma Cooper, was being admired by little ragamuffins! She could not but lift her head and walk particularly well, as together with Lizzie she crossed the pavement into the foyer.

As they ascended the wide staircase behind Lady Alston and Mrs Newcombe, together with a great many other well-dressed people making their way to the grand circle and boxes, Emma told Lizzie about the incident.

'It was wonderful, Lizzie. Whatever happens I shall never forget that night. It was when it all started for me, in a way . . .'

By then the four of them were being shown into a well-appointed box with an excellent view of the stage. From there they could look down into the stalls, and just see the pit, where the rather less fashionable families were sitting; looking up, there was the gallery, where poor families excitedly occupied the least expensive seats – also all set for a big night out.

The lights went down and the curtain went up on Scene One, The Village Green. Cinderella scurried across the stage, carrying a bundle of firewood, while the chorus of happy villagers sang a song of loyalty to their Prince Charming . . .

The Theatre Royal had a deservedly high reputation for its pantomimes, and this year's was no exception. The four women thoroughly enjoyed the evening.

When they had finished supper – cold chicken, potato salad and an orange soufflé – it was almost midnight.

Stratton appeared. 'My lady, the champagne.'

'Thank you, Stratton. Is it midnight?'

Taking out an elaborate silver fob watch, the butler solemnly replied, 'In two minutes, my lady.'

'I think you might do the honours, Stratton.'

White damask cloth in hand, Stratton carefully turned the bottle of Dom Perignon until the cork was soundlessly drawn, then majestically poured the champagne into four heavy gold-rimmed crystal flutes and handed them first to the two senior ladies, then to the younger ones, who both sat bolt upright, their gowns beautifully arranged, showing them off to full advantage.

Lady Alston stood up.

'My dearest new friends, let us drink to Emma – to her happy birthday – and to 1893!'

Emma, deep pink with embarrassment, meekly said thank you as Lizzie and Mrs Newcombe repeated the toast.

The two young women smiled broadly at each other and clinked their glasses, each reassuring the other.

'That will be all for the moment, Stratton. You may take a bottle of champagne for yourself and the others and have a little New Year celebration of your own. You may all rest until seven thirty tomorrow morning; it will be very late by the time you get to bed.'

'Thank you, my lady.'

'Now, my dears – these are for you,' said Lady Alston when Stratton had left the room. As if from nowhere, she produced two identical, small packages.

'But it's not *my* birthday, Lady Alston!'

'Well, think of it as an "un-birthday present" – you remember, in *Alice Through the Looking-Glass*?'

Tearing off the paper, the girls discovered they had been presented with almost identical brooches, both initialled 'E' in gold. Emma's was encrusted with purple amethysts, Lizzie's with yellow topazes, so that the gifts were the same yet not identical.

'You see, my dears, Emma's birthday stone is amethyst, while yours, Elizabeth, is topaz. I realised that you both have the same initial, but you are very different young women, so the brooches represent the qualities you share and those that are different.'

The girls' pleasure and thanks abounded.

Emma then received a silver fountain pen and propelling pencil from Mrs Newcombe and Lizzie.

'Now we have Joe's present,' said Lizzie. 'He wanted to give you violets – he thinks you must like violets – but he said they would die very quickly, so he asked me to find something that had violets printed or painted on it.'

Lizzie gave Emma a small but quite heavy package with a card.

'For Emma, on her birthday, from Joe.'

Inside was a beautiful little glass paperweight, with a group of three violets preserved in the glass.

The champagne had put them all into an even more festive mood.

'It's late, Lady Alston. We must go.'

Lady Alston rang for Stratton.

'Stratton, accompany Toby and the carriage – it's too late for him and Beauty to be out alone.'

As they left, they found Sybil, Mrs Green and, hiding behind her, Lottie, all in the hall to see them depart.

Lizzie nudged her mother to draw her attention to Lottie, whom Lizzie had not seen before. Once in the carriage, she said, 'That little girl, Mama – you saw her?'

'Yes.'

'Isn't she *tiny*? I suppose she's the kitchen maid. I felt so sorry for her.'

'Well, dear, she's much better off than many young girls of her age. Mrs Green will train her, and one day she'll be a useful cook.'

'But now, Mama, she seems so . . . so downtrodden. Did you notice Mrs Green pushing her into the background?'

'Yes, dear. Cooks are always terribly self-important. That's the way things are.'

After a pause, Mrs Newcombe went on, 'I felt really proud of you tonight, Lizzie. You looked beautiful, and – as I'd expect, of course – you behaved beautifully. I mustn't give you a swollen head, but it is nice when other people think well of you.'

Lizzie once more opened the silk-lined velvet box to look at her surprise treasure. She'd have a lot to tell Joe in the morning.

1893

Chapter Twelve

One morning during the first week of the Easter term, Miss Creeber called Lizzie into her sitting room.

'Miss Elizabeth, you will take the senior class for Old Testament Scripture during the last period this morning. Standards One and Two will work together with Miss Bethal. Miss Young is not at all well, and must rest for a few hours. The pupils will tell you what they were doing last term, and you can proceed from there.'

'Yes, Miss Creeber. Thank you. Is that all for the present?'

'That is all. You may go.'

At eleven forty-five, the beginning of the last period before midday dinner, Lizzie went into the senior classroom and settled herself into the teacher's desk. It was completely clear. Both seat and desk were high, and set on a wooden platform. There was a large blackboard and easel to the right. Some fifteen single desks and stools faced her, ready for the return of the pupils.

She was excited. This was the first time that she had been allowed to take the senior standard. Of course she realised that her three friends would, along with the other girls she'd known so well as a pupil, be facing her. They would expect a lot. Smiling to herself, looking forward to the challenge, she opened her large leather briefcase and took out her Bible.

'Right,' she said to herself. 'I'll make this interesting. I don't want the girls getting the better of me. They could all too easily start to tease – but we'll see.'

The girls filed in, surprised to see her rather than Miss

Young, whom they had expected. At once they started whispering and giggling.

'Quiet, please.'

Lizzie could be very authoritative if she cared to be, and was now quite the schoolmistress.

The girls took little or no notice. She repeated herself in a much firmer voice, and they responded.

'You may sit.'

They did so.

'I want to work on something very beautiful today.'

She had no intention of asking what they had been working on. From her own experience she knew it would have been Moses and the Ten Commandments.

'You will get out your Bibles and turn to the Song of Solomon. You will find that it follows Ecclesiastes and precedes Isaiah.'

Her pupils started to turn pages, and for two or three minutes there was only the sound of rustling paper in the room.

'Well, come along! Surely it's not that difficult? I can't give you the exact page because I don't use a school Bible nowadays. Annie Midgley, you're always quick – surely you've found it?'

'Er, no, Miss Elizabeth. I don't think it's here.'

'Of course it is. Don't be silly.' Lizzie was losing her patience. 'Bring your Bible here to me.'

'Look, Lizzie, it's not, honestly,' Annie was whispering under her breath.

At once Lizzie saw that Annie was right. The school Bibles went straight from Ecclesiastes to Isaiah. On looking at the page numbers, Lizzie saw that two or three pages had been cut out.

She was angry but undaunted.

'The Song of Solomon is a series of very beautiful poems containing some of the most lovely and moving phrases in the Bible. For some reason you are prevented from hearing or reading the poems. I shall put this right. We will not have time to discuss them fully, so it is up to you to go home and look them up in your family Bibles – or indeed when the sermon at church gets boring. They are, as I say, very

150

beautiful and I hope they'll make you think in a more positive way about love and its expression.

'You will find in some editions of the Bible an Introduction which states that we should think of these poems as an expression of divine love – the love of the church for Christ, and the inseparability of the two. That's good and beautiful – but the poems were written at a time when love between man and woman was considered beautiful too, and they actually describe that love in a . . . physical sense.

'This is the way we women, when the time comes, must learn to express our love for our husbands. That kind of love is special. It should not be simply a duty.'

Here some shy giggles broke out.

'No, it's not funny – nor is it rude, something not to be mentioned at any cost, though that's what you may be thinking. I suggest that you think about and learn from these beautiful words, so that when the time comes and you really and truly love your husband, you'll not be fearful, you'll not turn away from him.'

'But isn't all that a wicked sin, Miss Elizabeth?'

'It can be if it's misplaced, Elsie.'

'But we don't know anything about love – and what is that "special kind of love" you mention?'

'Stupid,' broke in a worldly-wise pupil from the back of the room. 'It's all about where babies come from. I know – I've got a big sister and she tells me. She's married. So there.'

'Clara, I'm glad that you have such an open-minded big sister, but there's no need to gossip. All you need to know at present is that when the time comes you must not feel upset or shy. Then, if you truly love your husband, you'll be far happier than a lot of young women who are fearful or prudish, realising that you're committing no sin if you express your love for him in a warm and caring way. I assure you that that doesn't go against anything written in the Old or the New Testament. There have been times in history when people have recognised this, though at present some people consider it improper for us women to allow ourselves to express our true and natural feelings.

'I will read you a little of the Song of Solomon:

*

151

'For, lo, the winter is past, the rain is over and gone; the flowers appear on the earth; the time of the singing of birds is come, and the voice of the turtle is heard in our land; the fig tree putteth forth her green figs, and the vines with the tender grape give a good smell. Arise, my love, my fair one, and come away.'

'Oh, Miss Elizabeth! That *is* beautiful.'
As Lizzie expected, it was Milly who spoke.
'*I* think it's silly.'
'Well as long as you think *something*. There's always time for you to change your mind, and you could well do so when you're a little older, Maria.'
Lizzie turned to the blackboard.
'I will copy these verses out for you. Read them in your own time and come to me privately after school some day, if you wish, and we can talk about them some more.'
It took only a few minutes to write the verses on the board. She allowed the girls – who were on the whole both mystified and intrigued by them and by Lizzie's provocative lesson – to talk quietly as she did so.
'Now, we have about fifteen minutes left before the end of morning school. Perhaps we can have a discussion about other Bible matters.'
Annie, who secretly admired Lizzie a great deal, stood up. 'Please, Miss Elizabeth, I have a question.'
'Go on, Annie.'
'Do you *really* think that God made Adam and Eve and put them into the Garden of Eden on the sixth day – as it says in Genesis?'
Lizzie had very strong views on the matter, and had from time to time talked the point over with both her parents, who, because they were very advanced in their thinking, had answered her questions in what they considered was the right way. She had even taken it upon herself to read a certain amount of Darwin's writing, though she had found his books difficult.
'That's a complicated question, Annie, and I can only give you my opinion – I may not be right. But I used to be very puzzled about that. Mr Darwin tells us that we humans

have developed, over many millions of years, from the apes.'

'Ugh!' the rest of the class responded, pulling faces and shuffling in their seats.

'Yes, the apes; and only very gradually over millions of years have we learned to walk upright and become civilised. Well, I thought that perhaps we did develop from the apes. But at first I was confused. Must we not believe what we read in the Bible? For a while, I thought that perhaps God created Adam and Eve as the first real people – who might have had apes as ancestors.'

'That makes sense, doesn't it? Both Darwin and the Bible are true,' remarked Annie.

'Yes, it would be nice to think of it in that way, but I don't think it's as easy as that. You see, Annie, those ancient writers and prophets had to describe the creation of the world and of man to their peoples, and not knowing any science, that was the way they did it. The story of Adam and Eve is beautiful, but I personally don't think it's true – I don't think it actually *happened*. I think it's a legend – just as the Song of Solomon is not really only about religious matters, or only has spiritual significance.'

'*Miss Elizabeth!*'

A hard, cold voice boomed out from the door.

'Miss Elizabeth – come to my sitting room *at once.*'

As Miss Creeber aggressively approached Lizzie, her eyes caught sight of the blackboard. She stopped dead in her tracks, shaking with rage. Pointing a skinny red finger at the board, she spluttered, 'And what is *that*, pray? *That*? Have you written *that*?'

Trying desperately not to shake, but feeling almost faint, Lizzie replied, 'Yes, Miss Creeber – it's from the Song of Solomon.'

'The Song of Solomon, indeed! Come, follow me!'

She turned abruptly, and all Lizzie could do was follow her into the sitting room, which had no fire even on that bleak January morning.

'I am extremely surprised and severely disappointed in you. You are an evil influence. Do you realise that you blaspheme, child? How dare you oppose the truth written in Holy Scripture? Preach heathenism to the girls? How dare you, child? How dare you? What right have you to take upon yourself such opinions? What will your parents say when they hear of your severe misdemeanour?'

'Please let me explain –'

'Explain! Under no circumstance will you explain.'

'But Miss Creeber, I was only expressing –'

'Expressing your private opinions, is that it? How *dare* you have such wicked, sinful opinions? And to spend time on the Song of Solomon! That is highly unsuitable for young persons. That is why it does not appear in any of our school Bibles.'

Miss Creeber's anger was far from subsiding. Lizzie tried to appear calm, and soon realised that it was as well simply to stand up very straight and keep her eyes on Miss Creeber's own. She knew that none of her explanations would make any difference, but at least was reassured that whatever the headmistress wrote to her parents, it would not make trouble for her, since she had already fully discussed these matters with them.

But Miss Creeber was going on:

'I cannot allow you to remain on these premises for another moment to contaminate my girls' minds. You have ruined your chances. Because of your wicked behaviour you will not now have the benefit of Miss Young's tuition and so you will not be going to Cambridge. I can do no other than to dismiss you instantly. Leave my Academy at once. Do you hear me? *At once!*'

Should Lizzie apologise? She felt she could not do so – it was as much a matter of principle for her as for Miss Creeber. She turned and, with dignity, but without arrogance, did as she had been told.

Distracted from his lunch by the crash of the front door slamming shut, Joe caught sight of Lizzie flashing by his open door and, without a word to him, rushing into the drawing room. Almost immediately he heard sobs, followed by the opening bars of Chopin's Revolutionary Study.

'Oh, dear,' he said, sighing to himself philosophically. 'Lizzie's in trouble again. She always plays that when things go wrong.'

He took another mouthful of his steak and kidney pie. His

154

sister's sobs got louder and louder; he called to her, but she didn't hear him, so he rang his bell with great ferocity.

Mrs Newcombe came running into the hall.

'Mama, what's wrong with Lizzie? She's just rushed in.'

'I don't know. Lizzie, whatever's the matter?'

'Oh, Mama! It was awful, awful!'

Lizzie's sobs were uncontrollable and almost hysterical.

Her mother ran over to the piano and nursed her daughter's head against her bosom.

'My darling girl, whatever's happened? Has someone frightened you? Why are you home at this time of day?'

'Mama – I can't . . . It was awful . . . I c-ca –'

'Darling, tell me everything. But first dry your eyes.'

Aggie came in.

'Whatever's wrong?'

'We don't know yet, Aggie. Quick, get a small bowl of warm water and a flannel! Lizzie's obviously had a dreadful shock of some kind, and I think she probably needs a brandy and water.'

Aggie, puzzled and concerned to see her dear girl so upset, disappeared at once.

Her mother's presence and touch was beginning to steady Lizzie a little, but she knew she had a dreadful story to tell, and she wasn't at all certain how Mrs Newcombe would take it.

'Now, wait a moment. Thank you, Aggie.'

Mrs Newcombe took the bowl and cloth and started to wipe her daughter's face and cool her burning forehead.

'Here, sip this, and just try to relax, then we'll talk.'

After a while Lizzie was breathing more regularly, and tried to begin to tell her tale.

'I'll never be able to go to Girton, Mama. I've been dismissed.'

'Lizzie, how awful! What a disgrace! You must have done something really dreadful. I don't know what your papa will say. But tell me all about it.'

Lizzie was frightened. It wasn't like her to be frightened of anyone or anything – least of all her mother – but the mention of her father and her mother's use of the word 'disgrace' was terrifying.

155

It took a long while to explain what happened.

'But what did you set as the Scripture lesson in the first place?' Mrs Newcombe's voice was far sterner than Lizzie had ever heard it.

'Oh, Mama, something beautiful – the Song of Solomon.'

'Lizzie! How *could* you? You know that both your papa and I love that poem, and we have taught you to love and understand it, too, but it's not really suitable to teach at school – especially a school like Miss Creeber's. It was a very tactless thing to do.'

'But Mama, the girls are just as old as I was when we read it together!'

'Ah, but you forget that most people aren't like us. And you must remember that Miss Creeber is – well, she's never been married, she doesn't understand. But then you went on to talk about Adam and Eve?'

'Y-yes . . . then suddenly there was Miss Creeber – and furious. She'd been listening for I don't know how long.'

'You should have apologised.'

'I couldn't, Mama, I simply couldn't. I can't deny what I think to be right – can I?'

In her heart Mrs Newcombe agreed with her daughter, but she realised that Lizzie's reputation was also at stake, and feared that her chances of being coached for Girton were now nonexistent.

'Are you sure you can't write and apologise? Miss Creeber might take you on again if you word your letter really tactfully.'

'No, Mama. And anyway, there's a lot wrong with that place. If I had a school, I'd –'

'You'll not be able to have a proper school if you don't get qualifications. Oh, you could set up a little one somewhere, like Miss Jenkins around the corner, but what good would that do you? It wouldn't be at all what you want.'

Lizzie knew that her mother was right. Her prospects were seriously damaged.

'Look, Mother, I can't – I *won't* go back there. So I suppose I'll not be able to go to Girton. But perhaps I could teach music, and I do love that.'

'I'm very disappointed and upset about all this, coming as

156

it does on top of our problems with Joe. Yes, of course you have your principles, and we have our somewhat unconventional beliefs – certainly where the Old Testament is concerned – and our opinions on . . . other matters too, but . . . Oh, Lizzie, I do wish all this hadn't happened!'

It was her mother's turn to cry.

'Promise me one thing, Lizzie.'

'Yes, Mama – what is it?'

'That you'll write a long letter to Papa explaining everything to him. He'll be angry and upset. You have a point, but you're simply too much ahead of your time in expressing it so forcefully – and to children who couldn't be expected to understand it properly. But I suppose it's our fault as much as your own.'

'I'm sorry, Mama, I really am. I'll make it up to you and Papa somehow – I don't know how, but I'll try.'

Mrs Newcombe was confused, but in her heart was pride in her daughter's strength of character.

She too would write to the Captain.

'Let's play judge and jury.'

Joe rearranged himself and sat up a little straighter.

'I'll cross-question you, like a barrister in court.'

'Must you?'

'Yes! I want to understand, too. Here we go.

'Now, Miss Newcombe, tell me – were you happy as a teacher at the Academy?'

'Well . . . I was and I wasn't.'

'Answer yes or no, please.'

'No!'

'Why not?'

'I didn't agree with their attitude.'

'So you wouldn't want to go back there?'

'No.'

'Are you sure? Especially as you won't be able to go to Cambridge?'

'Yes, I am sure.'

'Right. So what will you do with all your time, just go out with your friends?'

'No, that would be a waste. I'll teach music.'

'You'd like that?'

'Oh, yes!'

'Well, m'lud, I think our witness has answered all our questions, and the case rests.'

Taking on the voice of a very old man, Joe went on, 'I recommend you, the jury, to declare a verdict of not guilty of . . . of . . . er, insubordination.'

As ever, Joe managed to cheer Lizzie up.

Nevertheless she was now faced with the problem of collecting her thoughts and writing a letter of explanation to her father. It was not easy. She made several false starts, but, being honest, she knew that the only approach was a direct one – with no excuses. She simply had to tell him that she could not go against her principles and to apologise profusely to him for the distress she had caused her mother, especially at a time when such heavy demands were being made on her. She also had to admit that their plans for her going to college were now ruined.

It was with a heavy heart she eventually read through what she had written and addressed an envelope to HMS *Rameses*.

'Joe, you know Lizzie is very sad and I want you to cheer her up, just as she's been cheering you up in the last few weeks.'

'Yes, Mama.'

Joe was quiet for a while. The only sound in the room was the steady click of his mother's knitting needles.

'Mama, I've been thinking.'

'Have you, dear? About Lizzie?'

'Yes, but about me too.'

'What have you been thinking?'

'Well, Mama, if I can't go back to Dartmouth – at least for several more months – can they send my trunk home? It's still there, isn't it? Some of my favourite books are in it. I want them, and I want my technical-drawing book, and my *Round the World* book, and –'

'Yes, that's a good idea. I'll get it sent back. I thought that perhaps you wouldn't want it here.'

'I would like it, Mama.'

'In one of his letters your papa suggested that I should go

and see your old headmaster up at Hoe Grammar School to find out if one of the teachers there could come and give you some lessons. Would you like that? Do you think you feel strong enough?'

'Oh, yes please!'

'Well, we'd better ask Dr Higgins first. Shall I write to him?'

'Yes, please, Mama. Now?'

Mrs Newcombe put down her knitting and went to the desk in the drawing room.

'Let me hear E major over four octaves, please, Elizabeth.'

Professor Rowe looked at her from over the top of his half-spectacles. Lizzie flung herself into the scale. It was a key she particularly liked.

'You are uneven in the descending scale. Try it once more, and take it a little more slowly – at this pace, please.'

He set the metronome at 'presto', which slowed Lizzie down considerably – she had raced along the keyboard at prestissimo plus.

'That's better. You never lack speed, and your playing has excellent attack, but sometimes, you know, you are a little careless. You must try to overcome that. You play most expressively, even sometimes with too much feeling, but that's a good fault – so many of my pupils play as if they have no soul at all, and as if their hands and arms were made of wood. You, my dear, are not like that.'

'Thank you, professor.'

'Now, let's try C minor, harmonic and melodic this time. And I'll let you play just a little faster – but listen to the beat before you start.'

The old man turned the metronome up a shade, to two hundred and ten. C minor was another favourite key – and, being rather sad, it fitted in with her mood.

After a series of arpeggios and some Czerny studies, which gave Lizzie no problems, her teacher said, 'How are you getting on with the Chopin? Let me hear it. Can you memorise it yet?'

'Part of it.'

'Good. Well, play as much of it as you can without the music.'

159

Lizzie took a deep breath and, having placed her fingers over the keys, crashed down on the first dramatic chord with all the emotion that had built up within her during the last few days. She managed just over half of the study, then suddenly stopped.

'That was very, very good, my dear.' Professor Rowe peered at his pupil more closely, and went on, 'But I see you're crying.'

Tears had welled up in Lizzie eyes; she couldn't hold back. As briefly as possible, she told her old and trusted music teacher what had happened.

'My dear, would it help if I say to you that you are among my most talented pupils? And that while I do not think you could become known internationally, I do think that you will quite soon be able to give recitals to small groups of people, and of course teach. Indeed, I know you do a little teaching already. I see no reason why you shouldn't perform from time to time – and perhaps get paid for it. So you see, all is not lost, even if you cannot go to Girton.'

'Thank you, Professor! I'll tell Mama.'

'No need, my dear. I'll write to her.' He grinned and gave her a sly wink. 'Now, for a change, we should start work on some Mendelssohn – the *Rondo Capriccioso*. It's a beautiful work, and I think you'll cope with it very well. Do you have a copy?'

Lizzie hadn't.

'Then I'll give you one. Go through it at home, and we'll work on it next week. And don't worry. Frankly, I'm delighted you're not having to go to school to teach those wretched girls – you'll have more time to practise, won't you? And, of course, you are fortunate to have a very good piano to play on.'

'I've been playing a Broadwood, too, recently.'

And Lizzie told him of her experiences at Elliot Terrace.

'Number 5? Yes, I remember. The young son of the previous owner was musical. I taught him, and the family bought him that piano. He died, you know. I think he played the guitar, too.'

'It's still there. I saw the case. They keep it on the piano.'

The professor got up.

160

'Until next week, then. And don't worry – I'll do what I can for you. You deserve that!'

Lizzie felt a lot better. She'd always liked and trusted her music teacher – he was a sort of grandfather to her.

Chapter Thirteen

'Tea's ready, dear.'

Aggie called from the kitchen to Laura, who was peeling potatoes for dinner in the scullery.

'It's cold out there, Aggie.'

'Never mind, this'll warm you up.'

She slopped tea from the big brown pot into a huge old breakfast cup and passed it to Laura.

'Well, as I was sayin' this morning, I don't think –' She broke off in midsentence. 'Was that the front door?'

Laura cocked her ear. 'No, I don' think so. It's probably Joe dropping a book. The Missus'll cope – she's with him.'

'Well –' Aggie took a big mouthful of tea – 'as I was saying . . .'

Upstairs in the drawing room, Lizzie, who was practising her new piece, also heard the knock. At first she took no notice. It couldn't be their heavy front-door knocker; it was too quiet. But then she heard it again. She went to answer it, even though that was Laura's duty.

As she opened the door the wind caught it, and a flurry of hard, gritty snow hit her in the face.

'M-M-Mrs Newcombe?'

'That's my mother. Is she expecting you?'

Lizzie was confronted by a very round-shouldered, thin young man, wearing a frayed dark-brown Norfolk jacket. Mouse-coloured hair sprouted from beneath an ill-fitting cap, and as he crossed the threshold his steel-framed spectacles began to mist over from the change in temperature. His face was pale, but his nose was horribly red and sore-looking.

'Yes. I'm Eustace B-b-beaumont. I've come . . . Ahhh.' He let out a gigantic sneeze. Producing a wet, soggy handkerchief, he spluttered on. 'Excuse me, I've got a c-c-cold.'

'Goodness, you don't look too well! I am sorry.'

'Thank you.'

'I'm Elizabeth Newcombe. Oh, I expect you're from the Hoe Grammar School?'

'Yes.'

He started to unwind an extremely long red, black and white striped knitted scarf – the only really sensible garment he was wearing to protect himself from the coldest day they had experienced all winter.

The sight amused Lizzie, but at the same time she felt sorry for the young man. She felt she must say something to him, so, after he'd sneezed again – fortunately getting his hanky to his nose in time to catch some of the germs – she remarked, 'I do like your scarf – it's awfully jolly. Did your mother knit it for you?'

'Er, no. I knitted it myself. You see, I do rather a lot of p-plain knitting while I read.'

'How frightfully clever!'

The young man blushed, and she saw much warmth and appreciation in his nervous smile. She led him to the quiet room, where her mother and Joe were reading together.

'Mama, this is Mr Beaumont. I think you're expecting him.'

'How do you do, Mr Beaumont. This is my son, Joseph. I don't think you've met him – I believe you came to teach at the school last September, after Joe left?'

'I'll leave you to talk, Mama.'

'Yes, Lizzie. Ring for Laura to bring us a tray of tea. I think Mr Beaumont should have some. And I think some nice hot, toasted crumpets and jam. Yes, Mr Beaumont?'

'Yes, p-please, thank you.' Eustace nodded eagerly.

Lizzie did as she was bid, then went back to her practice.

'My dears, what a poor waif he is!'

'Mama, I don't think I've ever seen anyone so plain.'

'He's jolly nice, though. I think he'll be good at teaching me.'

'I'm sure he will, Joe. But Lizzie, I do know what you mean. I hope he hasn't given us his dreadful cold.'

Lizzie giggled.

'He's remarkably well qualified,' their mother went on. 'He's got a first-class honours degree. His papa was a vicar, but both his parents are dead. He went to Selwyn College at Cambridge – it was founded for the sons of clergymen.'

'Oh, I do hope he won't be too pompous and try to convince Joe that Adam and Eve really existed.'

'Lizzie! That's got you into enough trouble already.'

'Sorry, Mama. When's he going to start?'

'He suggested tomorrow, but I told him to wait until next week when his cold will be better.'

'Yes,' Joe put in, 'I don't want that.'

'You know, Lizzie, he may be an odd fish, but I do think he's really quite brilliant. He knows Greek and Latin, speaks French well, and says he can get by in German. He also asked Joe about algebra and trigonometry – which left me miles behind both of them.'

'Then, Lizzie, he said he thought could help me a bit with my technical drawing – so that'll be terrific.'

'You obviously got on very well with him, Joe. I'm so pleased.'

Lady Alston was keeping Emma busy, and she enjoyed her duties. Now they were living away from London there seemed to be even more letters to write and be signed by her employer. As a result, Emma found herself walking almost every day down towards the town centre to the large general post office. Beautiful mosaics of the Armada ships decorated the floor – a joy to gaze at while she waited to buy stamps and post the letters.

Of late Lady Alston had developed a liking for clotted cream, and quite often Emma would buy a quarter-pound pot in a branch of the Three Towns Dairy, next door to the post office. Another of her new responsibilities was to visit the Wiltshire and Dorset Bank near the bottom end of Lockyer Street – the street that led directly down from the Hoe towards the centre of the town. The Plymouth branch had

164

been given instructions from Messrs Stillwall, Stillwall and Keen, Lady Alston's men of business in London, to look after her financial affairs during the time she spent in the West Country.

On her first few visits, Emma entered the impressive building apprehensively. Usually she simply had to pass in an envelope and receive another with funds for the running expenses of the household – the staff's wages, which Mr Stratton would divide up, and other, smaller items that needed to be paid in cash. The bank clerks were always very polite, and she soon became accustomed to coping with them, returning any forms or documents that Lady Alston had to sign. She had a considerable number of investments, both domestic and overseas – in companies in the Far East, America and Australia.

In addition to all this, at home there was always the flower arranging, which Emma loved, and a certain amount of dressmaking, when she had time for it.

Emma and Lizzie met quite often, and enjoyed each other's company, though Emma felt a little inferior to Lizzie. She had a far more responsible job than Lizzie, and could do many things that Lizzie couldn't. For example, Lizzie lacked the patience to arrange flowers as beautifully as Emma, and neither could she sew. But when Lizzie had talked to her of her dreams of going to Girton, Emma was keenly aware that she herself would never get that kind of education.

One afternoon – a Saturday – Lizzie invited Annie, Elsie and Milly to tea to meet Emma. She had felt very nervous about this, for the three other Plymouth girls were of the same social class as Lizzie – and might not be as nice. But Lady Alston did her best to boost Emma's confidence. She pointed out that Emma had, after all, really beautiful clothes, as good as anything in any Plymouth wardrobe. She had a responsible job. These girls were still at school, and, unlike Lizzie, probably had few – if any – ambitions.

At tea, Emma found this to be true. And though she at first thought the other girls rather snobbish, as time passed they became quite wide-eyed and awe-stricken, especially when she talked of her successful sister. Lizzie, being kind and very quick-thinking, was a great help – and when Elsie had asked what Emma's papa did, before she could speak, Lizzie burst in:

'He's a shoe manufacturer. He has a factory in London and employs lots of people, and Emma's brother . . .'

Emma's heart missed a beat and a cold shiver ran through her body at the mention of George. What would Lizzie say next? She knew nothing about him – not even his name.

'He's the managing director,' said Lizzie firmly.

That satisfied their curiosity. Lizzie gave Emma a sly wink.

The more Emma thought about that afternoon, the more satisfied she felt. The climax had been when Lizzie played the piano – and oh, how well she played! – and they persuaded Emma to sing. Together, Emma and Lizzie managed 'Scenes That Are Brightest' from *Maritana*.

But in spite of the success of the tea party – mostly due to Lady Alston's encouragement and Lizzie's stimulating company – Emma felt that there was something lacking in her life. Lady Alston was beginning to think that way too, but decided to say nothing.

One morning, to Emma's delight, she received a long, newsy letter from Sarah. She'd written it in her dressing room at the theatre, and it was dated 2 February. In it Sarah told her how she had taken over from the leading lady, and how a few days later – on the night of her birthday, as it happened – the Prince of Wales had attended, and she'd been presented to him. He had congratulated her on her performance and given her his best wishes. She gave Emma some sound advice about saving money and told her to take special care of any valuable presents she was given, and added that she now regularly visited their mother, who had been delighted with Emma's and Lady Alston's Christmas gifts.

Lizzie felt honoured to be allowed to read the letter.

'Your sister sounds so nice,' said Lizzie. 'What a lovely letter – and how exciting for her to meet the Prince of Wales! Do you think we'll ever meet?'

'It's possible. Sometimes these big shows go on tour. Or perhaps you might come to London in the summer.'

'What a wonderful idea!'

They had a good practice of 'I Dreamt that I Dwelt in Marble Halls', and planned a short recital for Lady Alston. Emma was putting on her coat, about to leave, and the two of them were standing in the hall, when there was a timid knock on the front door.

'That'll be Mr Beaumont', said Lizzie with something of a sigh. 'Why doesn't he knock a little more loudly? Laura never hears him when she's downstairs. I'd better let him in.'

She strode somewhat impatiently to the front door and opened it.

'Good afternoon, Miss Elizabeth.'

'Good afternoon, Mr Beaumont, I think Joe's done all his homework.'

Eustace nodded to Lizzie, and as he passed Emma, he screwed up his eyes behind his spectacles and looked at her so closely that he almost hit her nose with his own. As he neared her, he became aware of a delicate hint of the light floral perfume she always wore. It was deeply attractive to him, and for the first time in his life he experienced an instinctive and sensational longing. Emma backed away, and Eustace severely knocked his shin on a wooden hall chair.

'Let me take your coat and scarf, Mr Beaumont,' Lizzie suggested as she straightened the chair. Eustace rubbed his leg, still gazing at the astonished Emma.

'Oh, yes. Th-thank you.'

Fumbling, he removed his new, thick overcoat and scarf, then knocked on the door of the quiet room and joined Joe.

When he was well out of sight and hearing, Emma remarked, 'What an *odd* young man! I wish he hadn't stared at me so intently.'

'That's Joe's new tutor. He's tremendously intelligent and clever – but isn't he a mess? He looked even worse the other day, but now he's got that new coat at least he's keeping warm.'

'Well, I don't think I like him very much. I thought he was *very* rude.'

But in spite of what she had said, Emma had, during that brief moment, noticed that he had beautiful hands, well shaped and strong. She always felt that hands were a revealing sign of character, and his said a lot to her about nobility and worth.

167

'Don't take any notice of him, Emma. I'm quite sure he's harmless.'

The two friends parted.

Lizzie did some music theory. About an hour later, Eustace cautiously slipped out of Joe's room. As he passed the drawing room, she looked up from the desk where she was busy with metronome and manuscript paper.

'Goodbye, Mr Beaumont.'

To her considerable surprise, clutching an untidy pile of books and bent over, he walked in with extra-long strides.

'Miss Elizabeth, Joseph is doing very well. He is a b-bright boy.'

'I am glad you think so.'

'Oh yes, Miss Elizabeth.'

Lizzie felt sorry for him because he was so dreadfully plain, and because behind his spectacles she could see two eyes that reminded her of Milly's spaniel. She was also acutely aware of the fact that he had to cope with a rather nasty stammer. Her warm heart wanted to make him feel a little more at home. After all, he was becoming one of the family in a way – he came to teach Joe every day, and was now well into his second week.

'Mr Beaumont . . .'

Not normally being one to hesitate, she did momentarily wonder if she was being a little forward, but went on nevertheless, 'Mr Beaumont, I don't like being called Miss Elizabeth very much. If you would like to call me just Elizabeth – or Lizzie – I'd like it much better. I don't think Mama will mind.'

'Oh, how – k-kind! Would that really be in order?'

A boyish smile broke over his pale, slightly blotchy face, which was looking somewhat healthier now his cold was better.

'Thank you. Er, tell me, Miss, er, Lizzie, that young lady – the young lady who was here when I arrived – is she your f-friend?'

'Yes, that's Emma Cooper. She's a companion to Lady Alston, who lives at 5 Elliot Terrace.'

'Oh, how interesting!'

Lizzie was a great tease and simply couldn't resist asking, 'Why, Mr Beaumont?'

'Oh, c-call me Eustace, please – that is, if you'd like to. Well . . . well, I think she's . . .'

He was lost for words.

Lizzie grinned. 'Go on, Eustace – you think she's pretty?'

'Oh, no! I mean – well, yes, I think she's b- b- . . . but you must excuse me, I must go.'

He rushed out of the drawing room and through the hall and before Lizzie could put in another word, was out at the front door.

The days began to lengthen. The first snowdrops appeared, followed almost immediately by colourful crocuses, and as February ended the daffodil spikes promised a glorious flurry of yellow both in the Newcombes' sea-facing garden and in the meticulously cared-for flowerbeds which tempted Plymouthians to promenade on the Hoe, even in early spring.

When Joe attended the hospital again towards the end of February, his hip had made such good progress that the amount of plaster encasing his lower body was much reduced; he could now sit up in bed, and was being measured for the crutches which would very soon enable him to move around the ground floor of the house. In due course he would be able to get out into the garden and perhaps be able to manage the stairs and return to his own bedroom on the top floor.

'By the end of March, Mrs Newcombe, we will know for certain just how Joe's leg is responding. It's true that there is some good knitting of the bone fragments, but I think you should now prepare him for the fact that he'll not be able to return to Dartmouth.

'He will probably need to wear irons for quite a while to support what amounts to a very weak leg; then, as he grows, we will just have to be patient to see if the leg is going to grow or remain stunted.'

'That's dreadful, Mr Blunsdon!'

'Well, my dear, I know it does sound very serious, but eventually a boot with a lift will work extremely well. Of course, it will have to be adjusted from time to time; but once he has reached his mature height, though he'll always walk with a limp, he will be able to move quite quickly.

Because he is such a brave young man and so positive in his outlook, I can see no reason why he shouldn't live a rewarding and fulfilling life.'

When they returned from the visit to the hospital, Joe, who felt that his mother had been unusually quiet on the journey, called her back as she was about to leave him in his room to give Laura orders for dinner.

'I'm going to have crutches soon, Mama, aren't I? That nice nurse said so when she measured my legs.'

'Yes, darling, you are – next week; then you'll start to move around a lot more. Spring will soon be with us and you'll be able to sit in the garden. Mr Blunsdon said that –'

Mrs Newcombe stopped in midsentence.

'Yes, Mama, what did Mr Blunsdon say?'

She paused and bit her lower lip. Joe noticed that she was blinking hard.

'Oh, Joe!'

'No, Mama, don't cry. Please don't cry or worry. I think I know. I think he said that I can't go back to Dartmouth. I think I can live without Dartmouth. But Mama, I don't want to just sit around or hobble about on crutches all my life.'

'You won't have to, Joe, no matter what happens to your leg. We don't know yet that it's not going to grow, but if it doesn't – and it might – you can wear a special boot with a lift in it and you'll only limp just a bit.'

'What about school? Will Eustace teach me until I'm sixteen?'

'No, after the Easter holidays you can go back to Hoe Grammar School.'

'Meanwhile, I go on working with Eustace so that I won't fall behind with my work – is that it?'

'Yes, darling.'

'Mama, you know I so wanted to go into the navy like Papa, but it's not God's will, is it? And I won't be able to run, or play cricket or rugby any more.'

'It doesn't look like it, does it? But, my dear, who knows what He has in store for you. I think it'll be something very special.'

Mrs Newcombe did her best to comfort him, cuddling him as if he were still a baby.

Biting his lip to fight back the tears, he said, 'I'll do my best, Mama.'

'Bless you, Joe. Now come on, sit up. You can now, you know.'

When she had left the room, he told himself, I mustn't cry any more. I mustn't cry ever again. It's only girls that are allowed to cry. But no navy, no sports, no seeing the world! I . . . I must *not* cry!

Joe, in the solitude of the quiet room, grabbed one of his pillows and stuffed it up against his face to smother his sobs.

During the weeks since Christmas, Lizzie had collected six little pupils for piano lessons. Professor Rowe, who was now teaching only advanced older pupils, was often approached by parents of young children who wanted them to learn to play, and for some time he had been recommending them to his senior students. He felt that Lizzie was well able to cope and, knowing that she was so enthusiastic about her music, he was certain that she would be a good and encouraging teacher. He had always been very impressed with her devotion and talent, and she had now passed all the grades set for piano by the Trinity College of Music.

'Goodbye, Tom. You *are* doing well! Don't forget to practice your C major scale, as well as that nice piece.'

'No, Miss 'Lizabeth. Thank you!'

Six-year-old Tom took his mother's hand as they left Lizzie at the front door of number 6.

'Mama, I've finished Tom's lesson. Shall I ask Laura to bring in the tea?'

'Yes, dear, and I think Eustace and Joe would like to join us.'

Mrs Newcombe had been writing to the Captain in the dining room – the drawing room was out of bounds while Lizzie was teaching.

Joe came cautiously in on his newly acquired crutches, followed by Eustace. The drawing room was bright but the rays of the afternoon sun made the fire look as if it were dying, though its warmth was welcome in the chilly spring afternoon.

'Come in, Eustace – and Joe, you'd better sit there.'

Mrs Newcombe pointed to a very upright chair. Lizzie instinctively rose to go and help Joe, but her mother restrained her – he must get used to moving about solely with the aid of his crutches.

Laura brought tea. Eustace clutched his plate nervously and, eager as ever, took a big bite out of a piece of Laura's sponge cake.

'Mrs Newcombe, Joe has been doing some technical drawing today. I found a p-picture of a cross-section of a Great Western Railway steam engine, and he drew it out to the half scale. It is a very good effort. P-perhaps you would like to see it?'

'Of course! Lizzie, go and get it from the quiet room – that is, if Joe doesn't mind.'

Joe, his mouth full of sponge cake and rather too much Devonshire cream, could only nod his answer.

'Look, Mama – it's lovely,' said Lizzie.

The drawing was perfect in every detail, and Joe glowed with pride at his mother's and sister's approval.

'Joe, you should draw something specially for Papa, and we'll send it to him. Why don't you look at your big book of photographs and copy a building or something from that?'

'Yes, Joe, that's a very good idea. D-do it for me by next Thursday.'

Eustace, shy as ever, complimented Lizzie on her teaching – he had seen and listened to her working with little Tom, and thought she was not only encouraging but also kind.

Mrs Newcombe agreed. 'I think Lizzie is a natural teacher,' she said as she poured more tea.

'I love teaching,' said Lizzie. 'I did some, you know, at –' She paused; she had been about to revive unpleasant memories, and didn't want to remind her mother of the unhappiness she had caused her.

'You were saying?' asked Eustace, meekly.

'At Miss Creeber's Academy. But, well, we didn't agree on . . . certain matters. Oh, I won't go into it now, but I wasn't happy there, and she wasn't happy with me, so well . . .'

'Lizzie was dismissed, Eustace.'

'Oh, I see.'

I wonder if he *does* see, thought Lizzie.

There was a pause, then, her emotions getting the better of

her, she told him the most distressing part of her story; that she would now be unable to go to Girton.

'It's been a huge disappointment for – for all of us, but chiefly for Lizzie,' added her mother.

Lizzie took her mother's hand and gave her a long look.

'I know I've let everyone down badly, and I'm sorry, but I couldn't go against my principles – just as Miss Creeber and Miss Young can't go against theirs.'

Eustace nodded thoughtfully. 'I d-do understand. But –'

Lizzie interrupted him – she too easily became impatient with his hesitant speech.

'So I'm now teaching music, and that's lovely, and I do enjoy it. But Eustace, my ambition was eventually to have my very own school. I saw all the mistakes that Miss Creeber and Miss Young are making, and my school would have a very different atmosphere – a happier one, one in which the children were far more aware of kindness and the beauty of . . . well, so many lovely things in life.'

'My daughter has very strong ideas of her own,' said her mother.

Eustace was still looking thoughtful. 'But you have had to give up the idea because you can't go to c-college?'

'Eustace, of course Lizzie could open a little school, like the one round the corner from here – you know it? But she would want a proper school, which she could run with the experience and confidence that Girton would give her. So now it's just going to be music. Well, at least she is very good at it, and loves it, as you know.'

'And it's evident that she's a good t-teacher.' Eustace was still looking thoughtful. 'But I wonder – if I'm not being impertinent – whether . . .'

He was silent for a moment; then he screwed up his face and closed his eyes so that his thick metal-framed spectacles fell forward on his nose. The three Newcombes exchanged amused glances.

'Mrs Newcombe, as far as I know, the requirements for entrance to Newnham and Girton are the same as those for men, at other c-colleges at C-Cambridge. You know, I think, that I have a first-class honours degree. I am familiar with the entrance examinations, and c-could certainly ascertain

173

whether there is any difference in requirements for male and female applicants. I wonder if . . .'

Lizzie could hardly believe what she was hearing. She already knew what Eustace – when his infuriatingly slow and stammering speech would allow him – was about to say.

'I wonder whether you would p-permit me to assist Lizzie towards taking the exam?'

'Oh, Eustace – *could* you? *Would* you – *really*?'

She was about to get up from the settee, rush over to the young man and fling her arms round his neck. Raised eyebrows from Mrs Newcombe – who foresaw exactly how her flamboyant daughter would react to such a suggestion – just restrained her. The shy, introverted young man would find such a gesture thoroughly embarrassing.

'If Mrs and Captain Newcombe would allow it, I am quite sure I could familiarise myself with the requirements – after all, it was only seven years ago that I sat a similar examination myself. And if I send for the syllabus, I don't see why I c-couldn't make any adjustments necessary.'

'Oh, Mama, what do you think? Do you approve? Do you think that Papa would approve?'

The anxiety in Lizzie's voice really touched her mother.

'Remember, Mama, that it was Papa's idea in the first place, and though I know that you have had some reservations . . .' Lizzie's eyes were bright with excitement.

'I understand that, Mrs Newcombe, if I may say so,' said Eustace gravely. 'There's a lot of p-prejudice against young women going to college; they are, as you know, not p-permitted to take a degree, no matter how well they do in tripos – the final examination. But I am confident that during the next few years more and more women will take that initiative, and that eventually they will be granted degrees, both at Oxford and Cambridge.'

'Isn't that wonderful, Mama?' said Lizzie excitedly.

'I suppose so, my darling. But Eustace, I imagine that every mother will have some doubts on the subject. I don't want Lizzie to ruin her chances of making a good marriage, even though I know she wants to have a rewarding career. Lizzie dear, you see I don't want to see you, when I'm old, like Miss Creeber or Miss Young – a spinster!'

'I don't think Lizzie could ever be like that, even if she didn't marry. She's so . . . so . . .'

Here Eustace's nerve let him down, and Mrs Newcombe completed the sentence for him.

'So full of life – is that what you were about to say, Eustace?'

'Yes, Mrs Newcombe.'

While this exchange was going on, brother and sister were soundlessly communicating with each other, knowing their respective thoughts and hopes and willing their mother to give approval.

'Mama, what do you say? *Isn't* it a good idea? Please, *please* say yes! You know Papa would approve, and he could afford to pay Eustace, couldn't he? Oh, *do* say yes!'

'Well, I know how disappointed your father was when he learned of your dismissal, so I don't really see why not. And I am quite sure we can come to some understanding about the financial side of things, Eustace.'

'Oh, Mama, you've made me so happy! Of course I'll continue to work hard with my music pupils. But to think that if I study hard enough I might – I just might – get to Girton after all!'

'I will have a good student, Mrs Newcombe, I know that. May I send for the p-papers? Then I can see exactly what's required, and with your approval p-perhaps I can order the necessary textbooks.'

Joe, who was as happy as his sister at the prospect, put in a word for himself. 'Eustace, if you're busy teaching Lizzie, and then there's the part-time work you do at Hoe Grammar – will you still have time to teach me?'

'Of course he will, darling!'

'Eustace, write *now* to Girton to get the details, please. There's still time to catch a late afternoon collection. Oh, please *do!*'

Lizzie took him very firmly by the arm and hastened him across the room to the writing desk, where without protest he at once put pen to paper.

That night Lizzie was so happy and so excited she hardly slept at all.

Chapter Fourteen

'Eustace, let me see, let me see!'

Lizzie snatched the thick envelope from Eustace's hand almost before he could get it out of his briefcase. She unfolded a sheaf of printed papers and started reading aloud.

'"The College course occupies three years, half of each year being spent in residence. The charge for board, lodging and instruction is thirty-five pounds per term."'

Mrs Newcombe, hearing Lizzie's voice, joined them.

'Look, Mama, the syllabus has arrived!'

With her mother looking over her shoulder, Lizzie continued reading:

'"Candidates for admission are required to pass an entrance examination, and to furnish a satisfactory certificate of character." Oh, Mama, who can give me that? Miss Creeber won't, for certain!'

'Professor Rowe would, or Dr Higgins.'

'Oh, yes – at least, I hope so. Shall I go on?'

She returned to the papers.

Mrs Newcombe said, 'It rather looks as if you will enter in October '94. Eustace, do you think Lizzie can be ready by next year?'

'Yes, Mrs Newcombe, I'm sure she will.'

'In that case, Eustace, please order the books you need and charge them to my account at Underhill's. I expect you'll have to work out a timetable – and see to it that Elizabeth sticks to it! Be strict. Don't let her take any short cuts – she will if she can, you know. She's pretty artful!'

'Right you are, Mrs Newcombe!' said Eustace, sticking his

chin out and grinning, lips tightly closed. He knew that Mrs Newcombe was teasing, but that there was more than a grain of truth in what she said.

'And don't hesitate to scold her if at all necessary! Remember, Eustace, her enthusiasm can get the better of her at times!'

Lizzie hardly ever blushed, but during this exchange between her mother and her prospective tutor she felt herself turning beetroot – something she hated, because beetroot-coloured skin definitely did not blend well with her hair.

'Mama – really!'

'No, Lizzie, it's true. You must go steadily. Keep her in order, Eustace!'

'Right you are, Mrs Newcombe,' Eustace repeated.

That evening as the sun was setting, Mrs Newcombe, sitting facing her favourite view, thought about Lizzie.

'How times have changed!' she sighed, comparing herself at seventeen to Lizzie. She had been schooled and trained solely for marriage. Now she was more modern in outlook, but she had her reservations.

That evening before dinner, she said to her daughter, 'Lizzie, darling, there's something I want to say to you.'

'Mama?' Lizzie was curious.

'Look, darling, during the coming months you're going to be spending a great deal of time with Eustace – alone. Now, he is a young man, you are a beautiful young girl. It's possible that . . . well . . .'

'Go on, Mama – but I think I know what you're going to say. You're going to say that perhaps he might . . .' Here Lizzie was the one to hesitate, but went on, 'that he might . . . get to like me? Is that what you're thinking?'

'Yes, Lizzie.'

'Well, yes, Mama, I suppose he might.'

Lizzie fell into one of her characteristic fits of laughter, and had to put the glass of sherry she was holding down on a nearby table.

'Oh, Mama! Mama! How funny! Honestly – really, honestly – I could never, ever, ever get to like him. He's so –'

'Plain!' both women chorused.

177

'Yes, Lizzie, I know he is – but darling, do be very careful, won't you? You could encourage him without realising it. Wear your more severe clothes when he's around, and don't show your ankles. You see, you might throw temptation in his way.'

'I do understand, Mama, but you know I *think*, I only *think* . . .'

'What?'

'That Eustace actually likes Emma!'

And Lizzie told her mother about the day that he came to the house just as Emma was leaving, and what he had tried to say.

Eustace and Lizzie were having their first session in the old nursery, which, it had been decided, was an excellent place for them to work. A new bookcase had been installed, and the small desk that Joe and his sister had used to play schools when they were little had been replaced by a smart, sensible table which stood by the attic windows.

This part of the house consisted of three rooms, one each for Laura and Aggie, and the large nursery – to which Joe and Lizzie still retired when they wanted to be away from the rest of the family, or to work on any project or idea that needed space and might make the smarter rooms untidy. The nursery also had a beautiful view over the sea, and from the top of the house the perspective was broader, so that from their windows the brother and sister could see approaching ships rather sooner than their parents down in the drawing room.

Eustace would become accustomed to teaching Lizzie in this setting, and here Lizzie, in isolation, would study, write her essays and complete all the exercises that would bring her up to the necessary standard for the entrance examination.

'Your essays are really very g-good.'

'I love writing. I love poetry, and Shakespeare. Wasn't Juliet brave?'

'Well, yes. I think you might write an essay on her and her attitude towards her p-parents.'

Lizzie was about to jump in at once with a lively response, but Eustace stopped her.

'However, it is your arithmetic that we'll have to work on. You know it is very weak indeed.'

'I *hate* it – I was never any good at it. I hardly understand simple fractions, let alone algebra, and the trouble I got into at school when we learned long division of money . . . And Joe is so good at mathematics, you know.' She sighed.

'Well, it's my job to help you. D-don't worry, you'll be right up to standard when the time comes.'

'Thank you, Miss Cooper. I have the name correctly, have I not?' 'Yes, I am Miss Cooper.'

The sleek, dark-haired bank clerk passed Lady Alston's account book and a considerable amount of cash over the counter to Emma, who was on one of her regular visits to the Wiltshire and Dorset Bank.

'Will that be all, Miss Cooper?'

Emma, who had not seen this particular member of the staff before, had made up her mind to open her own bank account. She was certainly spending less than she was being paid, and at present had a fair amount of cash in her room. Lady Alston had explained to her that while the chances of their being robbed were remote, it would be a good thing for Emma to start an account – in addition to being safe, once placed in the bank the money would grow at a steady rate of interest.

Shyly looking up at the handsome young man, she said, 'Well, no – not exactly.'

'So, Miss Cooper, what else can I do for you today?'

His dark eyes met hers, and she felt a nervousness and tension that had not troubled her for some months; but she knew what she wanted, and plucked up courage to explain her request.

'I would like to open my own account, if you please.'

'Certainly, Miss Cooper. Would you please step this way?'

The young man emerged from behind the wide, highly polished mahogany counter and led her across the banking hall to a tiny, welcoming office. Although it was quite a warm day, a glowing fire crackled cheerfully in a black-leaded grate.

The clerk gestured to Emma to sit in a studded leather

179

chair with wide arms. He sat down behind the desk opposite her.

'I would advise a deposit account, Miss Cooper,' he said, 'one from which you can readily withdraw cash at any time you wish. Would that be agreeable?'

'Yes, that would be agreeable.'

Sitting very upright and tightly gripping her handbag, Emma looked far more businesslike and self-assured than she actually felt.

The young man produced a paper and took down her full name and address.

'Do you need any references?' she asked. 'I am companion to Lady Alston, and there would be no difficulty –'

'That will not be necessary. But I need three specimen signatures. If you would sign here, here, and here?'

As he pushed the paper towards her, Emma noticed his slim, long hands, the nails of which were somewhat pointed and almost too well manicured.

'Thank you, Mr . . .'

'Webber, Bertram Webber. I do beg your pardon, I should have introduced myself just now. I will be looking after your account.'

As he spoke, he reached out his right hand to shake Emma's neatly gloved one.

'How do you do, Mr Webber. But before I sign, tell me, will this account pay me interest? I gather it is common practice for banks to do so.'

Bertram Webber was surprised; he didn't expect to be questioned like this by a mere girl. He had been thinking how attractive she was – and in his opinion young women shouldn't know anything about money.

'Yes, of course; your account will yield some two per cent annually.'

Emma removed her gloves and took the pen to produce the three signatures.

Looking up at her from below dark eyebrows that met in the middle, Bertram Webber thought that she must surely either belong to a wealthy family (was she related to Lady Alston, whose account the bank was administering in conjunction with an important London bank?) or have expectations of some sort.

He must be tactful. Trying to sound practical rather than inquisitive, he enquired, 'Miss Cooper, will you be making regular payments into your account?'

'That depends on my situation. It seems very likely. Once the account has been opened, I will let you have my initial deposit. Shall I call again soon?'

'Early next week, Miss Cooper.'

He stood up, indicating that the interview was at an end, and ushered her out of the office.

'Until next week, Mr Webber.'

'I'm much obliged, Miss Cooper.'

And he kept his eyes on her, admiring her slim, tall figure and her upright walk until she had disappeared out of the main entrance to the bank.

Emma made her way home up Lockyer Street. In spite of having bought several expensive presents for her mother and friends and added a few items to the fine wardrobe with which Lady Alston had provided her, she had twelve pounds with which to open her account. Soon Lady Alston would be paying her some more money. She felt pleased with herself.

Meanwhile, Bertram returned to his duties in a deeply thoughtful mood. He must get to know Miss Emma Cooper – and the sooner the better. He looked down at his papers and studied her signature. It was as beautiful and as elegant as its owner. Smiling to himself, he turned his attention to his duties.

'Very good, Lucy! Now let's play "Oranges and Lemons" together, as a duet – and we'll sing, too. Ready? One, two, three . . .'

'Hello, Lizzie. Am I disturbing you?'

'Oh, Eustace! No – Lucy and I are running a little late, but we won't be a moment.

> '"I do not know
> "Said the big bell at Bow."'

'There's a good girl. And next week we'll move on to "Here comes a chopper to chop off your head!"' said Lizzie, affectionately tousling little Lucy's dark curls.

The child ran out into the hall, where her mother was exchanging a few words with Mrs Newcombe.

'Eustace, before we get down to studies, would you mind if I played through the Mendelssohn? Can we spare the time? I've my lesson with Professor Rowe tomorrow.'

'I would like t-to hear it very much.'

He settled himself into an armchair, legs outstretched in front of him, feet crossed, hands folded across his chest, his small, sad eyes closed.

Lizzie had worked hard on the piece and it was nearing perfection. Eustace was entranced, but suggested that she could speed up a little on some of the arpeggios. She knew this to be true, but explained that Professor Rowe was encouraging greater accuracy rather than speed.

'You seem to know about music – I mean, as well as everything else!'

'Well, no, not really. But I have studied it.'

'Why didn't you tell me before? We could play duets.'

He paused again. 'No, I don't play the piano.'

'Well – what? The violin or cello?'

'The guitar, actually.'

'Oh, how beautiful! I would – we all would – love to hear you. Can you bring it round one evening and play for us?'

'Well, no, I c-can't.'

'Why ever not? Surely you're not too shy to play in front of an audience? I know a lot of musicians are, even though they are awfully good.'

'No, that's not it. You see, I haven't got a g-guitar any more.'

'Oh, no! Why? Did you have to sell it?'

'No.'

'Well, did you give it away?'

Lizzie had already realised during her brief acquaintance with Eustace just how infuriatingly difficult it could be at times to get any information out of him.

'You see, it was like this . . .'

'Go on.'

'Well, when I was leaving C–Cambridge for the last time, I was late for my train. I was c-carrying a big bag of books, an umbrella, a suitcase and my guitar in its case – a nice, strong, wooden c-case. But the handle had broken, so I was holding it under my arm.'

182

'Well, what happened?' asked Lizzie impatiently.

'I got to the p-platform and there was the train just about to move off – the guard had waved his green flag. I ran towards the train – I was at the end of the p-platform, facing the engine, and . . .'

'And?' Lizzie encouraged him.

'The guitar and its c-case slipped from under my arm and fell onto the track, and the engine ran over it, totally c-crushing it. It was dreadful. There were just some splintered remains after the train had pulled out.'

'Oh, Eustace, what an *awful* story!'

But how typical, thought Lizzie. It was her turn to be quiet for a while.

'And you see I can't possibly afford to buy another,' Eustace went on, 'not yet anyway, though now your mother is being so generous, I may be able to do so when I've got myself sorted out. But for the time being, that won't be possible.'

Lizzie had one of her sudden bright thoughts.

'Eustace, I might – I just *might* – be able to help you. But I can't say any more than that yet. Time for lessons now, eh?'

Eustace cheered up, and they went up to the top of the house to start work.

The two girls had enjoyed a walk in the early spring sunshine and were eating ice creams at the Three Towns Dairy. Lizzie took another mouthful and, leaning across the small marble table, looked pleadingly at Emma, who was sitting bolt upright, politely nibbling the wafer biscuit that garnished their mid-afternoon treat.

'Emma, please, *please* ask Lady Alston!'

'No, Lizzie. He's very rude – I don't like him. I can't understand how you put up with him.'

'But you've only seen him once, and then only for a moment. Just because he stared at you . . . He honestly wasn't trying to be rude, he's just dreadfully short-sighted. And he's so very, very clever – I'm sure he would play it beautifully, And you must admit that to have his guitar smashed by the train was awful!'

'Yes, it was, but he was obviously frightfully careless and disorganised.'

The two girls were quiet for a moment.

'He really does *need* that guitar, Emma, and let's face it, you don't play it, Lady Alston doesn't play it – I imagine she can't play it – it's simply just sitting there. Couldn't you at least ask if Eustace could come round and see it and perhaps play it to her? That could do no harm.'

'Well, I'll think about it. But I don't get on very well with men, you know, and I don't really like them.'

'I had gathered that, but I do think you're safe with Eustace. He wouldn't hurt a fly.'

Emma capitulated.

From the pavement outside the dairy, a young man in a severely cut morning suit and bowler hat caught sight of Emma through the large window and doffed his hat to her, smiled broadly. Instead of continuing his walk, he paused, turned and came into the dairy.

Lizzie noticed Emma grip her spoon and sit even more upright. She was surprised; could she know him? Who was he? What was he to her – she who had just that moment said she didn't like men very much? Lizzie felt she was about to be amused.

'Good morning, Miss Cooper. May I join you? If you and your friend do not mind.'

He drew up another little wrought-iron chair from a nearby unoccupied table.

Emma was overcome with embarrassment. She blushed profusely and felt droplets of perspiration break out on her forehead. Quickly, and with more success than she realised, she composed herself.

'Oh, Mr Webber. Yes, of course. Elizabeth, allow me to introduce Mr Bertram Webber. Mr Webber, Miss Elizabeth Newcombe.'

'Miss Newcombe, delighted to meet you.'

Lizzie could not fail to notice those dark, deep-set eyes and that heavy brow. They shook hands formally.

'Miss Newcombe, if I may be so bold – might you be Captain Newcombe's daughter?'

'Yes, my papa is a captain.'

'Ah, I thought so. We do business with the Captain at the bank where I work, and he has mentioned you. I believe you're a pianist.'

184

'Well, yes, I do play.'

'And very well, I gather from Professor Rowe – who has also spoken of you.'

Lizzie was surprised; this young man seemed to have informed himself very thoroughly about her. Meanwhile, Emma sat quietly by. She was glad that Mr Webber was talking to Lizzie; he made her feel nervous.

But now he turned to her, and slightly leaned across the table.

'Miss Cooper, your account has been prepared; if you would like to call at the bank at your convenience, we can take your business a stage further.'

'I will do that, Mr Webber, thank you.' Emma, frowning, leaned slightly away from him as she spoke.

'Miss Newcombe, I wonder whether . . .' Bertram Webber hesitated. 'The bank has been asked to look after the business of the newly formed hospital charity. A committee has been set up. One of the proposals is for a series of charity concerts in the Athenaeum in the autumn. Would you permit me to put your name forward as a participant?'

Lizzie was dumbfounded. Professor Rowe had told her she would be good enough to play in public; but there were her studies for Girton, which took up more and more of her time.

'You flatter me, Mr Webber.'

'Your mother is on the organising committee – we met at Admiralty House the other afternoon. I had been about to speak to her on the matter, but now, by chance, I've met you.'

'Well, Mr Webber, I will certainly consider it – if I can spare the time to work up a programme.'

'It's only March. I'm sure you have a lot of pieces in your repertoire anyway, and the series of concerts does not begin until October.'

'It would be most exciting, if the committee agrees and, of course, if Professor Rowe and Mama do as well. Thank you for asking me.'

Bertram got up. 'Young ladies, sadly I must leave you. Duty calls.'

Taking Lizzie's hand, he bowed to her; taking Emma's, he

seemed to her to hold on to it for a few seconds longer than was absolutely necessary before turning to leave, pausing first at the cash desk to pay his bill.

The two friends nodded to him from their table as he passed along the pavement outside the plate-glass window.

Bertram Webber felt very pleased with himself. The fact that he was on the hospital charity committee must surely have impressed them. He was now, at only twenty-four, on friendly terms with naval society and members of the medical profession, an excellent social advantage – and, in addition, he had learned that Miss Newcombe and Miss Cooper were friends. His next move would be to try and involve Emma (for that was how he thought of her) in some way in the charity work. But that would probably depend on Lady Alston.

He had a lot of thinking and planning to do. First, he must find some business reason for calling on Lady Alston and discovering what she was like. It was possible that Emma would be present at his interview with her employer. In any case he would try to ascertain whether Lady Alston was planning to leave a significant share of her money to the beautiful iceberg? For Miss Emma Cooper was just that – an iceberg glittering in the sun. He decided that if anyone could melt her, it was he, but he would not try unless there was a prospect of financial gain.

He would have to proceed with care. The unspoken messages he had received from Emma's eyes were so far anything but encouraging. In fact, he decided, he hadn't really received any messages at all. But at least that was better then a negative response.

'Pity, though,' he murmured to himself as he strode on, undaunted, swinging his ebony cane with a flourish. He walked purposefully to the Palm Court of the Royal Hotel, and ordered a luxurious afternoon tea.

'So, you have had a secret beau all the time! You're a dark horse, Emma!'

Emma was distressed, and showed it. Lizzie realised that she'd said the wrong thing, and apologised profusely.

'Oh, I am sorry. I really didn't mean to upset you.'

186

'Never mind, Lizzie. He's a handsome young man, and very polite. I met him at the bank the other day – he's looking after some business for me.'

There was more than a hint of pride in Emma's voice, but as she spoke, the vision of his slinky hands passed through her mind and made her shudder.

'That's nice. I think you should try to be a little sympathetic towards him. Do try, Emma! I'm sure he won't hurt you or upset you in any way, and I'm sure he'll be very successful later on.'

'Well, I'll try. But that sort of thing is just very difficult for me.'

'Would you like to tell me why?'

'No, I can't. I really can't. Some day, perhaps, but no . . . it's . . .'

Lizzie could see her friend trembling and her eyes growing heavy with tears.

'Emma dear, can I help? Do let me help.'

Emma shook her head. 'One day you'll understand. Be patient with me, please.'

She dried her eyes. Tactfully looking away, Lizzie reached for her purse.

'We'd better go.'

'No, let me.'

Emma had just had another payday. She called the waitress and asked for the bill.

'Oh no, that gentleman paid, miss.'

The two young women looked at each other wide-eyed, not quite knowing what to think. They were flattered, but didn't want to admit it – to themselves or each other.

'You are expected, sir. Please come in.'

Stratton opened the heavy front door.

'May I take your coat, scarf and gloves, sir?'

'Thank you.'

'Come this way, sir, if you please.'

Stratton led the way up the impressive staircase to the first-floor drawing room where Lady Alston and Emma were waiting.

'Mr Eustace Beaumont, my lady.'

187

'Thank you, Stratton.'

Emma coldly introduced Eustace. Overcome by her presence, he was trying hard not to gaze at her. Lady Alston, however, smiled warmly.

'Mr Beaumont, I have learned of the most unfortunate accident with your guitar. A great pity.'

'Yes, Lady Alston, it was, as you say, a g-great p-pity.'

Eustace stood round-shouldered, rubbing the tips of his fingers together as he spoke – one of his nervous habits.

'Please sit down, Mr Beaumont, and tell me more about your playing. Do you favour flamenco music or the more classical works?'

'Well, I . . . I . . .' He did not want to say something that Lady Alston might disagree with.

She smiled, and her expression was enough to encourage him.

'I do play a little flamenco, but it's rather noisy for my taste. I like Mr Sor's work, and that of many of the modern guitar composers.'

'Ah, good. I do not myself favour the flamenco, though in Spain in the sunshine it is beautiful, you know – I was there many years ago. Now, Emma, get the guitar for Mr Beaumont, please.'

Emma had been sitting in her most upright position, hands tightly folded in her lap. As she stood up, Eustace saw the guitar case resting on the Spanish shawl which covered the piano, and at once jumped to his feet to join her, thinking himself fortunate to have an opportunity to be near her.

'Miss Cooper, please let me – it's p-probably rather heavy.'

He was very anxious to see the guitar. He sat down on a low stool, placed the case on the floor in front of him, undid the two little latches and slowly opened the lid.

'Oh! Oh, it's b-beautiful.'

With the tender, loving care a mother gives to her newborn baby, Eustace lifted the guitar from its case and supported it on his knee.

'It's quite p-perfect.'

He was quiet for a moment or so, gazing at it with respect. Turning it towards the light, he examined the label.

'It's a Panormo, made in London in 1855. I have never, ever seen such a beautiful guitar.'

'Mr Beaumont, is it in a fit condition to play? I mean, the strings.'

Eustace put the guitar in a playing position and swept his right hand fingers across the strings. The sound was awful.

'No, they must be changed.'

Emma noticed some small packets in the case.

'Look, Mr Beaumont – are those packets of new strings?'

He picked them up and, bringing them very close to his spectacles, counted six.

'Yes, that's a complete set. Lady Alston, may I change the strings and tune the instrument?'

'Of course, Mr Beaumont. Then perhaps you will play us something. Emma, ring for tea. While it's coming, Mr Beaumont can prepare the guitar, and later we can hear him play.'

The instrument was very fine, and he soon realised just how easy it would be to play – far easier than the cheap guitar he'd spent so much time practising on over the years. Although he had not touched a guitar for several months, he played a set of attractive studies by Fernando Sor. Both women were very impressed, and even Emma was a little moved by his playing.

'Wasn't that beautiful, Emma? Thank you so much, Mr Beaumont.'

'Lady Alston, it is a beautiful instrument. I wonder if, p-perhaps . . .'

'Are you going to ask me if it's for sale?'

'Well, yes, although I c-c-c . . .'

Lady Alston smiled broadly. 'Although you fear that even if it were, you could not afford to make me an offer. Is that it?'

Eustace was pleased that she had spoken for him.

'Emma, do you think you would ever want to learn to play the guitar?'

'No, Lady Alston, I don't think I could manage to do that. It looks far too difficult.'

'Well, Mr Beaumont, Emma doesn't want to play and I'm certainly far too old to learn – my fingers, you know, arthritis. So there's no reason for me to wish to keep it. I know you will make good use of it.'

189

Eustace blinked, blushed and was very slightly shaking his head. 'You don't . . . You c-cannot possibly mean . . .?'

'Yes, of course you must have it. Instruments are meant to be played – which is one reason why Elizabeth comes here to play the piano sometimes. But I will lay down one condition.'

'Yes, Lady Alston – whatever you say.'

'That from time to time you come and play to me. We shall have musical evenings. Emma here sings beautifully, and with your guitar music and the piano we can have quite a concert. Will you do that for me?'

Would he not! Eustace couldn't believe what had happened to him. He hadn't been so happy since he was a child. And apart from his new acquisition, when he was invited to play he would also see the lovely Emma – though he realised she could never be even slightly interested in him.

Chapter Fifteen

Emma was enjoying her work and the increasing responsibilities that Lady Alston gave her. But she felt that in some respects there was a certain emptiness in her life. On a warm April day when she was walking across the Hoe in one of her few solitary moments, she fell into a contemplative mood.

Lizzie was studying – she had ambitions and goals; she was going to go to college. That week Emma had bought the theatre magazine *The Era*, which had a beautiful photograph of her sister on its cover. Sarah was achieving fame as well as fortune. Lizzie and Sarah both had their dreams.

What dreams did she, Emma, have? Her work was interesting, and there was much to do. But where was it actually leading her? Beyond the warm satisfaction of being a help-meet to her employer, she could see no other reward. Money, yes – Emma liked having money; who didn't? Perhaps she should make more use of it, and see it grow. It did not entirely satisfy her to spend it on fripperies. Fripperies were fun – she had seen a pretty hat in Popham's window which she'd decided to buy for Whitsun – but she wanted to get more out of life than just fun. To do that she knew she would have to set herself some firm objectives, and if necessary, spend some of her money in order to achieve them.

Thinking these thoughts, she found that she had walked right across the Promenade and turned down a tree-lined path which led to a narrow street called Windsor Lane, containing a variety of small, interesting shops: a fruit shop, a hairdresser's, a small laundry, a toy shop and next to it a

191

dolls' hospital. She peered into the last of them, and in the semi-darkness saw an elderly man with great care and devotion repairing a doll's broken arm.

Even he has an objective, Emma thought. He looks so fulfilled and satisfied. She became quite sad, and moved on.

The next shop was very different.

She gazed into its window with great curiosity. There was a collection of smart machines of a kind she didn't immediately recognise. A notice explained that they were the latest Remington Two Typewriters – 'As Used in the most Up-to-date Offices'. There were sheets of examples of the printing that could be produced by using them – formal business letters, writers' manuscripts – and a selection of testimonials saying that the owners, once having 'learned to type,' would never again write any business documents or correspondence by hand. Emma was fascinated. There was also a textbook, *How to Type using the New Remington Two Machine.*

Emma's handwriting was perfect. She had won prizes for it at school, and it had been one factor that had encouraged Lady Alston to offer her her present position. Emma was proud of this accomplishment, but surely learning to type – 'A Lady-like Occupation for the Woman of the Future' said another notice – would be something worth achieving? She could type Lady Alston's letters, she could type letters to her own man of business; any letter that was really important or formal would be better expressed and more impressive. Yes, typing would be a great asset.

She decided to go into the shop to discover the price of the machine and perhaps try one, to see just how difficult it might be to use.

Nervously she approached a middle-aged salesman behind the counter.

'I am interested to know rather more about your, er, typewriting machines, please – like the model in the window.'

'Certainly, miss. Would you come over here, please?'

He led Emma to a small table where there was a demonstration model.

'You place the paper in position, so.'

Taking a piece of paper he rolled it around the platen.

'Then you set the margin you require – the distance from

192

the edge of the paper to where the printing will commence – and simply start.'

He clattered away on the keys with great speed. But the action looked terribly difficult to Emma.

'Of course it takes practice. There are specially devised typewriting exercises, and you will progress slowly at first – but I assure you, you quickly get used to the procedure.'

'What if you make a mistake?'

'Well, you simply erase it! Like this.'

He produced what Emma thought was a pencil, but instead of lead it had an eraser with a sharp point, and carefully rubbed out the last letter he'd printed.

'Please do try the machine.'

'Oh no, I really don't think . . .'

'You will find you have no difficulty. Please take this chair.'

He got up, and Emma, nervously excited, did as she was asked.

'Why are all the letters arranged in that strange way? Why aren't they laid out in alphabetical order?'

'It is to prevent the keys from jamming when one is typing at speed.'

She wrote 'Emms Coippre', then 'Ksdy Tuewkk', and felt dreadfully stupid.

'Well, that's not what you really wanted to write, I suppose,' said the assistant. 'But you see, you're learning already – you've noticed how to use the upper and lower case.'

She blushed.

'There are some textbooks in the window?'

'Yes, one is supplied with the machine. And we hold regular courses in typing and other office skills – shorthand, book-keeping and so on – which you could attend.'

'That might be difficult. But I think I could teach myself.'

'I have no doubt. A lot of young women do, these days. I can see you're one of these modern "career women". Perhaps your employer would buy a machine for you, miss.'

Emma hadn't thought of that – and how did he know I had an employer anyway? she asked herself.

'Your employer, would he buy one for you?' the salesman persisted.

'Oh, I'm employed by Lady Alston.'

'I see!' The man was impressed by the title.

'I would really like to buy one myself, but it may be too expensive – how much is it?'

'This new model is fifteen guineas.'

'That is a great deal. I couldn't afford that much.'

'Well, miss, there is this one.'

He took Emma across the showroom to a shelf where there was another machine on show.

'This is a Remington Two, the same model as the one you've tried. It's not completely new – three years old – but I have thoroughly overhauled it.'

'And how much would that cost, please?' she asked apprehensively.

'I could let you have it for eight guineas – the same price as this little portable. This is new – a Halls machine, very inferior if you ask me; I wouldn't touch it myself. Best go for the reliable Remington.'

Eight guineas would seriously cut into Emma's savings, but her ambition and instinct told her this was the right thing to do. For a moment she wondered whether she should ask Lady Alston to buy it for her. No! She wanted to be independent.

'I'll take it, Mr, er –'

'Mullins. Thank you, miss. Shall I send Lady Alston an invoice?'

'Oh, no!' said Emma decisively. 'I will go to the bank and withdraw the money. I'll be back in fifteen minutes.'

'Of course, miss. I beg your pardon.'

She made her way to the bank, produced her deposit book and drew out eight pounds eight shillings. Putting the cash safely into her handbag, she returned to the shop and completed the transaction. The salesman promised to deliver the typewriter to Elliot Terrace later that afternoon.

Emma left the shop with several instruction books and a leaflet giving details of the courses the 'school' ran – though she knew the demands Lady Alston made on her time would prevent her from taking such a course.

She had started her walk feeling really quite depressed, but now she was excited, more excited than she had been for some time. She had spent a very great deal of money and she hoped that Lady Alston would not chide her for extravagance; but that her purchase had given her a fresh incentive – a real goal to aim for.

Bertram Webber stood up.

'Ah, there you are, Emma. Did you enjoy your walk?'

'Thank you, Lady Alston. It was most refreshing.'

'You know Mr Webber, I believe. We have been talking business, and he has something he would like to discuss with you.'

'I'm so pleased to see you again, Miss Cooper.' He took Emma's hand as he spoke.

Emma nodded, and they sat.

'Miss Cooper, as you know, I am on a committee which is raising funds for the local hospital. We need help in a great many areas. We had a meeting yesterday afternoon when it was officially decided that Miss Newcombe and Mr Beaumont should be asked to give, jointly, the first of our series of winter recitals in the Athenaeum, and I wondered if perhaps you might help us with the organisation of their recital.'

Emma was flattered, but had reservations.

'What would be expected of me, Mr Webber?'

'I would like you to liaise between Mr Beaumont, Miss Newcombe and myself. Work with them on the programme content, and generally help to organise the evening. Then on the evening itself you could welcome the audience as they arrive, and with one or two others show them to their seats, sell programmes – something of that sort.'

'Oh, Mr Webber, I've never done anything like that before.'

'Emma, you would do it beautifully. Besides, you would be working with our dear friends, and be such a help to Elizabeth.'

'Miss Cooper, the aim is to build a new maternity wing with the money we raise. Please say yes. The four of us will meet once or twice during the coming months, of course, and from time to time you can inform me of your progress.'

Emma's thoughts turned to the typewriter, and she smiled to herself. The idea was appealing in many ways.

195

'I will do what I can, but I'm sure Lady Alston has told you of our plans to return to London for the season. We will be away for many weeks.'

'Yes, we have discussed that. As long as we can get a certain amount settled before you leave, there will be plenty of time to make the final arrangements when you return.'

'In that case, thank you for asking me, Mr Webber. I'll be delighted to help you.'

He took his leave.

Bertram had had a productive afternoon. He was gaining Lady Alston's confidence in her business matters, and was in the process of conducting the sale of some shares that she had held for years in a Northumbrian mining venture. These showed a slow but steady decline, and on his suggestion she was instead to buy some in a large cotton mill that had trade outlets in the centre of Manchester.

He was clever, and his advice was sound. He accepted the fact that it would be a long time before he was treated with the confidence that her London banker and solicitor enjoyed – he was still only a senior clerk. But progress with her and the delectable Emma had moved forward.

'My dear, I think that helping to organise the recital will be excellent for you – it will give you a sense of purpose.'

'I think so, too – but Mr Webber . . .' Emma paused.

'What of him?'

'He . . . he's a little frightening – the way he looks at one with those dark eyes.' Emma shivered.

'Ah, my dear, I think you will soon discover otherwise. He thinks very highly of you. Do you not think he is charming?'

Emma blushed and tried to change the subject – something she was burning to do anyway.

'Lady Alston . . .'

'My dear, what is it? I do believe you're blushing! Perhaps Mr Webber is having an effect after all!' Lady Alston fell into her girlish, teasing mood.

'Oh, no! Lady Alston, I . . . I've . . .'

'Well, dear, and what have you done?'

'I've been shopping.'

'And what have you bought? That pretty hat we saw in Popham's the other day? I do hope so!'

196

'No. But I'm afraid I've spent rather a lot of money.'

'Emma, I do hope you've not wasted it. But no – I can't think that you would be silly with money.'

Lady Alston toyed with a long pearl necklace which had somehow become twisted up with the chain of her lorgnette.

'I've bought a typewriter, and I'm going to teach myself to type!'

There was a silence. The old lady's expression lost its gentle charm. She took a deep breath.

'A typewriter! *Whatever for*? You have absolutely no need of such an instrument!'

Her voice was surprisingly fearsome.

'But Lady Alston, I want to learn to type, to be more . . .'

Emma was genuinely surprised at Lady Alston's response and had extreme difficulty in finding words in which to continue.

'More *what*?'

Her employer seemed to be growing angrier by the moment.

'More, er, businesslike for you.'

'That is totally unnecessary, totally! Do you hear me? Your handwriting is quite perfect. It will suffice. I simply cannot allow you to learn something so . . . so lower-class – something that would perhaps have been suitable if you were still with your family. As it is, you are out of that sphere. No young woman of the class in which I trust you are learning to take your place, should allow herself to indulge in an activity suitable only for the commercial classes.'

'But I want to –'

'No, I won't hear of it. You will not bring such a thing into my house. I will not allow it. I do *not* want some sort of female clerk as a companion. You are to take it back from whence it came – and immediately, do you hear?'

Tears of disappointment gushed from Emma's eyes. She was about to explain that the machine wasn't yet delivered when Stratton entered.

'Excuse me, m'lady, there's a Mr Mullins –'

At this, Emma rushed out of the room and downstairs. She was surprised and shocked by Lady Alston's old-fashioned reaction, but between her sobs managed to explain her situation to Mr Mullins, who was most understanding and agreed to refund her money.

She became even more upset as she saw him leave, carrying what was to have been her lovely machine.

Her disappointment turned to angry frustration. She knew now that she was paying the price for her elevated position in life, her beautiful clothes and gracious living. She wasn't free to make any decisions that could influence Lady Alston's image as well as her own life. She was by no means as independent as she had thought.

But why? Lady Alston simply didn't understand that Emma had to think of her future. Without really realising what she was doing and without bothering to fetch her hat and coat, she rushed out of the house, slamming the front door behind her.

She needed fresh air. As her anger subsided, she realised that it was not only Lady Alston who had reacted uncharacteristically. Never had Emma expressed such a surge of angry emotion. She also realised that she had become self-confident enough to release her feelings. In the past, fear – the fear of her father's violence in particular – had prevented this.

Deep in thought and still crying copiously, she wandered further and further from Elliot Terrace. It was late afternoon; people from offices and shops were crowding the streets, hurrying to get home before the thick West Country drizzle saturated their clothes.

Emma had no idea where she was going, but she had made her way right down Lockyer Street and was now sitting on a tombstone in St Catherine's churchyard, directly opposite the Royal Hotel. Her neat white blouse was soaking, her hair hung in damp wisps over her face. She was feeling forlorn and crushed.

Should she go and see Lizzie, seek her advice and moral support? No – the problem was something she'd have to resolve for herself. But what action to take? How would she face Lady Alston? Perhaps she'd get her notice. The prospect terrified her.

'Miss Cooper, whatever is the matter? What are you doing here?'

Startled, Emma looked up to see Bertram Webber holding a large, black umbrella over her.

'You've been crying! That won't do at all – and we must get you dry. Come with me.'

Gently encouraging her to get up, he handed her a large white handkerchief, for which she was extremely grateful.

'No, Mr Webber, I cannot go with you.' She shied away from him.

'Well, you cannot sit here any longer – you'll contract pneumonia.'

She shivered, tightly crossing her arms and hunching her shoulders.

'It would be wrong – quite wrong. Don't you understand? – it's impossible for me to go with you. What would people say?'

'People will say nothing. They won't know,' he replied calmly.

He hailed a nearby cab, gave instructions to the driver, and opened the door for her. Weakly, she obeyed him, and got in.

Once inside she glanced apprehensively at him, suddenly realising the danger of her situation.

'No, please – I can't go with you – really. Stop the cab, Bertram, please, I beg you.'

Outside the cab, the rain was now pelting down, and the streets were now almost empty, the few people on the pavements striding along beneath their umbrellas, concerned only with getting out of the dreadful weather. Perhaps, after all, no-one would see them . . . Terrified, she attempted to open the cab door.

Bertram was gentle but firm and with difficulty managed to calm her down a little. After some minutes they arrived at a large terraced house where he had his lodgings.

'I really cannot – I mustn't come in with you.'

'Miss Cooper, under ordinary circumstances your coming to my rooms would certainly be improper; but you are very distressed – it is just as if I found you physically injured. You need to dry your clothes and your hair and have a hot drink.'

The landlady who brought a tray of tea looked somewhat

199

askance at Emma, tossed her head in disapproval and made a quick exit.

Bertram encouraged Emma to tell him what had happened.

'I understand, Miss Cooper. But I can see Lady Alston's point of view. It is somewhat unladylike for someone of your class to undertake such a study – why, if you want something new to do you might try watercolour painting or collecting butterflies.'

'No, Mr Webber, there you are wrong. I am convinced that learning to type would be an excellent thing for me. After all, Lady Alston isn't exactly . . .'

'Young, Miss Cooper?'

'Precisely, Mr Webber.'

She liked the way he had so tactfully put the opposing point of view and yet he was listening intently to her opinion. His expression seemed to have become more gentle and Emma felt less nervous in his company than previously.

'But I don't know what to do. I have severely displeased Lady Alston – of that I'm quite certain.'

'You must go home and try to convince her that she is wrong, and that you really do want to learn this new skill.'

'Oh, no! I really *couldn't* do that. I could *never* argue with her. I'll just have to apologise, I suppose, and explain my absence.'

Hearing a clock strike seven, she gasped apprehensively. 'It's so late, I should be at dinner by now.' Once more she burst into tears.

He got up from where he was sitting and went to comfort her. As he bent down to put his arm round her shoulders, he thought better of it and straightened up, taking a step away.

'Miss Cooper, my dressing room is at your disposal. Your hair is dry now, but it needs attention – please feel free to use the washstand too.'

He bowed slightly, gesturing her towards a door in the corner. She responded gratefully, and on returning said, 'You have been very kind, Mr Webber. I feel more composed. Yes, I'll apologise. Perhaps in time Lady Alston will –'

'Will you trust me, Miss Cooper?' he interrupted her.

'Mr Webber, I don't understand.'

200

'Trust me, Miss Cooper. I suggest that you say absolutely nothing about our meeting to Lady Alston.'

'Why? Is not honesty the best policy?'

'Yes, Miss Cooper – for ninety-nine per cent of the time. I will get a cab for you. Go back and do the right thing by Lady Alston. Be meek – eat humble pie if necessary – but under no circumstances mention our meeting.'

In the cab Emma tried to prepare herself for the ordeal to come. Thoughts of having to return to Hammersmith, to her father and the dreaded George, swished nightmarishly through her mind. She simply did not know what her reception would be – especially as it was now past eight o'clock and dark.

'So there you are at last! Where *have* you been? Stratton has just left for the police station. How *dare* you rush out like that? Really, Emma, I am most displeased. I should write to inform your father of your behaviour. It has uncovered a side of your personality that I find most distressing, a wilfulness which I did not suspect was present. I will *not* tolerate it – do you hear me?'

'Lady Alston, I am sorry – truly sorry. Please don't write to Papa. I was, well, surprised and upset that you were so angry. I thought that –'

'You thought that I would approve of your silly idea.'

At the word 'silly' Emma's penitence wavered and she became angry again.

'It is *not* silly.'

'Go to your room! We'll discuss this further when you have calmed down and are less inclined to defy me.'

For the second time within a few hours, Emma rushed out of the drawing room – this time to fling herself onto her bed and cry herself to an uneasy sleep.

She did not see Lady Alston again that day. She passed an uncomfortable night and eventually woke up an hour earlier than usual with a dreadful headache. As she stirred on her pillow, she became aware of her unhappy situation. Dragging herself out of bed, she ran a bath and tried to organise her thoughts. She would again attempt to apologise to Lady Alston and this time control her feelings.

201

'Eat humble pie.' Bertram's words came back to her. She decided that if her relations with her employer were ever to return to normal, this was the only thing she could do.

At breakfast she at once noticed that Lady Alston looked grey and tired and her eyes were red. It was obvious that she too had not had a good night and perhaps she had also shed a few tears.

'Lady Alston, I am so very, very sorry. Of course you are right; I was both impulsive and extremely rude. Please forgive me. You know how much I enjoy working and being with you.'

The old woman looked straight at her, knowing she meant what she'd said.

'My dear, I now know that you have strong feelings, but such differences must not come between us. I accept your apology, but that does *not* mean I've changed my mind. *No* typewriting. Is that clear?'

Solemnly and with resignation Emma replied in the affirmative.

Gradually during the coming days the two women somewhat uneasily rebuilt their relationship, but Emma was now feeling restless and still dissatisfied at having been thwarted.

'And perhaps you would kindly sign this?'

It was just over a week later and Bertram was handing Lady Alston a large sheet of paper.

Looking down, she noticed that the words were of perfectly even size and, although small, surprisingly easy to read.

She was very quiet for a moment then glancing up at him over her spectacles.

'Is this a *printed* document, Mr Webber? Surely something as important as this should be handwritten?'

'No, Lady Alston, it has been copied by our lady typists.'

'It is typewritten?'

'Why, yes. You know typing is becoming by far the most practical method for correspondence these days – apart from the most personal of communications.'

Pursing her lips, she replied curtly, 'No, I did not.'

Falling silent again, she studied the document in pretence of reading the details of the agreement. In fact it was the printing itself she was studying.

Bertram was amused.

'You see, Lady Alston, it is *so* much easier to read, and if one's sight is not very good –'

'I grant you that,' she interrupted crossly. 'Tell me, Mr Webber, who actually does this, this . . .'

'Typewriting, Lady Alston? A select number of our young ladies. There is an increasing interest in these machines, on all sides, and several of our best lady employees are eager to learn to use them. This is not only the case at the bank, I believe – indeed, only last week I was talking to the Countess of Mount Edgcumbe, who tells me that her niece is learning to operate a machine. Of course, the Countess was somewhat shocked at the idea at first – she thought such an occupation suitable for the lower classes only. But she has had to agree that it is a useful and genteel occupation for a young lady, especially if she is – ambitious, shall we say? Or wants to write poetry or perhaps even children's stories. The present mayor's daughter is also learning, in order to be able to assist her father with his correspondence . . .'

'Is that so? The Countess of Mount Edgcumbe's niece . . . and the mayor's daughter? Indeed.' Lady Alston took a deep breath. 'Well, thank you, Mr Webber.'

A week later Bertram Webber took Miss Emma Cooper's statement from the file and studied it. There was the original withdrawal of eight guineas – replaced. An entry for the close of business on the previous day showed a second withdrawal of eight guineas. He knew that his ruse had worked; he also knew that Emma was now indebted to him.

Chapter Sixteen

'Guess what?'

'What?' George and his father responded in bored voices as they ate their Monday evening cold meat and boiled potatoes.

'Our Katy's getting married!'

Will Cooper snorted and made no reply. George, however, did.

'Don't believe it, it'll never happen. He's no good – there'll be trouble there, and his ma's no saint.'

Crashing down his knife and fork on his half-eaten supper, George got up from the table as he spoke.

'Where are you going?'

'Got to see a man about something,' said George, and rushed out of the front door.

'Don't drink too much,' his mother called after him. She had noticed that George had been drinking quite a lot more in recent months.

After he'd left, she sighed and went on, 'Well, I think Jim's a nice young man for Katy. Do you think George is jealous?'

'Wouldn't be surprised.'

Will Cooper gulped down his last mouthful and pulled George's plate towards him to finish that off, too.

'It's a sin to waste good food.'

George strode down the street, going nowhere in particular. His anger had never been more seething, and it was matched by his frustration.

He was being led on by resentfulness and jealousy – emotions that would inevitably burst out of him in one way or another. He kept saying to himself, 'This *must* not happen. I *will* have her!'

As time went on, George became more and more morose. Even his father noticed it, and also noticed the great deal of noise George was making at work. Hammering brads into boots and shoes and wedging down rubber soles was noisy work at any time, but George was working with such aggression that he knocked the boot and the last from the bench onto his left big toe, severely bruising it. His language was foul, something that his father would not stand for.

'Mrs Knighton heard that. That was disgusting.'

'I don't care a bugger, I've hurt me fuckin' toe! I think it's bleeding.'

'That's enough of that, now, and I mean it, boy. Wonder you didn't crack the last. What's the matter with you? Making a fuss like that – I'm 'shamed of you. You mend your ways and cheer up, or you'll drive the customers away – over to old man Cornish. If you go on like that, we'll all be in trouble.'

'Don't know what you're grumbling about. I works hard, don' I?'

'Can't deny that – but you could be a lot better tempered.'

'All right, Pa, all right.'

'I thinks you're jealous of that Jim and Katy.'

This remark shook George, who thought that he had not shown his feelings. He had to think quickly. In his softest, warmest voice, and contrary to his first reaction to their betrothal, he replied, 'Oh, Pa, no, I'm real happy for them. Jim's a fine bloke – a fine bloke. Yeah, I was a bit upset last week, but, well, y'know . . .'

'Well, you think about what I've said, and calm down. Pray to the good Lord to help you.'

'Oh, I have, Pa, I have. Been on me knees every night! It was the good Lord that told me Jim's a fine bloke . . . yeah, a fine bloke!'

'Time you started to go to church with us again. I've made excuses for you long enough, simply because you lie abed till dinner on Sunday mornings. Time you thought about gettin' wed yourself, George. That'd calm you down and give you something else to think about, boy. Like as not you'll find a nice sensible girl at church instead of the likes of them you've been cavorting about with lately.'

George opened his mouth to speak, but his father went on.

'Don't you think I've not heard a thing or two. I know what went on on Christmas Eve – and you be grateful I've not told your ma. You get back on the straight and narrow, my son, that's what you got to do. I say no more.'

His father glared at him.

George, stupefied, and suddenly realising he'd been less clever than he thought, meekly agreed to go to church in future.

It was a Saturday afternoon. George, after the week's work, was relaxing on his bed and mentally working out if he could afford a trip up to the Edgware Road to the old Metropolitan Music Hall and then a tart. He got up, went over to his chest of drawers, where he kept his savings in a rusty cash box, counted out some coins and decided he could. Cheered by the thought, as he turned he glanced out of the window and saw Katy in Mrs Cook's garden, energetically beating a large carpet which was hanging across the washing line.

He opened the window and called out to her. 'Regular little Cinderella today, eh? Where's your prince? 'Ad a row, have we?'

'You mind your own business! It's nothing to do with you, George Cooper.'

'Oh, hoity-toity! No nice walkie in Kensington Gardens holding hands?'

'If you must know, I'm helping Mrs Cook with her spring-cleaning, and Jim's down the laundry painting it for Aunty T. *We* like to *help* other people what we loves – so there!'

'Aw, how nice,' he purred satirically. He slammed down the window and flung himself on the bed once more. Then he started to think. This was an opportunity not to be missed! Katy was next door, safely out of the way. Jim was in the laundry, which, like the Coopers' shop, was closed on Saturday afternoon.

George got up, went downstairs and, taking on a nonchalant air, left the house and walked down to Blythe Road. He wasn't sure what he was actually going to do, only that this

206

was *the* moment – the moment he could do something to put Jim out of the picture. He walked past the laundry, and from the corner of his eye saw Jim painting the white walls even whiter, whistling to himself as he worked.

He took out his key to the cobbler's shop and went in. If he was seen there, no one would think it at all unusual – he could easily be doing an urgent repair.

He knew that from the shop he could get into the laundry through the back door: each shop had a small yard, and the fence between theirs was broken down. At first he decided he would creep up on Jim and attack him. But although he was strong and stocky, Jim was taller, even more muscular and in better condition, and it would have been his strength against Jim's.

For a while he sat on his stool, thinking.

Picking up a heavy hammer, he thrust it into the palm of his hand once or twice. That would give a death blow if he aimed well. Then he saw a box of matches and the pile of cotton waste that they used to polish shoes. He remembered that in their back yard there was a can of paraffin. His plan began to take shape.

Without a sound he gathered the things together and, keeping well out of sight, crossed the fence into the next-door yard. There were several empty paint tins close to the building. He threw some of the cotton waste over the tins, making sure that they made contact with the wooden door which led directly into the laundry, then spilled the paraffin over them. He took one tin, stuffed it with the soaked cotton waste and, having set light to it, threw it in through an open window. It landed in the back room of the laundry, on a pile of dirty washing. There was a flash, and within seconds smoke started to billow out. As he retreated, he threw a lighted match on the other tins and waste, and hurriedly retreated to his own side of the fence, remembering to take the empty can of paraffin with him.

The street was deserted as he left the shop, locked the door, and put as much space between himself and the laundry as possible. He ran south for a while, then by a circular route made his way back to Craven Cottages. As he turned the far corner into their street, he saw one or two men and women

207

rushing out of their houses, calling out to their neighbours. A thick column of dense smoke was rising a few streets away.

'What's that? What's wrong?' he asked an elderly woman.

'Don't know George, but there's a nasty fire somewhere.'

'I think it's down in Blythe Road, by the look of the smoke. Cor, look at them flames!' shouted a young boy.

Flames were indeed now to be seen over the rooftops.

'Let's go and see,' George suggested.

As he did so, Katy came rushing out with Mrs Cook.

'Where is it? Where's the fire?'

'Blythe Road,' George shouted as he and the boy ran off together.

'Oh, my God, I hopes it's not the laundry!'

Katy rushed on ahead of the slow-moving but equally anxious Mrs Cook.

'Stand back, stand back! The fire brigade'll be here any minute.'

An authoritative policeman was doing his best to keep the increasing crowd of spectators at bay while some local men were spraying water from a hose through the broken laundry window. It had little or no effect. Sparks flew onto the pavement among the spectators, smuts settled on their clothing and smoke stung their eyes, blotting out the bright afternoon sun. Excited boys cheered as the flames leaped higher – they were enjoying the rare sight.

Katy, arriving at the scene, started to scream for Jim, and, pushing the policeman aside, tried to get into the laundry. She was immediately soaked with water, which momentarily stopped her in her tracks. As she was about to rush on into the burning building, a man managed to catch her skirt. There was a ripping sound, but the material held and she was halted, just as a burning timber crashed to the ground in front of her.

'You don't understand – it's Jim! It's Jim! He's in there.'

But as she shouted, the crowd was distracted. Two waving arms had appeared at a tiny attic window, and there were screams for help.

'Look! Look! There's someone up there!'

'It's Aunty T! Oh, my God, I thought she was out shopping! Do something, please!'

Katy was frantic – both her lover and her guardian were in the building.

At this, George decided to play hero. He started to climb up a drainpipe, and failed. Meanwhile, another man had brought a ladder.

'Here you are, George – this is safer.'

George grabbed it and climbed up several rungs, avoiding the flames from the first-storey windows.

The admiring crowd gasped at such bravery – then gasped again as the flames and smoke got the better of the hero and he had to retreat. The screams got louder and more fearful. There was the clanging of a bell and the clatter of horses' hooves. Soon the practised firemen had several hoses concentrating on the flames, which by now were pouring out of all the windows. People were forced back from the heat. Mrs Cook arrived, panting heavily, weeping and crying out to the firemen to save her boy. She too had to be restrained from entering the building.

'Well done, lad!' A fireman patted George on the back. 'You did what you could.'

The bystanders agreed. George pretended to be modest.

'George, what's happening? Where's Katy?'

George looked around, surprised to see a shocked and astonished Jim. He couldn't speak.

'Your Katy's over there, Mr Cook!'

A little girl dragged on Jim's coat and pointed a few feet away, where someone had brought a stool and a glass of water for Katy, who was just coming round from a faint.

'Jim! Oh, Jim, you're safe!'

'Yes, darling, I'm here. I went over to the market for some more paint, and I've just got back. Is Aunty T all right?'

They looked up at the attic window. A fireman on an extended ladder was nearing it, kept damp by spray from a hose. The crowd was asked to be quiet. But before the fireman could reach the window, the screams suddenly stopped and Mrs Tyrrell's arms and hands disappeared into the black hole in the fiercely burning building. A gasp of shock and horror ran through the spectators. Some hid their eyes; others, transfixed, cupped their hands over their mouths. Men comforted women and women comforted their children, shielding them from the dreadful scene.

A deathly hush followed, the only sound being that of the crackling flames and the swish of the water. The fireman, in spite of all his training, had been too late and had, like George earlier, been beaten back by the devastating heat.

'Oh, no, not Aunty T! Surely she's alive? She's got out at the back, on the roof. Go quick, and look!' Katy tried to break away from Jim.

'Katy, it's no good. It's no good. Aunty T . . .'

And with a few broken words, Jim burst into tears, and the two lovers held on to each other in their grief. Mrs Cook, also in a state of shock, but relieved that her son was saved, put her arms round them and tried to comfort and calm them.

'Come away, my dears. Let's go home together.'

'But this is my home! I've lost everything. Oh, Jim, Aunty T will survive, won't she? She must have got away from the fire. She must have! She's not dead, is she? She can't be!'

Katy gripped Jim's arms in terror, trying so hard to believe that her beloved Aunty T had miraculously escaped the fire, and conjuring up a picture of her being led down the back roof to safety by a helpful fireman.

Jim and his mother knew otherwise. All Jim could do was to say, 'You've got me, darling,' and hold Katy tight.

'Oh, Jim, Jim – yes, thank God you're safe! But how did it happen?'

'Don't let's go into that now. Come and rest. Jim and I will take care of you,' Mrs Cook comforted her.

And she led her grieving loved ones back to their cottage – away from the crowd, the flames, the smoke and the pervasive smell of burning.

George saw them go. He was mortified by increasing terror as he realised that not only had his plan failed, but he had been the cause of Mrs Tyrrell's death – a woman against whom he had no grudge whatsoever. He had completely forgotten about her when he planned his dastardly act.

'So, my dear, another Sunday morning. Now what's the news?'

Sybil had cleared away the breakfast things, and as usual Emma was opening the carefully ironed copy of the *Observer* to read selected paragraphs to Lady Alston.

'Very little, I'm afraid,' replied Emma with a slightly bored sigh. She was keen to slip upstairs to her typing exercises before matins. 'Let me see. Alexander of Serbia has declared himself of age.'

'Has he? Um, *very* interesting! My dear, I am glad – that father of his . . . Well, we shall see what we shall see. What else?'

'Anglo-Italian agreements have been reached over Abyssinia.'

'And who's died?'

'Timothy Salter, aged two, of diphtheria. Oh, how sad! And Lady Littleton, aged ninety-four, very peacefully after a short illness.'

'About time too! She was an old battleaxe. I shall *not* be sending a wreath.'

Emma turned the page. Suddenly she gasped and Lady Alston noticed her turning pale.

'My dear, what is it? Has a war broken out?'

Emma started to shake as she took in a small paragraph at the bottom of the page.

London, Saturday afternoon. A small laundry in Blythe Road, Hammersmith owned by a Mrs Tabitha Tyrrell, burned to the ground this afternoon. Crowds watched as Mrs Tyrrell screamed for help from an attic window, but the London Fire Brigade failed to reach her in time. Before the fire brigade arrived, a local man, Mr George Cooper, commended for his bravery, had attempted to save her, but was prevented from doing so by the fierce flames.

Emma was stunned. She read the report to Lady Alston, who at once got up from her chair and put her arms round her. She had heard a great deal about Aunty T, and identified with Emma's grief.

'You must be proud that your brother did all he could to save her, my dear.'

Emma was astonished at George's actions – so he did have some good in him, after all!

'Now, Emma, you must decide whether or not you wish to go to your friend. If you would like to, then of course I give you my permission – but if you hope to attend the funeral you must leave Plymouth today. The accident was yesterday;

there will be a delay over the weekend, but I would think that the interment will be either on Tuesday or on Wednesday at the latest.'

Emma burst into tears. She had to think, and think fairly fast. Lady Alston rang for Sybil and ordered brandy and water, for Emma had had a severe shock.

Wrapping a huge black cloak borrowed from Lady Alston tightly around herself against the unseasonably cold May wind blowing across the platform of Paddington Station, Emma hurriedly walked to the forecourt and engaged a hansom cab to take her to Craven Cottages. It had been a long, tedious journey, made longer and more tedious by her grief and by flooding on the line; but she very much hoped she would be in time to pay her last respects to someone who had been like an aunt to her, and to give support to her best friend and her family.

It had started to rain by the time the cab pulled up outside the Cooper home. It was four thirty.

Will Cooper was on the doorstep.

'Ah, Em, you've come, you've come. Thank goodness you got my telegram.'

'Your telegram, Pa? What telegram?'

'The one I sent you early this morning.'

'I know nothing about it. We saw about the fire in the newspaper.'

'Awful, awful!'

'Where's poor Katy and Jim? I must go to them.'

'I dunno. Em . . . Em!'

He was crying and sobbing in a way unknown to Emma. He gripped her arms in desperation.

'Pa, what is it? Tell me what's wrong.'

Emma was confused. She could understand her father's grief for their friends, but his reactions seemed disproportionate. Breaking away from his grip she said, 'Well, I'll go in to Ma and comfort her.'

'Em, no, you can't! Oh, Em, Em!'

'Pa, what *is it*? Tell me *please*, why not?'

'Oh, Em!'

She was beginning to lose her temper.

212

'It's yer ma.'

'What? Is she . . .? I don't understand.'

'Well, no, we don't think so – they've searched the ruins . . .'

'Then where *is* she?'

'That's it, Em, we don't know – she's disappeared. No-where to be seen. The police are looking everywhere.'

Emma took her father firmly by the elbow while he made heavy use of his handkerchief, and they went into the house. There was a tray of tea on the kitchen table, and she poured a cup for herself and one for her distraught father. Her hand shook as she held the heavy pot. Sitting down, she tried to calm herself and the confused, unhappy man. For once in her life she felt sorry for him.

'Now, Pa, try to calm down and tell me what's happened. I know all about the fire and how brave George was, and I'll go to Katy in a minute. But what's this about Ma?'

'Well, I went out yesterday afternoon, and yer ma said she was going over the Bush to see that Mrs Black who's just had another baby. When I got back, the fire was over, and we was all trying to comfort poor Katy, and Jim was having to work with the firemen and the police and –' here he started to sob again – 'fixing things with the ambulance people who took Mrs T away.'

'Go on, Pa.'

'It got late and George and I got worried. Yer ma didn't come 'ome, so George went over to Mrs Black and . . . oh, Em!'

'Pa, *please*, I must know. Do try to carry on.'

'She'd never been there.'

'What? And are you sure she didn't go to the laundry?'

'Well, of course we told the firemen and they came back and made a thorough search. No trace of another body, thank God.'

'Thank God!' Emma echoed.

'But still no sign of her.'

'Did anyone see her in the street before the fire?'

'No, we've asked all round. That was why I sent you a telegram. I can't manage without you.'

'Did you send a message to . . .' She hesitated to mention her sister's name.

213

Her father picked up Emma's train of thought.

'No, I did not – not 'er. I won't have 'er in the house. You an' me, well, we've had our differences, but, girl, you're not sinful – at least as far as I can tell.'

'Oh, Pa, please! Sarah must know.'

'No, we'll cope with this in our own way.'

'Where's George?'

'Out looking – gone back to the old place to see if she's visited any friends over there.'

'But she wouldn't stay out for – what? Over twenty-four-hours.'

A sudden thought struck Emma. 'Pa, did you and she have one of your quarrels? Tell me, did you hit her?'

'No, Em, God's truth.'

She believed him.

'Is there anything else we can do?'

'Em, Em, darlin'!'

Katy came in and rushed over to her friend.

'Thank you so much for coming. Isn't everything awful?'

Katy's tired, red eyes and bedraggled appearance said a lot. Jim followed behind her, and the three of them hugged each other in their grief.

'To think that there's no Aunty T any more! And your ma . . . is there any news?'

'No. George has gone over to the Old Kent Road. All we can do is wait.'

'And pray,' added Will Cooper.

'Pa, go and see the vicar and talk to him. He might have some suggestions to make.'

'I'll do that.'

He stood up slowly, as if he had suddenly become a very old man, and left the house.

'Katy, I feel so very helpless. What worry and sadness we're sharing!'

'Em, you're here, that's the main thing.'

The grief-torn hours slipped slowly by. Katy and Jim left when Will Cooper returned from the vicarage. Emma made a light meal for herself and her father, but they ate little. All they could do was to sit and await news.

214

At about nine o'clock the front door rattled. It was George.

'Any luck?'

'No, Pa, nothin' – I went everywhere. No news. They'd not seen her. God, I'm dead beat!'

'Would you like something to eat or a bottle of beer?'

'No thanks, Em, I'm for me bed.'

He turned, patted his father on his shoulder and lumbered upstairs.

Emma had never known George refuse a beer before, and was surprised to see the almost affectionate gesture he made to his father.

'Pa, I think we should turn in. There's nothing more we can do tonight. In the morning there could be news.'

'You go up, Em. I'll sit here for a while. I don't think I'll sleep much, anyway.'

Feeling desperately sorry for her father, she bent over and gave him a kiss, and made her way upstairs.

She looked round her old room. It felt cold and damp, but it wasn't only the temperature that made her shudder. What memories! Before getting into bed, she got the back of the little chair firmly under the handle of the door.

'Bless us, bless us, Holy Mother of God! What *is* happening?'

The front doorbell of the Convent of the Sacred Heart was clanging ferociously.

'Whatever time is it?' Sister Bernadette asked herself as she shakily jumped out of bed. Finding her wrap, she pulled it round herself. The bell clanged yet again.

'I'm coming, I'm coming! You'll wake Reverend Mother if you go on like that.'

She rushed down the passage, her bare feet making little slapping noises on the cold tiles. She undid the huge lock, lifted the latch and cautiously opened the heavy front door. A cold wind blew raindrops into the hall as she did so.

Standing in front of her were a middle-aged man and woman, with another woman between them.

'Oh, sister, can you help us, please?'

215

'Why, my dears, what do you want?'

'Well, you see, it's this lady ...' The man started to explain.

Sister Bernadette looked at the woman. Her hands were cut and very dirty, her feet were swollen and obviously blistered and her hair matted. She was looking straight ahead of her as if staring into the far distance.

'You see, sister ...'

'Please don't say any more – bring her in. She's obviously exhausted and in trouble of some sort.'

The nun led them into a small sitting room which also served as the convent's office.

'We found her just now, didn't we, Pol?'

'Yes, sister, just down the road – by Hammersmith Broadway. Staggering all over the place. We thought she was drunk at first, but she ain't – is she, Alf?'

'No. No, sister, we wouldn't 'ave brought 'er here if she'd been drunk.'

'You've done the right thing. Leave her to me. We'll take care of her. You go home, and God bless you.'

'Thank you, sister.'

Sitting the woman down, Sister Bernadette showed the couple out.

Returning to her new charge, she took her hands. The woman flinched. The cuts were painful, and needed to be dressed. This done, she summoned Sister Ulrika. They offered the woman a glass of warm milk. Still she sat, looking blank – seeing no one, nothing.

Without success they tried to get her to speak. There was no response whatsoever.

'Do you think she's been cursed?'

'Sister Ulrika, how *dare* you say such a thing?'

'Shall we wake Reverend Mother?'

'No, let's wash her and put her to bed. She's obviously very tired and needs rest.'

'But what do you think is wrong with her, sister?'

'She's certainly injured, but not seriously hurt. And look at her poor feet – she must have been walking for miles. Do you know, I believe she's lost her memory. Let's take her to the guests' cell.'

216

Emma awoke to hear heavy rain hitting the window. Looking at the clock, she saw it was a quarter to seven. Sadness, gloom and worry pressed down on her.

I'll run a bath, that'll – She checked the thought, scolding herself for her stupidity. That was something she couldn't do, here in Craven Cottages. She crossed the room to the washstand, poured cold water from the china jug into the matching bowl and, shivering all the while, washed, dressed and made her way down to the kitchen, where she lit the range and started to prepare some breakfast.

It was now Tuesday morning. She, her father and George had spent Monday travelling around various parts of London calling at hospitals, police stations and even shops, in the hope of finding Mrs Cooper, but to no avail.

Will Cooper joined her in the kitchen.

'Did you sleep, Pa?'

'For an hour or two, girl.'

'I've made some porridge – have some?'

'Yes.'

She stirred in a generous helping of golden syrup and milk and handed it to her red-eyed, confused father.

'We did everything we could yesterday.'

'I know, Em.'

'Today is Aunty T's funeral. Will you go?'

'I don' think I can face it – we've so much trouble on our own plate. They'll hunderstand.'

'Yes, I think they will.'

George joined them, doing his best to appear calm.

'I'm going right round to the police station again. No, I'll not stop for breakfast, Em. I'm off.'

In addition to carrying the guilt of Mrs Tyrrell's death, George was having to cope with the mystery of his mother's disappearance. He was plagued with the thought that it too was his fault. Was she dead? Would she ever come home? To avoid breaking down completely, he concentrated every waking moment on trying to find her.

Late that afternoon, Emma was looking out of the parlour window. She'd just seen Katy, Jim and Mrs Cook return from the funeral and was about to go in to them to make their tea as promised, when a hansom cab drew up outside.

217

The cabby opened the door and helped a nun to get out. Emma then saw a very fashionably dressed young woman leave the carriage. At once she recognised her sister.

'Sarah! Sarah, darling!'

The unlikely couple were supporting Mrs Cooper, one on each side, and making slow progress up the little garden path.

'Sarah! Oh, Ma! I'm so glad to see you! Where have you been?'

'Keep calm, Emma dear. Ma needs to be kept very quiet.'

Emma looked at her mother and saw her blank expression.

'Ma, it's me, your Emma.'

There was no response.

'I don't understand.'

'Emma darling, this is Sister Bernadette, from the Convent of the Sacred Heart in Hammersmith Road. We'll explain, but let's get Ma into the parlour first.'

'I'll find Pa.'

She called to her father and told him her mother was found but also warned him of Sarah's presence.

'Not going in there, Em. No, I won't.'

'Pa, you must.'

He calmed down when he saw Sister Bernadette. It was she who told the story.

'Mother Superior suggested we should see if Mrs Cooper had a pocket in her skirt. Why I didn't think of that before I just don't know – I'm really sorry.'

'Never mind, sister. Please go on.' Will Cooper spoke in his best Sunday going-to-church voice.

'There was only one thing in her pocket.'

'It was one of my postcards – a picture of me. Ma happened to be carrying it around with her.'

Will Cooper grunted.

'But sister, how *ever* did you find Sarah?' asked Emma.

'Well, of course, none of us at the Sacred Heart knows anything about the theatre, but on the card it mentioned the Gaiety Theatre, so we sent our messenger boy with a letter to Miss Cooper, just hoping that perhaps she might know who our visitor was. It was our only hope.'

'I went to the theatre as usual and there was the letter.

218

This morning I went to the convent, and spent some time with the sisters and Ma – and here we are. We can't thank you enough for what you've done, sister – can we, Emma?'

'It's all God's work, Miss Cooper.'

'Yes, that it was, thank you, sister,' Will Cooper responded.

'Mr Cooper, your wife has a very serious memory loss – it's evident she recognises none of you. She will need a lot of care and attention. Our doctor saw her. He says no medicine will help, it's just a matter of time.'

Sister Bernadette got up to go. As she did so, Sarah pressed a five-pound note into her hand.

'Sister, don't think of this as payment, but as a small contribution to your order. We are deeply indebted to you and your community.'

The three women made their way into the passage. As the nun left, Sarah turned to Emma.

'I'll not go back in there. There'll only be a row if I do and that won't help Ma. Let me know when he's back at the shop. Will you able to cope for a few days, or shall I hire a nurse for you?'

'Now I know Ma's back, I'll write to Lady Alston in the morning. I think I'll be able to stay here for a week or two – I hope so.'

'Give my love to those dear souls next door. What a dreadful time it is for them!'

Sarah slipped away just before George came back from another of his fruitless searches.

All that evening Emma sat with her mother. She re-dressed her cuts and her blistered feet, which were beginning to heal. She comforted her, she talked kindly to her, she did everything she could think of to try to get some kind of response. All to no avail.

Susan Cooper just sat. She sat upright looking straight ahead, her hands on her lap. Her eyes didn't move. They showed no emotion – not even apprehension or fear. Emma fed her, which wasn't easy. At around nine thirty she and her father guided her upstairs, where Emma washed and undressed her, and helped her mother use the chamber pot before gently easing her into bed.

A little later Will Cooper joined his wife, slipping between the sheets as carefully as possible so as not to disturb her.

Having done everything she possibly could for her mother, Emma had time to think and to write to Lady Alston. She hoped that her employer would be sympathetic and understand the situation. As she wrote, she realised that no one knew how long it would be before her mother's memory returned. Was she in duty bound to stay looking after her until that happened? She knew that her father would never let Sarah come and stay. No, everything that had to be done fell to Emma, and she knew it.

During the days that followed, Emma evolved a routine of washing and feeding her mother, shopping, cooking for the family, attempting to awaken her mother, and spending a little time with her dear, sad friend Katy.

She had an extremely sympathetic and understanding letter from Lady Alston, who realised that Emma certainly had to help her family at such a difficult time, though she hoped it wouldn't be too long before Emma could return to Plymouth, since in due course the time would come when Lady Alston would need help to pack and return to London. She added that she had sent a message to the Newcombes telling them of Emma's difficulties.

Emma was reassured. Her work at home was very tiring and strenuous, and it was beginning to seem pointless. After about a week she became almost numb and, although she was extremely patient, frustration was beginning to engulf her.

She managed to slip away to visit her sister.

'It can't go on for ever. It mustn't,' said Sarah as she fixed her false eyelashes. 'Darling, you're being simply marvellous, but you know you will soon have to begin to think of yourself. If within a few weeks there's no change, I'll go and have it out with Pa. I'll hire a full-time nurse – I can afford it. I don't want you to lose your job – your future is at stake.'

'He'd never let you hire a nurse. It's all up to me.'

And somehow Emma knew that that was the crux of the matter.

220

Chapter Seventeen

A few days later, Will Cooper went down to open up the shop as usual. He prepared himself for a long day's work. George had gone down with a bout of flu and was staying in bed. London was still in the grip of unseasonable weather and it was just as cold inside the shop as it was in the street. The atmosphere was dank and damp, and the smell of burnt wood and crumbled masonry had replaced the more familiar smells of leather, rubber, sweaty boots and shoes.

He surveyed the party wall he shared with the wrecked laundry. The ancient paintwork was blistered and peeling, and here and there deep cracks had appeared. He decided that he would have to get a builder in to stop up the cracks, then George could scrape and repaint the wall later on.

He shivered and went to the little junk room, which was really a rather large cupboard, to take out an old oil heater that they used in winter. He remembered emptying it of paraffin a few weeks earlier when the weather had, for a while, become warmer. Placing it by his bench, he went to the back door to get the can of paraffin to refill the heater. To his surprise he discovered that it was empty.

That was odd. He felt sure there would be plenty – in fact, he knew there would be, for he himself had drained the contents of the heater only a few weeks earlier.

Well, he thought to himself, I'm getting older – I must have forgotten.

He closed up the shop, put up the old notice 'Back in 5 mins', walked up the road to the local ironmonger and had the can refilled.

He returned to the shop. He couldn't find his matches for some time, but did so eventually, lit the heater and got to work on a pair of children's boots.

In about a half an hour he'd finished the work. He reached for the tin of black boot polish and the brushes and made the little boots look like new. To finish them off properly, he turned round to the back of the shop where they kept the cotton waste. There was none.

'Well, old man, are you turning stupid?' he asked himself, and started to look round amid the piles of tools, the sheets of rubber and leather hides, and all kinds of bits and pieces necessary for a respectable boot repairer to carry on his trade. No cotton waste.

Will Cooper was mystified. He got up and stretched. He was still desperately tired and unhappy, unable to understand his wife's condition. He took a breather, strolling to the very back of the shop and out into the little yard. He looked at the sad mess next door. It was a complete ruin, black, charred – awful. Grief hit him, and for a while he just looked and felt very sad, wondering why it had to happen. Mrs Tyrrell had been such a nice, kind, honest woman – and generous, too.

'The Lord works in a mysterious way,' he sighed. Then he saw something blowing in the chilly wind, something light and fluffy. It blew towards him and he picked it up. It was a half-burned piece of cotton waste.

He was puzzled. Mrs T wouldn't have used cotton waste. Examining it more closely, he recognised its mixture of colours – and a smudge of brown boot polish on it. Then he remembered the empty paraffin can, and how at first he couldn't find the matches. He sank down on his stool and buried his head in his hands.

'No, no – dear Lord, no! Not that! He can't be *that* bad. Oh, my dear Lord, deliver us from evil.'

He recited the Lord's Prayer.

He was a broken man.

George spent several days in bed. Emma put his sudden infection down to the shock he'd had, and thought he was overtired from his exertions on the day of the fire. Since he

222

ate virtually nothing and stayed in his room, he made little extra work for her. He wanted to see no one, and turned over to face the wall when she offered him food. He really did look extremely pale and wan – not at all like George.

After four days he began to look better, and got up on the following Saturday afternoon. Yes, he had been ill, but he had also had a lot of time to think. In fact, he had done nothing but think about the murder he'd mistakenly committed, and to wonder if his mother's illness was also the result of his action. He couldn't help thinking it was.

But what was done couldn't be undone, and in spite of all his guilt he still felt extremely smug that in the eyes of the neighbourhood he was a hero, and now, in addition, the family was getting a great deal of sympathy over Mrs Cooper's condition. He looked forward to going back to the Havelock Arms, where his cronies would stand him rounds of porter – even the odd whisky if he was lucky – and he'd receive many pats on the back. Yes, his standing in the community would improve, and that was no bad thing – especially as he now knew that Lil had done him quite a lot of damage. Oh, she'd gossiped – she must have if his pa had got to hear about that night. Thank goodness Pa didn't seem to have heard any of the tittle-tattle about him and Sarah and Emma! But people's memories were short – for good and bad – and that, George knew, was both for and against him at present.

The fact that he'd been ill would gain him sympathy. He could hear in his mind the comments that had been going on in the last few days: 'Oh, that George Cooper! Wasn't he brave? Did you see it in the paper? And now he's got this terrible flu – the smoke must have got on his lungs, poor man. Let's hope he'll get well soon.' George knew exactly how they would all react. And, of course, when he did reappear there would be all the more glory.

He decided to get up, and went down to the kitchen to get rid of the thick black stubble that had accumulated over his face in the last four days. He felt rejuvenated by his rest. He was alone in the house apart from his mother, in the parlour, who, as ever, sat motionless, hearing and seeing nothing. Emma was next door, with Jim, Katy and Mrs Cook. His father, he knew, was making up for lost time down at the shop. He'd been working single-handed all week, and it was a busy time of year for them – people found their winter boots and shoes were getting down at heel after the pounding they had taken since the autumn.

It was teatime when the three of them assembled.

'Nice to see you up and about again, George.'

Emma was wielding the willow-pattern teapot. 'Here you are, drink this. There's some Bovril sandwiches, and we can finish off that fruitcake.'

'Thanks, Em.'

He grabbed a thick round of bread and Bovril and scoffed it hungrily, then fell upon the cake and slobbered his tea. With his mouth still full of cake and tea, he went on, 'Yes, I'm feeling much better. Going out for an hour tonight.'

'Oh, you are, are you?'

'Yeah, Pa. Any reason why not?'

'George, I want you back by half past eight sharp. You've not been near the shop for days, and we have business matters to discuss.'

'But, Pa, I wants to go out and have a bit of fun, and it's gone six already!'

'There'll be time in plenty for that later on. I want to tell you about the takings and the work on hand. Eight thirty sharp, George, and if you're not here I comes up the pub to fetch you – right?'

He hit the table several times with a stubby finger as he spoke, and narrowing his eyes, looked straight at George, who could tell he meant to be obeyed.

'Yes, Pa.'

The furious George rushed out of the kitchen and slammed the front door.

'He's treating me like a kid,' he muttered under his breath.

Just before eight thirty Emma took her mother up to her bedroom to give her a blanket bath and settle her in for the night. The nightly ritual was a depressing task for her, and her thoughts always slipped back to when her mother was well and active. Had she known what Emma was having to do for her, she would have been shocked.

'I'm in the parlour.'

Since they were little, the three Cooper children knew that they were for it if their father wanted to talk to them in the parlour. He sat enthroned on a large chair with curved arms, emphatically the head of the household.

He was lighting the lamp as he spoke and asked George to pull the curtains.

'Now, look here! No, you stand there – don't you sit down. And take your hands out of your pockets.'

'Jesus!' George blasphemed under his breath.

'Don't you dare take the name of the Lord in vain, my boy. I've got something to say to you. Something important.'

'Why, Pa – are the takings down?'

'Nothing to do with the takings.'

'What then, Pa?'

George was beginning to feel a trickle of concern. Had his pa found out? No, not possible – he'd covered every inch of his tracks.

'I'll come straight to the point.'

Will was sterner than he'd been since the day he threw Sarah out.

George meekly cooed, 'Yes, Pa, of course, Pa. What's wrong?'

'My son, I have very good reason to believe that you deliberately started the fire. Oh yes, I know you was brave – everyone says so. But George, was that bravery the result of guilt?'

'Pa, Pa! What are you talking about? Me . . . me start the fire? How could I have? I was here, taking it easy – up in me room.'

Doing some quick thinking, he went on, 'You ask Katy. I saw her in their garden – I spoke to her!'

'Um, I dare say. But I have evidence, *solid evidence*, that you did.'

George was panicking. He was also a very good actor.

'But Pa, I couldn't have done.'

'Why then was the paraffin can empty? Why was them matches on the floor and not where I'd left them? And why was there bits of burnt cotton waste – with, I may add, brown boot polish on them – floating about the yard? Only you could have done it.'

George felt weak. Was he blushing? Were his lips trembling? He turned a little so that the light of the lamp wasn't falling on his face.

'Pa, I don't know what you're saying,' he protested after a moment's thought. 'The paraffin? The matches? The cotton waste? We have lots of cotton waste.'

'We don't any more – it's all gone. Gone to make the fire that killed Mrs T.' Will Cooper's voice deepened dramatically and he clenched his fists as he spoke the last sentence. Even more severely, he went on, 'And for all we know, because of your dastardly act, who knows, it could be all your fault that our dear mother is . . . well, like she is.'

'No, Pa, no! You've got it wrong. Not me! I wouldn't do a thing like that!'

George knew he had to be very convincing if he was going to get away with it.

'Pa – no!' he anxiously repeated. He put his hand over his heart. 'God's honour, it wasn't me. Someone must have broken in and used our things. Yes, that's it – someone must have broken in.'

His father fetched the large family Bible from its special plush-covered occasional table.

'Repeat after me – put your right hand on the Bible. Remember this is your solemn oath, my son.'

'Yes, Pa.'

'I, George Cooper . . .'

George repeated the words as his father went on, '. . . do solemnly swear that I did not cause the fire that killed Mrs Tyrell.'

Believing that no one would ever dare repeat an untruth under solemn oath on the Bible, Will Cooper sighed with relief.

'Thank you, my son. But we must find out who did it, and you must help me. It was no accident.'

George felt less comfortable than he'd done all week.

Emma picked up the letter. It had a Plymouth postmark, and she recognised Lizzie's writing. It was the most cheering thing that had happened to her in weeks. She took it into the parlour, where as usual her mother was sitting totally motionless. Lizzie said that she, Eustace and Bertram Webber had had a meeting to discuss plans for the recital, and she was not to worry because everything was under control. Lizzie and Eustace had worked out what they were going to play, and Joe was to design and decorate the printed programme. The evening promised to be very splendid and grand with supper afterwards. She told Emma that her friends were constantly thinking of her and that they hoped her mother would soon recover.

Emma was delighted to hear this news, but was concerned that she was letting them down, having promised to help organise the event. She felt compelled to reply to Lizzie right away, and thought that she ought also to send apologetic notes to Bertram Webber and Eustace. She was reluctant to write to Eustace, and argued with herself that it wasn't strictly necessary – besides, she didn't know his address. Bertram's she did know. Momentarily her thoughts slipped back to the night when she'd been in his rooms. But write to Eustace she must, in spite of her dislike of the fellow. She could enclose his letter with Lizzie's.

Eustace was making his way home after giving Lizzie her lesson.

I must wait till I get home, he told himself. I must wait. This is precious. I can't believe it! She's written to me! It's no good, I can't wait any longer, I must read it *now*.

He looked round for a suitable place to open his treasure. The street was crowded with busy shoppers. He was passing St Andrew's Church, so he entered.

The church was deserted. He went into a pew, knelt and said a quick prayer, then with loving care opened the letter. Emma had written merely a short note saying how pleased she was about the plans for the concert and how sorry she was to be inconveniencing them, but that she hoped to be able to come back to Plymouth at least for a little while before the summer, which she knew she would have to spend in London with Lady Alston. She ended the letter very formally with 'yours sincerely'.

'Sorry – you, Emma, saying sorry to *me*! Never will that be necessary.'

He got up and totally forgetting where he was, heard himself shouting out, 'Emma, Emma, I love you! I will always love you no matter what happens!'

There wasn't the slightest hint of a stammer as his voice echoed round the large church.

Chapter Eighteen

Every morning Emma hoped and prayed that this would be the day when her mother would give some sign of recognition – a little smile, a spoken word, no matter how hushed.

She was fast becoming desperate, and it wasn't only her mother's condition that weighed down upon her. She regularly wrote letters to Lady Alston, who until recently had been kind and understanding; but in the last letter she had received, there had been a hint of impatience in the old lady's comments. Emma knew how difficult it was for her to write letters. Her sight was so poor and her hands so crippled with arthritis – and it was of this she complained to Emma. She also pointed out that the time was fast approaching when she wanted to return to London, and she hoped that Emma could come back to Plymouth to organise the packing and the move. Mrs Newcombe had lent her Laura to give some assistance, and Lizzie had undertaken to buy and arrange flowers every week – not that she arranged them at all well!

'But surely, Emma, your ma will get well soon? Is there nothing else we can do?'

'I honestly don't think so, Katy; it really is a question of time.'

'Well, if you asks me, I think you should go back to Plymouth anyway, and let Sarah take over for a bit.'

'You know that can't happen. I hinted to Papa the other day that we should get a nurse and he wouldn't hear of it. "I'm not having any strange women in *my* house," he said.'

'Selfish and stubborn as ever.'

'He is, I'm afraid. But Katy, it's my duty. I know Sarah is

229

dying to help, and it's really wonderful when she comes round when Pa is at the shop, but it's fallen to me to do this, and do it I must.'

'Well, Jim and me, we thinks you're wonderful. But Emma, dear Emma – do think of your own future, and of Lady Alston too.'

'She'll be coming back to London in a couple of weeks, and wants me to help her with the move.'

'You must go back to her – you must! Otherwise who knows what will happen?'

Emma thought about what Katy had said. She knew that the chances of her getting away were small. If only her father weren't so stubborn, if only he'd allow Sarah to hire a nurse, which she was so willing to do ... She longed for her life with Lady Alston. She was grateful that Katy was next door living with the Cooks, but they were trying to come to terms with their own tragedy. How she missed Lizzie and her former elevated life, wearing her grand dresses – she'd recently bought some simple ones to wear while she did all her nursing, cleaning and cooking. She even missed Bertram. He had written to her – and so had Eustace.

She was resigning herself to the thought that her life with Lady Alston and her Plymouth friends was a thing of the past, never to be resumed.

As the days passed, she became more depressed. With her mother, she put on an air of cheerfulness, but her efforts were totally fruitless.

One day at the very end of the month the ultimatum came. She opened the letter. The message was simple.

If you cannot return to Plymouth within the next three days, then I am afraid that you are no longer in my employ. I am sorry about this, Emma, but I simply must replace you. My health is such that I cannot survive without help.

'Oh no, no! *Please*, not that!'

Emma rushed up to her room and flung herself onto the bed, distraught with grief and disappointment.

'But darling, I'm quite sure that Ma won't be like this for ever.'

230

'Sarah, it's been weeks now. I can see no improvement and I know you can't either – just look at the poor dear!'

'Let's go into the kitchen, Emma.'

Sarah thought that although their mother was not responding she might hear what they were saying.

'I really feel it's all my fault that you've lost your lovely job, Emma.'

'Don't, Sarah, please. We both know it's all because of Papa's stubbornness. I know I'm doing the right thing by Mama, but . . .'

'But you have made a very great sacrifice.'

Emma nodded sadly.

'Look, Emma, once Ma is better I'm certain you'll get another post. Why, you have so many skills now, and there's your typing.'

'I suppose so. But Sarah, it won't be the same, it really won't.'

She burst into tears, the first time she'd done so in front of another person. She'd managed to be brave, even in front of Katy – *especially* in front of Katy, who had her own sadness to cope with.

'Are you certain Lady Alston won't take you back?'

'I simply daren't ask her. Besides, I expect she's engaged another companion by now. Why should she take me back? I honestly can't blame her for one moment.'

Sarah sighed. 'Darling, I must go. I'm late as it is. I'll come again tomorrow, and sit with Ma. You and Katy might like to go out for an hour – it'll cheer you both up.'

'Thanks, Sarah.'

Emma closed the front door behind her sister. She looked at her mother from the passage. She walked back to the kitchen and started to peel some potatoes for her father's and George's tea. Tears and sobs overcame her again. She dropped the knife on the table and allowed her hands to sink into the bowl of muddy water and potato peelings.

'Oh, it's so unfair! So *unfair!*'

Two days later, just after eight o'clock, Will Cooper and George left for the shop as usual. Emma cleared up their breakfast things and went upstairs to wash and dress her mother. Having done that, she guided her down the stairs and sat her in the large chair by the kitchen range.

'I'll stoke up the range and boil the kettle for tea,' she said.

She went about her task, shovelling the coal and filling the heavy black kettle.

'Ssstoke . . . boil.'

Intent on her task, Emma didn't hear the nearly inaudible words. But, as she turned from the tap with the heavy kettle, her mother clearly said:

'Put on the kettle, dearie. Yes, p-p-put on the kettle.'

'Ma, oh, Ma!'

Emma dropped the kettle on the hob and hugged her mother. She noticed that her eyes were moving, but her body was motionless.

Emma knew she had to contain her excitement and her joy. Trembling, she quietly said, 'Yes, I'm putting the kettle on.'

'Then we'll have a cup of tea, dearie.'

Emma knew her mother never called her 'dearie'. The only person she had ever called 'dearie' had been Aunty T.

Mrs Cooper started to breathe deeply and then quickly. As if in a trance, she said, 'Burning – I can smell burning.'

Emma was both terrified and fascinated. Mrs Cooper moved to the edge of the chair, Emma still holding her around her shoulders. The breathing deepened and became frenetic.

'We must get out, come on, get out. No, no, dearie, don't go upstairs, don't go upstairs! Don't!'

Mrs Cooper was becoming hysterical and shouting.

'It's all right, Ma, it's all right!'

'Don't worry about the money, don't worry about the money, don't go upstairs. It's not safe, it's not safe.'

There was a pause.

'No, no!'

Mrs Cooper let out a heart-rending scream. Emma took her weight as all the tension drained out of her body. Beads of perspiration turned to heavy streams and ran down her face. Emma guided her back to a comfortable position in the big chair, grabbed a damp cloth and put it on her mother's forehead. After a few minutes, as Emma's pulse increased, her mother became more and more relaxed; then, for the first time for weeks, she looked at her daughter.

'Em?'

'H-hello, Ma.'

'Em, it is you? Where . . .?' Her expression was deeply puzzled.

'Oh no, no, no!' She burst into tears.

After comforting her, Emma said, 'It's all right, Ma, you're back with us again.'

'Back? Have I been away?'

'Yes, but don't worry for now. Let's have that tea.'

That evening Will Cooper, having been to church to thank the good Lord, came into the parlour and sat holding his wife's hand while George and Emma sat nearby. Mrs Cooper had been dazed but gradually became more and more coherent as the day wore on. They didn't want to tax her, but were anxious to know what had happened.

'It's 'ard to remember, Will.'

'You said you was going to see Mrs Black's new baby.'

'Mrs Black's new baby? Did I?'

George was doing his best to keep calm, although he thought that any minute his game would be up. Quietly he said, 'Yes, Ma, that's what you said.'

'Went to the laundry to see Mrs Tyrrell, show her the picture . . . picture of Sarah. Yes, that's it, I wanted to show Aunty T . . . picture of Sarah.'

'The postcard, Pa.' Emma got up and went to the sideboard drawer to fetch Sarah's photograph. She gave it to her mother.

'Yes – Sarah. That's it.'

'Went in. Mrs Tyrrell said she'd stoke the range, put on the kettle and make tea for us. Then . . .'

'Go on, Susan, go on.'

'Burning, we smelled burning. I saw flames . . . said, "Let's go." She said, "The money, I must get the money . . . in the attic." I said, "No, don't g-get the money." She went, she went upstairs . . . I ran out the back. Saw the floor collapse – she was all in flames.'

At that her expression became blank and she started to cry. 'Don' remember any more . . . no more.'

'Nothing about where you went after that? Nothing about the man and woman who found you – or the nuns?' Emma asked gently.

'No, Em. The nuns? What nuns?'

They told her. She was amazed. She remembered nothing after having seen Mrs Tyrrell in flames falling through burning floorboards.

'Ma, I expect you're tired. Let me get you up to bed and undress you.'

'Emma, you *undress* me?' Her mother's expression became its old alert self. 'What do you want to undress me for? And why are you 'ere? Has Lady Alston given you the day off?'

'Never mind that now, Ma. Do let me help you to bed.'

'Certainly not!'

'Coming, Will?'

'Yes, Susan. And you two, you fall on your knees and thank the good Lord before you gets into bed.'

Lady Alston replaced the neatly printed calling card on the silver tray.

'Very well, Stratton, show her up.'

'Miss Sarah Cooper, my lady.'

'Lady Alston.'

'Miss Cooper, how nice to meet you. Emma told me such a lot about you when we were together.'

She surveyed Sarah through her lorgnette and couldn't fault what she saw – a superbly dressed, elegant young woman with perfect features who moved liked a gazelle.

'Please sit down, my dear. What can I do for you? Have you news of Emma for me?'

'Yes, your ladyship, I have. At last her mother's memory has been restored. It's been a miracle, it really has. She has now fully recovered.'

'I am happy for you all. It must have been quite dreadful.'

'Yes – especially for Emma. You know, Lady Alston, everything fell upon Emma. Her father and I –'

'Yes, I do know all about that. It has been a very sad situation.'

'Lady Alston, is there any chance that Emma could come

234

back to you? She would so like to do so. She is dreadfully depressed.'

'Why are *you* asking me? Why can't Emma come herself?'

'Emma doesn't know of my visit. I came because I know she doesn't feel she should ask you.'

'This is a very difficult situation, Miss Cooper. I don't think it will be possible for Emma to return.'

With that, the double doors to the drawing room opened.

'Lady Alston, I've pressed your gown for this evening.'

'Thank you, Maisie. Miss Cooper, may I introduce my new companion, Miss Maisie Greenway?'

Sarah gave the girl a polite nod.

'That will be all, Maisie. I am sorry, Miss Cooper. I did feel that Emma and I shared a very special kind of relationship, but you see . . .'

'Say no more, Lady Alston, I quite understand. I wish you good morning.'

Stratton showed a very unhappy Sarah to the door. She took a cab to Craven Cottages. During the journey she tried hard to work out the best way to tell Emma the disastrous news. Sarah was now well connected and since Emma was so accomplished and had an excellent wardrobe – always an asset – she felt she would be able to find her sister another post; but it wouldn't be the same, as Emma had said a while back.

'Dear Emma, I am so very, very sorry. But, you know, I'm sure I'll find you someone else – someone younger, who perhaps travels and will need your typing skills? That would be exciting.'

'Sarah, you know how well I get on with older people, and I'm not keen to travel abroad. No, just leave me, please. I'll stay at home for a while.'

'But what about George? I'd hate you to have to cope with him all over again.'

'He's changed. He's been so quiet for ages now – especially since the fire. He's not been near me.'

'Umm, I'm sceptical. Oh, I believe you, dear, but a leopard can't change his spots. Meanwhile, I don't care how you're feeling now, I'm going to start asking around. Now you've tasted the rich life, you simply can't give it up, any more than I could, and you know it.'

Emma, tortured and upset though she was, knew her sister was right.

Chapter Nineteen

Will Cooper finished off his bread and ham and big slice of cheddar cheese, and folded up the cloth. Relaxing for a while before starting work again, he picked up a newspaper. His eyes rested on the report of a fire in the City. It brought back memories of the laundry fire and George's reaction when he had challenged him. Doubts were returning to his mind.

At that moment a small boy rattled the shop door. He got up to let him in – the latch was a bit stiff and the child could not lift it.

'Sole and heel, please, Mr Cooper. When can Ma have them, please?'

'Friday afternoon about four, son. Mrs Gregg, isn't it?'

'Yes, Mr Cooper.'

The boy ran out of the shop into the sunlit street.

He shut the door behind the boy. His thoughts returned to George and his excuses.

'No, Pa, someone broke into the shop and took the paraffin and cotton waste . . .'

Someone broke into the shop . . . someone broke into the shop . . . His thoughts lingered on the words as his hand still held the latch. If someone had broken in, the lock would have been damaged or a window broken. There had been no damage or evidence of entry anywhere. The only people to have keys were himself and George. George, then, was lying. But Will Cooper found it difficult to accept the fact that his son should be so wicked. Arson was a very serious criminal offence, and it had caused the death of an innocent woman – manslaughter, or even murder. And if that was the case, then

George was also guilty of causing his mother's illness, which in turn had lead to Emma losing her job. George'd get years in prison – he might even swing for it.

Will Cooper had never known such worry and confusion. He sat down on a stool, his head between his hands, not knowing what to do. He knew he *should* report all he knew to the police. But could a man accuse his own son?

If he did the right thing, he would have to cope with the scandal. The local people had loved Aunty T, and if George was found guilty of killing her, Will's trade would slip away and he and his wife would have nothing for their fast-approaching old age. No, he could never live with the shame and disgrace. Not only would George be in prison – or in Hell – but Will would have to struggle and do all the work by himself. If only Emma or Sarah had been sons to carry on the business! Employ a stranger? No, he was too old to train an apprentice – that wouldn't do – and he certainly wouldn't get enough business to pay for an experienced shoe repairer.

Everything he had built up while they had been living in Hammersmith would be ruined. He would never be able to face the community, much less the church, yet if he didn't do the right thing, would he be able to face his Maker when the time came?

There had been a lot of gossip about how the fire had started, but no one suspected arson. The common theory was that one of the coppers had boiled dry and eventually exploded, setting fire to the shop. The luck of the devil was certainly on George's side. Will Cooper was the only one to know the truth.

The truth – if that was what it was – could stay locked in his heart for ever, if he chose to let it. That was one solution. The next thing he had to decide was whether to confront George with his latest theory. If he forced his son to confess, then he would always be in his power – no bad thing, knowing the life that George was living these days. With power over him, he could make sure that he could rely on George's loyalty when he became old and could no longer work.

But how could he live with the awful secret? That would be a heavy cross to bear. Obstructing justice was a sin as well as a crime. His own soul would be blackened by his son's actions, and that was very serious indeed.

'Hello, Pa. 'Nother lovely day.'

George burped noisily as he walked briskly towards his bench.

'George, look at me.'

'Why, Pa? I've seen you before – and you've seen me.'

'George, I'm being serious. Very serious.'

'Not again! What now? What have I done wrong now? I works hard enough, don' I? An' I fixed that bloody wall where it got scorched.'

'Yes, George, you works hard – we all knows that you works hard.'

'Well – go on.'

'But you tells lies, lies!'

His father's voice rose in anger and tense emotion. He gripped the edge of the bench as he stood up to confront his son.

'Me? Lies, Pa? No, never. Truthful, I am. Couldn't face God if I wasn't.'

'Face God? You face God! You got to face me first.'

'Well, what's it all about then? Spit it out!'

George, feigning uninterest, put his feet up on his bench and swung back on his stool, pretending to pick at some thick dirt under his nails with a matchstick.

'You lied to me.'

'Well, so you keep saying – but what about?'

'I puts it to you that you did start that fire. Oh yes, you said someone broke in, and I, like a fool, believed you. But where, George, *where* did someone break in?'

Will Cooper walked over to his son, his face within inches of his son's.

'*Where* did someone break in? There was no broken lock. No smashed windows. Only you and me have got keys. If anyone got in, it was you. *You* started that fire.'

'No, Pa! Honest, I didn't.'

George, now sitting upright on his stool, tried to fend off his father's accusations.

'You did it, George. I knows in me heart you did it. I been asking myself why you did it. Now I think I know. You

239

wanted that Katy – oh yes, you wanted Katy, an' it was revenge and jealousy. You was jealous of Jim!'

George sighed heavily and furiously. 'So what if I was? What if I did?'

'I just don't know how you can live with the fact that you killed Mrs Tyrrell. Not to mention all the misery you caused to your dear mother, and Em and meself.'

'I didn't mean to kill Mrs Tyrrell. And I wasn't to know that Ma would go and see her before visiting Mrs bloody Black – that's not my fault. Nothin's my fault. Anyway, what will you do about it? Report your own son to the police and see him in the clink for years on end? How would you cope then, old man? All right, say you tell the police. Think of the shame I'll bring on you and the family.'

'What I do about it is up to me. I shall have to think about that – give it a lot of thought.'

'You'll never be able to show your face in the neighbourhood or the church again, will you, once I'm in prison? Have you thought of that, Pa?'

'Don't you worry, I've thought of that all right – and a lot more besides, like the way you'll make your dear mother suffer yet again.'

Looking shiftily around the shop, anywhere but into his father's eyes, George said, 'I really didn't think about Mrs T, Pa. All I knew was that Jim was in the laundry, painting. Yes, I wanted Katy – have done for ages, but she wasn't having any. Yes, I was jealous – I still am.'

'So you wanted him out of the way.'

'Pa, I done it on the spur of the moment. But then everything got out of hand. I did try to save Mrs T.'

'Oh yes, you tried to save her, but only to avert suspicion from yourself. Well, you've got away with it so far. I'm not saying I'll go to the police, but I'm not saying I won't, either.'

'Pa, keep it to yourself, eh? Please. I'll be good, I promise.'

'You, promise? Don't make me laugh. But until I tells you otherwise, this awful secret will remain between the two of us – and you thank the Lord I'm being so merciful.'

Without another word George picked up a child's shoe and got to work.

240

Will Cooper knew that he could not face up to the degradation of all this coming out into the open, and the loss of face that would follow. He decided to live with his son's guilt.

Mrs Cooper usually stayed up rather later than her husband. Earlier in her marriage she would find some excuse – there was always mending to do, or a bit of cleaning she'd forgotten which must be done before joining her husband. This was her simple way of keeping down the size of her family. If she got into bed about twenty minutes after him, she knew he'd be asleep and snoring, and would make no sexual demands on her. She was proud of the size of her family. Far better three children than a whole brood of ragamuffins.

Even nowadays she went to bed after Will; any lovemaking that went on occurred on Sunday afternoons when they went for their 'nap'. That night as she entered the bedroom she expected to find Will lying on his back as usual, snoring his head off.

She was surprised to find him kneeling by the bed, still praying.

He didn't hear her come in, nor did he look up as she undressed and got into bed. Eventually he rose stiffly from his knees and joined her. She noticed that his eyes were red.

'Are you troubled Will?'

'No, I'm fine,' he replied, biting his lower lip. But she knew he wasn't: turned away from her, his head buried deep into his pillow, he was sobbing.

'I believe you're thinking about Sarah again, is that it? Now that Emma's home I bet you've been feeling that you wish you could see her a bit more too, in spite of what you calls her sinfulness,' she said, none too gently. 'You know how successful and beautiful she is, an' you're feeling guilty about being on bad terms with her. Asking the Lord for forgiveness, were you? Well, that's no bad thing. You treated her rotten – and you know it!'

He made no reply. She put her hand on his shoulder and firmly turned him towards her.

'Will, look at me! Why don't you make it up with Sarah? Say you're sorry. It'll do you no harm to climb down. We could all be family again – that is, if Sarah'll make it up with

241

you. Please, Will, for my sake. I am proud of you, you know that. We've achieved a lot, what with this pretty house – some different to the Old Kent Road, eh?'

'Oh, Susan!'

Will cried and cried, trying hard to restrain his unmanly sobs. It was true about Sarah – at least, perhaps it was true – but now he had another problem to cope with.

'You close up at six. I got some business to attend to. See you at home, round half past eight. Tell your mother I've gone out, she'll understand.'

George was terrified. Had his father decided to go to the police? Nervously he asked his father where he was going.

'Never you mind. You just stay here and finish off the work. Don't you go sloping off anywhere. Hear me? I mean it.'

George had to agree. If he disappeared, and he knew there would be time to do so, he'd have every policeman in the country on the lookout for him. If he stayed put ... well, perhaps his father was only trying to frighten him. Marginally it was the lesser of two evils. His work for the rest of the day was not up to standard.

'Excuse me, Miss Cooper, there's a man down at the stage door who wants to see you. He says he's your father.'

'Pa here! My God!' Shakily, Sarah told the stage door-keeper to show him up.

Will Cooper stood at the door of the dressing room nervously clutching his hat, feeling totally out of place in the strange atmosphere of lights, glitter, silk and satin, piles of hats and feather boas and the smell of Sarah's greasepaint.

'Pa, I am surprised. Never thought you'd cross the portals of this den of iniquity, as you'd call it. Well, now you're here, sit down. I can spare you a little while before I finish getting ready. What do you want?'

'I've come because your mother wanted me to.'

'Oh, not because *you* wanted to – is that it? Well, what do you want? Some money or what?'

'Sarah, this is difficult for me.'

'Oh, so you don't think it's difficult for me too?'

242

'We was talkin', your mother and me. She said I ought to be ashamed of myself – you being so successful and beautiful, and that. Not that I approve of all this, mind you, it's sinful.'

'Is it sinful to make people happy, Pa? Well, never mind that now. Go on.'

'Your ma says she wants us to make it up, she says it would be better for us as a family if . . .'

'Well?'

'If I apologised for being so hard on you.'

'Bit late in the day for that, isn't it, Pa?'

All the while Sarah knew what her proud father was going through – to climb down like this and actually come to the theatre! If she did agree to forgive him, she knew that on the credit side it would be easier for her to see her mother and Emma, but she was torn three ways: she loved her mother, she still felt a lot of animosity towards her father, and she was totally unable to forgive her brother. But there was something far worse on her mind, and before she could make things up with her father she knew she would have to bring it out in the open. If her father couldn't accept what she had to say, then they would stay as they were for ever, going their separate ways.

'Pa, you know as well as I do there were other reasons why I left home. Oh, yes! I know you hated my dancing, and I knew that I was good enough at it to make a living, but there was another reason I left so suddenly, and you know what it was. You knew that George was interfering with me.'

'No, never! What are you saying? George is a good boy.'

'Pa, you know he's not.'

'I don't! He'd never touch you, you lying bitch!'

'Don't raise your voice. I happen to be respected here, in my own domain.'

She narrowed her eyes grimly as she spoke.

'You know full well that George got at me on the night before I left home for good – and on lots of other occasions too! Do you want me to spell it out? No, that's not necessary, is it? Because *you saw it all*!'

'What?'

Will Cooper was shaking all over and very red in the face.

'You partitioned off that bit of the room, but what you

243

didn't realise was that from my bed I could see through the little heart-shaped hole in the door. Night after night I saw you spying on us. Oh, you'd make sure you crept away in good time before George left me, and how you never disturbed Ma, goodness knows – but you saw. I know you saw, and you can't deny it. By the way, this is something Emma doesn't know. I didn't bother her with the sordid details. I want her to still think reasonably well of you, even if you did knock her about just before she went to work for Lady Alston.'

He was astounded. He hadn't had the slightest idea that Sarah had discovered his voyeurism. He hung his head in shame.

Sarah went on, 'So perhaps you can understand why I cleared out, and why I thank God Emma got that job – just in time. But now, goodness knows what'll happen if George gets up to his tricks again. Thankfully so far that doesn't seem to be happening.'

'Emma? Emma? What's she got to do with it?'

'You don't know about that? I'm surprised. But of course, Pa, there's no hole in the door of Emma's room at the cottage, so you didn't get your cheap thrill, did you? Yes, Emma and Katy came to see me for advice when Emma was bothered by George, who started up his old tricks with her. At least she got out before . . . well, before he really harmed her, but now she's at home again . . . well, we'll just have to hope for the best, and that she'll make a fuss if he as much as goes near her. Unlike me.'

'Sarah – oh, Sarah, stop it, stop it! I'm so ashamed!' Instinctively he covered his ears with his hands.

'You've every right to be. And you go on about sin and the good Lord. Well, Pa, you've got a lot of praying to do. If you were a Catholic I'd suggest that you went straight to confession, but there you are. At least you've had the guts to come and see me, and we've cleared the air.'

She paused for a moment, then, rubbing salt into her crushed father's wounds, she went on, 'Oh, and don't think that Ma doesn't know all about George. I went to see her not long after Emma left. But you thank the Lord that I didn't tell her her old man was a peeping Tom. Only you and I know that, and I suggest we keep it that way.'

'What can I say?'

'"Sorry" would help, you know. You may feel a little better now that your guilty secret is out, Pa. But If I do decide to make it up with you, I can never ever forgive George for spoiling me. I can never forget how terrified I was. I was fortunate not to get pregnant. That would have given you something to think about. It could have blighted me for ever. As it is, I'm doing fine, thank you. But after what George attempted with Emma, I don't think she'll find it at all easy to become close to a man or fall in love.'

Sarah was near to tears. The scene had been a tremendously strenuous and emotional experience for her, yet she was proud that she discovered the strength to confront the pompous hypocrite with his sick weakness.

'Pa,' she said quietly, 'what happened to me all seems a long time ago now. But do understand how degraded I felt, and how disappointed that my upright, churchgoing father could be so despicable, at a time when I was suffering from all those problems with George. Thank God I was talented enough to make my own way in the world, even if it was in a way you disapproved of.'

'You forgive me then? You forgive me?'

Will Cooper fell to his knees at her feet where she sat, turned away from her dressing table.

'I'll try hard, Pa – but it won't be that easy.'

'Thank you! Oh, thank you, my girl! Oh, my Sarah . . . I'll tell Ma she can come and see you.'

'Oh, do. But actually we do see each other quite often, you know – every first Monday, while you're down the old Kent Road!'

He should have been furious, but only heaved a sigh of relief.

'I'll come and see you very soon, I promise. Perhaps you can repair some shoes for me.'

'Willingly, willingly, Sarah!'

'Goodbye, Pa.'

A tearful father gazed at his daughter. They did not embrace or even shake hands. He left the theatre relieved in many ways, but bearing yet another burden of guilt and shame.

Chapter Twenty

Emma's life had now fallen into the bland, boring routine which had been all too familiar before she lived and worked with Lady Alston. She was in no way the lively young woman of last year, nor was she the young girl her mother knew when they first came to Hammersmith to live. She had nothing to look forward to.

Not long after Lady Alston had given Emma notice, all her things had arrived at Craven Cottages by a carrier. It was heartbreaking for her. She felt as if a part of her had died, the part that had been sustained by her interesting and exciting life. Among the cases was her typewriter. This was her one joy, and although she felt little hope, she made herself practise every day. Her skill was improving rapidly – but to what end she had no idea. It was just something useful and sensible to do.

She was delighted that her mother was now completely recovered. Their relationship was as good as it had been before she left home, if not better; Mrs Cooper felt sorry for her, and sad that because of her Emma had missed out on the biggest chance of her life.

Sarah had the unhappy task of breaking the news to Emma that Lady Alston had a new companion. That was a black day, indeed, but Sarah was constantly buoying her hopes, doing as much as she could to find Emma another suitable job.

The summer sunshine, the green trees and the flowers did little to cheer Emma. Letters from Lizzie, who was working hard in Plymouth, brightened her life; she gave Emma a great deal of support and encouragement, but every time Emma had news from her friend, she felt the remoteness of the chances of seeing her again.

Several weeks went by, with Emma becoming more and more depressed, relieved only by Katy, who, because she was so much in love with Jim (they planned to marry soon), was much happier.

One morning Emma had taken all her best gowns out of her tiny wardrobe to press them and to check that no moths were invading them. She became tearful, thinking that they would go out of fashion long before she had the opportunity to wear them again.

A knock on the front door made her jump. Blowing her nose and wiping her eyes, she answered it.

'*Toby*, oh, Toby! How wonderful to see you!' She took both his hands in greeting.

'Miss Emma, it's nice to see *you*.'

'What brings you round these parts? How's Lady Alston? And Sybil, and Mrs Green?'

Out on the street she noticed a cream-coloured horse pulling the smaller of Lady Alston's carriages.

'Surely nothing's happened to Beauty?' Without giving him a chance to answer, she ushered him into the parlour. 'Now, tell me everything – how are they all?'

Toby said everyone was well, and so was Beauty, but she was having a holiday in Devon and would stay down there. The new horse was called Pearl and was borrowed from Lady Cricklewood.

'I've a message from Lady Alston. She says can you come and see her this afternoon, at three?'

Emma's eyes were now glistening with joyful emotion. Toby was an emissary from the world she felt had cast her out, and she was thrilled that Lady Alston wanted to see her.

'Miss Emma, I don't rightly know, but . . .' He hesitated.

'Toby, do go on – *please*.'

'Not sure as I should say, really, but, well, it's that Maisie Greenway. Sybil hates her.'

That didn't surprise Emma, knowing how badly she and Sybil had hit it off in her early days.

'Well, I expect Sybil will get to like her in time.'

247

'It's not only that. You see – oh, Miss Emma, I don't like to gossip.'

'Please tell me, Toby.'

'Well, all right, but strictly between ourselves. Miss Maisie, well, she's so . . . so *stupid* – not like you.'

That made Emma smile.

'Yesterday she ruined one of her ladyship's ball gowns' Toby continued, – she scorched it very badly, and her ladyship had wanted to wear it to Lady Cricklewood's first reception of the season. There was a dreadful row.'

'Toby, you know it's easily done. I'm pressing my dresses now and I must be careful.'

'But that's not all. She's broken two cut-glass vases, she can't do the flowers, and when she does she forgets to put water in the vases so they die too quickly. Then she forgot to put stamps on four of her ladyship's letters, and her friends were furious. I could go on and on . . .'

'I see.'

'So, Miss Emma, can I tell her ladyship that you'll come?'

'Of course I will, Toby. Thank you.'

'I'll be back at two thirty to call for you.'

'So nice to see you, Miss Emma!'

'Thank you, Mr Stratton. Is her ladyship in the drawing room?'

Sybil appeared.

'Emma, dear!' She hugged her. 'It's been awful, it really has.'

'Now, Sybil!' Stratton shook a finger at the exuberant parlour maid.

'Emma.'

'Lady Alston, thank you for asking me to call on you. How are you?'

Emma could see that she looked drawn and tired.

'Somewhat exhausted, my dear.'

She paused. Emma was sitting on the little chair she'd sat on the first time they met.

'My dear, I'm glad your mother is quite recovered. It must have been a dreadful time for you. I was so sorry for you.' She took a deep breath akin to a sigh. 'I was also sorry I had to dismiss you, but . . .'

248

'I do understand, Lady Alston. You couldn't go on for ever without help and we certainly didn't know how long Mama would be ill.' Feigning naivety, she continued, 'But now you have a new companion – that's nice.'

'Well, no, Emma, it's *not* nice and it *hasn't* been nice. I've had to dismiss her.'

Emma then heard the stories she'd been told earlier that day.

'So, you see, she was worse than useless, and caused me so much embarrassment – stupid girl!'

'I am sorry to hear you've had so much trouble.'

'Emma, I too am so very sorry – that I dismissed you. I really should have been more patient. So ... would you? Could you, that is, if you can see your way clear, come back?'

'You really would like me back?'

'Please, dear Emma, if you'll come.'

They hugged each other, tears merging on their cheeks as they did so.

'Now, Ma, are you sure you can cope without me?'

'Of course I can, girl, and I'm relieved. Oh, Em, you don't know just how awful I've felt about all this. Me and yer pa, we were both so pleased to see you getting on like you have, then there was the accident and, well, it was all my fault for calling on Aunty T before –'

'Don't go on, Ma, please. Do you think Pa will mind?'

'Tell him your news yerself, he's just coming in now.'

'Well, girl, you've done yer duty like a good Christian. We'll miss you, but now ...' He paused. 'Now things is better between me and yer sister, I looks forward to Sunday teatimes when we can all get together sometimes.'

'Thank you, Pa.'

'You go, girl. You've proved yourself to me, Ma and Lady Alston. Cor, I bet she had trouble with that other little empty-head!'

'She did, Pa!'

It took no time at all for Emma to get back into her old routine, and as a celebration she now had several new summer outfits in her wardrobe.

249

To Emma's delight, Lady Alston said she would like to see Sarah's show, and with three neighbours – Commander Sebastian Gasslot and his wife Ella, and a younger gentleman, the Right Honourable Alexander Staveley – they made up a party. It was Emma's duty to book the box and a table at the Café Royal for a theatre supper afterwards.

'My dear, do you think Sarah would join us for supper?'

'I'm quite sure she would. May I write to her?'

The show was quite magnificent. Emma's heart was bounding with pride as she sat on the edge of her seat waiting for Sarah's first entrance. A round of applause greeted her, and there was another when she started her increasingly famous skirt dance, making several complicated turns and waltz movements while wearing a very full, long, accordion-pleated circular skirt which she held in her fingers. It rose and fell, making wonderful flowerlike shapes, as she floated around the stage.

As the curtain went down on the first half, the Honourable Alexander said to Emma, 'I say, Miss Cooper, don't you feel jolly proud of that sister of yours? She's a real winner, isn't she, what?'

'Yes, Mr Staveley, she is – and a very generous and kind person, too.'

'Bet she has an admirer or two, eh, what?'

'I would think so, but I do not intrude on her personal life.'

'Quite right, my dear young lady, quite right!'

Then he and the Commander left the box while the ladies stayed seated. Conversation was light-hearted, mostly centring on the delights of the show. Emma glanced across the circle to the box opposite, having been aware of someone looking at her.

'Lady Alston, may I please borrow your opera glasses?'

'Of course, my dear. Is there someone you know?'

'I think so.'

She focused them.

It was, as she suspected, Bertram.

'Lady Alston, it's Bertram Webber. Oh, he's getting up.'

There was more than a hint of nervousness in her voice.

'I expect he's coming over to speak to you. How *nice!*'

He was. There was a knock.

'Do come in, Mr Webber.'

Lady Alston introduced Ella Gasslot. Having politely acknowledged her, he turned to Emma.

'Miss Cooper, I am so delighted to meet you like this. I was going to call on Lady Alston tomorrow. I have some business to finalise with her. But perhaps I may hope to see you afterwards?'

'If my duties permit, Mr Webber, of course you may.'

Emma nodded very stiffly and formally. The interval bell rang.

'I must leave. Until tomorrow then, Lady Alston. Goodbye, Mrs Gasslot.'

Thunderous applause greeted the cast as they took numerous curtain calls, and there were cheers for Sarah when she was led forward by the leading man. A liveried footman brought a huge basket of red roses onto the stage for her; she graciously took them and bowed to the audience again – then, turning straight to Lady Alston's box, gave a deep curtsy specially to its occupants.

The atmosphere of the Café Royal was something that Emma had not encountered before. The décor consisted entirely of rich, red plush, gold carving and mirrors. The air was thick with expensive cigar smoke and French perfumes. The chatter was lively and noisy, highly educated accents vying with the clatter of cutlery, glass and china. Here and there flames flared up beneath pans of exquisite food being cooked at the tables by waiters in long, white aprons while others scurried to and fro. There were very few empty tables.

'This way, Lady Alston,' said the head waiter, who knew her well. 'How nice to see you again – and looking so well. We've not had the pleasure of your company for well over a year. If you'll permit me, you look as beautiful and as young as ever.'

'Ah, Armand – the flatterer, as ever! But if what you say is true, then it's all due to my young companion here, Miss Cooper.'

'Miss Cooper, delighted.'

The head waiter bowed low and, taking Emma's hand, repeated her name.

251

'Are you by chance related to Miss Sarah Cooper?'

Blushingly Emma made the appropriate reply.

'Ah, I can see the family likeness. She comes here so often.'

'She's joining us this evening.'

The group settled at the table. Emma was in seventh heaven. Her eyes darted around, taking everything in, and when she caught sight of herself in a nearby mirror, she asked herself, Is this really me?

'Bosie, over here, dear! No, not that table – it'll be far too draughty.'

The rich Irish tones of Oscar Wilde's voice made heads turn as he entered. Seeing Lady Alston, he swept over to greet his old friend.

'Rosamund, my dear! How wonderful to see you catching up with life again!'

'Oscar – how nice. And dear Lord Alfred too.'

Lord Alfred Douglas bowed, somewhat sullenly.

'Masses of news. Can I come to dinner? I've not seen you for positively years.'

'Of course.'

Turning to Emma, the notorious playwright exclaimed, 'Young lady, you look charming. What a simply glorious gown!'

With that, he and his companion found their table.

If Oscar had turned heads on his entrance, Sarah made the diners gasp, the women admiring, the men lost in romantic and sexual reverie. She was wearing a pale silver-grey cloak edged with ostrich feathers and a matching gown trimmed with purple velvet. Armand whisked away the billowing cloak as she joined her hostess and the other guests.

Lightly kissing Emma and Lady Alston, she sat down and was bombarded with questions about the show, what she was going to do next, who was to play whom. The menu chosen, the supper was soon under way.

Halfway through the main course of jellied chicken with champagne, Armand brought Sarah a note. She read it, and asked for notepaper and an envelope to reply. Excusing herself momentarily from the rest of the table, she wrote a sentence or two, signed and sealed it, and gave it to Armand, who immediately disappeared with the envelope.

The evening wore happily on, and the meal ended with a dessert of syllabub and macaroons.

Emma, having had two and a half glasses of champagne, felt a little light-headed by the time coffee was served. She'd had no chance to speak to her sister at all intimately over the meal, but as they rose from their table she was delighted to hear that Sarah would be having Sunday-afternoon tea at home with their parents.

'Lady Alston, I fear I must leave. Thank you so much for such a happy evening.'

She bade her farewells to the rest of the guests and walked ahead of them from the restaurant. When the ladies had been handed their cloaks, Sarah, still a little ahead of the others, stepped into Regent Street to be greeted by a top-hatted servant, who gestured her towards a waiting carriage drawn by two black horses. As she stepped into it, Lady Alston and Emma saw a somewhat plump, bearded face smilingly welcoming her. Lady Alston at once recognised Sarah's escort, but, realising that her younger sister hadn't, decided to say nothing. The carriage clattered away towards Piccadilly.

'Thank you, Lady Alston, the arrangements are now complete. I have settled the matter with Messrs Stillwall, Stillwall and Keen, and they in turn have informed Coutts. I will collect the papers tomorrow and take them to our bank, where they will be more accessible to you over the winter months, should you need to revise anything. I gather that duplicate copies will be in safekeeping at Coutts. That is what you require, is it not?'

'Yes, Mr Webber; thank you. You are very efficient.'

'I do what I can. Lady Alston, I wonder if Miss Cooper is in the house at present?'

'She's in her suite. No doubt you would like to see her.'

'I would, Lady Alston. Our plans for the recital are progressing, but as Miss Cooper has been out of touch for a while – I gather her mother has quite recovered – may I take her to tea to discuss further the arrangements for the evening?'

'By all means take a cup with us, Mr Webber. Miss

253

Cooper is not always free to leave the house; like you, she is very efficient, and I give her a great deal to do. And next week we are giving a dinner party.'

'I understand.'

Lady Alston rang for Sybil, who summoned Emma to the drawing room.

'Miss Cooper. How fortunate I am to be able to mix business with pleasure!'

'Pray sit down again, Mr Webber. Shall I ring for tea, Lady Alston?'

'For yourself and Mr Webber, dear. I am a little tired. The heat is exhausting me today, so I will rest. Mr Webber, we shall meet again in Plymouth in the autumn, I expect.'

'Lady Alston, it's been a pleasure.'

He rose as she got up from her chair and turned to leave the young people. Smiling wryly to herself, she pretended to yawn volubly and went to her room.

'Miss Cooper, our plans progress. I met Miss Newcombe the other day, and she was able to tell me what music she and Mr Beaumont had decided upon.'

'She told me. That's good – I mean, that she and Mr Beaumont have planned their programme.'

There was a slightly awkward pause.

'I'm staying with my aunt, you know, not far from here. I was so pleased to see you at the theatre the other evening. Wasn't it a marvellous show? Especially Sarah Cooper . . .'

'She's my sister, you know.'

Bertram gasped. 'I'm amazed! But now you mention it, I see the likeness.'

'Thank you. Perhaps so. We're very fond of each other.'

Sybil brought tea, and Emma served it – rolled bread and butter, delicious little maid-of-honour cakes. But conversation did not flow.

At last Bertram asked, 'How is your typing progressing?'

'Very well. I have quite a high speed and I'm accurate. I cannot thank you enough for changing Lady Alston's mind about my learning.'

'You know, you are a very remarkable and very individual person, Miss Cooper. Modern in outlook – very modern.'

'Both Miss Newcombe and I feel much the same way

254

about the role of women in the future, and we want to play our part in the development of greater independence for women, but she has a brilliant mind. She's academic – oh yes, and artistic, as you know. We want to be women of the twentieth century, Mr Webber – and that century is not so far away, is it?'

'No, Miss Cooper, it is not. Miss Cooper, please . . . may I call you Emma?'

'That is a little forward of you, Mr Webber.'

A hard line appearing between her brows, Emma froze at his request. She wondered if Lady Alston would approve. She thought for a moment, and although she wasn't enamoured of the idea, she didn't want to seem priggish.

'However, yes, you may – but perhaps, in front of Lady Alston, *Miss* Emma might be more suitable.'

She wasn't going to let him have it all his own way, especially since she was now – very belatedly – realising that he was attracted to her. She didn't want to encourage him, but she recognised that he was beginning to do well in his profession. He was polite, smart and made a good impression – and, yes, good-looking, with a fine aquiline profile. And his eyes, which had frightened her at the start, now seemed to her to take on a gentler, kinder look, in spite of the fact they were so penetrating, while the heavy brows gave him a certain smouldering darkness which she found both intriguing and difficult to cope with.

'Emma, I am to holiday in London for two more days. Would it be possible for us to go perhaps for a drive and afternoon tea? I have my aunt's carriage at my disposal – may I call for you tomorrow? It would give me great pleasure.'

Emma was perplexed. In a way she wanted to go, yet she was fearful. She realised that her fear sprang from her unfortunate experiences with her brother, and Katy's words rushed through her mind: 'It only *nearly* happened to you. Be thankful for that, and don't let it spoil your life.' Taking a deep breath to calm herself, she answered:

'Well, I don't know whether Lady Alston will approve.'

Bertram leaned towards her. 'I have already asked her permission, and she says you may accompany me.'

255

'Well, er, Bertram . . . thank you. You may call for me at two thirty.'

He got up, bowed, took her hand and kissed it. Emma, sitting characteristically upright, rang for Stratton to show Bertram out.

He was both light-hearted and light of foot as he all but danced out into the late-afternoon sunlight. He was making slow progress by his standards, but Emma was no ordinary, flighty girl. Would she prove too much for him? Would she turn out to be bossy and dominant? Was he about to bite off more than he could chew? Well, he would take the risk. It was not simply that his access to certain important documents of Lady Alston's had persuaded him to put two and two together and make five, without having to assume very much. He also very much wanted to take Emma in his arms and kiss her. However, he decided that if she allowed him momentarily to hold her hand or steady her arm, he would be making considerable progress.

But now, here he was in London! Why not a visit to the Bedford Music Hall? Why not a little pleasurable adventure afterwards with a pretty young filly wearing a red hat? He'd go back to his aunt's to change and then London would be at his feet.

The large, open carriage drawn by two chestnut horses impressed Emma. She took her place with Bertram, smart in white with a college tie and boater.

'I thought we would have tea at the Richmond Hotel. It has a pretty garden reaching down to the river, and tea is served on the lawn.'

'I'll enjoy that, Bertram, thank you. This is a beautiful carriage.'

'Yes, my aunt is – well, quite well off, you know. Lives not far from Regent's Park – a very convenient area for a visitor to London. She always lets me use rooms at her house and one of her carriages when I'm in London – provided, of course, she's not going off to polo or whatever. She enjoys a good social life, goes to the races, Henley, Goodwood, things of that sort. Perhaps Lady Alston knows her.'

'I doubt it. Lady Alston's friends are either in society or

the arts – the arts mostly. She doesn't usually mix with people from the City or in commerce. You did say that your uncle was in banking, did you not, Bertram?'

'Yes, he's chairman of the Dorset and South Devon. He's keen for me to make my way as he did – no short cuts, you know.'

'That's good. It is very character-building to make one's own way.'

His uncle was indeed in banking – the manager of a small branch in Islington.

They drove west, passing Hammersmith parish church, then crossed the huge structure of Hammersmith Bridge and drove alongside the river. At Barnes, some rowing crews were practising. Having driven through Richmond town and up the hill, the carriage halted on the front drive of the hotel, and they were escorted by a pleasant receptionist into the back garden, where under huge willow trees they took a table beautifully set for tea.

While eating smoked-salmon sandwiches, Bertram kept the conversation light by talking about the Richmond Theatre – had Emma visited it? No? He'd been taken to a pantomime there when he was ten, and could fully recommend it. Richmond Park was also delightful as a place of recreation. At last, he decided that the time was right to find out more about Lady Alston.

'A wonderful person, Lady Alston, isn't she?'

'Yes, she's so kind and very generous.'

Generous: that was a word he wanted to hear.

'I expect she gives large donations to charity.' He knew she did from her bank statements. 'And no doubt she has many relatives to whom she is equally generous and kind.'

'She does most certainly give a lot of money to charity – to children's charities, mostly, but also for the betterment of conditions of the poor in the East End. We supported a charity fête a few weeks ago, in just that cause. It was most enlightening. She's also very generous to animal charities – for the improvement of the conditions of working horses, in particular, and free veterinary treatments to poor people's pets.'

'But surely her relations must command at least equal sympathy and assistance?'

257

'She hasn't any relatives at all. Oh, look, Bertram – there's a big paddle steamer. It must be an outing of some kind. Can you hear them singing?'

Emma thought that perhaps Bertram was getting a little too inquisitive. However, Bertram needed to ask no more questions. No relatives! He was delighted to hear it.

The passengers on the paddle steamer were singing the 'Eton Boating Song', and as it came to an end, 'The Boy I Love Is Up in the Gallery' was wafted to the listening couple on the warm summer breeze. Emma smiled to herself as she heard the singers' thick cockney accents, and thought of one of the rare summer outings she'd had as a child with Sarah, her parents and George – down to Southend by boat.

The conversation turned once again to trivial subjects. Bertram was enjoying her company, and got the impression that she wasn't exactly bored.

She wasn't. She had relaxed quite a lot in his company, but still found it extremely difficult to look him straight in the eye. She didn't give herself away by blushing, and now, because she was fast becoming more confident, she realised that she could face up to the intensity of his gaze.

About an hour and a half later they were driving up Kensington High Street. She felt him gazing at her once more. She sat up even more upright, and said, 'You know, you really shouldn't gaze at me like that.' But all the while she felt flattered.

'How can I help myself? You're so beautiful.'

She knew he meant it. She also realised that she was beginning to succumb to his charm.

'But I wish you wouldn't, it's dreadfully embarrassing.'

'The coachman's back actually gets very boring after the first half-mile.'

That made her laugh.

'You should laugh more – it suits you; and that smile of yours really is bewitching. Do you know you've only managed to smile at me three times since I've known you? Honestly, I think I'm due for a few more. You're in credit and I'm definitely in debit, putting it in banking terms!'

So he has a hint of a sense of humour after all, she thought.

They turned the corner into Queen's Gate.

'Emma, I *have* enjoyed our afternoon. Thank you for allowing me to escort you.'

As he spoke he cautiously took her gloved hand in both his own.

'Thank you, Bertram. It has been delightful, but . . . excuse me.'

'No, don't take your hand away – please, Emma!'

In spite of feeling attracted to him, nervousness and fear of men overcame her once more.

'I'm sorry, but I must. I cannot let you hold my hand in that way. Please, Bertram. Do try to understand that I cannot be anything more than a friend to you. I cannot think of you – or any other man – in any other way.'

'I'll try, but I don't really believe you.'

'Don't let's spoil a lovely outing, and let us look forward to the recital; but please, Bertram, strictly as friends.'

He sighed deeply, released her hand reluctantly, descended from the carriage and opened the door for her, taking her hand again to help her down.

'Until Plymouth in early October?'

'Until October, Bertram; and thank you again.'

He kissed her gloved hand and saw her to the door. Getting back into the carriage, he made sure she saw him ride away.

'You can stop here, my man,' he called to the coachman when they were just a little east of the Royal Albert Hall.

'Right you are, guv'nor. That'll be one pound eleven shillings and sixpence, please. Any time you wants to hire me for the afternoon, you know where to find me.'

Chapter Twenty-One

'Oh, Lizzie the views were astounding. I'd not been to the Alps before, but they are quite b-b-beautiful. I stayed at a boarding house right on Lake Lucerne. There were little flowers everywhere and I swam in the lake – it was wonderful. I feel t-terribly well, you know.'

'You look it, but . . .'

Lizzie examined his face more closely. His skin was clear and tanned, and somehow he looked less plain. Then she realised what it was.

'Yes, you do look well – but Eustace, where are your spectacles?'

'Oh, that was a d-disaster. I was on the lower slope of an Alp, lying flat out on my back enjoying the sun. I'd taken my spectacles off and put them on a nearby rock. All was very quiet, then I heard a sort of snuffling noise and a strange crunching, and when I looked up I saw a large mountain g-goat with the spectacles in his mouth. I got up so quickly that he started to run off with them. Well goats can run very fast and he got away. I think he p-probably ate them. Other tourists helped me to look, but we couldn't find them any-where. One man said that the same goat had eaten his wife's hat, complete with a hatpin, the d-day before. So that I could read on the train, I bought a large magnifying glass in Switzerland before I left. Look, here it is. I'm still waiting for my new spectacles. I went to Coombe's, the opticians, yester-day as soon as I got back, and I'll be getting them the day after t-tomorrow.'

'Eustace, I am sorry. Please excuse me – I must get a hanky!'

Lizzie rushed out of the nursery to find Joe and her mother downstairs. They looked surprised to see her bending forward holding her tummy, and thought for a moment she was feeling sick.

'What do you think?' A goat ate Eustace's spectacles!'

'Typical. But he only needed to wait . . .'

'Don't be vulgar, Joe!'

Then Mrs Newcombe couldn't hold back any longer, and the three of them laughed and laughed.

Lizzie smoothed her green velvet dress, patted her hair and took a deep breath.

Bertram was addressing the packed hall.

'My lords, ladies and gentlemen, may I present Miss Elizabeth Newcombe.'

Emma standing by her, momentarily took her hand. 'Good luck, Lizzie!'

'G-good luck from me t-too, Lizzie.' Eustace gave her a warm, brotherly hug. Walking as tall and as confidently as the butterflies in her stomach would allow, she made her way onto the platform where the full concert grand piano, black and shining, was ready.

She stood by its side and bowed to acknowledge the applause. She recognised many faces in the audience, and gave a special smile to her mother and Joe sitting at one end of the second row. Not far away she caught a glimpse of Professor Rowe, seated next to Lady Alston.

Remember what Professor Rowe said; don't start to play until they've really settled down. If someone coughs, wait, hands poised over the keyboard. Make sure your dress is spread out and that you are sitting really comfortably with the stool at precisely the height you want it. Take your time. Don't be rushed.

All was at last completely quiet.

The opening of her first piece was a series of restrained arpeggios, then it melted into a slow and very beautiful melody. She got through it, and went straight into the second of the *Songs Without Words*, which contrasted vividly with the first – a delightfully happy piece.

The audience was bewitched. It had already warmed to

her, and as she struck the final chord and lifted her hands from the keys, a storm of applause rewarded her. It gave her confidence for her third piece, one that she had worked hard and long on – the *Rondo Capriccioso*. She loved it, and could tell that the audience loved her interpretation of it. The applause that followed seemed almost undignified from a 'society' audience.

After this first group of pieces, she returned to the ante-room, where Eustace and Emma had been listening. She was breathless and excited.

'Lizzie! Oh, Lizzie, you're doing so *well*! It's all so beautiful!'

'Quick, Emma – a glass of water, please. Thanks. Yes, I think it's not too bad, though I did slip two notes halfway through the *Rondo*.'

'D-don't worry, it was fine.'

'Right! Now I'm ready for the big one – this really is a test.'

She returned to the platform. Once again with her hand on the piano, she bowed to her audience. As she raised her head, a glint of gold flashed, caught in the gaslights as they were dimmed. She blinked. By now the audience was quietening.

'Oh!'

Her mouth opened wide as she let out a loud cry of surprise. The audience gasped, fearing something was wrong.

The light had caught the gold braid on the sleeve of Captain Newcombe's jacket. Her parents and Joe just grinned, and those of the audience who had noticed him slip into the hall or had seen an extra chair brought for him during the pause, smiled warmly to each other. Lizzie wanted to rush down from the platform and hug her father, but she realised that would be childish and unprofessional – indeed, she had been unprofessional enough as it was! Blushing deeply, she addressed her audience.

'Ladies and gentlemen, I do apologise. My papa has just appeared – and I simply didn't know he was about to return home. I am sorry.'

Cries of 'Ah!' and warm applause.

Lizzie, now seated once more at the keyboard, took several

262

deep breaths and waited – rather longer this time – for her audience to settle before striking up the slow opening movement of the *Moonlight Sonata*.

Mrs Newcombe looked at her Peter, knowing him to be so proud of their daughter. It was a strange first meeting for them after a tour of duty, but wonderful that he could be there on this special evening. She hadn't been at all sure that he would arrive in time for the concert. Much depended on his duties and the time that HMS *Rameses* docked – it could have been on the midnight tide. As it was, all was well. They gazed lovingly at each other and squeezed hands as their daughter continued to captivate her audience.

As she finished the sonata, the applause was greater than she had expected. She took two or three bows, and exchanged a broad smile with her father, then once more joined Eustace and Emma in the anteroom.

'We knew all the time, we knew all the time! Joe told us, but we were sworn to secrecy – weren't we, Eustace?'

'I'm quite dazed, I really am. How did it go? I have no idea. Was I tolerable, Eustace?'

'T-terrific! Now go and knock them out with the Chopin, then it'll be my t-turn. Oh, dear!'

The vestibule of the Athenaeum, its plaster casts of the Elgin Marbles and the Medici Venus all swathed in swags of flowers, was echoing with the buzz of delighted conversation. The prosperous business people and gentry of the town had flocked to the occasion and during the interval were glad to see and be seen. The elegantly dressed women were eyed and criticised by the less prosperous members of the audience occupying the cheaper seats towards the back.

'Papa, Papa! I knew you were in Malta, but I thought . . .'

'You thought I had to go back to Suez again.'

Father and daughter kissed each other. Setting her at arms length, he went on, 'Lizzie, you look so grown up in that dress! It's beautiful. And I'm amazed at your playing.'

'I have worked hard, Papa. Oh, you must meet all our new friends. Eustace – well, Eustace won't want to be seen now, he's still got his share of the work to do. But I simply must find Emma. Mama, Joe – while I look for her, take Papa over to meet Lady Alston.'

A group of admirers milled around Lizzie, offering congratulations. Politely she thanked them, but made her excuses. Emma was across the room thanking Elsie, Milly and Annie for their help and giving them instructions for later, when most of the audience would file into another room for supper. Lizzie rushed up to her friend.

'Emma, I've just noticed your gown – I suppose I was too nervous to look at it properly before. You really do look fabulous.'

'It is nice, isn't it? But may I meet your papa, just briefly? The interval will be over very soon, and I must look after Eustace – he's pretty nervous.'

Again pushing through the crowd, they were introduced. The Captain was impressed, and later remarked to his wife how handsome Emma was, though somewhat aloof – she didn't have Lizzie's warmth.

It had been decided that Lizzie would sit at the end of the row for the second half, as she was keen to listen to Eustace. Yet another chair was added so that she could join her parents and Joe. The interval bell was rung.

In the anteroom, Emma found Eustace fine-tuning his guitar, sitting on a low stool and looking nervous.

'Eustace, are you very . . .'

'Oh, Emma, d-do you think I'll be good enough?'

She smiled reassuringly. 'Of course you will. You play so well . . . like an angel!'

'Do you really think so?'

His face glowed with pleasure. They heard Bertram's voice from the platform.

'We come to the second part of our recital, when we are delighted to welcome Mr Eustace Beaumont. I know some of you present will know Mr Beaumont as a teacher at Hoe Grammar School, where he is very popular with the boys.'

While Bertram was speaking, Eustace was delighted to have Emma to himself. She felt sympathetic and sorry for him because he was so anxious. He stood up, carefully holding his guitar in his right hand. They were facing each other. Almost without realising what she was doing, she lightly kissed him on the cheek. Momentarily he gazed at her, dumbfounded. The welcoming applause rose, and, keep-

264

ing his eyes on her for as long as possible, he made a somewhat shambling entrance.

He suddenly felt confident about his playing. Emma had actually kissed him. What bliss! It made him forget his nerves and think of something quite different – of how much he loved her. Now he would play for her, and her alone. In his mind he conjured up a picture of the pair of them on a balcony, the Alps in the background . . . just the two of them, he playing his guitar. That would be living and loving. That would be happiness!

He sat down, positioned his guitar, placed his footstool where he wanted it, and struck up the first piece. It was a piece he particularly liked, a Sor study he'd learned as a young teenager. He played it well, probably better than he had ever played it in his life.

Emma, appalled at her sudden action, tried to calm herself. She was annoyed and flustered. How could she have done such a stupid and undignified thing? But, she reasoned, she could just about cope with Bertram's friendship, so she *should* be able to cope with Eustace's. And she *had* felt sorry for him. She had to admit that he looked smart tonight in his evening dress, and though he was still as plain as plain, his hair had been well cut and the new spectacles were also an improvement.

But what she had done was wrong. Fast and unladylike! She had never kissed a man before, other than her father. She would have to apologise to Eustace for her forward behaviour.

Eustace, meanwhile, had begun his second piece. He liked it rather less than the first, but it was in good contrast. He was well into it when quite suddenly the first string on his guitar snapped, sprang up and hit him across the face.

The audience's reaction was an audible gasp.

He looked up, his eye watering from the sharp sting.

'I'm so sorry, ladies and gentlemen. This can happen at times. P-please excuse me – I will have to retire to change the string.'

Lizzie was at once on the edge of her seat. She saw Emma appear from her vantage point at the entrance to the ante-room and they exchanged glances. Lizzie, always ready to take action, at once stood up and returned to the platform. The buzz of conversation in the audience ceased.

'Perhaps I might play for you again while Mr Beaumont is changing his string.'

There was a round of applause. She went over to the piano, which had been wheeled to one side of the platform, opened it and sat down. Doing some quick thinking, she announced Chopin's A Major Prelude. It was very short, and as there was no sign of Eustace when she had finished, she continued with the D Flat Major – the 'Raindrop'. As she came to the end of it, she saw from the corner of her eye Eustace standing on the platform, smiling broadly.

'Thank you, Lizzie,' he said under his breath as he led her centre stage to take a bow. The audience had been delighted – a bonus.

The rest of his programme went extremely well, becoming more and more exciting as he expressed his skill and tenderness – at its most powerful in the delightful variations on a theme from *The Magic Flute*.

'I don't have to tell you how good you are – listen to that!'

Emma spoke firmly to him when he returned to the anteroom after an impossibly difficult piece. The audience went on applauding for the whole of the short pause he took to collect his thoughts.

'Thank you so much, so very much, Emma.'

He ended his recital with a delightful and exuberant Guiliani overture – odd to end with an overture, but it made a good finale.

Then Lizzie joined him on the platform again, and together they took their final bows.

They were thanked by the chairman of the board of governors of the hospital, and once more the applause rang out. Someone shouted, 'Encore! Encore!'

Eustace gestured to Lizzie, who sat down at the piano yet again, and played a set of variations on 'The Bluebells of Scotland' – a piece both fun to play and to listen to. By then she was quite exhausted, and felt she couldn't play another note. It was Eustace's turn.

He sat down at his place and, having re-tuned his guitar, looked up at the audience and announced:

'These are my own variations on a beautiful piece by the Russian composer P-Peter Ilich Tchaikovsky. I expect most of you will know it, it is a song called "None but the Lonely Heart". As the guitar is particularly sympathetic to the key of E major, I have written my theme and variations in that key, and it is d-dedicated with great admiration to someone whose initial is E.'

When the audience had applauded their fill, those who were not staying on for supper filed out of the building. Annie, Millie and Elsie encouraged the rest to move into to the supper room. This was high and spacious, and very familiar to Lizzie, for it was here that she had sat on numerous occasions at an upright piano to take her music examinations. Now it was festive, with long white tables set out ready for the participants to take their places for the supper.

Everyone was greeted with a glass of champagne, which helped the conversation to flow. Lizzie broke away from her admirers to look for Emma. She found her alone in the anteroom.

'Oh, Emma, what are you doing here by yourself? Wasn't Eustace marvellous? And his encore so beautiful.'

'Yes – and dedicated to you. He so admires you, Lizzie!'

Lizzie frowned and shook her head. 'No, no, Emma – it's dedicated to *you*.'

'Me? Why should he dedicate it to me? No, of course that's not so. You must have heard it lots of times – you work together so much. Surely you know it's your piece?'

'I've *not* heard it before. Eustace and I get on well, but I'm quite certain it's *your* piece.'

Emma slumped down on a chair and started to cry.

'Emma, dearest, what's wrong?'

'Lizzie, I did a terrible thing – an awful thing. I don't think I can ever forgive myself.'

'I can't believe you've done anything awful! Whatever can you mean? Tell me, please.'

Emma could hardly speak for crying.

'Tell me, dear, if you can – and quickly. We must circulate, and I do want to talk to Papa.'

'No, you go on. Leave me here for a while.'

'I can't leave you so upset on a lovely evening like this when we've all been so successful.'

'Lizzie, don't tell a soul, please, especially Lady Alston – she'd be horrified, I know she would!'

'I don't think Lady Alston is easily shocked. But go on.'

'Well, just before Eustace went onto the platform I . . . I kissed him!'

Lizzie was amazed. She almost wanted to laugh, but knew she mustn't. What Emma had just said had taken her totally by surprise.

'But Emma, I didn't think you liked Eustace very much.'

'I don't – or at least I don't *think* I do. But he was so nervous and I felt sorry for him. I wanted to encourage him, to give him more self-confidence, I suppose.'

'Well, you certainly did that. He wasn't a bit nervous, and when he had to speak he hardly stammered at all.'

'But I was so very forward. He'll have no respect for me. I don't know how I'm going to apologise to him – it's dreadfully embarrassing.'

'Emma, listen to me.' Lizzie knelt down in front of her holding Emma's hands. 'You don't need to apologise to Eustace. Why, he was delighted, I'm sure! And it worked – you did give him confidence.'

'But –'

'No buts! Don't say anything about it. Why, he might even thank you for being so kind. And he is, I assure you, the last person in the world to think badly of you, and the last to take advantage of your action. He's much too polite and kind. And you know he hasn't had much real love in his life. Why, your little kiss was probably one of the nicest things – like that, anyway – that's ever happened to him. Don't worry. I think you did precisely the right thing. It was very sweet and kind, and I'm glad that you did it.'

'But it's s-sinful!' said Emma, still half-sobbing.

'Of course it wasn't. You couldn't be that, Emma! Look, dry your eyes, there's a cloakroom over there, go and bathe them, and fix your hair – it's a bit untidy. So many people want to talk to you, and I'm sure Eustace will want to thank you for being so kind. Remember, *don't* apologise – just smile that lovely smile which all of us love so much. Promise?'

268

'I promise.'

At supper, Bertram sat between Emma and Lady Alston, and across the table Lizzie had her father on one side and Eustace on the other, with Joe next to him. Mrs Newcombe was on the Captain's other side. Not far away, Professor Rowe was enjoying praise for his student.

The meal was beautifully served by immaculate waiters, and the room lit by a high chandelier and by candelabra spaced at regular intervals along the tables, which were decorated with neat little flower arrangements. While attending to her social obligations, Lizzie glanced at Emma as often as possible. Now aloof and in a formal mood, she talked chiefly to Bertram, who glanced angrily at Eustace from time to time. Eustace seemed not to notice him – he simply drifted in his own little world, and more than once when Lizzie spoke to him he confessed he hadn't heard what she'd said. The general buzz of conversation was his excuse. But Lizzie knew that in reality Eustace was in his seventh heaven.

Towards the end of the evening, when coffee had been served and votes of thanks proposed and seconded, Bertram leaned across the table and hissed to Eustace under cover of the applause, 'Beaumont, I want to talk to you – outside!'

Eustace took no notice. Bertram repeated his request.

'Oh, all right,' Eustace replied absently.

They made their excuses – which weren't really necessary, since everyone was leaving the tables. They left together – much to Lizzie's surprise.

She called after them, 'Eustace, don't forget that we can take you home in our carriage.'

Eustace waved an acknowledgement.

Once they were outside, Eustace realised that Bertram was furious.

'You've got some explaining to do.'

'What? What do you mean, Webber?' Perplexed, he could hardly manage to answer.

'How dare you? How *dare* you? I saw you, and you needn't think I didn't. I saw you kiss Emma. You've no right to do so. You're only a common, ill-paid teacher – right out of her class. Besides, I'm her beau. I've spent a lot of time

269

with her, *alone*, during the last few months – so keep your filthy little hands off her, otherwise there'll be real trouble.' He narrowed his eyes as he spoke and glared threateningly at Eustace.

Eustace was devastated. What Bertram had just said made him feel miserable and he certainly couldn't tell Bertram that it was Emma who had kissed him, for that would be damaging to Emma's reputation.

'I say, old chap, I didn't mean anything, I'm really sorry. It was just that she –'

'Oh, yes? Don't make excuses. Just that you had her alone and were about to go off and play, and knew that she couldn't shout out or prevent you! You're a coward and a cad to take advantage of her like that. Keep off! She doesn't care for you and never will. Coward and blaggard that you are – you can't control yourself!'

Calm, sensitive Eustace, shy, self-effacing Eustace, was suddenly very angry indeed. He didn't like Bertram's expression any more than he could tolerate what he'd just said. What was worse, he instinctively mistrusted Bertram. So what if he had seen Emma's kiss? Bertram was obviously no gentleman. Not too long ago, words like 'blaggard', 'cad' and 'coward' would have been enough to provoke a duel. Eustace loved Emma with all his heart. The thought that Bertram was smarming his way into her affections infuriated him.

'How dare you call me a blaggard and a coward? Take that back, Webber!'

'No, I won't.'

'Right!'

Eustace landed Bertram a heavy blow right on the nose.

Bertram turned and attempted a return blow, but Eustace managed to block his arm before it landed. Blood was streaming down Bertram's face.

After a few minutes, the two young men were missed.

'Where are they? Shall we go and look for them?'

'Yes, let's – I can then see if Toby and Beauty have arrived.'

As they left the Athenaeum, they heard raised voices coming from the side of the building, concealed from the departing concert-goers.

270

'Look, Emma – they're there! Oh, goodness! How awful! Stop it, you two! Stop it at once!'

The combatant were surprised to be interrupted and ashamed to be seen by Emma and Lizzie.

'Bertram, your nose is bleeding,' Emma exclaimed crossly.

'Emma, please excuse me, I'm going home at once. Mr Beaumont and I have had – what? – a little argument, shall we say? Please don't trouble yourself over me. Good night Emma, good night Lizzie. Please make my excuses to your family, Lady Alston and the committee. I'm not feeling very well.'

Frowning and grunting at Eustace, who just stood quietly by, Bertram walked quickly away in the direction of Derry's Clock.

Eustace suddenly grinned.

'I hit him! I've never hit anyone in my life before. I hit him. I hit him! Ha ha! And I feel all the better for it. Blast him!'

The two young women were appalled.

'Eustace, really, that's ghastly! Why did you hit him?'

'He annoyed me, he said . . . unpleasant things. He said I was a coward.'

'We will not ask for what reason, will we, Emma? The pair of you have behaved abominably. Just like silly schoolboys.'

'It was a question of honour!'

'Honour?'

'Yes, Emma. But if I have upset both of you, you must forgive me, please. Both of you. You will forgive me?'

'Well, you must have had a dreadful quarrel to fight in that stupid way, and I suppose it's not our business. But look, you and I have had the most successful evening of our lives so far, and so has Emma. Let's try and forget this disgusting scene ever happened. I think that's only fair to both of them, don't you, Emma? We must not take sides.'

Emma agreed.

Lizzie breezed ahead of them back into the building.

Emma was feeling very shaky. She decided that in spite of Lizzie's advice, she must explain to Eustace.

'Eustace, I also owe you an apology, I also behaved very badly this evening. I'm so sorry. It was quite dreadful of me.'

271

'Emma, on the contrary, I c-can't thank you enough for tonight. You *couldn't* behave badly – not to me – ever. You were kindness itself. I will never forget what you did – ever. I p-played for you all evening, you know. You gave me confidence.'

'Thank you for being so understanding. Rest assured that it will never happen again.'

'I understand,' he replied with a sad, resigned sigh, then went on, 'did you like my composition?'

Without meaning to, she gave him one of her special smiles.

'Oh yes, Eustace, it was really beautiful – but rather mysterious, too.'

'It was meant to be!'

They joined Lizzie inside, who was surrounded by an admiring crowd and autographing their programmes.

1894

Chapter Twenty-Two

6 June 1894

The train journey was such fun – we had a wonderful picnic lunch. The house here is big and I have settled in well in a beautiful guest room on the second floor. I have already seen this statue and the Albert Hall. Lady Alston and Emma are well and send love.

More news later,

Your ever-loving

Lizzie.

Mrs Newcombe turned the postcard over: a sepia photograph of the Albert Memorial. She was concerned about Lizzie. The girl had been tired when she left for London with Emma and Lady Alston, whose return to town happily coincided with the approach of Lizzie's entrance examination.

Her thoughts drifted back over the past six months. Everything had gone according to plan. Christmas had been heavenly, with her husband at home and Joe so much better. The four of them had had good cause to celebrate and enjoy themselves. They had spent happy times with their two friends: the pantomime, again so much more fun than last year because Joe and Peter were with them, and the excitement of Emma's nineteenth birthday. Best of all was Joe setting his heart on becoming an architect. It delighted and relieved Mrs Newcombe and the Captain to know he was aiming for a rewarding profession. And how Joe had laughed when Lizzie and Emma demonstrated what they had learned at their ballroom-dancing lessons and mimicked some of their less nimble partners!

Eustace had been encouraging and kind, but had worked Lizzie hard. Winter had turned to spring almost before they had realised it. And now Lizzie was in London, and the Captain was at Rosyth. Mrs Newcombe hadn't been so lonely for ages. Though she was always optimistic, she was trying to imagine how she would cope with Lizzie, should she fail the examination – it would be a shattering blow for her.

Thank goodness she has her music, she thought.

'My dear, in the morning Toby will take you to the examination hall, and he will be waiting for you when you've finished.'

'Thank you, Lady Alston; that will be a great help, if it's not putting Toby to too much trouble.'

'Elizabeth, these are very important days for you. We must do everything we possibly can to make your life comfortable and to ease the strain.'

'Do you feel nervous, Lizzie?'

'Apprehensive, Emma, but also a little excited at the opportunity to show them what I can do. Once the maths paper is over, I'll be much happier. You know, I think I'm more nervous about being nervous than anything else!'

'Something I've learned in life, Elizabeth, is that if one has a difficult or unpleasant task, the amount of time it takes cannot last any longer than if one has something exciting or pleasant to do. The time until Thursday afternoon will pass very quickly for you.'

'What a nice thought! Thank you, Lady Alston.'

The next morning Lizzie awoke at seven thirty. She looked out of the window to see the milkman with his horse and cart and churns serving Lottie, and Lottie giving the horse a carrot. One or two hansom cabs were trotting down the road. She washed and dressed in a plain cream linen skirt and white cotton blouse, and was joined by Emma, who told her that Sybil was bringing breakfast for the two of them to Emma's sitting room.

'Oh, Emma! So much rests on what I do today . . .'

'You'll do well, Lizzie, I know you will. Look, I'll come with Toby and Pearl to meet you. Meanwhile, have you got your pens, ruler, pencils and things?'

'Yes, everything's ready.'

'Here's your hat. It's a beautiful day – your linen jacket will be quite warm enough.'

By half past eight she was ready to leave.

'Good luck, Lizzie!'

Emma kissed and hugged her friend; Stratton and Sybil also wished her good luck; and Toby drove her to Bloomsbury and London University in great style and comfort.

Twelve young women met in the classroom, some looking nervous, some trying rather obviously to be brave. One rushed out of the room retching. They sat at two rows of six worn wooden desks and chairs, each with an inkwell, a piece of blotting paper and several sheets of lined foolscap.

An elderly woman, severely dressed but with a warm voice, encouraged the candidates to sit down.

'In a moment, ladies, the arithmetic paper will be given out. Please do not touch it until I tell you. I remind you that you must not write your name on the paper, simply the examination number that you are about to be allocated. Talking and conferring is of course strictly forbidden, and would merit instant disqualification. You have three hours in which to complete this paper and we will commence at nine o'clock precisely. We wish you the very best of luck.'

Lizzie's pulse quickened. She read the questions right through, then through again. She glanced around the room. Other candidates were already scribbling rough notes. She picked up her pen and began work . . .

She glanced up at the clock as she was finishing the last question. She had two minutes left. There would be no time for her to read over what she'd done, or to prove any of her answers. She just finished writing as the invigilator said, 'Ladies, please put down your pens.'

Had she done well or badly? She wouldn't know until the results came out; but at least the dreaded paper was over.

'There will now be an hour's break for lunch. Be ready to start again at one o'clock, please. Tea and coffee are being served in the canteen; you may eat your packed lunch in the canteen, or, of course, as it's warm, in the garden. The lavatories are down the corridor on the right.'

The easing of tension in the examination room was very noticeable. Lizzie smiled at a girl at a nearby desk.

'I can't wait to get out of here. My goodness, it's hot, isn't it?' The girl with red hair heaved a sigh as she spoke.

'I'm certainly ready for lunch and a cup of coffee. Let's find that canteen.'

They walked together down the corridor and introduced themselves.

'Lucy Dearman – I'm from Nottingham. What did you think about the paper? My guvvy told me something about what to expect, but nobody can know until they turn the thing over, can they? I think that'll be my best paper – I want to read mathematics.'

'It's probably worst – at least, I hope so! I think I've scraped through. I'm for Classics – if I get a place, that is.'

They found the canteen, bought coffee and took it into the garden. They barely had time to eat and drink and relax for a few moments in the sun, before it was time to return to start the second paper, which was English grammar and composition. Lizzie executed this with ease and inwardly thanked Eustace for all his excellent teaching.

Next day Lizzie had to take the geography paper and after lunch, English history. On the third day she and her fellow candidates completed the first part of the examination with the New Testament Scripture paper.

By now the dozen girls were beginning to be friends. They sat around in groups during the lunch hour in the sunny garden, exchanging ideas about what they hoped Girton would be like, and discussed in great detail the questions they had been answering.

Part Two of the examination offered a choice of two papers from a list of five. Lizzie had chosen Latin and French. The Latin was easy: passages to be translated into English and some simple English sentences to be put into Latin. Lizzie finished with quite a lot of time to spare. She read through what she'd written, then, folding her arms over her desk and putting her head down, she actually fell sound asleep.

She awoke with a start to the now familiar words, 'Ladies, please put down your pens.'

She simply couldn't believe that she had slept so soundly. As she sat up she felt a sharp pain in her upper back – she'd obviously been sleeping in a very odd position. Still, she felt refreshed for the nap, and was especially cheerful when Emma and Toby called for her.

The final paper, French, which was taken on Thursday morning, was also reasonably straightforward. At last it was all over. The die was cast.

That evening, after a wonderfully happy dinner, Lizzie suddenly felt the room blur. For a moment she was merely dizzy, then she fell to the floor from where she was sitting on a sofa. She had blacked out completely. She knew nothing.

Emma rushed over to her. Lizzie was so still that she thought she was dead. Lady Alston went very pale and immediately rang for Stratton to send for Dr Minton.

Emma managed to lift Lizzie back on the sofa, but still she did not move. Lady Alston handed her some smelling salts, and very slowly Lizzie started to come round. As she was doing so, Dr Minton, who lived a few doors away, rushed in, panting, and at once felt Lizzie's pulse.

Lizzie stirred, and after a while rubbed her eyes. Then she let out a pitiful cry, 'I can't see!, I can't see! I'm blind!'

Her friends couldn't believe what they were hearing. Dr Minton reassured his patient.

'Miss Newcombe, I know this is very frightening, but it is not as serious as you think. Just keep very still for a while. Your sight will return quite soon. Some water, someone, please.'

Lizzie sat upright on the sofa, being calmed by Emma. After about ten minutes her vision started to return. Dr Minton asked her if she had been ill recently.

'No, but I have been quite busy.'

'Augustus, that's an understatement,' said Lady Alston, much relieved. 'Miss Newcombe has been working very hard indeed for well over a year for an examination, quite apart from studying the piano.'

'Ah! My dear, you are totally exhausted. You simply must rest completely for some weeks. Just recline during the day, with a little light reading, and I'll recommend a special diet.

You probably need extra iron – you look somewhat anaemic. I will call on you again tomorrow.'

'Thank you, doctor.'

'So how's the young lady who was surprised to faint after having worked so hard for so long?'

Lizzie smiled weakly.

'I feel much better this morning, thank you, Dr Minton. Tomorrow I'll be my usual self again, ready to enjoy several weeks of what London has to offer!'

'I'm afraid not, Miss Newcombe – that is, if you really want to go up to Cambridge in October.'

'Do you mean that I cannot go out tomorrow?'

'I mean just that. You must continue to rest. The fact that you so easily fainted tells us that your body and whole system are at an extremely low ebb. If you do not rest you will become vulnerable to all kinds of infections which could ruin your health for the rest of your life. I have suggested to Lady Alston that she write to your mother, and that you should go home as soon as possible. If you stayed here, there would be too many distractions. You and your friend would be up and doing all the exciting things you young girls like to do in these modern times.'

'My dear, I am sorry, but I do think Dr Minton is right – he's a very wise man, you know. I have written to your mama. I expect she will travel up to take you home; if not, we can send you on the train with a qualified nurse.'

Lizzie was terribly disappointed, but above all hoped that her mother wouldn't be too upset. She knew she'd be dreadfully worried, but she also knew that Lady Alston would have written a sympathetic letter.

'Oh, I'm sure I can manage the journey alone. After all, Emma did when Mrs Tyrrell died.'

'Yes, my dear, but Emma, although shocked, was in excellent health. You are not, and we simply must get you well for Girton.'

'If I pass.'

'I know you will – won't she, Emma?'

'If she doesn't, then, well . . . well, I'd . . . Oh I don't know what I'd do, I'd be so angry!'

Three days later Lizzie and Mrs Newcombe left Paddington, complete with one of Fortnum and Mason's luncheon hampers. As the train steamed out of the station and Emma waved goodbye, they both realised that they might not meet again until just before Lizzie had to leave Plymouth for Cambridge. Lizzie – tired, exhausted, frustrated Lizzie – was sadly realising that she would miss out on what had promised to be such an exciting summer.

Chapter Twenty-Three

'Joe! Come quick, Mama! Oh, where is she? Mama! Go fetch her down, Aggie, *please!*'

'Lizzie, why don't you open it instead of just standing gawking at it?' Joe suggested.

Lizzie was bursting with emotion, tears springing into her eyes. 'I can't, Joe, I can't! It'll be just too awful if . . .'

'Give it to me, then.'

And he snatched the letter from her as their parents appeared, looking as anxious as Lizzie and Joe.

'Well, what does it say?'

Joe was having some difficulty with the thick envelope, but eventually wrenched out its contents.

'Well?'

'Dear Miss Newcombe,

We are pleased to inform you that you have been a successful candidate in the entrance examination for Girton College. You should present yourself at the College no later than five p.m. on Tuesday October the 9th, when we will welcome you. You may be accompanied by a parent or guardian. The Mistress, Miss Elizabeth Welsh, has asked me to congratulate you.

Yours sincerely,
Agatha Hale White (Mrs),
Assistant Secretary.'

'Rosamund, it's so kind of you to delay your return to Plymouth in order that Lizzie and I can break our journey here.'

'My dear, I knew the girls would want to see each other before Lizzie's great adventure, and it's been no problem. We can all have an easy evening together before you take the train tomorrow morning.'

Mrs Newcombe remarked to her hostess how similar the house was in layout to that in Elliot Terrace, and how much she admired Lady Alston's beautiful paintings.

'I particularly like the portrait of you as a young woman, with the little girl on your lap.'

'That is special.' The old lady sighed deeply, paused, then went on, 'That was my daughter. She died not so long after the portrait was completed, when we were abroad. It was very sad, but – well, one survives these tragedies. Do you know, I think that, had she lived, she would have looked very like Emma. She too had blonde hair and a sweet smile.'

Lizzie and Emma were walking in Kensington Gardens.

The trees were showing autumn tints, and leaves were scattered along the paths. It was the last time the girls would meet before the Christmas vacation.

'I know you'll love the life. You'll meet such interesting people.'

'I think I will – and very different types of girls. I expect some will be very wealthy, but others'll be like me, and I know that there'll be some particularly clever ones who will be there because they've won scholarships.'

'Lizzie, I'll never be clever in that sort of way, nor seriously musical, like you – but, you know, I would like to learn shorthand and perhaps book-keeping. I just don't like to suggest that I take time away from Lady Alston, especially after the truly dreadful difference of opinion we had when I first attempted to buy my typewriter.'

'I'm sure you could confide in her. You know, she *is* really quite old – even if she's looking younger and younger every day – and you must think about what you'll do when she dies. If you have shorthand and book-keeping as well as your typing, then you'll be in a position to get a really good job – if you don't marry, that is.'

'You know how I feel about *that*. And, yes, I've been thinking along those lines for some little while myself. Well, we'll see.'

'Yes. And look after Eustace for me – and don't ignore Bertram either. If you like, you could see Elsie, Milly and Annie sometimes – they're quite sweet, and very impressed by you. They love your clothes! So do meet them for coffee if you feel in need of younger company – if *Mr* Webber and *Mr* Beaumont give you time, that is!'

'You're teasing me. But, you know, I'm coming to the conclusion that Bertram is *quite* nice.'

'Oh, good! But what about Eustace?'

'No, Lizzie, I respect him and I love his music, but no . . .'

Once she had spoken, Emma asked herself, was she as definite in her mind as she appeared to be in her statement?

She paused, then went on, 'Those three girls are good fun, and were certainly helpful last year – but they aren't like us, are they, Lizzie?'

'Not at all. No ambitions, no real interests. Well, I expect they'll make good mothers when the time comes, but you and I, Emma, we're friends for life. No one and nothing – college or shorthand or book-keeping or men – shall ever part us. Let's shake on that!'

They stopped dead in their tracks, shook hands, and gave each other a sisterly hug – right in front of the Albert Memorial.

'I'll take you up to the porter's lodge, madam – miss.'

'Thank you, cabby. Oh, Mama, look! It's jolly impressive, isn't it? Such a beautiful building, and so modern.'

As the cab turned from the main road into the drive, Lizzie saw the long red-brick building standing before her.

There were young women everywhere – chatting in groups, staggering along paths with heavy suitcases, reading, carrying piles of books. Two girls struggled with a heavy armchair, which needed considerable manoeuvring to get it through a side entrance, while another girl waited patiently behind them holding a huge potted palm.

The cabby jumped down and assisted them with two large cases and a patterned carpet bag, placing the luggage just by the porter's lodge.

'Hello! Your name, please. I'm Miss Jackson, the junior bursar.'

284

'I'm Elizabeth Newcombe.'

The efficient-looking young woman wearing a dark green skirt and a stiff white blouse and tie consulted a list.

'Oh, yes – Miss Newcombe, from Plymouth. Classics. Well, I expect you'd like to see your rooms. Cyril'll take you up, then at four thirty we assemble for afternoon tea and a welcome from Miss Welsh, the Mistress!'

She went on, 'Mrs Newcombe, would you like to stay for the welcome – or at least the tea? But perhaps you have a train to catch?'

'It's at six o'clock – I'm returning to London tonight, then to Plymouth tomorrow morning. Yes, I would like to stay for tea, but I may have to miss the welcome.'

Cyril, the porter, appeared with keys. 'Come this way, please.'

Picking up Lizzie's cases, he led the way from the main entrance, with its shining tiled floor and large fireplace, up a flight of stairs, turning left into a long corridor. Having passed one door, which looked as if it might lead to a cloakroom, and another pair of doors, he stopped and unlocked the next.

'These are your rooms, Miss Newcombe. I'm sure you'll be very comfy here.'

They were shown into a sizeable sitting room with pair of tall, narrow windows, a fireplace, and some basic furniture. He opened a door to the right of the fireplace. 'And here is your bedroom.'

The iron bedstead was very plain, but there were sparklingly clean pillows and a mattress. Across the room was a washstand with a jug, bowls, soap dish, slop bucket and a towel rail. Underneath the bed Lizzie noticed a chamberpot.

Mrs Newcombe looked around somewhat apprehensively. This was definitely not the sort of room her daughter was used to.

'Well,' she said doubtfully, 'you've everything you need, but the place does need a lot of cheering up, doesn't it? Let's measure the windows for curtains, and I'll get some sent to you in a few days – these are terribly worn. Your sheets and pillowcases and things are in the trunk, which no doubt will turn up in due course.'

'Yes, and I think, when I've unpacked the trunk and hung my clothes in the wardrobe, the place will come alive – and I'll certainly fill that bookshelf! Actually, there's far more space than I expected.'

'But Lizzie, there's no fireplace in the bedroom! How on earth will you keep warm in winter?'

'Mama, there'll be a fire in the sitting room – I'll just keep the door open at night.'

Her mother was not convinced. Ever since Lizzie had been more or less grown up, she had had the luxury of a fire in her bedroom. This was something Mrs Newcombe and her husband had had words over: he thought his wife was being far too soft on the girl. But she remembered her own chilly youth, before she married.

There was a knock on the door.

'Hello, Lizzie!'

Lucy Dearman had been allocated the next set of rooms. The girls greeted each other, Lucy was introduced to Mrs Newcombe, and the three of them went down to the dining room for tea.

'I suppose we'll get to know everyone soon. Look, I think that's Miss Welsh. I recognise her from a photograph in a magazine.'

'She doesn't look much like a headmistress, does she, Lizzie?'

The slim, very young-looking woman was darting between groups of girls and speaking to parents. Her laugh was a delight to hear, and she had expressive gestures and a very bright, shrewd expression which suggested that she missed absolutely nothing.

She rushed up to them.

'Now let me see – who are you?'

'Lucy Dearman – I'm from Nottingham.'

'Good, good. Mathematics, isn't it?'

'Yes, Mistress!'

'And you are?' Turning to Lizzie she asked.

'Elizabeth Newcombe – from Plymouth.'

'Classics, yes? Welcome to Girton, ladies, and – is it Mrs Newcombe? How nice to meet you, too! Please don't worry about your daughter. She'll be very happy here – we all are, I

286

assure you. I'm right in thinking she has not been away from home before? Well, all will be well. Miss Newcombe, Miss Dearman, you will soon get to know our little ways.'

And Miss Welsh breezed on to the next group of young women, who were accompanied by two fathers.

'Lucy, isn't she a lovely person? So full of vitality.'

Mrs Newcombe put down her cup and saucer. 'Look, darling, I think it's time I left. I don't want to miss the train – and Toby is picking me up at King's Cross. Now, are you sure you'll be able to cope on your own? Oh, Lizzie, I'm going to miss you so much! And now Papa is away, too.'

'Mama, you've got Joe, and do invite Emma and Lady Alston to visit you from time to time. Look after Emma for me, too, won't you? I'll write very often. The term isn't that long, you know.'

Mrs Newcombe embraced her daughter, said goodbye to Lucy, and tried hard not to cry as she and Lizzie walked arm in arm to the porter's lodge, where several cabs were standing for hire.

'Until Christmas, Mama.'

'Until Christmas! Oh, Lizzie . . .'

Lizzie suddenly felt very vulnerable, but smiled bravely as her mother stepped into the cab and told the driver to take her to the station.

Half an hour later, Lizzie stood, hands on hips, looking round her sitting room. Her clothes were now hanging in her wardrobe, and she'd unpacked her sheets and pillowcases, putting them on the bed ready to make it up a little later on. She placed a row of books on the bookshelves and a pile of her precious music at one end of the shelf. There was a knock on the door.

'Hello, are you new? I'm Gwen Crewdon.'

'Lizzie Newcombe. Yes, I'm new today too.'

'What are you going to read? I'm for Classics.'

'So am I.'

'Hello, you two. Freshers?'

'Yes.'

'Well, I'm Matilda Kent – Miss Kent to you. That's one of our little rules, you know: you call us seniors by our surnames unless we give you permission to use Christian names. But look, don't hesitate to knock on my door – it's just along the corridor on the far side of the lecture room. Oh, here's your set of rules and information about mealtimes and so forth.'

Miss Kent, superior but kind, swept out.

'What does it say, Lizzie? I suppose I can call you Lizzie, can't I?'

'Of course, Gwen. Have you met Lucy yet?'

The two girls moved next door to Lucy's room, and the three of them read the sheet of paper which set out various instructions and college rules.

After dinner that evening, Lizzie, wanting to be alone, excused herself from her new friends and walked a fair distance from the dining hall. At random, she opened a door on the right to discover a simple kitchen. She heard laughter and, opening another door, found about eight or ten maids giggling and gossiping. They stopped when they saw Lizzie, who apologised for her intrusion.

'That's all right, Miss, er?'

'Newcombe, Elizabeth Newcombe.'

'Right you are, Miss Newcombe. We'll look after you, won't we, girls?' This was said with the friendliest of grins.

'I was wondering if you could tell me where there is a piano, please?'

'Go out and turn down to the right. There's a little room beyond the far staircase, and there's one in there.'

'I must congratulate you on passing our entrance examination. We have high standards, and girls who have only been educated by a governess or, like you, have attended a private academy where national examinations are ignored, often find the prospect particularly daunting. You must have had a great deal of help, surely?'

Miss Welsh smiled kindly.

'Yes, Mistress.' Lizzie told her about her work with Eustace.

'You have done well, my dear, but now you face new and even more daunting challenges. As you know, we women are not admitted to the university, but we do take the tripos, and it gives us excellent standing for our future careers. Do I take it you want to teach?'

'Yes, Mistress, very much.'

Lizzie went on to describe her teaching experience and her reaction to the conditions and out-of-date attitude at Miss Creeber's Academy. She was quite honest about her impulsiveness and the Mistress was inwardly very amused when she heard about the Song of Solomon incident.

'I'm delighted that you have such an independent and modern spirit – I recognised it, of course, from your answers, especially in your essay about the role of women in the modern world. I see too that you're a musician. We shall certainly want to make use of your talents.'

Lizzie was told that in addition to a timetable of lectures in college, she and her group would also attend the lectures of Dr Postgate at Trinity College.

'My dear, I'm sure you're going to be happy here. We certainly want you to be. Now that you have some idea of your timetable, study will begin in earnest tomorrow. Is there anything you want to do during the rest of the day?'

'I want to finish unpacking, and I would very much like to find a furniture shop in Cambridge – to buy an armchair and some things for my room. May I have permission to go into the town after lunch?'

'Yes, of course. I would suggest you find another student to go with you. You do not need an older chaperone for visits of that sort. Attendance at lectures is a different matter. You will be informed tomorrow about our routine for attending lectures in Cambridge. Is that all quite clear, Miss Newcombe?'

'Yes, quite, Mistress, thank you.'

As Lizzie left the Mistress's study, Gwen was waiting to go in.

'Was she nice? How did you get on with her?'

'She's a dear. Look, do you want to go into Cambridge to buy anything for your room?'

'Yes, and so does Lucy.'

'Ask her permission, then. I have, and she says I can go – preferably with someone else. The three of us could share a cab.'

Lizzie walked down a passage lit by a narrow slit of a window and along a short part of the long corridor to her rooms. She was in high spirits, thinking just how different Miss Welsh was from her forbidding grim old Miss Meany Creeby!

A little later she met up with her new friends for their first expedition into Cambridge.

'We all want a furniture shop, please.'

'Well, missie, I'll take you down to Skelton's in Bridge Street. He'll have everything you need – of that I'm sure.'

The three of them bundled into the cab, and after quite a long journey the cabby pulled up his horse outside a small but well-stocked furniture emporium. The three girls split up once inside, for they all had rather different requirements. At Girton, each pair of rooms was slightly different from the others; some new students were fortunate to inherit quite reasonable pieces of furniture from previous owners who simply hadn't bothered to take their chairs, rugs and so forth with them when they left. But Gwen badly needed a large rug, while Lucy wanted an upright chair.

Lizzie went to the parlour-furniture department and found a very comfortable armchair upholstered in dark-red plush. It cost thirty shillings, which she could easily afford from a sum of money her parents had given her. Then she joined Gwen in the rug department and found a very shaggy goat's skin which would do a great deal to give the room a warm and friendly look when it was placed in front of the fireplace. She also invested in three brightly coloured cushions with deep fringes. By that time Lucy had chosen her upright chair, and on paying their bills the three were promised that the things would be delivered next day.

Leaving the furniture shop, they walked down Bridge Street towards the centre of the town, and eventually reached Trinity Street, where they browsed in Tomlin's bookshop. Feeling adventurous, they wandered on until they came to the market, where they bought apples, gingerbread, tea and cocoa. They wanted to lay in some kind of a larder in order to be able to entertain the circle of friends they hoped to find.

After breakfast on Monday morning Lizzie called at the porter's lodge to pick up her post. There were two parcels for her, and she rushed back to her room to unwrap them. The first disclosed a box which contained dark-rose velvet curtains from her mother – two pairs for the windows of her sitting room and one for the single bedroom window. At the bottom of the neatly packed box were some pictures she had requested. She was delighted to see how well they completed her furnishing scheme.

She looked curiously at the other parcel. Its very creased brown paper, rough string and tied-on label puzzled her. It was soft to touch. She hastily opened it. Inside the first wrapping she found a scrawled note:

Dear Lizzie,

I so hope that you are beginning to settle down to Cambridge life, and I hope that you are not feeling too cold – yet! I've heard tales of those long, draughty corridors at Girton, so I set to work and made this for you. I hope you will like it. I am sorry that I did not finish it in time to give it you before you left Plymouth. Do write to me soon, please. I miss teaching you and Joe at West Hoe Terrace, but he is working very well at school, where, of course, I often take him for certain lessons. I am *so pleased* that you were so very successful.

    Your friend and ex tutor (!)

    Eustace

Lizzie tore off the layers of tissue paper to find an enormous hand-knitted, striped scarf in the Girton colours of pale blue and fawn.

She hugged it with delight.

Chapter Twenty-Four

Robert Townsend was enjoying the warmth of the autumn sun as he sat on his windowsill, idly gazing down on the immaculate green lawn that filled the impressive quadrangle. His eyes rested on a group of young women led by a formidable-looking older one dressed completely in black. They were walking briskly along the path immediately beneath him. One girl at the end of the double line stopped momentarily in her tracks to look at the buildings. As she did so, a sudden blast of wind caught her beret, which flew off and landed on the lawn. She started to run towards it, but was stopped by a college scout.

Robert knew what was happening. Only college members and fellows were allowed on the grass. He rushed down two flights of stairs and joined them.

'It's all right, Jones – leave me to deal with this.'

'Right you are, sir. I don't mind breaking the odd rule for you, sir,' he replied knowingly, and left them.

Within seconds Robert had retrieved the velvet beret.

'Oh, that was kind of you. Thank you so much. I didn't know I wasn't allowed to walk on the grass.'

'Stupid, isn't it? Never mind, here you are.'

He handed her the hat and, noticing her scarf, said, 'You must be a Girton girl. Not seen you before. Are you a fresher?'

'Yes, I've just come for –'

'Don't tell me – old Postgate's lecture.'

'Miss Newcombe – at once, if you please!'

'Sorry, Miss Bland. Look, I must go! Thank you again.'

He liked the way she looked up at him. Warmly he returned her smile.

'I'll see you later,' he said, a mite overenthusiastically.

'You won't be able to – that's my –'

'Yes, I know. Your chaperone.'

He heard her giggle as she ran to rejoin her group, now waiting for her at the entrance to the lecture room where Latin grammar awaited them.

'. . . So the structure of that particular phrase should take this form.' Dr Postgate walked to the board to rewrite a few Latin sentences without the common mistakes made by his students.

Although Robert had opened the old door of the lecture room with the greatest of care, it creaked. The back row of desks and chairs was unoccupied, so he sat in the end seat. The noisy door had attracted the attention of the girl sitting next to the one he'd just met, and he saw her nudge her friend's arm and gesture to her to turn around. She did and, slightly raising her eyebrows, smiled at him. She was delightful! He admired her lively expression and her abundant chestnut hair. But she quickly turned away again, just as Dr Postgate started to speak once more.

The lecture over, Dr Postgate left the room, and Robert watched as the girls' chaperone, who had been quietly knitting in a far corner, got up and gathered her charges round her. As the girl neared him, Lizzie smiled broadly to him once more and said, 'Thank you again, Mr –?'

'Townsend – Robert Townsend. And you are?'

'Elizabeth Newcombe.'

They shook hands. As they did so, Miss Bland spotted them.

'Miss Newcombe, I cannot allow you to fall behind. It will not do at all.'

'I must go.'

'Yes, of course. Goodbye.'

He followed them at a safe distance as they emerged into the afternoon sun, and saw Miss Newcombe and her friend in animated conversation. He made a mental note to be around on the following Monday at precisely the same time.

*

293

One Saturday afternoon the three of them and another student, Helen Cartwright, got permission to go into Cambridge to spend some time in the Fitzwilliam Museum to look at the Greek and Roman pottery, and to shop for a special Sunday-afternoon tea to which the Classics freshers had invited the second-year Classics students. Lucy was to join them, although she was on a different course.

They marvelled at the ancient pottery and made useful notes. By the time they left the Fitzwilliam, the weather had deteriorated, so they quickly made their way back along Trumpington Street to King's Parade and turned down Market Street. Helen saw a stall selling toffee and purchased a pound, sharing some of the rough-cut pieces among her friends. After turning into Sydney Street they passed Miller's Music Shop. Lizzie stopped at once.

'Oh, come *on*, Lizzie, we're freezing! Let's get a cab home.'

'I can't yet, Gwen. I must go in here.'

Lizzie had seen a new Broadwood grand piano. Suddenly she was homesick – she missed her own piano dreadfully. She stalked into the shop, went straight up to the piano and sat down on the stool – but just as she was about to play, a salesman came up to her.

'Excuse me, miss, but we don't allow –'

But Lizzie had already struck up the Mendelssohn *Rondo Capriccioso*. Her friends, watching from outside, rushed into the shop. The salesman stood amazed, and was soon joined by his colleagues and customers, who had been either browsing through music or trying other instruments. Lizzie went on and on. Her audience was completely silent, and when she'd finished they broke into a round of applause.

'Well, miss, I was going to stop you, but that was wonderful! Thank you so much. Am I right in thinking you want a piano?'

'There's nothing I'd like more, but we have a lovely piano at home. Unfortunately at the moment I have to make do with a dreadful old thing out at Girton.'

As she spoke she noticed someone pushing his way through the little crowd of people around her, clearly wanting an encore.

'Yes, go on, play something else, Miss Newcombe. I'm

sure Mr Miller here won't mind – he'd like to hear his stock being played beautifully for once!'

'Oh! Mr Townsend – how nice to see you again.'

She felt herself blushing, her pulse quicken. What shall I play, what shall I play? I wonder what he'd like. She decided on the Chopin 'Harp' study.

More applause when she finished. Her friends were delighted, and crowded round to congratulate her. But she wasn't really very concerned about them.

'Miss Newcombe, that was beautiful. Thank you.'

'Well, thank Mr Miller, really.' She turned to the shop owner. 'It was good to work on a real instrument once more.'

'Call in any time, my dear. Perhaps I could arrange for you to practise sometimes.'

Tactfully, the three other girls slipped out of the shop ahead of Lizzie and her new friend.

'I say, that really was frightfully good, you know.' Robert Townsend looked straight at her, taking in the details of her face as he spoke.

She was experiencing feelings that were new to her, and she couldn't quite understand them. She knew she liked Robert but there was something else, something she had certainly never felt during all the time she had spent with dear, plain Eustace.

'I'll look out for you on Monday afternoon.'

'Oh yes – Monday afternoon.'

With a hesitant yet hasty goodbye, she hurried to catch up with her tactful friends.

As they re-entered the college, they glanced at the porter's noticeboard, which had a scribbled note on it saying:

DON'T FORGET
DANCING TONIGHT
IN THE GYMNASIUM
9 'TIL 10

'Right, everyone, let's start off with the Lancers. Take your partners, please.'

Miss Stansfield, the gymnasium instructress, was in charge.

295

'Come on, Gwen – can you do the Lancers?'

'Yes, Lizzie!'

Almost all the students were in attendance, and in a party mood. Most of them were wearing rather more colourful clothes then usual, which added to the spirited atmosphere. One girl was playing an even more ancient piano than the one Lizzie used, while another obliged on the violin and a third on the trumpet. It was an odd but lively combination.

Lizzie and Gwen took the floor.

Lizzie's mind drifted back to the dance classes she and Emma had attended. The last time she had danced this dance, her partner had been a shy young naval lieutenant. Now, Robert Townsend came into her mind. She thought how nice it would be if he were dancing with her, and imagined he was. She remembered his thick, wavy hair, and that smile – it really lit up his eyes! He was tall and powerfully built. What colour were his eyes, she wondered? Brown like his hair? She wasn't sure – but she knew she liked them. He really was very handsome indeed, and there was a deep richness to his speaking voice. Lizzie always responded to beautiful, resonant sound. Just the thought of him made her smile and feel . . . comfortable. He had liked her playing – of that she was certain . . . As the music drifted on, she forgot she was dancing with a girl.

'Grand Chain, everyone, please! Now, don't go wrong – remember right hand, left hand . . . yes, that's good! Keep it going, ladies!'

Eventually the sequence came to an end. Gwen and Lizzie found seats for a while.

'You obviously enjoyed that. You looked as if you were miles away!'

'I was, Gwen – sorry about that!'

'Right! Now, the Gay Gordons.'

And everyone obeyed Miss Stansfield's energetic command.

The lecture room was filling up with the male students, who sat in the front rows. Robert who ought not to have been there, slipped in at the back and made himself as inconspicuous as possible, with notebook and pencils at the ready.

The Girton contingent started to file in and, as was the custom, all the men stood up. Lizzie was about halfway down the short line of girls. Robert soon spotted her, and was more than pleased to see a big smile of delighted surprise. They could only say a quiet hello before she must take her place with her fellow students. Throughout the lecture he constantly looked at her. It was quite easy. He didn't attract her chaperone's attention because he was sitting well behind the girls, so he could only see Lizzie's back and her lovely hair.

She managed, by occasionally dropping a pencil or pretending to adjust her skirt, to turn and glance at him once or twice; but he could see she was trying hard to concentrate on the complicated concepts that were being put to her. Every movement she made thrilled him. He badly wanted to meet her properly – preferably alone. He certainly got the message that she wasn't indifferent to him, but he would have to tread with great care. It was easy for him to come and go as he pleased, provided he didn't get locked out at night, but was it possible for her? She was a fresher, and would not be at all keen to break any college rules. And he knew just how hard the women students worked: they had to if they were to hope to gain real recognition at the university.

After the lecture had ended, Lizzie passed by him again. He had been quite determined to ask her if he could write to her, but finally decided it would have been too forward. Yet he knew he mustn't lose her – she was quite the most lovely young woman he'd ever met. Full of impatience and eagerness to develop the relationship, but knowing that he could so easily ruin his chances, he just gave her his best smile.

'Next Monday?' she suggested tentatively,

'Oh yes, I hope so, but I may not be able to come to this lecture. You see, this isn't my course, and I should really be elsewhere.'

'Oh. I'm sorry. Goodbye.'

And she was out of sight. He followed the line of girls across the quad to the main entrance, keeping at a safe distance. They made their way along Trinity Street towards Bridge Street, where the carriages were waiting that would take them back to Girton. Miss Bland and three other

297

students got into the first one, and Lizzie and two friends in the second. He ran and tapped on the window just as the cabby instructed his horse to walk on. Lizzie looked out, startled and surprised, but waved enthusiastically. As the little procession of carriages made its way up the hill, Robert, hands deep in his pockets, turned and went back to his rooms in Trinity.

Chapter Twenty-Five

'My dear,' said Lady Alston thoughtfully, 'I hope you don't feel in any way inferior to Lizzie, because, you know, you're not. You have a great deal in common, though, as I've said before, you have different qualities. I'm sure that as your friendship continues you will greatly help each other in life.

'Now I've been thinking,' she went on, 'your typing is extremely good, and I know you're keen to learn shorthand. No, don't interrupt me. It will take time, but I really do think that you should go to classes, and perhaps take book-keeping also. I know I was dreadfully against your learning to type but I recognise my mistake, and I've been feeling for some time that you would like to further your studies. If so, why not go and find out when the next course starts? I expect it will be after Christmas, don't you?'

Emma was delighted.

'Thank you, Lady Alston. You are right, I have been thinking a great deal about that. May I go and find out the details today?'

'Of course. And I've been thinking about something else too. You know I've only worn the Alston rubies once since we've been here in Plymouth, and I feel a little uneasy about keeping them in the house, so would you call at the bank and give them to Bertram to put in my safe-deposit box? And if he asks you out to tea, by all means join him. You've not seen him for several weeks, have you?'

Emma hadn't been out very much since Lizzie had gone up to Cambridge, and apart from accidentally meeting Eustace in the market one morning and having a coffee with him in Spooner's (he had spilled more than half of it over an immaculate white tablecloth because of his sheer delight and nervousness in her presence), she had socialised only in the company of Lady Alston.

The new course at Mullins' Business School in Windsor Lane turned out to be due to start on Monday 14 January. Emma enrolled, purchased several books and was given a collection of leaflets to read and study in the meanwhile. She would attend on three afternoons a week – twice for shorthand, once for book-keeping. She felt really excited at the prospect.

Clutching the case containing the ruby necklace, she then went on to the bank and was escorted to the small office which Bertram now occupied permanently.

'Emma, how nice to see you! It seems such a long time since we met.'

'You know, I have to look after Lady Alston particularly carefully at this time of year. I've very strict instructions about her health from Dr Higgins here and Dr Minton in London.'

'And so what can I do for you today, Emma?'

Bertram was in a very formal and, Emma thought, particularly pompous mood, which she put down to his recent promotion to undermanager.

'First, congratulations, Bertram! We heard that you had been promoted.'

'Thank you. Yes, one day this important branch will be solely in my charge. I will have considerable standing in the town, Emma.'

Emma made no reply. She was impressed, but had learned years ago to recognise when people were showing off. She came straight to the point, producing the case containing the necklace and putting it in front of him.

'Lady Alston wishes you to put this in her safe-deposit box, please. It contains a valuable necklace which she doesn't often wear, and is nervous about keeping it in the house.'

Bertram opened the case and blinked as the light caught the beautiful ruby necklace set with diamonds.

'It's quite remarkable,' he said, lightly but longingly touching one of the gems with a finger.

300

'Yes, it's very grand. I believe it was originally made in India. The setting is a little dated, perhaps.'

'That could be changed very easily. But of course I will put it down in the strongbox right away. Let me give you a receipt for it.'

He took a pen from its stand and wrote out the necessary document.

'Emma,' he said, handing it to her, 'I would so like to give you tea again. Today would have been ideal, but I have to work late. Might we say tomorrow?'

'Tomorrow would suit me very well, Bertram, thank you. At about this time?'

He got up and shook her hand. He was tempted to kiss it, but thought it best to resist the impulse.

It was three o'clock. The bank was just closing to the public, but the staff continued to work, making up the books. After Emma had left, Bertram sat for a moment deep in thought. He realised that he had been given an opportunity that might well not occur again.

He waited for just over an hour and a half, by which time most of the staff had left the building. Then, taking the necklace in its case, he used his newly acquired key to the main safe where the bank kept the keys to their customers' individual safe boxes. There was a special code for senior staff which told them which key belonged to which box. He had only been entrusted with this information that week. He used it for the first time to discover which was Lady Alston's key.

The dusty basement room was dimly lit, but he easily found the right door to the box, which was about halfway along at eye level in a line of twenty others.

He unlocked the box. There were several jewel cases labelled Cartier, some plain black ones and three little chamois leather bags, all containing valuable pieces of jewellery. In a separate compartment were a great many papers some of which he recognised as the share certificates he had collected from Lady Alston when he was in London the previous year. He lifted each one in turn. At the bottom of the box he found what he had thought might well be there – a large envelope with her name on it in handsome copperplate and,

301

in engraved print, 'Stillwall, Stillwall and Keen, Solicitors and Commissioners for Oaths, Chancery Lane, London, E.'

He opened it and removed a document headed 'The Last Will and Testament of Lady Rosamund Louisa Alston.'

This was what he wanted. It was quite in order for him to go to the safe-deposit boxes for a customer – in that respect he was breaking no rules. However, he knew full well that wills were held by the bank in the strictest confidence. He also knew that his future plans depended on the knowledge he would glean from the document he now held in his hands. Once he had discovered what he wanted to know for certain, he could simply return the will to its proper place, and no one but he would be any the wiser. Looking furtively around, he slipped the envelope under his jacket, turned the key in the lock and put it back in his pocket. He would soon know how much or how little Emma was due to inherit. If it was little he would discontinue his pursuit of her, especially since she was so shy and distant.

He made his way upstairs and across the banking hall to his office, and shut the door. The gas lamps shone brightly from the two brackets at either side of the fireplace, and for extra light he lit an oil lamp that stood on his desk.

Cautiously he removed from the envelope the impressive document, written on thick handmade paper in perfect copperplate.

'This is the last Will and Testament of Rosamund Louisa Alston, of 1 Queen's Gate, London, W., and 5 Elliot Terrace, Plymouth, Devon . . .' He turned the page. 'I bequeath to the Orphan Homes of East London Charities Commission for the Poor the sum of . . .' No, that wasn't what he wanted. He turned the page again. Several generous donations to a variety of charities, to St Mary Abbot's Church, Kensington, annuities to servants . . .

Then he found what he was looking for.

'To my dear companion and true friend Miss Emma Cooper . . .'

At the precise moment when his eyes fell on Emma's name, the door of his office opened.

'Ah, Webber, pleased to see you working so diligently. How are you getting on?'

The manager, Mr Donkin, had seen the light in Bertram's office shining out from under the door as he passed by on his way home, and had called in to have a friendly word.

'So what's occupying you this late, eh?'

Bertram was lost in confusion at his unexpected visitor. He at once tried to cover the will with other papers, but Donkin walked around behind his chair and, peering over his shoulder, at once saw the document, which was far too impressive to hide easily.

Bertram's heart raced, his hands shook.

'What have we here?'

The kindly Mr Donkin was still simply curious. He picked up the will and read its title page. Seeing the name he took a deep breath, and was very quiet for a moment.

'Webber, why is this will in your hands? It was not drawn up by the bank. It is an entirely private and confidential paper, the concern only of Lady Alston and her solicitors. It has nothing to do with us whatsoever. If she wished to make any changes to it, she would consult her solicitors, and certainly not us. You have some serious explaining to do.'

Bertram, quick-witted though he was, was at a loss. He paused and licked his dry lips.

'I had to put some jewellery in her box for Lady Alston.'

'And did she ask you to get the will out for her?'

'Ah. Oh, yes, yes, she did, so I've just taken it out to take up to her on leaving the bank.'

'Why then was it removed from its envelope? You were reading it. This is inexcusable curiosity and impertinence. And if, as you say, she requires it, she will have sent a written authority to remove it from the safe. Kindly show it to me.'

Bertram fumbled with other papers on his desk.

'Well, it doesn't seem to be here, Mr Donkin – I must have mislaid it. Or perhaps the cleaner removed it by accident . . .'

The manager straightened his back. 'You have until tomorrow morning to find the authorisation. Bring it to me at nine o'clock. Now give me the will at once – I will take care of it.'

It was a very worried Bertram who went out into the cold November evening. His whole career could be in danger of ruin – and he hadn't even managed to discover Lady Alston's intentions for Emma. Then he remembered he had a sample of Lady Alston's handwriting in a small book of poems she had inscribed for him as a gift some months ago. He would go back to his rooms and spend the evening forging a letter from her. It was all he could do.

'Good morning, Mr Webber. I trust you found the authorisation?'

'Yes indeed, sir. It was on the floor under my desk.'

Bertram had been up for most of the night practising Lady Alston's handwriting, and had been quite pleased with the result. It was very shaky and unevenly spaced, owing to her poor eyesight, and that had made it easier for him. Fortunately he had some quality notepaper on which to make the final copy.

'Here it is, sir.'

Mr Donkin took the letter and studied it very carefully. He was extremely suspicious. After he had left Bertram on the previous evening, he had immediately gone to the safe to get the key to the deposit box in order to return the will to its proper place. The key was not there. If Webber had really been instructed to take the will out of the box for Lady Alston, surely he should have returned the key? Since it wasn't in its place, Webber must still have it in his possession. So it seemed that he must have removed the will for his own purposes, planning to return it only when he'd read it – which implied that he was at the very least guilty of the most severe breach of confidence.

However, he wasn't going to accuse Webber until he was quite sure.

He looked at the faked letter for a long time. All the while Bertram felt more and more uncomfortable, and was soon perspiring heavily.

'Right, Webber. Take a couple of hours off. Report back to me here at noon precisely.'

Bertram was confused. He didn't know whether he'd got away with it or not.

He just nodded to Mr Donkin and went straight out into the cold, wet street.

*

'My lady, Mr Donkin from the bank is here to see you on urgent business, and asks if it would be convenient for you to see him.'

'Why, of course, Stratton. Show him up. What can he want, Emma? I do hope the necklace is safe.'

'I'm certain it is, Lady Alston.'

'Mr Donkin, my lady.'

'Good morning, Mr Donkin. What can we do for you? You know my companion, Miss Cooper?'

'Yes, we have met. Lady Alston, the business on which I have to see you is most private.'

'Emma, would you mind . . .?'

'Of course, Lady Alston.'

Emma tactfully left the room.

'Lady Alston, I apologise for this intrusion, but I would be grateful if you would examine this document.'

He produced Bertram's authority.

'Will you look at this and confirm, please, that you wrote it?'

Somewhat confused but curious, she took the letter and, placing her lorgnette to her weak eyes, examined it for some minutes.

'Mr Donkin, I admit the writing is very like my poor shaky hand – my sight is not good. But no, I have never seen this letter before. It is not on my own notepaper, which I would have used for such a purpose, and, as with all my correspondence these days, Miss Cooper would have typed such a letter – even such a personal and important one as this pretends to be – and I would simply have signed it.'

'Thank you, Lady Alston. That's all I need to know.'

'So this authority has been forged in order that someone may interfere with my private affairs? That does not please me, Mr Donkin – in fact, I have never heard of anything so disgraceful. It does not inspire confidence in your bank.'

'Lady Alston, I quite agree with you. In thirty-five years at the bank, I have never come across such a dishonourable occurrence. Rest assured that the culprit will be immediately dismissed.'

'Mr Donkin, I hear you; but I expect a written apology and an assurance that such a thing will never recur. If I am

not entirely satisfied, you and your bank will hear from my
solicitors. Good morning, Mr Donkin!'

As arranged, that afternoon Emma went to the bank to meet
Bertram. She expected to discover rather more about the
unpleasant incident. She went to his office door, and was
about to knock when a clerk came up to her.

'Excuse me, Miss Cooper, did you wish to see Mr
Webber?'

'Yes. I have an appointment with him.'

'I'm afraid that Mr Webber is no longer in the employ of
the bank.'

Emma was dumbfounded. It was obvious that there was a
connection with the forged document which had so concerned
Lady Alston. Could he really be the culprit? Bertram had
treated her so well, so politely – indeed, had been the first
man to do so. She felt she could trust him and was beginning
to enjoy being with him. His kindness and encouragement
when she had most needed it was something she'd not forget,
but now this . . .

Why should he have done such a dreadful thing?

Chapter Twenty-Six

'It was a wonderful surprise, Mr Harper, but I do think the brakes are slipping just a little. Could you adjust them, please?'

'Of course, Miss Newcombe. It's a fine machine – the best on the market. When your mother contacted us, she said she wanted us to choose one that was both strong and safe – and this is it. The adjustment'll take an hour or so. Can you wait?'

'I'll call back later.'

Lizzie's bicycle had been delivered earlier that week, on the morning of her birthday – a special present from her parents. She and Gwen – who was using one of the four college cycles – had ridden into town together, and had just separated, something they weren't strictly supposed to do. Gwen was going to the Fitzwilliam, and Lizzie was off to spend another hour or two in Mr Miller's instrument warehouse, at the back of his shop. There she had the choice of a great variety of pianos, some brand new, waiting to find space in the showroom, some restored and merely awaiting a final polish.

She left King and Harper's cycle-repair and sales shop in Sussex Street and walked the short distance to Miller's, where the owner welcomed her. In the large, chilly warehouse her eyes fell upon a superb full concert Bechstein grand which had just arrived from Germany.

'What an opportunity! How marvellous!' she said aloud, and sat down and started to exercise her rather stiff, cold fingers on a series of scales.

'Keep the pace even, don't rush. The slow way is the quick way, eventually.' Professor Rowe's words came back to her.

She had been given the Beethoven *Pathétique Sonata* to work on and had spent quite a lot of time on it, often very early in the morning before breakfast. She forgot the cold of the warehouse and, inspired by the superb instrument, absorbed herself in her music.

'Mr Townsend, the parts for the Trinity Orchestra you ordered are here.'

'Thanks, Mr Miller. Will you enter them to college account, please?'

How is the orchestra? Coming along nicely, I trust?'

Miller spoke on equal terms – not only the successful businessman, proud to a fault of his prosperous emporium, but himself no mean organist.

'Yes, thank you. They're giving a concert in Trinity Chapel just before we go down for Christmas.'

'Well, there's still talent around, I suppose. Mind you, it's not what it was . . . you young people these days, you lack the discipline. Not that that applies to the young lady in there.'

He jerked a strong thumb in the direction of the warehouse.

'Just listen to her!'

He opened the connecting door, and the notes of the beginning of the beautiful slow movement of the *Pathétique* were heard.

'May I . . .?'

'Of course, go in, Mr Townsend; she'll be pleased to see you, no doubt.'

Robert needed no second invitation. He stood behind Lizzie for quite a while, listening. Her concentration was so deep that she didn't hear his footsteps on the hard cement floor. At last the movement came to an end, and he applauded. She gave a jump, and turned.

'Oh! Oh, how long have you been there? How nice, I've not seen you for ages. How are you?'

'Very well, Miss Newcombe, thank you. I say, you're playing even better than the other week!'

He smiled nervously. There was a pause, which Lizzie managed to break.

'Do you play an instrument, Mr Townsend?'

308

'No, I'm just a music lover. But I'm secretary to the Trinity Music Club, and it's up to me to obtain the parts for the orchestra, arrange the rehearsals and so forth.'

'Mr Townsend –'

'Let's drop the formality. Please call me Robert.'

'Thank you, Robert. I know we hardly know each other, but I'd like it if you would call me Lizzie.'

'What a pity!'

'What's wrong?'

'A beautiful name like Elizabeth, and you say "Call me Lizzie!" Elizabeth – probably the best name in the English language!'

Lizzie laughed nervously to cover the stunning impression his presence and deep rich voice were having on her.

'That's what my papa says. It goes back to when my brother Joe was little – he couldn't say Elizabeth, but managed Lizzie. Papa dislikes it too, but even he calls me Lizzie, though he tends to get very cross if he hears Aggie or Laura say it.'

'Who are they?'

'Aggie was our nurse – and she's never left us. Laura is our cook and general housekeeper.'

'Tell me more. Where is home? What does your papa do?' He could not take his eyes off Lizzie as he spoke.

Lizzie explained.

'And where is *your* home, and what does your family do, Robert?'

'I come from Stamford. My parents own a very old inn there. It's been in our family for generations. I think my brother and sister-in-law will take it over when Father wants to retire. I came up to Trinity on a scholarship.'

'They must be very proud of you.'

'I think they are – more than they should be, really. They gave me a very good education – I was a boarder at Harrow, and the plan is, if I get a good degree, for me to teach modern languages there. The head said there would be a vacancy in the autumn of '96. Do you want to teach too?'

Lizzie told him of her plans and ideas on education.

'Of course I'll start in a very small way, in Plymouth. I hope to find a building there that I can rent, just to begin.'

'I so agree with your ideas.'

She felt nervously excited. Her heart thumped at his close proximity as she tried to concentrate on what he was saying.

Robert leaned on the end of the piano and looked down at her.

'There is a great deal wrong with education. I was dreadfully unhappy for a lot of the time at Harrow, and when I get there as a teacher, I'll certainly do my best to make life a little more pleasant for any of the boys who may be being bullied as I was at first. I expect I'll encounter opposition, but I shan't worry about that. I have hopes of becoming a house master in due course – then I'll be able to do a great deal more. But all that's a long way in the future. Tripos first.'

He paused for a while, then went on, 'But I'm stopping you from playing.'

'Oh, please don't worry about that. But this is such a wonderful piano, I would like to play some more. Look, draw up that stool and sit down and listen – if you'd like.'

'I'd like to very much.' He gazed right at her as he took up her suggestion.

This was no time for scales, or for staggering through the last movement of the *Pathétique*, of which she was still unsure. She played the Chopin C sharp minor waltz.

'That was wonderful! Thank you so much. Look, can I see you here again next Saturday? It'll be the last of term.'

'Well, if Gwen wants to come to town, too. Oh, my goodness! She'll be waiting for me at the cycle shop. My parents have just given me a bicycle, and we've both learned to ride!'

'Marvellous – how brave of you!'

Lizzie smiled. 'I'll be here next week. I hope that this piano will be too!'

'Goodbye, Elizabeth – until next Saturday.'

He took her hand, which she had just encased in a thick woollen glove, shook it, and gave it a little squeeze.

'Goodbye, Robert.'

Tactful and discreet, he left the shop just ahead of her while she picked up her music. Closing the lid of the superb instrument, she gave it an affectionate pat before hurrying to the cycle shop.

'Here you are, Miss Newcombe. The brakes did need a little adjustment. No charge, of course. Your friend is waiting in there. I thought she was beginning to look cold outside the shop, so I asked her into our snug.'

'You've been ages! How did the practice go?'

'Wonderful, wonderful! I say, Gwen, you do want to go to the Fitz next Saturday, too? Please say yes!'

'No, I'm definitely not going to the Fitz next Saturday, and you won't be going to Miller's.'

'Oh, why not?' Lizzie was crestfallen.

'Well, it's the Mistress's at home, and we all have to do our bit to get the place ready for it – remember?'

'I quite forgot!'

They rode on up Bridge Street. As they pedalled along a straight stretch of road, Gwen drew up beside her friend.

'What's wrong, Lizzie? You sounded so happy back there, but now you're . . . well, morose. That's not a bit like you.'

'Can I trust you, Gwen? Can you keep a secret?'

'Of course I can, Lizzie – you know that!'

Lizzie told her friend about the arrangement with Robert.

'So you won't be able to see him next Saturday – is that it?'

Lizzie nodded sadly and her bike wobbled.

Gwen laughed out loud.

'You could – and quite easily. If you'd really read the notice, it said that we can invite guests – men, if we want. It's going to be a big night, Lizzie. Do you think he's got a friend he could bring? I'd like a beau too, you know, just for the evening!'

'Shall I write to him at Trinity, then?'

'Oh, do! And ask him to bring someone!'

After their Saturday-evening hop, Lizzie wrote a letter to Robert, wording it very carefully. In the same post she sent a postcard to her mother asking her urgently to send the green velvet dress.

From early the following Saturday morning, the whole college took on a different atmosphere. Students were running around everywhere. Many of those who could sew were finishing off their evening dresses for the party and helping

311

others who weren't so proficient with their needles. They were also transforming the building. The entrance hall was decorated with large blue and white Chinese jars filled with indoor plants and arrangements of holly, mistletoe and ivy; and to welcome guests as they arrived, a huge crackling log fire blazed away in the impressive grate.

The hall where the food and dancing was to take place was decorated with a vast Indian quilted bedcover, and a great many Indian shawls were artistically draped along the walls, making the place look exotic. Curtains had been removed from unused rooms on the top floor to add a certain mystery and enchantment to the normally uncurtained windows, and some long strips of blue carpet, borrowed from a corridor guests were not expected to visit, made an impressive border to the floor, now waxed and polished, for the dancing. Ingeniously draped walls gave two reading rooms the air of Bedouin tents, furnished with groups of sofas and cushions and lit by candlelight.

Around seven o'clock all the women – staff and students – retired to their rooms to get ready. For once femininity took over where a studious outlook on life usually reigned.

'You look lovely' was the most common phrase as girls emerged from their rooms; the excited atmosphere was highly spiced with giggles and a surprising amount of blushing. It was as if everyone had shed a few years, becoming about fourteen or fifteen again, their serious attitude towards their work and their ambitions forgotten for a few hours.

'Do you think they'll come? Do you really think they want to spend the last Saturday night of term with *us*? It could well seem dreadfully dull to them. I expect they have a far more exciting time than we do, you know.'

'Robert accepted, didn't he? And you know as well as I do that the men don't get many opportunities to see the inside of Girton. They'll come all right – probably hordes of them, and from a great many colleges. I dare say the Mistress and lecturers will be enjoying each other's company, as well.' Gwen was reassuring her friend.

At eight thirty the first of many carriages drew up at the main entrance, containing a party of third-year students from King's. They were enthusiastically received by a group

312

of third-year moral sciences Girton girls and whisked away to the hall, where they stood around in groups drinking a light, well-spiced punch.

At about ten to nine, when Lizzie was just beginning to think Robert wasn't going to turn up, she spotted him walking briskly up the main drive with another young man. She had to restrain herself from rushing out of the front door to meet him.

'I say, Lizzie, I'm sorry we're late. There's such a crush of carriages along the main road. I think the whole of the university is here. You look stunning! What a frock – green is definitely your colour!'

'Thank you, Robert. Let me introduce Gwen Crewdon.'

She noticed that Robert's friend was looking eagerly at Gwen.

'And let me introduce Matthew Summers,' said Robert. 'Miss Newcombe, Miss Crewdon.'

The young men left their opera cloaks in an improvised cloakroom and the four of them walked into the crowded hall just as the dancing began. The music was played by a pleasant small orchestra now performing a jolly schottische.

'May I have the pleasure?' Robert bowed with teasing formality.

'Certainly, Mr Townsend!'

Soon the floor was very crowded. At first a few students were nervously waiting to be asked to dance, and trying to enjoy themselves; but as the excitement built up, most became rather more informal than their parents might have thought proper. Close contact with the opposite sex was rare, and they seized the opportunity to experience the pleasure of feeling a young man's arm about their waist. Youthful energy and exuberance made for an unforgettable evening.

'You dance well!'

Lizzie and Robert spoke together, laughed, then in the sheer joy of each other's company danced on until supper, when a lavish buffet was served. Young men and women spread themselves into the other rooms, some finding places on sofas in the transformed reading rooms, some sitting on the floor on cushions, some on the stairs leading to the first and second floors of the building. They gossiped about

313

favourite and not so favourite lecturers, swopped stories about their studies and the various sporting occasions they had attended.

'We beat Newnham at hockey last week. It was great fun, wasn't it, Gwen? Some of our friends are in the team, but I daren't risk my hands.'

'Because of your playing, Miss Newcombe?' asked Matthew Summers.

'Yes, I have to be careful.'

'You've not heard her play, Matt – that's something really special.'

'A waltz! Robert, I love to waltz! It really is my favourite dance. Do let's go back.'

They left Gwen and Matthew and hurriedly rejoined the couples on the dance floor.

Lizzie was in a dream. She did love the Viennese waltz – and it was fast taking on a new meaning for her. Robert danced extremely well, and led her round the room, carefully avoiding the many other couples. The pace was fast, and if she looked anywhere but at him, handsome in his black tie, she knew she would soon become very dizzy. She *was* dizzy – but for reasons quite other than the whirling of the dance. Two pairs of eyes smiled at each other; there was no need for words.

Lizzie couldn't remember being so happy – and in a way unrelated to being happy with her music, to her love for her parents and Joe, or her friendship with Emma. Momentarily Eustace flashed into her mind. And in that flash she now realised just how he felt about Emma.

About halfway through the lilting strain of the 'Emperor Waltz', Robert drew her very slightly nearer to him. She gave a tiny gasp, then laughed in sheer joy. He caught her excitement and laughed too. He'd been to college dances before; he had danced with several very pretty young women, and flirted with considerable success, but the girl he was now holding in his arms was special.

'Thank you, Lizzie. That really was awfully jolly, wasn't it?' He squeezed her hand as they left the floor. 'I would like some lemonade, wouldn't you?'

Slightly breathless, Lizzie looked up at him and nodded.

Having been served some and drunk it, he suggested, 'Let's go somewhere where we can talk. I so want to find out more about you.'

They made their way out of the hall towards a curving staircase. Halfway up, there was an open arch from which they could look down and see the ground-floor corridor, crowded with groups of students laughing, talking, eating and drinking. Although so many people were only some fifteen or twenty feet below, the corner was private and there was a welcoming padded seat immediately in front of the arch. It was as though (Robert said) they were sitting in a Gothic castle and looking down on some medieval court enjoying a secular celebration.

'As long as it's not Bluebeard's castle!' she replied.

'And as long as you're not Rapunzel – having to let down your long locks to let me in.'

They were quiet for a moment or two.

'Lizzie?'

'Yes, Robert.'

He hesitated, and she encouraged him with a smile.

'Lizzie, I don't know what you think, but I really feel that there is something, well . . . special between us.'

'I think so too. I do hope that we can be friends – really good friends, don't you?'

'Yes, Lizzie.'

'I have some other very dear friends. There's Eustace . . .'

He frowned.

'You'll like Eustace – he coached me so well for the entrance exam!'

Robert looked even more serious.

Lizzie smiled to herself, realising what he was thinking. Quickly she went on to tell him about Eustace and Emma.

'I'm so glad that Eustace likes Emma.'

They were looking deeply at each other. He lifted her hand to his lips and kissed it.

Her heart was racing as if she'd just cycled up the steepest hill in Plymouth.

'Oh . . .'

'No, don't say anything. I'm so glad that . . . well, that we like each other quite a lot?'

'Yes, Robert, quite a lot!'

She tossed her head and laughed, a happy, rippling laugh.

'I think I hear the Lancers being called. I'd like to do them.'

'Of course, But I'll scold you if I see you flirting with any other undergraduate – especially Summers, he's the biggest flirt in the university. Let's go and find him and Gwen.'

Carriages had been called for a quarter to twelve, but no one wanted the evening to end. They kept shouting for yet one more dance, and, with friendly nods to the little orchestra from Miss Evans, who seemed to be enjoying herself quite as much as her students and the rest of the staff, yet another dance was begun – the Gay Gordons, the military two-step, an energetic polka . . . But eventually, at well after one in the morning, the very last waltz was announced.

Robert and Lizzie took the floor, knowing that the time was coming when they would have to say goodnight – indeed, goodbye until next term, for Cambridge went down for the Christmas vacation on the following day.

'Lizzie, this has been the most wonderful evening ever. Will you write to me at Christmas? The vac will seem quite endless now.'

'But you'll have some happy times with your family, especially at the inn – it's sure to be a perfectly splendid Christmas for you. I know it will be for me, too, but I'll long to come back next term, won't you? Even if we can only meet in Mr Miller's warehouse.'

By now he was one of a long line of young men, and quite a few women guests from Newnham, waiting to retrieve their coats and cloaks. Lizzie stood closely by him, and he squeezed her hand. They looked fondly at each other, and were snapped out of their reverie by Matthew and Gwen.

'There you are. Look, I've got my cloak. We'll wait for you outside.'

'Go down the drive and try to find our carriage, will you, Matt?'

Robert collected his cloak, and he and Lizzie walked slowly towards the front door and down the drive. Crowds of other young people around them were all saying their goodbyes.

'Goodbye, Lizzie – until after Christmas.'

'Goodbye, Robert. Happy Christmas!'

As she spoke, he nervously and quickly bent down and lightly kissed her on the forehead. He went on firmly holding her hand until the very last moment, when the door of the carriage had to be closed.

1897

Chapter Twenty-Seven

'Welcome home, sir, madam!'

'Aggie, it's good to see you after all this time.'

'Sir, you *do* look well – and you too, madam. It's wonderful to have you back again from those foreign parts. What a time you must have had – all those strange places!'

'Eustace, be careful with that case, it's very heavy. Now, Joe, don't you strain yourself.'

Mrs Newcombe shouted a warning as the two young men got out of the second cab, in which they'd ridden from the dockyard with the Newcombes' multitude of cases and carpetbags.

'Tea's ready in the drawing room. I've made one of my special sponges, and there's Devonshire cream.'

'Thank you, Laura. Yes, it is good to be home – and *tea*! I've not had decent tea on shore since India – a long time ago!'

Tea was brought, and Aggie and Laura retired downstairs, leaving the four of them to re-cement their bonds of family love and friendship.

'Joe, stand up, please.'

'Mama, don't embarrass me!'

'Joe, *please*, because I do think you've grown.'

Eighteen-year-old Joe did as he was bid. It was almost ten months since his mother had last seen him. He was standing much straighter, and now walked well and quite fast, wearing his surgical boot and using only one stick.

Mrs Newcombe eyed her son with pride. 'My dear, you have grown! And how quickly you're walking!'

'I don't think any quicker than when you went away, Mama.'

'I'm not so sure.'

'You certainly look well, son. How's the work going?'

'Loving every minute of it, Papa. Mr Pooley gives me more and more to do. At the moment I'm designing a butcher's shop which is to be built in Market Street. Of course, he's still supervising me, but I think he's pleased with my efforts.'

'Eustace, I can't thank you enough for looking after Joe all this time. It was good of you.'

'Mrs Newcome, it's been a great pleasure. Joe and I have always been good friends, ever since . . .'

'Of course.'

'Well, my dear, don't feel that now we've come back we're going to throw you out on the street tomorrow. We know you'll have to find some new rooms, but take your time. After all, Lizzie won't be home for several weeks yet, so she won't be needing her room. And I'm so pleased that things worked well for you and Joe.'

'The vacations were great fun. We've all had some happy times, as of course you know from our letters. I suppose they all arrived?'

'We often had several together – but that's shipping for you, Eustace,' replied the Captain, settling himself even more comfortably in his favourite chair.

'I've some news for you, Captain and Mrs Newcombe.'

'What is it, Eustace? I hope it's good! Does it concern Emma?' asked Mrs Newcombe excitedly.

'Well, no. Though we have been really good friends for a long time, as you know, and we are, I think, beginning to reach some kind of an understanding.'

She looked knowingly at her husband. Turning to Eustace, she urged, 'Well – tell us.'

'I'm to be head of the English Department at the Hoe Grammar School after the Easter holidays. It will mean quite a lot more money.'

'My dear, that's excellent! But there's something different about you. You look particularly well.'

'I feel it, Mrs Newcombe – so very well, and happy!'

322

'And successful. Jolly good, old chap,' said the Captain as he signalled to his wife to pour him another cup of tea.

'But it's something else . . .' She was quiet for a moment, then went on. 'Ah yes, of course. I don't want to be rude, Eustace, but since we've met this afternoon, do you know I've not heard you stammer? Not even once.'

Eustace blushed, which gave his face something of a schoolboyish appearance.

'Mrs Newcombe, I'm pleased to say I've overcome it. I'm not quite sure how. Emma has been very patient, and has given me certain breathing exercises to do; and on her last vacation Lizzie helped too. They made me take deep breaths and take my time. We worked every day. And Emma, well . . .'

'Many congratulations again, Eustace. That's real progress. And Joe, with your studies going on so splendidly, why, you'll be designing – I don't know quite what! It seems they've done very well without us, doesn't it, Peter?'

There was a knock on the front door. Laura hurried upstairs from the kitchen to answer it, and soon came into the drawing room looking white and frightened.

'It's a telegram, madam. The boy's waiting.'

'Give it me, quick.'

'No, Laura, I'll take it,' the Captain interrupted, remembering all too well the effect telegrams had on his wife since the one that had announced Joe's fall. He tore open the envelope. His face relaxed into a smile.

'Tell the boy he can go, Laura.'

His wife looked anxiously at him. 'What is it, Peter?'

'"WELCOME HOME DEAREST MAMA AND PAPA STOP LOVE LIZZIE."'

'Ah, how lovely!' She heaved a sigh of relief.

'Would you excuse me? I have some English compositions to mark before school tomorrow morning.'

'Of course, Eustace.'

Eustace went up to the old nursery where he did all his studying and marking. The strong wind on that cold, dark February day caused the rough sea to thrash wildly against the rocks not far from the end of the garden, but the weather didn't in any way reflect his mood, nor the mood of the rest of the household.

*

'My dear, how lovely to see you again!'

Lady Alston started very slowly to get up from her straight-backed chair to greet Mrs Newcombe. Emma rushed over to help her.

'Rosamund, please don't get up.'

'But I must, I must! We haven't met for so very long – how long is it, Emma?'

'Ten months, Lady Alston.'

'Now, I'm so anxious to know . . . You managed to find it, Caroline, but please tell me more than you were able to in your letter. Everything you say will mean such a lot to me.'

'Rosamund, yes. It's being beautifully kept, I assure you.'

'That pleases me. But go on.'

'Well, the day after we arrived I made some enquiries, and my hostess, Lady Marchant, took me to St Mark's – which was just as you had described it, on a hillside, and in a beautiful setting. The churchyard is still very neat and well laid out, because, of course, the church is used regularly. It was very hot, even up there in the hills. I spoke to the vicar, who, though he didn't actually remember you, had heard your name mentioned from time to time. He took me to the grave.'

A tear trickled from the corner of the old lady's eye, but she was very anxious to hear everything her friend had to say. Mrs Newcombe spoke softly and as gently as possible.

'The pink rose tree you planted at the time is very big, but is pruned regularly, so it's strong, healthy and beautiful. The acacia which stands just behind the headstone must also be very much bigger than it was when you were there. I took the liberty of arranging to have another rose tree – a white one – planted, just at the foot of the grave. I thought you might like that. The stone and inscription are in excellent condition, but I asked the sexton to clean them, and Lady Marchant has promised me that she'll make quite certain they're scrubbed at regular intervals.'

More memories flooded back to Lady Alston. It had been a dreadful year for the plague, and while she and her husband and household had fled to the hills as soon as the outbreak occurred in Bombay, the sickness had spread rapidly to Poona itself. Within a matter of a few weeks their darling

324

only child, the four-year-old Juliet, became sick and died in three days.

Emma, who had sat very quietly through the touching conversation, got up and put her arm around her friend. Mrs Newcombe passed Lady Alston a narrow box neatly wrapped in tissue paper.

'I thought you might like to have these.'

Carefully, with her shaky, distorted hands, she unwrapped the parcel. It contained six carefully pressed pink roses. She held them to her cheek.

'How beautiful! How thoughtful of you! Over all that distance . . . My dear, I cannot thank you enough.'

'And I've brought this for you, Emma. We bought it for you in Singapore.'

Excitedly Emma undid the smooth string and removed the brown paper to reveal a length of very fine pure silk taffeta in a pale shade of blue.

'There's fifteen yards there, my dear. Have it made up as it pleases you – perhaps when you have a special party or ball to attend. We have something similar for Lizzie, but I'll not send it to Girton, we'll wait for the Easter vacation to give it to her.'

'What a wonderful surprise! Thank you so much. You must be looking forward to seeing her again, Aunt Caroline.'

'How nice to hear you call me that once more, Emma! Yes, it has been a long time. We did think of going up to Cambridge for a few days, but as Lizzie's examinations are so close, we felt it would be better not to disturb her.'

And after a pleasant afternoon's conversation and tea, Mrs Newcombe made her way home to West Hoe Terrace.

In the carriage she thought just how much Rosamund had aged during the ten months while she and her husband had travelled halfway round the world. Her visit to little Juliet's grave had obviously been very reassuring, and she was glad she had made the effort. She thought of her own successful and exuberant daughter – how would she have coped if Lizzie had died so young? At once she dismissed the horrible thought. But everything was so different for her Lizzie. Her fears that Girton would spoil her daughter's chances of marriage had soon been quelled. Robert was such a splendid young man, and Lizzie was devoted to him. As a woman, she could understand that. He was so open and honest, so uncomplicated and studious – as well as handsome!

Mrs Newcombe had also watched with interest the slow development of the relationship between Eustace and Emma. She felt that Eustace would wait for ever for Emma: she could see it in his eyes every time she saw them together. And now Eustace was beginning to be successful too – and between them, Lizzie and Emma had actually cured his stammer!

'Now, Lizzie, I know you're twenty-one, but that doesn't mean you shouldn't take my advice. Of course you'd have a wonderful time if Robert came down here for a week or so, but honestly, I think you'd try to do too much. You'll need that fortnight for study – quietly and without distraction. Besides, I'm going to be just a little possessive for once. We haven't seen you for almost a year, you know, and we have a lot of catch up on. So let's keep this time special, for the four of us.'

'Mama's right, Lizzie. Robert's a great chap, and we all like him; but for the present – well, let's just be us!'

The reunion with her parents – and their traveller's tales were exciting. She had gasped at the beauty of her length of silk, extremely fine and the palest shade of ivory. She knew just what she was going to do with it. But when?

So she fell in line with her mother's wishes, and, while feeling lovelorn, enjoyed the closeness of her family circle. Having her father around was always rewarding, and they began to talk about the coming summer months, when she would come down from Girton for the last time. When the tripos was over, all she would have to do was wait for the results. At that time the whole nation and Empire would be ablaze with the festivities surrounding Queen Victoria's Diamond Jubilee.

One evening after dinner, Mrs Newcombe raised the subject.

'I think we should rent rooms in London for a few weeks. Joe, how much time could Mr Pooley spare you, do you think?'

326

'He's been thinking of closing the office for three weeks. You know, he feels that if he spends time in London he might meet people who would give him commissions in other parts of the country, then he could spread his practice.'

'I'd like to be there for longer. I'm sure I could always stay with Lady Alston and Emma.'

'That doesn't surprise me. I suppose that young man of yours will join us?'

Lizzie smiled at her father. 'Well, he might,' she replied coyly, knowing that he would. 'And Emma was saying that she can arrange even more concerts for Eustace and me this year. Three last summer, you remember? We're still in demand, and with all the celebrations there will certainly be more opportunities. And there'll be so much to see . . .'

'Then even if Joe can only spare three weeks, I think *we* should go for six. Aggie and Laura can join us while Joe's with us, and when he has to come back to Plymouth they can return with him, and we'll get some temporary domestic help.'

Turning to her husband, Mrs Newcombe continued, 'As you have work to do at the Admiralty, everything should fit in very well.'

'My dear, we'll have a wonderful summer – once again!'

Meanwhile, just up across the Hoe, Lady Alston was saying, 'Now, Emma, it's time we planned our jubilee celebrations. I would like to give a dinner and a ball.'

'Will you want to hold it at an hotel, or at Queen's Gate?'

'I think at Queen's Gate, don't you? If the furniture is cleared from the drawing room and the double doors into the sitting room opened back, it will be quite sufficiently large for dancing. Now, have you your notebook and pencil ready? We must note my ideas as they occur to me. I'm sure to forget things if we don't.'

After a lengthy discussion, Tuesday June the 29th was the date decided upon; then they drew up the list of guests. Some would come to dinner and stay on for the ball, while others, less close to Lady Alston, would attend the ball and supper later.

Emma's studies at Mullins's Business School had been well

worth while. Not only had she a certificate acknowledging that her shorthand had reached a speed of one hundred words a minute, but she had organised Lady Alston's household with great skill. She had a file containing the addresses of all her employer's friends and acquaintances, and another for those businesses and tradespeople where they had accounts. She kept the books in order, and balanced the household finances. In addition to all this, she had begun a record book of those who had commissioned Lizzie and Eustace to give recitals, the date of each, and the payment they received, with copies of the programme.

For Lizzie, the present time was an anxious one. She was catching up on her studies and revision, and was encouraged and helped by Eustace. The time of the tripos examination was so close that she badly wanted to sit it, and get it over and done with.

And so, in mid-April, the day arrived when she must return to Girton for the last time.

Chapter Twenty-Eight

'I can't believe we've actually done it, I simply cannot! I feel like . . . like . . . like waltzing!'

And as she spoke, Lizzie gave a twirl and whizzed round several times so fast that the college buildings and the large evergreen trees became a blur and made her feel dizzy.

'But what fun we'll have for the rest of the term, Gwen! Though I do have decisions to make, don't I?'

'You most certainly do! If I were you, I'd open my own school and wait until Robert is promoted to house master, then get married. I'm sure there would be someone from here to whom you could sell your school, knowing that it would be in good hands, then you could go off as Mrs Townsend, living in the rarefied atmosphere of Harrow. And, who knows, he could become headmaster in due course. Your role as his wife will be useful because of your achievements here, and your musical talents are sure to impress. You could achieve a very great deal there.'

'But Gwen, I *don't* want a long engagement – but at the same time I do want to be independent and make my own way in the world.'

'Oh, I know it's difficult for you two lovebirds to be apart, but there seems to be no other way. Besides, if you were to give up your ideas now, why, I doubt if he could support you at all comfortably on his present salary. You'll have the holidays to be together. And you'll be achieving your ambitions.'

Their discussion had helped Lizzie to consolidate her ideas; but she knew that it would be the lack of Robert's physical presence, and their inability to express their love fully, that would be difficult and frustrating for both of them.

Gwen went on, 'Meanwhile, I'll be back at my old college working in the library there. If my plans work out, you can come and see me later on, when I've achieved my ambition to be the librarian of *this* college. The Mistress does know that I would like to do that when the position becomes available.'

So their futures were beginning to take shape.

Lizzie and Robert, along with the rest of the audience, filed out of gymnasium where the concert marking the end of the academic year had been held, and made their way over to the hall for the buffet supper and the dancing.

A little later, she and Robert were dancing a pleasant, lilting veleta.

'I remember when we heard this band for the first time, don't you, darling?'

'Yes, I'll never forget that night. How I hated it when you eventually had to leave! I was so lonely that Christmas, even though I only just knew you – well, hardly knew you at all, really, and yet . . .'

'And yet you did know, didn't you? Just as I knew!'

The veleta ended, and they returned to a sofa where their other three friends were sitting. But after a few minutes the strains of a Strauss waltz began to fill the air, and they looked at each other.

'Oh, Robert! I don't suppose we'll ever have the chance to dance to this again here, will we?'

The 'Emperor Waltz' enhanced their memories of the Christmas dance of 1894. Hand in hand, they took the floor. Lizzie caught up the skirt of her pleated pink silk gown and they danced towards the centre of the floor. The harmony between them perfectly matched the music and it was noticeable to the other dancers. Robert turned her and guided her with great speed and precision as they gazed at each other, often laughing and always smiling because of the true love and affection that was uniting them. They were so expert at the waltz that gradually other couples left the floor to give them more space and to admire their skill. They waltzed on, totally enraptured by each other's presence and the beauty of the music.

Eventually they were the only couple dancing. Robert became aware of it, and made an even more flamboyant effort. He was proud of his Lizzie and he wanted people to know it. When the music ended, Lizzie looked around her to discover that everyone was applauding them. She hid her eyes with embarrassment, hunching her shoulders forward as she did so.

'Stand up straight, Lizzie, and curtsy – just as you did after your piano solo.'

'But I'm no dancer!'

'Don't underestimate yourself, my girl.'

And she acknowledged her unexpected triumph. They moved back to their seats.

'Lizzie, this summer my parents and I are going to stay with my grandmother – my mother's mother – in Hampstead. I'll be there for most of the vacation, and my parents are coming for two weeks.'

Wide-eyed and excited, Lizzie replied, 'Then we'll have time together.'

He took her hand and whispered, 'Let's go out for a while. It's full moon, and a beautiful night.'

'Where will we go?'

'Oh, just into the grounds . . . or round and about.'

'I'm not supposed to go out this late, even though the party isn't due to end until a quarter to twelve.'

'Trust me?'

'No – but I'll come.'

'Get a wrap from your room – quickly, before the others come back.'

Lizzie scurried back to her room, picked up a shawl, went to the bathroom and rejoined Robert in the hall.

No one was yet leaving the party, so the entrance hall was deserted. As they slipped out, Robert winked broadly at the friendly porter.

'Everything's in order, sir, Miss Newcombe. Go on – you enjoy yourselves while you're young!'

'What's that supposed to mean? I know he's a friendly old thing, but . . .'

'But nothing – come on, quickly.'

They rushed down the drive, where an open carriage was waiting, the coachman smoking his pipe while the horse nibbled the sweet grass at the side of the road.

'You know where, please.'

'Right you are, sir.'

Astonished and puzzled, Lizzie said, 'Where are we going? I don't want to get sent down – I mustn't be locked out. Please!'

'Darling, relax! Everything's taken care of. Look at that moon through the trees.'

The situation was irresistible. Lizzie did relax, and even managed to forget about college rules. They were alone; she was lying back on the comfortable cushions with Robert's arm around her, her head on his shoulder, and from time to time his lips were lightly caressing her temple.

The horse trotted steadily on towards the centre of the city. They spoke little.

Up to now, while they had spent quite a lot of time in each other's company, more often than not there had been other friends present – even if they were close friends like Eustace and Emma or Joe. There had been a few private moments now and again on the Hoe, on a visit to Torquay, and on moorland picnics, and there had been their secret meetings in Mr Miller's piano warehouse – but never anything as beautiful and solitary as this.

Having driven right along King's Parade – not that they had noticed it – the driver made a right-hand turn into narrow Mill Lane. At the end he turned left and after a few yards stopped his horse. Robert spoke confidentially to him and pressed some money into his hand.

'I can wait, sir,' he replied resignedly.

'Come over here. Be careful.'

Robert led the way to a little wooden jetty built out a few feet over the river. There was a punt moored to it.

'I thought we'd have a trip on the Cam.'

'We won't see much at this time of night.'

'We'll see enough – the riverbank swans, the moon, stars . . .'

As he spoke, he led her carefully into the punt and settled

332

her down on the leather cushions. He took the long, smooth pole, and punted off towards Grantchester. Lizzie felt she ought to have been shy and nervous, but she wasn't. She thought of her friends and how they would have reacted to this situation, and felt that she was the only one, apart from Gwen, who would react as she did – excitedly and happily; not nervously, prudishly or shyly.

Robert punted masterfully onwards, passing under the mathematical bridge, and after about twenty minutes they came to a beautifully quiet stretch of water where he moored the punt – disturbing a pair of swans who momentarily hissed their disapproval. Not wanting to upset the punt, he cautiously stepped over to where Lizzie was reclining, and lay down beside her.

The air was still and very quiet. It was particularly balmy for late May, and the stars and moon shone brightly. The only sound was the lapping of the water against the punt. Instinctively, the couple closed in a warm embrace that was tender and loving, and very meaningful. Lizzie responded to Robert, at once circling her arms around his neck. Their faces were close, and within a few seconds their lips met, and they held a long kiss.

'Oh, Lizzie, I've waited a long time for this. We've already had a lot of happiness, but so little opportunity to express our love.'

Lizzie felt sensations she'd not experienced before. But she was not ashamed to feel them. She was now in a situation where she wanted to express her love to Robert – the man with whom she knew she would share the rest of her life. Her body began to ache with a longing to be even closer to him. She tightened her arms around his neck as he held her to him. They found each other's mouths again; this time their lips parted and their tongues met. Exploring this new experience occupied them for a long while.

Lizzie could feel the excitement mounting in Robert's body as he slipped her gown from her shoulders. It fell to the top of her stays.

'Robert, we can't . . . we must wait.'

'My darling, trust me, I won't hurt you, I promise; but we can go further.'

It was only now that she realised how passionate she was, and how much she wanted sexual fulfilment; but she knew that it would be quite wrong to experience this before they were married. Besides, pregnancy was a risk not to be contemplated.

As he spoke, he put his hand inside her stays and caressed her breasts. This increased her excitement; she was very much aroused. She felt her nipples react to his touch.

'Hold me, hold me, please, darling.'

She didn't understand, but Robert guided her in the right direction. The feeling of him in her hand came as quite a shock. She had mixed responses. She felt she ought to be ashamed and fearful, but she wasn't. In fact, it was a wonderful sensation. Meanwhile he had lifted her skirt, finding his way through many layers of petticoat and drawers, and gently stroked her. In spite of his excitement, Robert was sensitive and careful.

They stayed lying together for sometime. As well as appreciating each other, they now enjoyed the glint of the moon and stars between the branches of the overhanging willow trees, and the reflections on the water. After kissing several times, and just lying gazing at each other, they eventually had to leave the beautiful spot which had afforded them such an idyllic place for their encounter, and begin to make their way back to the patient coachman.

'Happy?'

'What do you think? I should be feeling guilty – and I *am* feeling guilty, because I'm *not* feeling guilty!'

'You know you can be very verbose at times, darling. But I suppose I'll have to put up with that – a price to be paid for having a well-educated wife!'

'Do you know you've not really proposed to me? I'd like to be proposed to.'

'I will propose to you formally, one day. In the meantime, the future Mrs Townsend will just have to be patient!'

Suddenly a wave of horror swept over her and she took a sharp breath. 'Robert, have I . . .?' she asked anxiously.

'What?'

'Am I not a . . .?'

'What? Go on.'

She gulped, the word wasn't easy to say. 'Am I not a . . . a virgin any more?'

'Don't be silly, of course you are!'

'But it was so . . .' She smiled smugly.

'Well? Enjoyable? Delectable? Naughty?'

'All those things – and wanton of me; but you did . . . touch me!'

'And you touched me too, so we're equal, and we're both now . . . well, not inexperienced, if not experienced, er, if you get my meaning.'

By now they had reached the quay. Robert stood up, steadied the punt and anchored it safely. After helping Lizzie ashore, he readjusted his twisted shirt and re-tied his tie. Lizzie straightened her dress and, as most of her hair had fallen down, pulled out what hairpins remained and let it hang freely down her back.

They got back into the coach, and the tired coachman encouraged his horse to a trot.

Lazing sleepily in her Robert's arms, she asked him the time.

'I don't know, and care less.'

At that moment a college clock struck two.

Immediately she sat bolt upright. 'Oh, no! I can't believe it! How will I get back into college? I'll be in really serious trouble, you know.'

'As I said earlier, you won't be. Now relax!'

And as he spoke he pulled her back into his arms and once more they kissed passionately. He stroked her long hair, never having seen it loose before.

'Here you are, sir,' the coachman called to him. 'I think I'd better stop here.'

They had just turned off the main road and were skirting the grounds of the college.

'Can't thank you enough, old man. You've been very patient.'

'What are we doing here? I'm getting cold, it's awful, I know I'll be in trouble. Why, only last term –'

'I said you won't be, darling, and you won't. Stand here.'

He wrapped her shawl more tightly around her as he spoke, then let out a long, low whistle.

335

After about a minute there was a rustling sound from inside the hedge at the other side of the wall. The undergrowth was pushed back to reveal a very old, unused door.

'Good morning, sir! Come on, Miss Newcombe, through here.'

It was the porter's thick Cambridgeshire accent that greeted them.

'Goodbye, darling, see you in London. Cyril'll look after you now and see you get in safely.'

'Goodnight, darling, see you in London!' repeated Lizzie.

The porter escorted her through the gardens to a back door and up a staircase that she'd never used before, to the door of her room. They didn't make a sound, and disturbed no one.

'Lizzie, Lizzie, wake up! It's a quarter to eight, you'll miss prayers.'

Gwen was knocking anxiously on her friend's door. She heard a contented moan.

'Um, uh? What . . .? Is that you, Gwen? What time is it?'

'Lizzie, wake up, It's gone a quarter to eight!'

'Oh, no! Thanks, Gwen.'

Sleepily Lizzie fell out of bed, grabbed her dressing gown and started to get into something resembling her usual morning routine; but she had only about ten minutes, whereas she usually spent at least half an hour washing, fixing her hair and deciding what to put on. She was about the last person in college to slip into assembly.

Since it was Sunday morning, the students were in a relaxed mood, and she was not the only one to be feeling somewhat different.

'So you enjoyed yourself last night! We missed you. Where did you go?'

Lizzie felt that Gwen was being just a little too curious, but was aching to tell her what had happened. She compromised, deciding that it would be safer for both of them. After all, if it did leak out that she'd been with a man until well past two in the morning, and that Cyril had been involved . . . She dreaded the thought.

'Oh, we just took a walk round the grounds. It was a lovely night, you know.'

'Yes, full moon – all very romantic. You must have had a very long walk.' She was teasing Lizzie.

'Quite long.'

'Kissin' an' cuddlin'?' Gwen put on a Southern American accent.

'Oh well, yes, some . . . Stop it, Gwen!'

And they both dissolved in shy girlish giggles. As soon as she could, Lizzie changed the subject.

Lizzie had packed her trunk and was closing the last of the three cases containing her clothes. She had decided to take her goat-skin rug as a reminder of her days at Girton, and the room now looked very bare. Her paintings were in the trunk, wrapped in the rug for safe travelling, and the potted plants that she had collected over the years were given to the gardener for care during the summer, so that a fresher wanting something green to enliven her room would not have to buy it.

She decided to leave the pretty curtains that her mother had made three years ago, and as she looked around the room she thought she'd also leave her comfortable chair where it was.

She went downstairs to the porter's lodge.

'Cyril, my trunk is closed and locked. It can go on the next van to the goods yard, please.'

'Right you are, Miss Newcombe.'

Then, leaning across the narrow counter, he said in her ear, 'How's that fine young man of yours? He's a good one, that he is. You'll be 'appy with him, that you'll be. I won't say a word. Head porter sees everything, says nothing!' He winked and tapped the side of his nose with his stubby forefinger.

Lizzie blushed. 'Yes, he is a dear. We're very happy already!'

'Coo, I bet you are! Lucky chap, that's what he is. My mate down to Trinity remembers him – he was 'is scout, you know!'

'I didn't know that.'

At once Lizzie began to understand how Robert had been able to plan their little adventure so carefully.

337

As she spoke, she happened to glance into his office. There was an indescribably worn and broken easy chair which was obviously where Cyril sat during his rare quiet moments.

'Look, Cyril, after I've left – in about half an hour – go up to my room. There's a very nice easy chair in there that I bought new, when I first came up. Please have it – with my appreciation for all your help.'

'Very, very kind of you, Miss Newcombe. Thank you, and all the best.'

Lizzie went back to her room for the last time. She looked around, sad yet happy, confident yet apprehensive. Confident in what she knew she wanted to do, confident in her love for Robert, and in the knowledge that it was fully reciprocated; but apprehensive about how her plans for her school would work out. She did not know how difficult it would be to find just the right premises, and in the right district in Plymouth. But she was looking forward to the summer months, to playing the piano and enjoying the jubilee celebrations with her beloved family and close friends.

Taking a few steps backward to keep the room in view for as long as possible, she put her hand behind her to locate the handle of the door, turned it, and backed out – closing the door on a beautiful and important phase of her life.

Chapter Twenty-Nine

'Birf-day cake, birf-day cake, Ma, taaa?'

'No, Charlie-boy, no – not now. Eat up your porridge. You can't have birthday cake at breakfast. We'll wait till teatime and share what's left of it with Grandma and Pa. Finish your porridge, like I said, while Ma sees to Tabitha – there's a good boy.'

Three-year-old Albert Charles James Cook grinned broadly and whacked his spoon into the middle of the plate of porridge, causing it to splatter all over his face and bib and the tray of his high chair.

Katy was feeding little Tabitha, and was about to scold her son for making such a mess and wasting his breakfast when she heard the letterbox rattle. Putting the small child on a nearby large chair, she went to pick up the letter. At once she saw from the typed envelope that it was from Emma. Hurriedly, she tore it open and excitedly read the contents, her eyes darting along the lines of neat typewriting.

'Ma, Ma!' she called to Mrs Cook senior, who was in the back yard up to the elbows in soapsuds from a huge tub of washing.

'Yes, dear? What is it?'

'Letter from Emma. It seems Lady Alston is giving a big party in her house up to Queen's Gate on the 29th of the month, and she wants me to do the flowers. It'll be a very special job. She says I can spend as much as I need to make it really nice.'

'Oh, my dear, what a hopportunity! That *will* be good for

business. Jim'll be so thrilled. Now don't you worry about Charlie and little Tabitha. I'll look after them.'

'Emma says I must go up to Queen's Gate on Wednesday to talk to her and Lady Alston about what I think would be best. Look, Ma, can you take care of the little 'uns while I go down the shop and tell Jim?'

'Course, darling. Put her in the bassinet out in the yard while I finish off the washing. And you, young man, drink up your milk, then I'll wipe up all that mess you've made.'

Katy grabbed her sun hat and danced out of the house, delighted at the prospect of a big job. Her step was light and airy. Her reputation as a florist was growing fast. She'd found an elderly retired expert to teach her how to make wreaths and wedding bouquets; she had learned about potted plants and how to arrange large displays. In the last year or so she'd decorated several civic functions and the Society of Fruiterers and Greengrocers' annual dinners and dances. She and Jim were making good progress, becoming prosperous, and now badly needed bigger premises. A family of four, they wanted a place of their own, and the tiny area of the shop that was given over to flowers needed to expand. So they were saving up hard for the day when they could afford to rebuild the still boarded-up and ruined laundry. There they would have their own home upstairs, and a separate florist's business.

Katy was proud of her husband and children, and enjoyed her work with flowers. When she arrived in Kensington on the Wednesday, Emma was glad to see her old friend looking so happy.

After they had made arrangements for the floral displays, Katy asked her friend, 'Any wedding bells for you yet?'

'Oh no, Katy. But I do have a good friend.'

'That's Eustace, isn't it?'

'Yes. I'm fond of him, and I know he likes me, but I can't leave Lady Alston – she's getting quite frail, and it would be horrid to desert her. Besides, I'm not keen on marriage, and you know why.'

'Still bothered by that – after all these years?'

'Yes. But it's really Lady Alston.'

'Well, be that as it may; but you remember, my girl, that Eustace of yours mayn't want to wait for ever. I bet he's really madly in love with you. I'm good at reading between the lines – oh yes, even your neat typed lines! From what you tell me in your letters, I know.'

She gave her old friend a smacking kiss and left.

'And how's my godson, eh?'

Emma picked up young Charlie-boy and sat him on her knee.

'You know he's a real little man already, Katy.'

'Yes, he's almost too grown up. He's been very good and sensible since Tabitha came along – a real big brother, not a bit jealous.'

'Do you love your sister, Charlie?'

'Say "Yes, Auntie Emma",' the proud young mother instructed.

'Yes, Auntieeee Emmmma!' The little boy chuckled with laughter.

'Now, go and play with Pa in the garden. He'll fill the tub, then you and Tabitha can sail your boat.'

The happy three-year-old toddled out to find his father and baby sister.

'Katy, how do you think they are? I'm worried about Papa, you know.'

'To be honest with you, he looks, well – clouded, dark somehow. He only grunts to me if I see him in the street. And your ma, well, she talks a lot, private like, to Ma Cook, but Ma never tells me a thing. I think she's looking much better these days. Your pa making things up with Sarah a few years back has helped her such a lot, and she's real proud of you Em, you know that. But I know she wants to see you and Sarah married before she goes.'

'I'll go in for tea in a minute, then Pa'll want to go to that special service this evening – the first of the thanksgivings for the Queen. What's going to go on round here?'

'A huge street party in Masbro Road – we're helping out with that, and the little 'uns are going. It's going to be lovely. Then there's going to be a Blythe Road Traders' Association street party on Wednesday afternoon for the children, and a real old knees-up in the evening for the grown-ups – all under fairy lights when it gets dark.'

341

Swallowing the second of what would be many cups of tea that afternoon, Emma left her friend and went next door to spend an hour with her parents. Sarah was visiting, too, and their mother was full of admiration of her two fashionable and successful daughters, who greeted each other warmly.

'Oh, Emma darling! How glorious to see you!'

'Sarah, you look wonderful!'

'Like it? The wardrobe mistress ran it up for me. The silk came from Japan – it was actually left over from Marie Tempest's kimono! Oh, you must come and see me when I take over from her next week. *The Geisha* really is a wonderful show, Emma. Ma and Pa are coming on Jubilee night – at *last* we've got Pa to say he'll go to the theatre. But he still thinks it's wicked – doesn't he, Ma?'

'Oh, you know your pa, girls. I heard him praying last night; he was asking God to forgive him for saying he'll go. Even the Reverend couldn't convince him there was no harm in it – even though his daughter's the leading lady.'

Coming downstairs after his Sunday-afternoon nap, Will Cooper managed to smile at his daughters.

'Well, I must admit you two looks really ladylike.'

'We are, we are, thank you,' they chorused, allowing hints of their early cockney accents to colour their remark.

'Um, well, I've got to get ready for church. Any tea going, Ma?'

'Yes, Will. George said he'd be back in an hour or so, but we'll have ours in a few minutes.'

She went into the kitchen, and Emma took the best tea set from the glass-doored cupboard in the dining room while Sarah went to the sideboard drawer and produced the crochet-edged tablecloth that was used only at Sunday tea-time. They came face to face as they began to lay the table.

'I say, Sarah, I don't want to see *him* – do you?'

'Not bloomin' likely! We'll try to get away before he comes. Leave it to me!' The two sisters fell into girlish giggles.

Sarah went on, 'I say, Em, do you remember that time when George had toothache and we said we could cure it? He believed us and we –'

'Blindfolded him, tied string to his tooth, and then tied the

342

string to the handle of the door – how he let us, goodness knows, but even then you were a good actress.' Reminiscing, Emma ached with laughter.

Sarah took up the story again. 'We shut the door and the tooth flew out. It was good Ma came in, otherwise he'd have belted us. But it kept him quiet for ages, didn't it? Must have hurt like hell!'

During tea Sarah said to her mother, 'I have to go right down to Richmond to see one of the cast who's been off ill for a while, and Emma has an adjustment to make to the gown Lady Alston's wearing to see the procession on Tuesday.'

'Sew on a Sunday and you're stabbing Christ through the heart!'

'Oh, Pa, don't! Surely we can be forgiven in this of all weeks, when we're really preparing to thank the good Lord for the long reign of our blessed Queen. I'm sure He won't mind – do you think He will, Sarah?'

Emma lightly kicked her sister under the table.

'I think He'll forgive you, Emma. Look Ma, Pa – we must go. See you again very soon!'

Once outside the cottage, Emma and Sarah collapsed in laughter.

'I don't know how I kept a straight face, do you?'

'No, not after you reminded me about George and his toothache. But poor Pa – he'll never change, will he, Sarah?'

'In some ways, I think he has. In others, never.'

'Captain Newcombe, your seats are along there.'

'Thank you, lieutenant. Joe, you go in first, then Caroline, Emma, Rosamund, then Lizzie, and I'll be at the other end.'

They had front-row seats in a stand about halfway down the west side of Whitehall. It stood about ten feet from the ground and was separated from the general public by wooden rails covered in royal-blue fabric. They were able to sit comfortably and had an uninterrupted view above the heads of the crowd. By now the service in St Paul's was coming to an end, and they would eventually see the procession on its way back to Buckingham Palace.

The morning had begun very dull with a chill in the misty

343

air, but by eleven o'clock, when the procession left the Palace, the sun had burned away the cloud and the weather became truly royal.

There was plenty to look at. Marines lined their part of the route, and the atmosphere was one of jollity and happiness that a reigning monarch had occupied the throne for an unprecedented sixty years. Bunting and garlands of flowers adorned every lamppost and swags of blossoms hung heavily from post to post, many with ribbons fluttering in the light summer breeze.

'It's all so exciting and beautiful!'

Joe had been miles away admiring the historic Banqueting House further down Whitehall to the south. He turned to see a young girl of about seventeen sitting next to him and realised that she was speaking to him.

'Oh yes, isn't it? We'll get a good view of the Queen and the bands, soldiers and everything, from here.'

'I like it in London, but I expect you live here, don't you?'

She's not exactly shy, he thought to himself, and noticed that she had an accent he'd not heard before. He thought perhaps she was an American.

'We'll, no, I don't live here, actually, we're – that's my papa, and sister over there, and Mama's next to me here – we're from Plymouth. Papa's a captain – he has to take his ship to the Spithead review on Saturday.'

'My papa's a captain too,' she said.

He noticed dark, curly hair tied in a wide white bow at the nape of her neck, laughing brown eyes, and thought how pretty she was.

'What's your papa's ship? Perhaps they know each other. But you're not English, are you?'

He asked the last question apprehensively, thinking that it was his turn to be less than shy – and perhaps a little too forward.

'No, we're Australian. Papa's ship is one of those representing the foreign navies at Spithead. We're going on his ship – are you going?'

'Yes, I'm looking forward to it.'

'What do you do? Oh, if that's not a rude question. Please forgive me. Mama keeps saying I'm too forward for my age, but I like to come straight to the point, don't you?'

344

'Just like my sister – she's forward. I'm an architect.'

He didn't say he was only articled to an architect and that it would be another two years before he was fully qualified.

'That's impressive. I've just left school. I went to Melbourne Ladies' College – it's the oldest school for girls in Australia. It was very strict. When Papa's ship was chosen to be in the Jubilee review, Mama and I came too. I never thought I'd get to *England* – but here I am! It's wonderful, and it's hot – but it's June.'

'And it's winter in Australia? But I think we ought to introduce ourselves, don't you? I'm Joseph Newcombe – and you?'

'I'm Nancy Peterson. So pleased to meet you, Mr Newcombe.'

'Delighted to meet *you*, Miss Peterson.'

'I hear a band in the distance.'

'Mama, listen! Lizzie, they're coming!' Joe called across to his sister and mother.

The procession was long and consisted of several bands and contingents from the armies and navies of the Empire. Eventually eight cream ponies came into sight, pulling a beautiful open landau. Sitting in it on one side were two members of the royal family, but the centre of attention was the tiny old lady in black, a black lace parasol protecting her from the sun. She held it in such as way as to prevent it masking her face, which in spite of her age was radiant with happiness at the show of loyalty and affection of her people.

Cries of 'Isn't she wonderful?' and 'God bless her!' and cheers rang out. People in the thick crowd below jumped up and down to try for a better view. Every bit of brass harness, the guardsmen's red uniforms and white gauntlets, sparkled in the strong sunshine.

When the procession had passed, the Admiralty guests made their way into the main building to enjoy naval hospitality and an excellent cold luncheon.

They were placed at a round table, with Lizzie sitting on one side of her brother.

'I saw you flirting, brother Joe. She looked nice. Tell me about her.'

At that moment a voice across the table said, 'Here we are, Mrs Peterson, Miss Peterson – you're there, Nancy.'

345

Joe beamed with delight. Nancy had been placed next to him on his other side.

The huge, high room buzzed with conversation as people found their places at the twenty large tables. Standing behind their chairs waiting for grace to be said, Peter glanced over at his son to see him in animated conversation with the young girl. An elegant lady stood next to him, and by her side another captain.

'I see our daughter is getting to know a young man who I assume is your son?' The other officer reached out a hand. 'Peterson, on permanent attachment to the Royal Siam Navy.'

Captain Newcombe introduced his party to his new acquaintance and to Mrs Peterson.

'Well, those two are getting on well, aren't they? It's quite something to have an exuberant daughter,' Captain Peterson remarked.

'We know that only too well!'

Grace was said and the meal began. It was a very happy occasion, formal yet relaxed. Joe and Nancy weren't the only ones to be enjoying themselves.

'So you're an architect, eh? We have beautiful buildings in Australia, Joe.'

'Yes, sir, I know. I've been studying the Melbourne Public Library, which was opened in 1856 – a very fine structure. Then there's the New Town Hall in Sydney – what an impressive main entrance!'

'You do know your architecture, young Joe.'

All the while, Nancy was looking on and listening in quiet admiration.

Conversation flowed as the courses came and went. Towards the end of the meal, after coffee and the toasts, Lady Alston, who was sitting right across the table from Emma, beckoned to her. Emma got up from her place and went over to her.

'My dear, what nice people! Such good company! Of course we cannot invite them to the dinner, but do take down their address: I would like to invite them to the supper and the ball. I somehow think that Joe would like that too, don't you? She is a pretty, lively little thing, don't you think?'

Emma, in her usual efficient manner, discreetly requested the Petersons' address. The two captains exchanged views on the coming naval review at Spithead, where Peter Newcombe's current ship, the large armoured cruiser HMS *Magnificent*, one of the new Sovereign class, would be in line with the rest of the fleet and the fourteen visiting ships from foreign navies. The captains' families and friends were to be allowed on board.

It was almost four o'clock when the lunch party split up. That evening the Newcombes gave an informal supper party at their rented house in Edwardes Square.

'Oh, Lizzie, do you think she'll be incovenienced? I hated leaving her.'

'Of course she won't. The house is quiet, and if old Nurse Brown is as reliable as you say, she'll sit and knit while Lady Alston sleeps. And she wants you to have fun. Emma, what's the time?'

'You asked me that a minute ago. It's twenty-five past seven.'

'How do I look?'

'Lovely, but a bit flushed.'

'I think I caught the sun this morning.'

'That's your excuse.'

'Heavens, there's the bell!'

Lizzie looked out of the window. 'It's your Eustace!'

'He's not *my* Eustace – but I'll let him in.'

Lizzie kept her eyes on the square, and when Emma had gone downstairs she saw Robert and his parents walking towards the house from the north side of the colourful central garden.

'They're here! I wonder how they'll get on. I'm so nervous!' she said aloud to herself. It was the first time she'd seen Robert since their night in Cambridge. She felt she'd waited an age for this moment. Excited and happy, she took a last quick look in the mirror. Her new blue and pink striped dress made her look tall and elegant, yet youthfully pretty. She rushed downstairs, hurriedly greeted Eustace, then opened the front door to let in her lover and to introduce her future parents-in-law to her own parents. She so wanted to throw her arms around Robert's neck, but they both knew that would be indecorous. With pounding hearts, they just squeezed hands.

Lizzie needn't have worried. All was to be well. The members of older generation, although from very different backgrounds, were obviously going to be good friends. Champagne flowed, the buffet supper was delicious, and at ten o'clock the five young people went off to join the celebrating crowds and see the lights and decorations of central London.

They took their leave of Emma and Eustace at the end of Queen's Gate, and Eustace escorted Emma the short distance to the front door of number 1.

'This has been a very special day, hasn't it, Emma?'

'I'll not forget it ever, will you?'

'No.'

Eustace was silent for a moment, and purposely slowed down their pace.

'No,' he repeated. 'I won't.'

He fell silent. Just as they reached the entrance to the house, he stopped and turned to face Emma. He wanted to make it an even more memorable day.

'You know, I'll never forget that night b-back in 1893 when . . .' His stammer became just noticeable.

'When what, Eustace?' But she knew what he was about to say.

'When I was nervous and you kissed me. I can't tell you how much that meant to me. How I played for *you* that night. How I *always* play for you.'

'I do know, and I respect and admire you a very great deal. I also like you very, very much.'

'Emma, do you think you could ever love me?'

'My dear, if I could ever love a man it would be you. But I am not free to love – not like Lizzie and Robert.'

'Because of Lady Alston?'

'I owe everything to her, Eustace. I can't leave her. Not that things have always been easy between us, as you know, but I can't allow myself the sort of love you want from me.'

'I shall never love anyone else but you. I will wait for you, Emma.'

'You mustn't.'

'But why not?'

'There are other reasons.'

'What are they? I can't believe that there's anything to keep us apart, other than Lady Alston – and I understand and of course respect your loyalty.'

'Eustace, there are things about me you don't know and wouldn't understand. I don't think I'm capable of returning a man's love. No, don't wait for me.'

'I'm not taking that for an answer. I love you with all my heart. I'll be patient. Perhaps one day you'll explain. But for now, please, Emma, please give me that kiss again – for waiting nearly four years already.'

His tender speech, his patience, kindness and gentleness touched her heart, and made her relax and smile.

'I'm waiting.'

'As you have for almost four years?'

'Precisely. And it *is* Jubilee night, and I can't promise to wait another fifty-six!'

He took a small step closer to her. Summoning all her courage, she leaned forward and, standing on her toes, brought her lips to his cheek.

He cautiously held her around the waist, and felt a surge of nervousness in her body as he did so, but nevertheless he very gently and lightly pressed his lips to hers and held on to the delicate embrace for three or four seconds. Breaking away, he smiled so warmly and looked so blissfully happy that in spite of all her inhibitions and fears she managed her warm, loving smile.

'People are quite right. You have a more divine smile than anyone I've ever met.'

'Good night, Eustace – dear Eustace.'

'Good night, Emma. And I will wait, you know!'

She turned and unlocked the heavy front door to let herself in. The house was quiet. Slowly she started to mount the stairs to her rooms. She could still feel the warmth of his lips on hers. It was a good feeling. She was happier than she'd ever been – but memories from her teenage years still clouded her emotions. It was as though an icicle had stabbed her and frozen her heart. But now she began to wonder whether it was just possible that some time, somewhere, Eustace could melt it and perhaps even kindle a fire in it.

349

Chapter Thirty

The preparations for the important evening were well under way. Emma had engaged a parlour maid for the day to assist generally and to serve at table with Stratton and Sybil. Lottie, now eighteen, was to cook one of the courses – an *Apfel Strudel* – and, for the first time at any major dinner party, was to help to serve. (She had made excellent progress under Mrs Green's strict discipline and instruction and recently her wages had been raised to eighteen pounds a year.) Somehow Emma had managed to find time to make both young women new lace headdresses and aprons, which increased their confidence and enhanced their appearance.

'Now, Effie, the orchids are for the hall here, and I want you to give this box of posies to Miss Cooper. Tell her to have them put in the cellar, or somewhere very cool, so as to keep them fresh for tonight. Oh, and if you can carry the box of carnations, give them to her as well. I think she's down in the kitchen at the moment. But don't you get in the way down there, or we'll be in trouble.' Katy and her young assistant were already extremely busy.

As the morning wore on, Sybil and the temporary maid got on with setting the dining-room table, now extended to its fullest. A blue, gold and white Sèvres dinner service looked magnificent, and to complete the appearance six matching flower vases were taken up to Katy to fill with delicate pink and white rosebuds and maidenhair fern. These alternated with matching compote dishes which would contain crystallised and fresh fruits. Silver candelabra completed the central display of the long table. During the early afternoon Toby and Stratton polished and arranged the glasses.

The busy pace of the house increased further after three o'clock, when two waiters and two waitresses from Fortnum and Mason came in carriages bringing the first load of food for the buffet. They set out what would not deteriorate; the rest of the food would be brought while the dinner guests were eating, well before the supper and ball guests were due to arrive, so that everything would be ready in time for the much later supper interval.

But the kitchen was the real centre of activity. Mrs Green and Lottie had been up since four peeling potatoes, shelling peas and trimming beans. Then they moved on to stuffing six chickens, to be roasted later in the day, and to dress two full legs of lamb with rosemary. The house had been built with large-scale entertaining in mind, and had ample capacity in the roomy kitchen. Two huge ranges allowed plenty of space for the roasting, and the hobs were more than adequate to accommodate pans for sauces and vegetables. As the day wore on, the heat of the kitchen, with both ranges going at full strength, became intense.

Emma knew just how important it would be to keep Lady Alston as calm and relaxed as possible, and at three thirty managed to persuade her to rest for an hour. After tea, they toured the house, just as Katy was finishing clearing up discarded pieces of foliage and unsuitable flowers.

'My dear Kate, you have done well. Thank you so much! I've never known this old house look better – it's so much more beautiful than when I gave my Golden Jubilee ball, ten years ago.'

'So glad you're pleased, Lady Alston. Doesn't the room look large now you only have seats around the walls? And the floor'll be lovely for dancing, won't it? But before I go, would you care to see if downstairs is to your liking?'

Lady Alston, Emma and Katy made their way down to the dining room, where they saw the full splendour of the elegant table.

'Ah, excellent! And what a nice touch to have these tiny posies by each lady's place.'

'Yes, I've not done that before.'

'Now, my dear, call round late tomorrow afternoon with

your account, and Emma will pay you right away. I must start to get ready. Show Kate and her assistant out, will you, Emma? I so hope that the staff are able to have a rest before the fun begins.'

'Yes, they are – I insisted.'

'Good luck for tonight, Em – and enjoy yourself. You've seen to everything, so just have fun and dance with that Eustace chap as much as you like!'

'Thanks, Katy. I'll tell you all about it tomorrow evening.'

At half past five a hairdresser came and dressed Lady Alston's hair, then Emma's.

The old lady looked at herself in the large cheval mirror. Her pale-grey gown with its fashionable leg-o'-mutton sleeves stood crisply out from the edge of her shoulders, the neckline modestly filled in with a fine lace. She had not wanted her wrinkled skin and protruding bones to be apparent, even though she was wearing an elaborate piece of jewellery. She was an unfashionably thin woman for her age and time, but though her arthritic condition forced her to stoop, she fought it, and at this moment made herself stand up straight.

'Your ladyship is pleased with the gown?'

'Thank you, Madame Elise – you look after me very well.'

A few minutes later, after the dressmaker had left, Emma came in. She was now completely ready. Her pale-blue silk gown was cut low in the front and shaped to show off her tiny waist, and made her look more beautiful than she had ever looked before. Its panelled skirt was much fuller as it reached the floor and fell into a train at the back. She had white doeskin evening gloves, and wore a white gardenia in her hair.

'My dear, you look truly wonderful. I hope you've powdered your nose and put on the merest touch of rouge. Come close, let me see . . . Ah, yes, excellent! That's quite discreet. We must always help nature just a little on these occasions, you know.'

'Lady Alston, you look truly lovely, you really do!'

'Well, I must admit I think I'm not looking too decrepit! Now, my dear, come here for just a moment. I have something for you.'

She opened a black leather jewellery box lined with satin.

352

It contained a choker of four rows of pearls with a diamond and sapphire clasp, and a matching bracelet.

'Emma, I want you to have these. They were given to my grandmother a hundred years ago by a French aristocrat, before she went to the guillotine. Lord Alston had them reset for me like this, and now I want you to have them. It will give me great pleasure to see you wearing them – my old neck . . . Well, no matter. They're yours.'

Lady Alston kept most of her jewellery in the bank, and Emma had never seen the pearls before. She was stunned. The old lady clipped them round her slim neck and placed the clasp at the centre, in the front. Emma looked in the mirror, her eyes shining with delight as she put the bracelet over her gloved wrist.

'What can I say? I'm so very, very grateful. Thank you so much.'

'No, don't hug me – we might disarrange ourselves!'

Emma took both the old lady's hands in hers and squeezed them with delight.

They went downstairs.

Just before seven o'clock they took their places in the hall, ready to receive their first guests. Stratton in his new blue and silver livery announced the arrivals, while Toby, looking very dashing in his, stood by ready to take cloaks and put them on rails in the ground-floor cloakroom.

'Captain and Mrs Newcombe, Miss Elizabeth Newcombe, Mr Joseph Newcombe.'

'My dears, I'm so pleased you've come on the hour. It's lovely to have nice, lively people around as some of the old fogies arrive. It cheers them up.'

As the older people talked of recent events, Emma showed off her necklace and admired Lizzie, who looked spectacular in a pale-green and silver-shot taffeta gown. Mrs Newcombe was in a shade of deep peach and the Captain resplendent in his dress uniform.

They began to move upstairs for the reception.

'Sir Edward Coley Burne-Jones and Mr Edwin Lutyens.'

'How nice to see you again, Sir Edward – and Edwin.'

'The Lady Cricklewood.'

'Good evening, Rosamund, Emma. You haven't told me

353

about the procession. Of course, *I* was in St Paul's, you know!'

'Doubtless I would have known, if you had a telephone, Hester.'

'Well, you both look quite nice, I must say.'

'Thank you, Lady Cricklewood.'

As Hester Cricklewood turned to glide up the stairs, she noticed Emma's pearl choker and bracelet.

Surely Rosamund hadn't been that foolish, she muttered to herself under her breath. No! She must simply be wearing it for this evening, of course.

And so the guests poured in.

Emma was getting concerned. It was ten past seven.

'Mr Eustace Beaumont.'

She heaved a sigh of relief.

'Ah, Eustace. Don't you think our Emma is looking beautiful tonight?'

'Yes, Lady Alston – but no better than her best friend.'

'Oh, Eustace, I didn't know you were such a flatterer!'

'Emma, my dear . . .'

They held hands for a moment, but he had to move up the stairs as more guests arrived.

'Your Ladyship, everyone has now arrived. Would you and Miss Emma care to go up for a while, and I will slip up in about a quarter of an hour to announce dinner?'

'Thank you, Stratton.'

Taking Emma's arm, Lady Alston mounted the stairs. They ascended slowly, their long trains swooshing out behind them, and joined their guests in the drawing room.

'You looks lovely, Miss Emma, if I may say so,' Sybil whispered in her ear as she passed by with a tray of champagne.

'Thank you, Sybil – but you do, too; really elegant, you know!'

Sybil, resplendent in black taffeta with white lace accessories, moved over to Mr and Mrs Keen and recharged their glasses.

'Ladies and gentlemen, dinner is served.'

'Augustus, would you take me in to dinner, please?'

'Of course, Rosamund.'

354

The hostess and her doctor led the way.

The menu listed caviare followed by a clear consommé, salmon with mayonnaise and cucumber, roast lamb with peas, new boiled and buttered potatoes, roast chicken with haricot beans and a side salad. Then *Apfel Strudel* and whipped cream, anchovy salad, cheeses, raspberry water ice, strawberries and clotted cream, and finally fresh and glacé fruits.

It was a full but not overelaborate dinner. Each rich course came and was cleared very smoothly. Conversation flowed. All was great gaiety and laughter.

Emma talked a great deal to Archibald Stillwall, who was sitting at the top end of the table on Lady Alston's left.

'My dear, I cannot say just how highly Lady Alston thinks of you. She has watched your development and growing self-confidence over the years you have been with her, and is, I know, very proud of you.'

'It's flattering of you to say so, Mr Stillwall. I certainly love her dearly, and we are such good friends, in spite of the difference in our ages. I owe so much to her. Look, she gave me this, this evening. Isn't it beautiful?'

'Yes, as a matter of fact, she discussed the idea with me, and I thought it an excellent one.'

Lady Cricklewood from across the table happened to catch a glimpse of Emma showing Mr Stillwall the necklace, and heard her comments. She was inwardly furious, but conversation with her dinner partner, Commander Gasslot, and her enjoyment of the food helped to distract her. Mrs Newcombe, further up the table on the other side, smiled to herself as she saw her husband melting under the effect of Ellen Terry's charm and superb looks.

Lizzie was fascinated by her dinner partner.

'Well, you see, Miss Newcombe, I won first prize for piano at the Paris conservatoire last year. Next week I give the recitals at the Queen's Hall. Do you like Liszt?'

'Very much, Mr Cortot, especially the B Minor Sonata, which I'm hoping to start work on very soon.'

'Ah – you are then a pianist?'

'Yes, I suppose the piano is really my first love.' Lizzie told the young pianist about herself and her and Eustace's recital engagements.

355

At the far end of the table, conversation was equally interesting, if rather more serious.

'You must come and see us all at work down at Kelmscott, Mr Newcombe.'

'May I? Oh, I say, that would be awfully jolly, Sir Edward.'

'So you're an architect too, Mr Newcombe?' Edwin Lutyens put in.

'Yes, but I'll not complete my indentures for another two years. I find your country houses a delight, from the pictures and plans I've seen in the architectural magazines.'

'I must say they are getting very popular. You see, my dear fellow, I'm finding that more enlightened people are now also in need of a greater feeling of space and simplicity. There's a very clever chap in Glasgow – Charles Rennie Mackintosh, a wonderfully innovative architect and furniture designer. We hope to do a great deal of work together.'

At the top of the table, the conversation had turned to the recent celebrations.

'Do you know the City's spent over a quarter of a million on decorations? I wonder if the Queen really approves of such expenditure?'

'Knowing her, Rosamund, she will be extremely grateful, and possibly would have liked more – to impress the masses, you know, and of course the colonials. But what really astonishes me is the extent to which society has hobnobbed and taken their pleasure *with* them – quite disgusting! I really fail to understand today's society. However, I also hear that the poor people were in no way disrespectful – never disorderly or offensive. When we left St Paul's – yes, please, I will have another slice of that *Apfel Strudel*. When we left St Paul's, our landau could scarcely get through the crowd.'

Hester stopped to take a large mouthful of the pastry dessert smothered in whipped cream. Augustus Minton was about to speak, but she, swallowing hastily, went on, 'Then there was the Garden Party yesterday. Her Majesty drove round the garden at five thirty, and stopped her carriage every so often to speak to people.'

'What did she say to *you*, Hester?'

'Well, I didn't feel inclined to push my way to the front –

356

so undignified, though of course there were those who did. No, I didn't detain Her Majesty. I shall wait for my invitation to Windsor. But do you know, the Princess of Wales was wearing a – what d'you call it? a *sari* – a heathen Indian woman's garment. I thought it was quite disgraceful – I can't imagine what Canterbury thought about it. I saw him eyeing her with disgust.'

'I expect it was pretty, though.'

'Well, I suppose you *could* call it that. It seemed to be made of a sort of gold gauze.'

'Perhaps one of the Indian princes gave it to her, and she was paying homage to the subcontinent.'

'Well, whatever the intention, Augustus, it was *most* indecorous as well as being disrespectful to British Christian values. Don't you think so, Mr Glyn?'

'Possibly so, dear lady,' the vicar replied, daintily dabbing his mouth with his napkin as Sybil set strawberries and cream before him.

As the meal drew to a close and the guests nibbled a grape or a piece of crystallised fruit, Lady Alston got up, and Stratton moved her chair back.

'Ladies, shall we retire to my boudoir for coffee? The gentlemen may join us later.'

The dozen women went up to their hostess's large boudoir to relax, tidy themselves, make use of the bathroom and gossip. It was the first time that Emma and Lizzie had had a chance to exchange a few words.

'It was nice of Lady Alston to ask the Townsends and indeed the Petersons to the ball. I can't wait to see Robert again.'

'That was a lovely evening – it went so well for you and Robert. After all, your respective parents could have loathed each other, or just been coldly polite.'

'Yes, they were fine. But tell me, did you get home safely? Did Eustace look after you?'

Emma blushed, and sat gazing down into her lap at nothing.

'Ah, I see he did well. What have you got to tell me? Or can I guess?'

'He was very kind.'

'I think that's probably the understatement of the evening!'

A little later the eleven men joined the women, and for a while they enjoyed coffee. Soon it was time for Lady Alston and Emma to welcome the ball and supper guests. As the little orchestra was striking up, their friends moved down a floor to the drawing room, now serving as the ballroom.

The floral decorations filled the room with a fresh, delicate scent. The large French windows opening out onto the balcony were banked by palms, their fronds gently waving in the warm summer-night breeze, and the light net curtains softening the whole effect. Garlands of flowers graced the walls, while yet more arrangements of white and red roses and blue scabious stood on tall stands in the corners.

The room was lit by huge rings of candles set in chandeliers hanging from the centre of the ceiling, and by candle fixtures on the walls. Although more modern forms of lighting were available, Lady Alston had been eager to create the special atmosphere that only candles could give. The musicians were placed on a small platform in front of the large fireplace, but still there was plenty of room for dancing.

More and more people gathered. Most of them knew each other or had met on odd occasions. Emma embraced Sarah, who was looking magnificent in white trimmed with pink.

'And did Papa enjoy the show, Sarah? I'm most anxious to know.'

'It was very interesting. Of course, Ma was speechless. He grunted a bit, and had to admit that he thought everyone dressed far more modestly then he'd expected. Perhaps he was disappointed. He actually managed a smile or two – I could see him from the stage. But it was all worth it for Ma, you know.'

Upstairs, Lizzie was doing her best to be polite to everyone, though her eyes were on the door, waiting for Robert's arrival. She saw his parents first, and went to speak to them. And Joe, while he was fascinated by everything that Lutyens was still telling him about his enterprises, was almost as excited as Lizzie as he waited for Nancy.

When they came, the three families joined each other.

'Hello, darling. Isn't it perfectly splendid? Did you have a good dinner?'

358

'Marvellous,' Lizzie replied as they pressed hands and looked at each other.

'Ladies and gentlemen, your hostess will now lead the dancing with Dr Augustus Minton.' Stratton made the announcement.

The band struck up Strauss's 'Gold and Silver Waltz', and Lady Alston and Dr Minton waltzed slowly round the room to the admiration of the guests.

Eustace and Emma looked at each other.

'Well, you're the second hostess, you must go next – so may I have the pleasure, Miss Cooper?'

Picking up the loop on her train and slipping it over her wrist, she joined Eustace on the floor.

'Come, darling – it's not the 'Emperor' but . . .'

'Yes please, Robert.'

And they were away, soon to be followed by the Captain and Mrs Newcombe, the Townsends and many other guests.

'Nancy, look – Mr Cortot is without a partner. You should dance with him.'

'Oh, Joe, no – I'll sit this one out with you. But didn't I read somewhere that Lord Byron could dance in spite of his club foot?'

'Yes, I think so – though I'd hate to fall down. But you must have fun.'

'I want to sit with you!' When their eyes met, she blushed, and shyly turned to smell a rose.

'Aren't these lovely?'

'Yes, very pretty . . . just like you! Excuse me – I shouldn't have said that.'

'Well, as you know, I like people to say what they think.' Nancy gave him a broad smile.

The conductor saw that Lady Alston and Dr Minton were now sitting down, and increased the tempo, which pleased the whirling Robert and Lizzie.

Lady Cricklewood had been engaged in conversation with the Stillwalls, but now they had taken the floor and she was alone. She caught sight of Emma and Eustace. As they passed, Lady Alston gave Emma a big smile and a wave. A beam of bright-blue light momentarily blinded Lady Cricklewood, making her jump. She realised it was from the large sapphire clasp on the pearl necklace adorning Emma's throat.

'Look at her,' she muttered to herself, 'the little fortune hunter, look at her, making up to Rosamund like that. And now she's got *that* – of all things. She's probably got the Alston rubies, too, for all I know, and I bet the little bitch has pawned them already. Yes, that's just what such a little ragamuffin would do. Why didn't Rosa keep that nice girl Maisie? Why on earth did she take *her* back?'

While these thoughts rushed through the jealous woman's mind, her fury continued to mount. Her breathing shortened and her face reddened. Finally, she could contain herself no longer. Suddenly she stood up and, in a voice that overpowered the orchestra, cried:

'I can stand this no longer! I cannot and I will not. *Good night*, Rosamund.'

Though only a few other people heard her over the sound of the music, Lady Alston was appalled.

'I don't understand . . . Hester, whatever is wrong?'

But Hester had gone.

Lady Alston staggered and almost fell.

Emma and Dr Minton took her to her bedroom, where a short rest recovered her, though the incident marred her evening.

Meanwhile, the orchestra was playing 'The Mikado Lancers'. During this, Robert pulled Lizzie out of the grand chain as they passed each other, and took her out on the balcony. It was deserted: everyone was either dancing or sitting, gossiping, fanning themselves with large feather or lace fans. The night was clear, but they couldn't see many stars – the lights of the big city blotted most of them out.

'It's warmer than it was in May, isn't it?' Lizzie remarked.

'I don't want to talk about the weather.'

'Oh, Robert – neither do I.'

Glancing round to make sure that they weren't being overlooked, he took her in his arms and they enjoyed a long, passionate kiss.

'I really love you very, very much, Lizzie.'

'And I you.'

'Now – this is the moment.'

Smiling broadly, he got down on one knee, and she started to laugh.

'Silly, get up! You'll make your dress trousers dusty.'

'No, I won't – there's carpet underfoot. Besides, I don't care.'

Calming down a little, and allowing an air of tenderness and romance to return, he continued, 'Miss Newcombe, my feelings for you are deep, meaningful and honourable, so will you do me the honour of becoming my wife? There – I said I'd propose properly, didn't I?'

Lizzie, her heart brimming with love, amusement and adoration of his sense of humour, smilingly replied, 'Of course I will. But you'll have to ask Papa.'

'I have already. We had a man-to-man chat!'

'Oh yes – and when?'

'I'm not telling you. But both he and your mama approve, and so do my parents. They are all prepared and expecting it.'

'Then I suppose we'd better go and tell them. I know it'll be a long engagement, but it will be marvellous to know we're so close. Oh, do come on! I can't wait to tell them!'

'Wait a moment. I have something for you.'

He put his hand in his pocket and brought out a little case containing a diamond-cluster ring.

'Oh, Robert – it's beautiful! Put it on for me.'

It was a tiny bit big, but that was no problem.

'Darling, I'm so happy! Thank you a million times.'

They kissed again, but had to break their embrace as two other couples joined them. Smiling somewhat embarrassedly, they scurried to find their parents.

It was two thirty.

Stratton, in his most resonant voice, announced, 'Ladies and gentlemen, supper is served.'

A huge carved ice swan was glittering in the light of the chandelier and the many candles set around the room. The Captain spied Lizzie and Robert in the throng, looking flushed and excited.

'I think they have something to tell us. I wondered if he'd ask her tonight.'

'Mama, Papa – look!'

'Dearest girl, I'm so happy for you! What a lovely ring!'

'Congratulations, old man. You've certainly taken on something there. Your life won't be dull, that's for certain.'

The Newcombes and the Townsends gathered around, and were soon joined by Joe, who kissed his sister and congratulated his brother-in-law to be.

'We're privileged to be witness to this family rejoicing, Captain Newcombe.'

'Thank you, Mrs Peterson, Captain.'

'I must find Eustace and Emma,' Lizzie said rather breathlessly.

It wasn't easy, but eventually the other couple heard the good news, and soon it had spread to Lady Alston, now once more with her guests. She gave her blessing.

'I think we should announce it to everyone here, my dears, and allow you and Robert to lead off a dance. Have you a favourite piece of music?'

'Oh yes, Lady Alston.' Lizzie didn't take long to decide. The butler was summoned, 'Ask the orchestra to play the "Emperor Waltz".'

The conductor shook his head.

'Lady Alston, is there a problem?'

'Mr Cortot – Miss Newcombe here and Mr Townsend have just become engaged, and I suggested that they start a dance to their favourite piece of music, but the orchestra don't have it.'

'What is the piece, Miss Newcombe?'

'Strauss's "Emperor Waltz", Mr Cortot.'

'I shall play.'

Lady Alston stood up and Stratton called for quiet.

'My friends, I have an announcement to make. There are two especially happy young people here this evening. Mr Robert Townsend has just proposed to Miss Elizabeth Newcombe and she has accepted. As a mark of our affection, I think we should allow them to start the next dance, the music for which will be played by Mr Alfred Cortot.'

There was a round of applause as Lizzie and Robert took the floor.

'This really will be our piece now, won't it, darling? It always seems to catch up with us in one way or another.'

362

She glanced at the spectrum from her ring as the diamonds responded to the candlelight.

He twirled her round with his usual dexterity and grace. Their parents were next to join in and soon the floor was crowded.

As they danced, Eustace said to Emma, 'I'd like us to be like Lizzie and Robert – you do know, don't you?'

'Yes, Eustace, I do know – and you do make me happy. But I must do my duty.'

'Well, at least we know how we stand,' he said resignedly.

And they waltzed on.

It was getting quite late, but Lady Alston had one more surprise for her guests.

'Dear friends, we cannot allow this occasion to pass without hearing the lovely voice of Miss Sarah Cooper, who, as you know, is now the leading lady in *The Geisha*, playing at Daly's Theatre. She has agreed to sing for us that delightful song "The Amorous Goldfish".'

Emma was full of pride. Sarah's voice was even more beautiful than when she'd heard it on previous occasions. The song, which every errandboy in London was whistling, came over as fresh and charming. Sarah was greeted with a huge round of applause when she finished. Having bowed, she joined her hostess.

'My dear, that was quite lovely! Thank you so much.'

'Thank you for inviting me, Lady Alston.'

'You are being well looked after?'

'Excellently, thank you. Of course, he has been very busy lately, but all is well. And if the Prince – if he tires of me, well, I'll have my career, and some generous gifts. He has commissioned Mr Sargent to paint my portrait; I go for my first sitting in a few weeks' time.'

'How exciting for you, my dear! You are extremely talented in many ways, Sarah, and I understand – completely.'

Just as they finished the discreet conversation behind their fans, Sir Arthur Sullivan joined them and asked Sarah for the next dance.

It was now almost four o'clock, and the guests began to take their leave.

'Good night, Joe.' Nancy's big, bright eyes were shining at her hero.

'Good night, Nancy.' He took her hand, and on an impulse kissed it.

They both blushed, and she joined her parents, who were saying good night to Lady Alston and Emma. Sir Arthur Sullivan congratulated the conductor on the performance of 'The Mikado Lancers' and Ellen Terry joined Sarah as they waited for their carriages.

The Newcombes and the Townsends left together, teasing the lovebirds about having soon to part them.

Gradually the house became quiet. Eustace was the last to go.

'It's been simply marvellous, Lady Alston.'

The clock in the hall struck four as he took his farewell. Dawn had broken. He turned to face Emma.

'Good night, Emma dear, You were wonderful. I will see you tomorrow.'

'It *is* tomorrow, Eustace. And I'm so happy for Lizzie and Robert.'

'Yes, so am I.'

He stole a light kiss on her flushed cheek, and Stratton shut the front door after him.

Lady Alston and Emma very slowly began to mount the stairs to her bedroom.

'It was a wonderful evening. But I wish Lady Cricklewood hadn't behaved so very badly. It was most hurtful – are you sure you've quite recovered?'

'Yes, Emma dear. Apart from that horrid incident, I think it was the best party I've ever given. We'll have many *happy* memories of tonight, won't we? Hester can be dreadfully unpredictable at times, you know. Nevertheless, I wish I understood what annoyed her so much. It was *most* embarrassing.'

She was quiet for a moment. As they reached her bedroom door, she said, 'Apart from that, which we must at once forget, it was perfect. Well, almost perfect.'

'Not absolutely perfect?'

'No, Emma.' She hesitated, then went on, 'Someone was missing.'

'You . . . you mean Lord Alston?'

'No, not Lord Alston, nor Juliet. You're my Juliet nowadays. No someone else . . . Good night, dearest girl.'

364

Chapter Thirty-One

Shakily Lizzie tore open the envelope, her eyes darting across the lines. She let out a loud exclamation.

'Well – good news or what? Tell us, Sis!'

'"We are writing to inform you that you have achieved honours in the recent Classics tripos, and congratulate you on your success."'

'My dear, congratulations!' Her parents and brother clustered around to hug her, and Joe at once told Aggie and Laura, who joined in the excitement.

'Mama, I must go to the post office and send Robert a telegram to let him know.'

'Lizzie, you'll faint if you don't eat something before you go out. Have some toast and marmalade, then you can go.'

'Oh, all right. Then I'll go on up to Emma and Lady Alston; I know they'll want to know. And I ought to send word to Gwen and Lucy. Wonder how they've got on.'

'You'll take the omnibus to Queen's Gate, of course.'

'No, Mama – can't wait around for that. I'll go on my cycle.'

Lizzie had her bicycle with her in London, having gone straight there from Cambridge.

'Lizzie, no! You've not ridden in London – it mayn't be safe. There's more traffic than in Plymouth or Cambridge, you know.'

'You should see Cambridge on Saturdays, Mama! I'll be fine.'

'Well, wear your cycling skirt and make sure you attach

365

the tapes to your ankles. We don't want you chased by street urchins.'

'Street urchins in Kensington? Well, really, Caro! But just be a bit careful, Lizzie, eh?'

Lizzie pedalled off.

'Come in, Miss Newcombe. Miss Emma is up in the drawing room.'

She made her way up the stairs. To her surprise the room was dark, with only thin shafts of sunlight streaming through joins in the shutters, and it had an usually quiet, eerie atmosphere. The furniture had been replaced; the flowers and garlands were still in position, but were now drooping. A withered petal fluttered to the floor, catching a flash of sunlight as it fell. For a moment she saw or heard noone.

'Emma? Stratton said you were in here. Why don't you pull the shutters back? It's a lovely day, and guess wh –'

'Lizzie, I'm here on the sofa. Please come over.'

'Whatever's the matter? Even Stratton seemed glum. I've got some wonderful news!'

Emma stood up, greeted her friend and held her tight. Lizzie could feel her whole body shaking.

'What is it, Emma? Tell me. What is it? Is your mama ill, or is Lady Alston?'

Emma nodded.

'Tell me, Emma, you must tell me. She's . . .?'

'Yes, she's dead.'

'But when? How? She was so well on Tuesday night.'

'Yes, she was – until . . . until . . .'

Emma couldn't go on, but she wasn't crying.

Lizzie sat beside her and held her hand.

'Until – well, we don't know exactly when, but . . . Oh, it was awful for Sybil.'

'You mean she found her?'

Emma nodded again and went on, 'At half past eight – an hour or so ago. She took her morning tea in to her as usual, and there she was. Sybil thought she was still sleeping, but when she couldn't rouse her, she . . .'

'She called you?'

'Yes. I too thought she was just deeply asleep. She looked so peaceful. Then Sybil got that little dressing-table mirror and put it to her lips, and . . .' Emma sat staring blankly ahead of her.

'We got Stratton to telephone Dr Minton, and, well, he confirmed it. He's just left. He'll come back soon with the undertaker. Oh, Lizzie, what am I going to do? I'm so alone now.'

'We'll all take care of you, Emma, you know that. And I'm sure Dr Minton and Mr Stillwall will be kind and helpful.'

She gave Emma a reassuring hug, whereupon Emma started to sob, grief and tears pouring out of her. Lizzie was relieved that this was happening. She'd heard of the effect of a death on people who couldn't cry when they lost a loved one.

'Has Dr Minton given you a sedative?'

'No, but he will when he comes back. He says that Sybil must have one as well – it was a dreadful shock for her in particular.'

'I don't want to leave you, but would you like me to go and see them below stairs?'

'It would be kind, Lizzie dear. Thank you.'

Lizzie left Emma sitting on the sofa in the semi-darkness and made her way down to the basement, where Lady Alston's staff were in their parlour. Mrs Green, Lottie and Sybil were trying to comfort one another. Toby and Stratton sat at the table with them, silent and miserable.

'Oh, it *is* nice of you to come so soon, Miss Newcombe. Thank you so much.'

Lizzie didn't tell them the real reason for her visit.

'It's as if the blessed Virgin sent you to us, to give us love and kindness,' Mrs Green added.

'I'm stunned too. Look, let me make you all some tea – you don't want to bother to do that now. Just sit quiet for a moment.'

'Thank you, miss. Lottie, you help Miss Newcombe.'

Together they made tea in the kitchen. Lizzie noticed, standing on the large kitchen table, the neat, pretty tray with its little silver tea service and dainty cup and saucer. She touched the pot. It was still warm.

When the tea was ready she carried it on a heavy wooden

tray with big breakfast cups and saucers back to the servants' parlour, and returned to Emma.

As she crossed the hall, the front doorbell rang. She called downstairs that she would answer it.

Dr Minton had a strange man with him. Lizzie assumed he was the undertaker. He at once went upstairs.

'Miss Newcombe, I am glad that you're here.'

'Is there anything I can do to help, Dr Minton?'

'My dear, if you can use the instrument, I would ask you to telephone this number, enquire for Mr Stillwall or Mr Keen, break the news to them, and ask them to come here as soon as possible. I want to give Emma and Sybil these sedatives to calm them – such a shock!'

Lizzie hadn't used a telephone before. Gingerly lifting the receiver and putting it to her ear, she heard the voice of the operator and asked her to connect her with the number on the paper Dr Minton had given her. She made the call to the solicitor, and then, finding a book called the Telephone Directory near the instrument, looked up the telephone number of the vicar, Mr Glyn, and spoke to him. Within half an hour he was at the house to comfort Emma.

'Eustace, do come in, dear. Lizzie should have been back ages ago – she went up to Queen's Gate to tell them her news.'

'Her news? Her exam results? Tell me, how did she get on?'

'Well, it would be so nice if she told you herself – I know she'd like to.'

'I can't wait, Mrs Newcombe. Please tell me!'

She handed him the letter.

'But that's marvellous! Are you worried about her not getting back for luncheon, Mrs Newcombe? As you know, we were going to the Wigmore Hall this afternoon to hear Mr Cortot.'

'Yes, I am rather. You see, she went on her cycle. She might have had an accident.'

'Well, I'll come right back if she isn't there or . . . anything.'

Eustace was greeted by a very pale-faced Lizzie, who opened the door to him.

'Are you training to be a butler, Lizzie?'

'No, Eustace. Come in.'

'What's wrong? You look awfully pale!'

Lizzie told him.

'Emma's asleep at present. I'm helping in the drawing room.'

Stratton and Toby were now in the drawing room, pulling down the half-dead floral garlands. Lottie and Mrs Green were unfolding huge pieces of filmy black gauze. As the garlands fell to the floor, sombre draperies were placed over the chandelier, the paintings and the large mirror over the fireplace.

'I think they'll bring her in here later on, Eustace. Isn't it sad? She was such a lovely lady, and so full of life on Tuesday. I can't believe it.'

'It's too awful. How's Emma?'

'She's had a good cry, and of course a sleep will help.'

They left the drawing room and made their way downstairs, away from all the grim activity.

'Do you think I could possibly go and sit by her bed? Do you think she'd like to see me when she wakes?'

'I think she would, you know. She's going to need all our love and support – especially for the funeral.'

As Emma stirred, Eustace got up from the nearby chair where he had been reading, and went to her bedside. She opened one sticky eye and then the other. Seeing Eustace, she gave him a little smile; then, as she became more conscious, sorrow flooded back, and her eyes started to swell with tears.

'Eustace . . .' she said, through her sobs.

'I know, dearest. I said I'd sit with you until you woke. The sleep has done you no harm.'

Hurriedly she sat up.

'How did you find out? What time is it?'

'It's half past seven in the evening.'

'I've been asleep for hours. Oh, I shouldn't have been! I should have –'

'Dr Minton's sedative was a good thing. Earlier today I telephoned the theatre, and as soon as Sarah arrived there, she had my message. After the show she'll go home and get

369

some things, and she'll come and stay with you here for as long as you need her. Of course she'll have to go to the theatre as usual, but when she's not here either Lizzie or I or Mrs Newcombe will come. You won't be alone, we promise.'

'Thank you so very much.' She bit her lip. 'Oh, Eustace, I'm so unhappy! I don't know how I'll get over this. I'll have to get a job as a typist, or something. But this house and the house in Plymouth . . . and what will happen to the staff?'

'Dear heart, those things are not your problem. They're for Mr Stillwall to see to, and whoever Lady Alston's executors are. Now, I think you should have something to eat. Look, I'll go down to Mrs Green – I expect Sybil is awake by now, too. She had the same medicine as you. A plain omelette and some toast would be a good idea.'

'I can't eat a thing.'

'You really must,' he replied, becoming gently masterful, 'otherwise your physical strength will let you down. Get up. Shall I run you a bath? Don't bother to dress – just put on your dressing gown and slippers for now. You must move around, otherwise you'll not sleep tonight.'

He went to her bathroom, found some refreshing pine essence and turned on the taps, then made his way to the kitchen. On the stairs he met an equally red-eyed Sybil, and tried to comfort her a little as well. She appreciated his kindness, thinking what a pleasant and caring man he was.

He carried the tray with the light meal into Emma's rooms, put it down on her lap and put his arm around her. She was glad of his comforting warmth.

He had a great many things to tell her.

'My dear, the funeral is to be on Tuesday at two o'clock. It appears that Lady Alston left some very clear instructions about the order of service. Dr Minton is coming very soon to tell you about some of the other arrangements that have been made. Do you think you can cope with hearing about them, now?'

'Yes, the sooner the better. Stay with me, Eustace, while he tells me, won't you, please?'

'As if I would do anything else! Unless, of course, such things are confidential.'

'Eustace, I must dress.'

'You know, you're perfectly decent as you are. Look, I'll put your coverlet over your knees, and if you've an extra bed jacket, put that over your shoulders. And you are in shock, so don't bother about dressing just for Dr Minton. I'm glad you were able to eat something, anyway.'

'Yes, and I do feel a little more settled because of it.'

Dr Minton greeted Emma in a kindly, fatherly way, expressing support as gently as he could.

'Now, Emma, after you had your sedative, Rosamund was taken by Mr Chalker to his chapel of repose. On Tuesday morning she will be brought here to rest in the drawing room, where friends can come and pay their last respects.'

'Am I right in thinking she had a heart attack, Dr Minton?'

'No doubt about it, my dear. While it is a dreadful shock to all of us, it was wonderful for her – no suffering, and so soon after the splendid evening we had. Tell me, was she at all unwell yesterday?'

'I do wonder, Dr Minton, if Lady Cricklewood's strange behaviour could have been the cause of her attack. Did you overhear her? Lady Alston was dreadfully upset.'

'If that were the case, she would, I think, have had her attack at that moment. But the incident certainly might have been a contributory factor, I must admit.'

'That really is quite dreadful.' Emma paused thoughtfully. 'She was very tired yesterday, and we both took some extra rest – I was tired too. Later we went over much of what had happened, and read the papers. There was an account of the ball in *The Times*, by the way, which gave her great pleasure.'

'Did she complain of any pain in the chest? Or of indigestion, perhaps?'

'No . . . wait a moment, she did. And she took a dose of Milk of Magnesia. That wouldn't have hurt her, would it?'

'It couldn't possibly have done so. But what she thought was indigestion could have been a sign of trouble.'

'If only I'd have realised that, she might be still alive.'

'No, my dear, that's not the case. You must not put blame on yourself. Her heart was weak – it had been so for years. We must be thankful that she ended her life on such a happy

371

note – and, my dear Emma, that you made her last five years such fun for her.'

'It wasn't difficult, Dr Minton – she and I got on so well. Yes, I loved her dearly. I'm only sorry that I shall never, ever, be able to thank her enough for these five wonderful years. As to the future, well . . .'

Eustace came and sat on the little settee beside her.

'Emma, don't worry. Please don't worry. I will take care of you, if you will allow me. I have my teaching, and we can go and live in my little house in Plymouth – its very comfortable that is if . . . in due course . . .'

He gently placed his hand over hers, which were neatly folded in her lap.

'Very good, my boy. Take care of her, won't you? And Emma, I think I'll give you another sleeping pill for tonight, and I'll come round and see you again tomorrow. Before I go, I'll visit the servants. They might like a little help with sleeping, too.'

'Thank you so much. Good night.'

As he made his way down to the servants' quarters, Dr Minton thought what a remarkable young woman Emma was. Such dignity, such inner strength – and so delightful and charming. How well Rosamund had chosen!

On his way back to his boarding house that evening, Eustace dropped a note through the Newcombes' letterbox telling them that Emma, with Toby, would call at nine thirty in the hope that Mrs Newcombe and Lizzie could go with her to Whiteley's to choose some mourning.

Sarah liked to be in the theatre an hour and a half beforehand.

'Now do you think you'll be all right?' asked Sarah as she got up to leave.

'Of course I will. I've a great deal to do. Don't worry about me.'

'Now, I must go and cheer up the waiting masses, so it's off to work and "The Amorous Goldfish"!'

Sarah immediately wished she'd not mentioned the title of her favourite solo – it brought back such a poignant recent memory. Emma's eyes reddened.

372

'My pet, I *am* sorry. But what a way to die, so soon after what she herself admitted was one of the most joyous evenings of her life. And without pain – do look at it like that, Emma.'

'Of course you're right, but everything seems so uncertain. Mr Stillwall is dreadfully evasive about the future, and so is Dr Minton.'

'Darling, they know what they're doing. Don't worry. Now, I simply must go.'

'Why don't you have a little rest, Miss Emma? You've been so busy, what with all your letter writing and things.'

'Thank you, Sybil. And why don't you and Mrs Green go and have tea somewhere nice, somewhere really nice?' She reached for her purse and gave Sybil five shillings. 'Stratton'll let Mr Stillwall in and out. Now, do you need new hats for Tuesday?'

'Well, miss . . .'

'I think perhaps you ought, even if you do have suitable ones. Look, call in at Barker's and choose something. You'd better have some more money.'

She gave Sybil an additional half sovereign, then had an afterthought.

'Perhaps you should get a black tam-'o'-shanter for Lottie. She could go with you, but I expect you and Mrs Green would enjoy being on your own. Besides, you must go to a really nice café for tea – or even an hotel, if you'd like. Lottie can be on hand, should I want anything.'

The idea of new hats was very cheering for Sybil, who at once thought that after a few weeks she and Mrs Green could put some coloured flowers or feathers in them. And tea out would be a pleasant treat.

As she prepared for her rest, Emma suddenly thought that it would be appropriate if Lady Alston were buried in the new gown she had worn to her own ball. She had looked so lovely in it – everyone had said so – and, after all, young brides who died were often buried in their wedding gowns. She went into Lady Alston's darkened bedroom and, to see her way to the huge wardrobe, pulled back one section of shutter and the heavy velvet curtain. The July sunlight

373

dazzled her for a moment. She went to the wardrobe. The delicate scent of Lady Alston's favourite eau de Cologne greeted her. There, quite near the front, was the gown. With great care she took it down on its heavily padded hanger and placed it lovingly on the bed. On the top shelf of the wardrobe she found the large box in which it had been delivered. She packed the gown almost as meticulously as it had been when Madame Elise had brought it. As she folded it, she noticed some creases at the back of the skirt, where Rosamund had been sitting. The simple little marks at once stabbed her heart.

'My dear friend – I never thought you'd wear this to your grave!'

Some tears fell on the gown, and in a strange way this seemed to console her. It was as if a little of herself would be buried with her friend and benefactress.

On Saturday and Monday messages poured in. Many people called and left cards. Some asked to see Emma, but in most cases Stratton made her excuses.

She was using her own sitting room all the time now; the drawing room was prepared for the arrival of the coffin the following morning, and Emma couldn't face sitting in the room, hung as it was with black drapery.

Eustace made himself generally useful, taking countless messages and writing a number of short letters.

Emma went to bed fairly early; he waited up until Sarah returned from the theatre.

'Tomorrow is going to be a great strain for all of us, Eustace, but especially for Emma.'

'She is a remarkable person, Sarah.'

'You love her very much?'

'Yes, very much. I will never leave her.' He paused for a moment, then went on, 'In fact, my heart is on fire for her – it has been since the first moment I set eyes on her.'

'I thought so. Do you know if she loves you?'

'She has said that if ever she marries it will be me, but – this was before Lady Alston's passing, of course – she said that she had her duty to her . . .'

'That's very typical of her – she's extremely loyal. But has she said anything else to you?'

'She's been very mysterious at times. She says there are other reasons, but she seems unable to go on to explain them. I can't understand it, especially as she seems to love me.'

'I'm quite sure that she loves you, and that she will be as loyal and faithful to you as she has been to Lady Alston these last five years.'

'But now she owes no more loyalty to her, does she?'

'No, Eustace; she's done her duty.'

'So now what? We have to resolve the other problem, I suppose?'

'Yes, you will.'

Sarah paused, then went on.

'Eustace, Emma will have to tell you herself, and that is going to be very difficult for her. But, believe me, her difficulty is very understandable. I think she will only finally resolve the problem if she *can* tell you herself. It is not up to me to go into details.'

'You obviously know about everything, but at times I'm at my wits' end trying to work out what is so seriously bothering Emma. It's dreadful not knowing, when you feel you could help and when it's someone who means so very much to you.' Becoming increasingly passionate, he continued, 'Sarah, I so want to marry her, but I simply can't get through the barrier, and we've known each other for almost five years. There are times when I think I'm breaking it down – I believe I came near to doing so the other night, when she made me very happy.

'Oh, I know most women are shy, but quite honestly I have felt for a long time that there's something else. Now you say that is the case; it's more than I can conceive. I accept the fact that you cannot give me details, but please, Sarah, put me out of some of my misery. Is there or has there been another man in her life? Is that it?'

There had been, of course, 'another man', as Eustace had put it, but not in the sense that he could guess. Sarah's own early suffering came back to her. She felt and smelled George's ugly, unwelcome presence from all those years ago. But she had come to terms with those early, revolting experiences. She could only be honest; she could only hint, but in

375

hinting she knew she could help Eustace to understand, and in doing so he could just perhaps encourage Emma to unburden herself.

'My dear, Emma is living with a very dreadful problem. To put it bluntly, there was another man.'

Eustace opened his mouth to respond, but at once Sarah put her hand on his arm to reassure him.

'But it wasn't at all what you might think.' She paused. 'Both Emma and I had a very serious problem within our family at the time. I suffered even more than she, but she has suffered far more since; she feels that she cannot express love towards a man. I think she's even more confused about it now that she finds she is so fond of you. And if, as you say, she made you happy the other evening –'

'Oh, it wasn't . . . I mean, we didn't . . .'

'Quite. But it does look as if she wants to exorcise the problem. I think you'll just have to be patient for a while longer – especially now she's so unhappy and unsettled. If you're content to wait, when the time is right I'm sure you can help her.'

Eustace, whose early life in the Gloucestershire manse had been very strict and simple, was dumbfounded. He half guessed at Sarah's meaning, though at first he could not grasp the idea, the horror.

'A man within the family? Oh no, not –'

'No, not her father. But I can say no more, Eustace. And of course, as far as Emma is concerned, we have never had this conversation.'

'I understand completely, Sarah, and I cannot thank you enough. You have given me a great deal of food for thought.'

He bade her good night. He would be back early next morning, to give Emma as much support as possible during what was to be the most demanding day in her life so far.

Chapter Thirty-Two

The darkened room was lit by four large candles, one at each corner of the bier, which had been placed in the centre of the room. Some upright chairs stood nearby.

Emma was at once struck by the heavy scent of lilies and roses. Tall vases of arum lilies softened the hard lines of the candlesticks and gently bowed, as if in sombre farewell, towards the open coffin. On the floor beside it was the large, long wreath of pink and white rosebuds, which had been made at her request and brought to the house by Katy.

Although there was so much atmosphere, Emma felt that the room was empty. There was no one there – apart from herself, and Dr Minton standing by the door. She turned to him for reassurance. He encouraged her to move forwards to the bier.

The sides of the open coffin were covered in flowers, and it was from them that the scent permeated the air. Looking down into the coffin, Emma for the last time came face to face with her much loved friend. She was at once struck by Lady Alston's peaceful and young expression. Emma was too unhappy to cry; but her unhappiness was not of the heavy, morbid kind. She knew that Lady Alson had lived her life to the full, and she felt with conviction that the person lying in the elaborate coffin dressed in the lovely gown was not her dear friend. She was in another place, and probably young again – as young as Emma herself.

'My dear,' she sighed. 'I am going to miss you so very, very much. Thank you for everything.'

She bent forward and lightly kissed her on the forehead.

The feel of the cold flesh ran as a shudder through Emma's body.

The elderly doctor joined her.

'Emma, if you would now like to sit here while the others come through, I'll summon them.'

She sat down. The staff came in first, the women muffling sobs into their handkerchiefs. Having paid their respects, they took their places standing back against the closed folding doors. Friends, who in a subdued mood had been taking a glass of sherry in the sitting room beyond, entered to pay their last respects.

Emma stood up to greet Lady Cricklewood, but the defiant old woman completely ignored her and walked past her as if she weren't there. Bravely Emma shook hands with everyone else as they filed by.

People talked in muted whispers, and remarked how peaceful and happy Lady Alston looked. Eventually it was the Newcombes' and Eustace's turn, and Emma gained strength from their warm embraces.

'Are you bearing up, my dearest?'

'Yes, thank you, Eustace.' She managed a weak smile.

After about an hour everyone had filed through and for a while returned to the back sitting room. Emma was left alone with Dr Minton.

'My dear, the undertaker and his assistant are here now; I think we should leave them to close the coffin.'

This was too much for Emma. Tears rolled down her cheeks.

'Of course, Dr Minton, I understand. But can they wait just a moment or two? There's something I so want to do.'

'Of course, my dear.'

She went up to Lady Alston's bedroom. Not far from her bed was the long; narrow box that Mrs Newcombe had brought for her from India. Carefully opening it, with great tenderness Emma lifted out the fragile pressed roses which had blossomed on Juliet's grave. She returned to the drawing room, now totally empty, and approached the coffin. She placed the flowers under the crossed hands, saying, 'I think these should be with you always. Goodbye.'

She joined the other mourners, soon to follow the coffin to the hearse and the waiting carriages in the sunlit street.

Six bearers, wearing black frock coats and top hats with long black silk weeper ribbons, carried the coffin to the elaborate hearse. It had cut-glass panels and decorations of silver and gilt emblematic flowers, and iron scrollwork on the roof, on which also was crowded a great number of wreaths.

The funeral procession was lead by the undertaker, walking at a slow, steady pace and carrying a black-ribboned staff. The hearse was pulled by four elegant, shining black horses, which from time to time tossed their heads, causing the feather ostrich plumes on their bridles to flutter majestically. It was followed by five mourning carriages also drawn by plumed black horses.

Emma rode in the first carriage with Augustus, Lady Cricklewood, who ignored her completely, and Mrs Glyn. It was a short journey to St Mary Abbot's Church, where the choir and a crowded congregation were waiting.

At the end of the service, the slow procession made its way down the long aisle. As the coffin neared the west door, Emma noticed a tall, elegant man, who must have been well over seventy, standing in the pew just behind Sarah and her parents. She was quite sure he hadn't been there when they entered the church. Then she distinctly heard Hester Cricklewood hiss under her breath, 'Gaston, you! How dare you?' As the coffin passed, he crossed himself with his left hand, so Emma noticed that he had only one arm.

The carriages took them to the main entrance to Kensal Green Cemetery, and they processed on foot to the Alston tomb – a large, impressive monument with Italianate weeping cherubs and a white marble angel embracing a broken column, to which was attached lichen and straggling ivy.

They stopped at its dark entrance for the committal. The atmosphere was formal and cold, and in spite of only close mourners being present, it seemed to lack the intimacy and love that Lady Alston deserved. Emma thought how much nicer it would have been if she could have had a grave in some pretty country churchyard. There were trees and a great many beautiful rose bushes and flowers all round the tomb; but there was also a severity, with none of the tender emotion and sympathy which so often softens grief. The

379

dark-grey stone walls of the tomb, its metal grills and grim contents seemed alien to all Lady Alston had stood for and everything that Emma knew about her. Her final resting place, although very grand, was somehow not right for such a sweet, kind and very human lady. But she gathered that it had been both Lord and Lady Alston's wish that they should lie together, and such wishes must be adhered to.

As the interment came to an end, the mourners gathered round the wreaths, lined up around the base of the tomb. Across the leafy path, Emma saw the man she had seen earlier in church, again standing bolt upright, top hat in hand, abundant white hair catching the afternoon sunlight. He looked calm and composed, but Emma could feel his grief.

Should I go and speak to him? she thought. But before she had made up her mind, it was time to leave. She was not sorry: this was a dreadful place which made her feel even more unhappy, though she knew that Lady Alston was now lying with her husband.

The mourners filed back to the waiting carriages, Lady Cricklewood on Dr Minton's arm. As they turned to retrace their steps, Emma noticed that the man gestured, raising his one arm as if to plead with Hester. She merely gave him a basilisk stare and tossed her head, narrowing her eyes, her whole face seeming to shrink in wrinkled bitterness. When she had gone by, Emma noticed the man's serene calm break, and tears began to roll down his cheeks. There was no response from Dr Minton or anyone else. A few paces further on, she gingerly turned to see him placing a single red rose tied with a black ribbon at the entrance to the tomb.

Back at Queen's Gate, Emma was surprised to find that the shutters and windows, tightly closed since the death, were open, and the trappings of death had been entirely cleared away. Friends gathered upstairs in the drawing room, where fresh bowls of flowers had appeared as if by magic. The grim solemnity of the funeral ritual had been completed, everything was now lightness.

'This too is what Rosamund wanted, my dear; it was another of her very precise instructions.'

'The room looks wonderful, Dr Minton – wasn't that typical of her?'

380

Emma's curiosity got the better of her. 'Dr Minton, may I ask you something?'

'Of course, my dear.' His round, rosy face looked down gently smiling at her, knowing that her ordeal wasn't yet over.

'There was a man in church, and I saw him again at the cemetery – do you know who he was? I noticed that Lady Cricklewood seemed to know him and to dislike him, but to me he looked . . .'

She felt she was saying too much.

'I do not think we should intrude on these matters. He was certainly someone who knew Rosamund, perhaps from years ago – an old friend, I expect, but I have absolutely no idea. After all, Rosamund had a great many friends over the years. I expect he just wanted to pay his respects.'

Emma remembered Lady Alston's cryptic remark after the ball.

There must be a connection. She was sure the mysterious man had been in Lady Alston's thoughts. But why had Lady Cricklewood been so cruel to him – especially when he looked so sad?

The very best vintage champagne was served, and the company was then taken down to the dining room for high tea.

Among the party were four men to whom Mr Stillwall introduced Emma, they represented four charities dear to Lady Alston.

Because tension has eased, the meal passed quite pleasantly, with everyone present recalling their favourite memories of their friend. There was a certain lightening of the atmosphere – helped no doubt by the champagne, and clouded only by Lady Cricklewood, who sat steely-eyed throughout, saying as little as possible.

Most people now began to take their leave, greeting and thanking Dr Minton and Emma.

'Aunt Caroline, please don't leave me – and you, Lizzie, can you stay? I would be so grateful if you could sit with me until after the will has been read.'

'Peter and Joe, go back and tell Aggie and Laura that Lizzie and I will be late.'

381

'Eustace will look after you while I'm with the others. Perhaps you could all go to my sitting room?'

'Emma, you were so brave!'

'Lizzie, I so *hated* that tomb! I'll never forget it, dear Lady Alston in that dreadful place.'

Mrs Newcombe put a reassuring arm around Emma. 'But she's not *really* there, you know.'

'Yes, Aunt Caroline, I *do* know, but . . .'

Tears caught up with her.

'My dear, will you summon the staff?'

'Yes – which members, Dr Minton?'

'All of them, please.'

'All of them?'

'Yes, Emma.'

They assembled in the drawing room, where rows of chairs had been placed to occupy them, and a table had been set up with three chairs facing them.

'The staff are here, but please, Dr Minton, may I go to my friends now? I really can't face any more formalities today, especially as I'm something of an outsider. Why, I haven't been with Lady Alston even as long as Lottie.'

The elderly man stood facing Emma, and put his hands reassuringly on her arms.

'My dear, I'm afraid you must be present.'

He gave her a glass of brandy, adding a little water. 'Keep this by you, and don't be shy about taking a sip when you feel you need it.'

Everyone was now seated, Hester Cricklewood in the centre chair of the front row, upright, firmly resting a black-gloved hand over the round gold top of a cane which stood as erect as its owner's heavily corseted torso. The room was quiet.

Mr Stillwall stood facing them, holding a document, and announced:

'This is the last will and testament of Rosamund Louisa Alston.'

He paused, unfolding the thick paper, then read out the copperplate writing.

'"I, Rosamund Louisa Alston, being of sound mind and body, hereby bequeath my estate as follows . . ."'

382

Lady Alston had made generous donations to the church and to her favourite charities, whose trustees smiled warmly at each other.

'"The loyalty and faithful attention of my personal staff over the years deserves reward, and I want publicly to acknowledge and thank them for their love and hard work. I therefore bequeath the sum of one thousand pounds to my butler, Mr Alfred Stratton, and the same sum to my cook, Mrs Bertha Green, as a reward for their impeccable service.

'"To Miss Sybil Andrews and Mr Toby Matthews I bequeath the sum of five hundred pounds each. In addition I wish to donate such a sum as my executor deems fit for the care of my horse, or horses, for the rest of their days, this to be administered by Mr Matthews.

'"To Miss Lottie Christmas I bequeath the sum of two hundred and fifty pounds to remain in trust until she becomes twenty-one years of age, should she not have reached her majority by the time of my passing."'

There were little cries of pleasure and surprise as the staff heard the news. They exchanged excited glances, and even the usually austere Stratton gave Mrs Green and Sybil a broad smile. Lottie, however, looked confused. Sybil whispered, 'It's all right, Lottie. Mr Stratton will explain after about the trust – you'll see!'

'"To my old friend, Lady Hester Cricklewood . . ."'

At the mention of her name, Hester shifted in her seat and then sat up even straighter, fat nose high in the air.

'". . . I offer my sincere thanks for the help she has given me at times during my life. To her I bequeath my black lace fan, in the hope that she will accept the gift with love, and that it will bring back many happy memories of the times we have spent together."'

Hester Cricklewood looked as if she was about to have an apoplectic fit. The doctor was ready for such a reaction and produced smelling salts. Mr Stillwall noticed that she was about to stand up – for her instinct was to make another of her dramatic exits.

'Lady Cricklewood,' said Mr Keen, 'there is more. Please wait.'

'"The residue of my estate, my paintings, furniture, works

of art and jewellery, my two houses and all remaining monies and investments both in this country and overseas, I bequeath to the constant companion of my fading years, Miss Emma Cooper, who will, I know, make good use of said properties."'

The room was abuzz. Emma was stunned and confused. The statement hadn't sunk in – 'my two houses . . . all monies and investments . . .'

She sat blankly. Dr Minton smiled.

'Take some brandy, my dear.'

Emma did as she was told, still wide-eyed, automatically putting the glass to her lips.

At this point Lady Cricklewood did sweep out of the room, like a galleon going to fight the Armada.

Mr Stillwall handed an envelope to Emma.

'Ladies and gentlemen, the will is properly signed, witnessed and dated 10 July 1896, and supersedes any previous will made by Lady Alston. The executor is Dr Augustus Minton. There are no codicils. That concludes this ceremony. Thank you.'

The sound of excited voices filled the room.

'My dear, you are a very wealthy young lady – very wealthy. Many congratulations.'

'But Dr Minton, I just don't deserve it. She was always so generous anyway, and she made me happy. I can't – I *can't* accept it.'

'You can, and you must. Lady Alston has put her trust in you because you have proved your worth. You must never forget that you made her the happiest of women during the last five years. Emma, you should have seen her a while before you came into her life – I thought she was going to die then, she was so melancholic, especially after her previous companion left. Don't worry, I will help you – and Mr Stillwall will advise you, especially with the investments. The staff will continue to receive their salaries – and so will you, of course – until the will is proved. Now, go and tell your dear friends, and then get an early night.'

She staggered upstairs to her sitting room, finding the doorhandle without eyes.

'Emma, you look so pale. Are you unwell?'

'I . . . I don't think so.'

And with those few words the heiress fell into a dead faint at their feet.

That evening Lady Hester Cricklewood wrote a letter.

Two days after the funeral, Emma retired to her bedroom after lunch. Sarah had gone to the theatre for a performance, and Eustace and Lizzie had a teatime recital at the house of a cousin of Lady Sullivan. So for an hour or two she was alone, apart from the staff, who were going about their tasks.

She relaxed on her comfortable bed, and felt that now she was strong enough to open and read the letter that Lady Alston had written to her – when? She presumed at about the time she revised the will.

Her assumption proved correct. She carefully cut the envelope open and unfolded the familiar stationery. It was dated July 1896.

My dearest Emma,

By the time you read this, I will have departed the earth, and my wishes for the funeral will have been carried out.

I so hope that my leaving the bulk of my estate to you will not come as too much of a shock; but Emma, it is my wish. I cannot impress upon you too strongly just how much your lively, loving company has meant to me during these last years of my life.

I have watched your confidence grow, as I have watched your skills in typewriting and your other practical studies develop.

As you know, I am as fond of your friends Elizabeth and her family and Eustace as you yourself are, and if, in some way, you young people can find a way to work together, I am sure that all of you will lead particularly fulfilling lives – assisted by my legacy to you.

Of course, you must not forget your parents – they are getting older and may need help. Discuss this with your dear sister. Both you and she probably have cause to be forgiving towards your father and brother. Be kind to them, Emma, but be firm too.

Now, Emma, believe me when I say that the greatest thing in life we can experience is the joy that a meaningful, loving relationship can bring. I know that Eustace loves you with all his heart and soul. He is a good man, Emma. Do not reject his love. Receive his tenderness, affection and devotion with open arms and heart, so that in time any unpleasant black memories of your youth will be wiped out. All heaven will rejoice with me when you and he become one for ever.

Do not, Emma dearest, allow yourself to be distracted from that love. During my long life I have made mistakes – and one in particular, which I bitterly regret. I have had to live with it and to rise above it; but it has, unknown to you or others, always haunted me, and my secret will, I hope, be buried with me in the grave. Believe me, it has been a heavy burden to carry. I would wish such remorseful feelings on no one, and least of all you.

My dear, I know from this time forward life will never be the same for you. Be guided by my old friends Dr Minton and Mr Stillwall – they are fond of you. Think of them as uncles! Live your life to the full.

May God bless you, always.

My eternal love to you. I will watch over you and guide you if I am permitted to do so.

Yours for always, and with more thanks than you can possibly imagine,

Rosamund Louisa Alston.

'I simply couldn't read it right away, Sarah; but isn't it a beautiful letter? So helpful and kind. She seems to have remembered all of us – that was typical of her. But I still don't know how I'm going to cope.'

'You will, you know. Life will be wonderful for you, Emma – one huge challenge. Of course, you have a lot of decisions to make – especially once the will has been proved, which will take a while – and if I were you, I'd start to think about the future and what you want to do.'

'I can't, I can't! It's all too much.'

'Of course it seems so, but soon the mists will clear and you'll see your way ahead.'

Emma managed a smile.

'Darling, the money will cushion your grief, believe me. I know.' Sarah paused, as if finally to make up her own mind, then went on, 'I don't tell you much about myself, but I've had to make important decisions from time to time.'

'And have you ever regretted any?'

'Not one. For all his faults and his strict discipline, Pa has a lot of common sense, and we have inherited it, and Ma is no fool either. You'll do well, Emma. As I have.'

'Yes, you have done well.'

'Now I can tell you something. You knew I left my rooms near Sadler's Wells, didn't you?'

'Why, yes.'

'But you haven't been to see me at my new address. It's a lovely house, a large one, in Cheyne Walk on the Chelsea Embankment, and I'm not renting it – it's mine!'

'But how? How did you get it? It must have cost a great deal of money.'

'It did, and I've worked hard for it. I haven't wanted to tell you before, and anyway I've not had it long; but now it's properly decorated and very comfortable, and I look forward to entertaining you and the others there.'

For the first time since the death, Emma was really cheered.

Sarah was holding Lady Alston's letter.

'I think it would be nice to show this to Eustace and Lizzie. After all, she speaks so well of both of them.'

'No, I can't do that – Lady Alston speaks too freely of Eustace and his feelings for me. I'd feel embarrassed.'

'Well, do take note of what she says about you and him. She's right, you know. Don't reject his love, Emma.'

That night, tossing and turning in her bed before sleep came, Emma had those words rushing through her mind: 'Don't reject his love . . . Don't reject his love.'

Emma had felt ever since the funeral that she must reassure the staff – *her* staff, as they now were. She was very fond of them, and though she knew she had, in some respects, to keep a distance between herself and them, she hoped that they would prove as loyal to her as they had been to Lady Alston.

At ten o'clock they all filed into the drawing room, which was sunny and warm and had, as usual, several large floral displays in big vases to make the atmosphere bright and colourful.

'Now, I know that you all are feeling as unhappy as I am, but I don't want you to feel insecure. I think you have been told that you will continue to get your wages as usual until the legal matters are settled. What I want you to know is that I am not going to turn you out – you'll continue to work for me as you did for Lady Alston. I have not yet decided what I actually want to do, but your futures are quite secure. We have all worked together well during these last five years; we are a good team, and whatever the future holds for us, we must look to it with hope, and be ready to accept any challenges that may come. I am not the kind of person just to sit around and allow you to wait on me. I like to do things, and I shall be in a position to make an interesting life for myself – and, I hope, for you.'

'That's very reassuring, Miss Cooper, I'm sure I speak for all the staff. Thank you.'

'Thank *you*, Stratton. Although it is a little unconventional, I would very much like it if you continued to call me simply Miss Emma, as you have done in the past. Now, I think we can all get back to work. I have many letters to write. So for the moment, thank you all.'

Chapter Thirty-Three

Emma crossed the strange, large room and walked towards
the heavy door. She had to use some force to push it open
and enter the second room. In the distance, upstairs, she
could hear children's voices. She thought they might be
singing. As she mounted a wide flight of stairs, the sound
became clearer. The children were singing – not a song, but
the four-times multiplication table.

She entered the room at the top of the stairs. A little girl
got up from her desk. She was wearing a pink and green
dress – the skirt was made of rose petals. She took Emma by
the hand and led her to a window. Outside was a choppy sea,
and in the distance a menacing black pillar of rock. Eustace,
in a small boat, was having some difficulty in rowing towards
her. He waved to her. She smiled and blew him a kiss. Now
at her feet were several heavy bags which she knew contained
golden sovereigns. One by one she took them and placed
them on the floor of an empty room in the pattern of a large
number two.

She turned over, opened her eyes and looked at the clock.
It was one minute past two. Suddenly she was wide awake.
The dream had been very vivid and given her a lot of food
for thought. The scenario and some of its symbols struck
very clear chords for her. She lay tossing and turning, the
words, 'If only . . . I wonder if I could . . . Would that be
practical? Dare I suggest such a thing?' rushing through her
mind.

'Now, what can I do for you, my dear?'

Mr Stillwall had arrived in response to Emma's summons. He sat down, thinking how odd it was to see young Emma instead of his old friend and client sitting on the sofa facing him.

'Mr Stillwall, I'm beginning to have ideas about the future, but I need some help before I approach certain people who might like to join me.'

'Go on, my dear. You know it's very early days – you must be careful not to rush into anything.'

'Of course you're right, but if I am to follow up this particular idea, I shall have to take action fairly quickly.'

'Tell me all about it.'

She told him that her London neighbours, Commander and Mrs Gasslot, were about to sell number 2 Queen's Gate and retire to the country.

'You want to buy the Gasslots' house?' Mr Stillwall raised his bushy eyebrows in surprise.

Emma smiled rather smugly.

'Yes. Miss Newcombe plans to open a school in Plymouth, but I think she might be persuaded to do so here in Kensington. It would give her far greater scope, and her fiancé might be interested in joining her – as might Mr Beaumont. However, this house alone would not be big enough for such an enterprise. If I could acquire number 2, we could have a very impressive establishment. I feel quite capable of coping with the business side of running the school and the others are more than well qualified to do the teaching.'

'My dear Emma, I congratulate you on the notion. Your thinking is excellent. But you know it's not the done thing for a woman to run a business. I am not at all convinced that it would be quite proper.'

'Mr Stillwall, for the last three years I have run all the accounts of this house and the Plymouth house. I have learned book-keeping and have been practising it regularly. My shorthand is competent and my typing extremely accurate – although I suppose I shouldn't say so myself. Indeed, if you remember, last week when I handed the ledgers over to your partner, he asked me who our clerk was, and couldn't believe that the accounts had been kept by me – a mere woman.'

Mr Stillwall couldn't deny it.

'Now, the will is unlikely to be proved until – when? Late September at the earliest? If my friends decide to join me, it will probably be necessary for me to make an offer on the property within the next few days. Houses around here sell very quickly, as you know. So what can you do to help me?'

'The matter doesn't rest with me, my dear, but with the executor. We will have to consult Dr Minton.'

'May I telephone him and invite him to dinner this evening – if you yourself are able to stay?'

'I think it would be possible, if I may telephone my wife.'

'Of course, Emma, we must remember that as yet you do not know if your friends will want to accept your proposal.'

'But if they do, Dr Minton?'

Emma leaned over the dinner table and willed the doctor to make some constructive suggestion.

He laughed. 'Oh, the enthusiasm of youth! How right Rosamund was, wasn't she, Stillwall?'

Stillwall nodded. Emma blushed.

Dr Minton was quiet for a moment.

'I think there is a way round the problem.'

'Please go on!' Emma's pulse rate was increasing, her eyes shining brightly for the first time since they had been dimmed by tears.

'First you must gather your friends together and get their opinion. Then we will go and see Mr and Mrs Gasslot and *I* will make them an offer for the house, and when the will is proved you can purchase it from me. Or, if you think it would be simpler, Stillwall, I will simply lend Emma the money for three or four months against her expectations – as our beloved Dickens would have said.'

'Dr Minton, thank you so much. I'll summon my friends to a meeting tomorrow. Now I'll leave you. Do join me later for coffee in the drawing room.'

She rang for Stratton to bring the port for her two guests. Augustus Minton lifted his glass, a quizzical look in his old eyes.

'To the young people of the twentieth century,' he said.

They clinked glasses and drank in silence.

391

'It all came to me in a dream, Sarah – or at least a lot of it. The dream wasn't easy to understand – there were children singing their four-times table . . . all sorts of things.'

'Four-times table? Well, that makes sense, doesn't it? There will be four of you, if you go ahead, and you four will be dealing with a lot of others – quite like the multiplication of four.'

'I hadn't thought of it like that.'

'My dear, I'm delighted. I can't wait to hear what the others'll say; but Emma dear, they simply mayn't like the idea. Look, it's gone midnight. I expect everyone's gone to bed. I'll go down to the kitchen and make us some malted milk. The show went well again tonight, by the way. The Prince of Wales came yet again . . . Emma, will you be all right if I go home to sleep tomorrow?'

'Yes, of course. You mustn't neglect your own house for too long.'

In spite of the malted milk, Emma had so much on her mind that she did not drift off to sleep until five o'clock.

'Miss Lizzie Newcombe and Mr Robert Townsend.'

'Eustace, what *is* all this about? We're mystified!'

'I've been here ages, and I can't get a word out of her. I don't know why! I took her for a walk in Holland Park this afternoon, but her lips were sealed.'

'Oh, poor Eustace!'

'Thank you, Lizzie; I knew you'd understand.'

'I wanted you all together, and I knew that Robert would be still at school, but now, well – sit down, and I'll explain.'

Excitedly and not always coherently, Emma told them of recent developments and her idea.

'Lizzie, I know your plan is to open a school in Plymouth, but how would you feel about opening one right here in Kensington?'

'Emma!'

'This is an excellent location – plenty of wealthy families live nearby. Now, Eustace, how would you feel about teaching at our school?'

It was his turn to be speechless.

Emma turned to Robert.

'I know you're established at Harrow, but would you consider joining such an enterprise?'

The three of them now started to speak at once. Emma called them to order and looked at her notes.

'Even if I can acquire the extra property, a great many alterations would have to be made to the two houses, and of course we wouldn't be ready to open for some time – a year at least. If you like the idea, I can support the school until it supports itself – pay you proper salaries, at least as good as those you two men are getting at present, and I would hope rather more. As time goes on and the school becomes a profitable business, we can think about forming a limited company, all working together, and each becoming a shareholder.

'Lizzie, would you be prepared to sacrifice living in Plymouth quite soon? I would need you here for the planning period.'

There was a short silence, which Robert broke.

'You know, Lizzie, if this really came to pass, we could get married much sooner than we expected. You would be fulfilling your ambition and we needn't be parted while you did so.'

'You like my idea?'

Lizzie and Robert gripped each other's hands so tightly that Lizzie's strong pianist's fingers became red.

'I can't believe it – a big school here in London! Oh, Emma, are you sure?'

'Of course I'm sure. I'll have the money, I can acquire the property, you three have the necessary qualifications . . .'

'And you can cope with the business side of things, Emma.'

'Yes, that's what I thought.'

Eustace sat staring at Emma, unblinking.

'Am I hearing correctly, or am I dreaming too? If so I want never, ever to wake up. Emma dearest, of course – it's the most wonderful plan! Of course I want to be part of it. I can go back to Hoe Grammar until you feel I can be of use here, and I can come in the holidays; Robert is close at hand even in term-time. But Robert, old chap, how do you feel about sacrificing the possibility of becoming a house master at Harrow?'

393

'I won't mind at all, if Emma is sure she'd like me to work with the three of you.'

'Definitely – why, we're almost family, anyway. I'm certain we'll be set for success. But there's so much to discuss, so many decisions to make. Then there's the conversion – I don't think that too much will be called for, but there will be some structural alterations to the houses.'

'Perhaps we can consult Joe.'

'Of course, Lizzie – I'd not thought of that. There, you see, we'll all have so many ideas.'

Emma got up and rang the bell.

'Serve the champagne now, please, Stratton. This is the beginning of a new era. And open a bottle for yourself and the staff. I have some exciting plans to tell you about, very soon!'

The four friends stood up solemnly, raising their glasses.

'A toast, my friends, to our enterprise: to – to the Alston Academy, a seat of learning for the twentieth century!'

'The Alston Academy!'

Chapter Thirty-Four

'Lizzie, Lizzie!'

Emma was knocking on the guest bedroom door.

'Yes, come in, Emma.'

'It's arrived, it's here! We have the confirmation that number 2 Queen's Gate now belongs to Dr Minton.

Problems and questions crowded around Emma like hungry children crying for food. What about the house in Plymouth? How many extra domestic staff would be needed when they opened the school? What about Lady Alston's jewellery? How many additional teachers would be needed? Books, books, books! They'd have to buy hundreds!

There had been a tempestuous meeting at which the four partners argued fiercely over whether the school was to be for boys or girls. Lizzie had stormed out in a temper when the men said they didn't want to teach only girls, but eventually they compromised. There would be a school for boys at number 2 Queen's Gate and one for girls at number 1.

Now that Lizzie had moved into the house with her, Emma was getting a lot of support from her. Sarah had returned to her Chelsea home, but still visited frequently. And it was Eustace's custom to arrive at number 1 around ten in the morning.

'Dearest, what good news!'

He took both her hands as he spoke.

'I've already written to Joe. We should hear tomorrow if he can spend the weekend with us.'

'Oh, the weekend? Yes, I suppose we must devote it to business?'

He sounded disappointed. Emma noticed his disgruntled tone of voice and remarked on it.

'It's just that it'll be our last weekend together until half-term. I have to go back to Plymouth.'

'Yes, I know, on Monday, for the start of the new term. But Eustace, our plans must go forward.' She sounded brisk and businesslike.

'But I wanted, well, I wanted to t-take you out on Sunday and to spend our last day together, just the two of us.'

His eyes, which at the least provocation looked sad, couldn't have looked more so.

'I'm sorry. But we'll see. If we do well on Saturday, we might just be able to manage a few hours somewhere.'

Joe produced a large sketchbook from his portmanteau. The others craned over the dining table to see. His ideas for the conversion were both imaginative and practical. Emma had written to him saying that it was essential that the boys' and girls' classrooms should be totally separate. They also wanted a library, a gymnasium which could be used as a theatre, a science laboratory and an art room. With adjustments to the two buildings and careful timetabling of the two academies, these facilities could be shared. Joe's ideas for the gymnasium were inspiring. He planned to build it at the back of the two houses with separate entrances. The prospect of a real stage with proper lighting and exercise equipment was thrilling to all of them.

At the end of the long, very productive meeting, Emma said, 'I don't want to be too selfish, but I would like to have my permanent home on the first and second floors of this house.'

'It doesn't worry Lizzie and me. We'll be making our own arrangements in due course.'

Robert squeezed Lizzie's thigh under the table as he spoke, causing her to jump in her seat and let out a little cry.

'But perhaps Eustace might have an opinion on the matter.'

'Whatever Emma wants is fine with me.'

'I could use the back sitting room adjoining the drawing room as a dining room, then all the ground floor including the back study and the morning room, which has been shut up since Lord Alston died, can be used for schoolrooms. I want to teach sewing, embroidery, and later on business studies too, and perhaps sometimes social graces and household management, in what was my suite on the third floor, and of course the fourth floor can also be used as classrooms.

'So, Joe, what is the next stage?' asked Emma.

'You must ask Mr Stillwall to write to the manager of the Harrington Estate, the freeholders, informing him of our plans. Get him to reassure him that we shall make no alterations to the front exterior façades of the houses – that's very important – and he must also add that we are fully aware of the Public Health Act and intend strictly to adhere to the legislation laid down in it. There should be no difficulty about using the premises as a school – there is already one in a similar house at the other end of Queen's Gate.'

'I will do that tomorrow, and send you a copy.'

'Emma, tomorrow you and I are going out, remember?'

'Very well, Eustace. I'll write the letter before I go to bed tonight.'

The meeting broke up.

That afternoon they all paraded into number 2. Just as Emma, surrounded by the others, was unlocking the heavy front door, a carriage drawn by two palomino horses passed by. The passenger, recognising them, rapped with her fan to order her footman to stop.

'Help me down, help me down! I want to know what's happening.'

She strode up to the group of friends.

'And what is going on here, pray, Miss Cooper?'

'Lady Cricklewood, how *nice* to see you. This house has just been purchased for me, and I am about to show it to my friends. Please excuse us, our time is limited.'

Hester Cricklewood was furious, but she restrained herself, merely looking Emma up and down as though she was the meanest of servants, before climbing back into her carriage.

'Take no notice, Emma,' said Eustace, 'she's just very jealous of you.'

'That's right, don't worry – come on, let's go in.'

Hester Cricklewood nearly missed her footing as the footman helped her back into her carriage. In her fury she gripped and twisted the fan in her agitated hands. The struts immediately fractured in two. Her inheritance lay shattered on her lap.

'Don't ask questions. Everything's under control. We leave at nine thirty precisely.'

'What time is it now?'

'You've fifteen minutes to prepare.'

'But . . .'

At nine thirty, with the late-summer sun spreading a golden glow over Kensington's plane trees, Emma and Eustace left in the carriage driven by Toby, with Pearl trotting happily.

'I said we were going to have a day out and I meant it. Sybil and Mrs Green were delighted when I told them, and they've packed us lunch and there's a basket for Toby too.'

'But aren't we neglecting Lizzie, Robert and Joe?'

'No, they're going to go rowing on the Serpentine. Today is for us, and for you to get away from all your splendour.'

'I'm going to miss you so much!'

Eustace turned and grinned.

'I'm glad to hear it, Miss Cooper, and it's so nice to see you in white, even with black trimming.'

'I know I shouldn't, but it's still hot, and black draws the heat, especially on picnics.'

'White is quite in order – in some countries white is used for mourning anyway.'

He took her hand, and she turned and smiled her special smile, which encouraged him a great deal. Pearl trotted on, and after about an hour Toby asked if they could stop to give the horse a break and a drink. They found a little cottage café and had coffee, then went on their way.

Hampton Court glowed, its warm red bricks catching every glint of sunlight. The grounds were colourful with dahlias and late summer flowers, and roses smiled at them from bed and standard trees. They strolled to the Diana fountain, its spray making miniature rainbows, and Eustace did everything he possibly could to relax Emma by attracting her attention to nature and the wonders of the palace itself. Like most visitors, they entered and eventually left the maze, and then found a seat on which to have their picnic lunch, and enjoy a beautiful view of the Thames near where, in Henry VIII's time, ceremonial barges were moored.

'You really will come back at half-term, won't you?'

'Of course I will. It's only seven weeks away, you know.'

'I know, but that seems such an age.'

'But you've got Lizzie, and she's a tower of strength.'

'Yes, and Robert'll come and see us at weekends when he's not having to supervise sport or take evening prep at Harrow.'

'So you won't be lonely or too sad, will you, Emma?'

'I'll miss you dreadfully.'

'You said that earlier, and I'll repeat what I said.'

'That you're glad?'

He nodded and grinned. Then he became reflective. 'Dearest, are you any nearer to loving me?'

'I *do* love you. I couldn't feel about any other man what I feel for you.'

'I know that, and I'm grateful. But what I meant was –'

'Am I any nearer to loving you in a more . . . a more physical way?'

'Yes, Emma, that's what I was trying to say.'

'Dear Eustace, I so want to – but it's difficult for me, so very difficult. I know that it should be the most natural thing in the world, when we love someone, to express that love in, er, that way, but I just find the idea somehow . . . well, dirty.'

'Dirty? Emma dearest, no, it's not, it's quite beautiful.'

She shuddered. He instinctively put his arm round her.

'I'm not cold.'

Her tone was tense and nervous. She moved away from him a little.

'But is there a reason why you feel like this? I can understand your natural modesty – that's really charming and a delightful thing in a young woman. But for two people like us, who have grown so close together over such a long period of time . . . Well, Emma, if there is something wrong, perhaps it would be a good thing for us to talk about it, and the sooner the better.'

'Of course I agree with you. But it's so hard for me. You don't know, you can't imagine . . .'

399

'Well, why don't you try and tell me? I'm not easily shocked, you know, and I do have quite a good imagination. Look, if you'd committed murder, even if you'd had a child before we met, I promise faithfully that it could not possibly stand between us. I won't be jealous, or want to stop seeing you or being with you.'

He could not bring himself to go back to Plymouth with this problem keeping them apart. The next few minutes would be difficult for both of them, and he was more than thankful that Sarah had taken him into her confidence, even without telling him all the details.

He wanted to draw Emma out as soon as he had had the conversation with Sarah, but it would have been cruel to put an even greater burden on her at such a time. Even now, five weeks later, he wondered if he was asking too much of her, but he knew that if he succeeded, their relationship would be on a far more settled footing.

She sat bolt upright, biting her lip. 'Do you *really* mean what you say? If only I could believe you!' She looked at him, frowning.

'You *can* believe me, Emma.'

'Eustace, it's *too* awful. You see, you see, I'm not, I'm not . . . I can't go on.' In shame she hid her face with her hands.

'You can and you must, for both our sakes. There's too much at stake, believe me.'

After a while she recovered slightly and confessed, 'I'm not a virgin.'

'My darling girl, as if that matters to me! It might to most men, but that doesn't bother me at all. So what? You had a little encounter when you were young and probably regretted it –'

Between sobs she continued, 'No! It's not as simple as that. It's far, far worse. I've not spoken of it for years. At the time Katy helped me, and so did Sarah.'

'And they understood?'

'Katy was practical and Sarah sympathetic – she suffered more than me.'

'From the same man?'

'Yes.'

'Within the family?' Eustace pretended not to know.

400

'Yes.' Tears rolled down her cheeks.

'Well, you know, that's not all that uncommon. It happens all too often, I believe. Was it your father?'

'No, not him.'

'Who then?' He paused, handing her a clean white handkerchief, then realised what she was implying. 'George?'

Emma nodded.

'My darling, darling girl, how awful! He actually –'

'No, but, well, it hurt, and . . .'

'He took your virginity?'

She nodded.

'Oh, Eustace, what must you think of me? You can't want to touch me now you know that.'

'Dearest, it couldn't possibly make any difference to the way I feel about you. No wonder you loathe him so much. I could kill him!'

'You *really* mean you don't mind – *honestly*?'

'Honestly! I love you so very, very much – as you know.'

She fell quiet for a minute or two, then heaved a deep sigh. Quite suddenly her eyes brightened. She took his hand and slowly moved her face closer to his, her eyes fixed on his. He rather nervously took her in his arms, and for the first time ever she gradually put her arms gently round his neck. He could feel her relax into their embrace. They kissed long and tenderly.

'Wonderful! That makes me very happy! It wasn't so awful, was it?'

She shook her head, surprised and dazed at what was happening to her.

'No, it was lovely,' she replied, slightly smugly.

They kissed again, tenderly and romantically. For the present, that satisfied Eustace. It was so much more than he had experienced over the five years of their relationship.

'You have been so *very* patient. From the little I know of men, I can't imagine anyone else putting up with me in that state for so long. I can't thank you enough for that – but please don't rush me. I know now that we can fulfil our love, though before I told you, I thought that wouldn't be possible. At the same time I didn't want to lose you, I couldn't imagine life without you, even then. Now, well . . .'

401

He was exploding with happiness.

'It can happen, Emma, yes?'

'Yes . . . yes, it can.'

'You've always said that if you married any man it would be me, and that gave me hope. I know you're not ready for marriage yet – but, come to that, neither am I. And we have so much to do over the next year or so. But in due course?'

'Yes, Eustace, in due course.'

'And with that in mind, will you wear this for me?'

Shaking with excitement and nervousness, he produced a little case, and looked down at it rather disconsolately for a moment. 'I expect there are at least a dozen in Lady Alston's jewel case far more valuable, but it's the best I can afford, so . . .'

He took a delightfully pretty sapphire and diamond ring from the box and slipped it on her engagement finger.

They hugged each other, both of them sobbing for sheer joy, not noticing that there were other people around – not even aware of the Thames flowing ever onward to the sea.

It was past six when Emma and Eustace joined Lizzie, Robert and Joe in the drawing room.

'Emma, you look different – really quite flushed. Have you been out in the sun for too long? I do hope you're not feverish.'

'Er, I think we both are, a little.'

'Feverish, Eustace?' Robert enquired.

Eustace gave one of his characteristic grins combined with a series of nods that made his head look like a stringed puppet's.

'We didn't think you'd notice anything.'

Emma started to wave her left hand around in the air, pretending to catch a moth. Lizzie sprang up from the sofa and grabbed it.

'Emma, darling, darling Emma – at last! I can't believe it! What a lovely ring!'

'It's true, Lizzie!' Eustace was nodding even more vigorously.

'Splendid news! Good chap – let me be the first to congratulate you.'

'Thanks, old man, but you're not the first, actually. Toby nearly drove the carriage into the wall when we told him!'

Joe joined in the congratulations.

'Tell me all! Will you marry soon?' Lizzie asked impatiently.

'No, we've decided to wait until the school is open and we know it's running successfully.'

Stratton appeared. 'Miss Emma, Mr Eustace, may we see you a moment?'

'Of course, Stratton – come in.'

He was followed by Mrs Green, Sybil, Toby and Lottie.

Stratton cleared his throat. 'Miss Emma, Mr Eustace, I hope it's no impertinence, but Toby has ... well, we have heard your news, and I speak for all of us when I say that we wish you every happiness, and we look forward to the day when you are joined in holy matrimony.'

'Thank you all so much. Yes, we *are* very happy.'

And, although it was by no means the done thing, Emma got right up and kissed the women members of her staff and, with Eustace, shook hands with the men.

'Champagne all round!'

Chapter Thirty-Five

Emma and Lizzie watched as the carriage taking Eustace and Joe to Paddington for the Plymouth train turned the corner.

'Seven weeks, Emma, before you'll see your Eustace again – he is *your* Eustace now, you know!'

'Yes.'

She shyly looked down at the third finger of her left hand. 'Let's continue our planning in the dining room.'

'Yes, let's. We must work out a library list, then there's the –'

Stratton joined them. 'Excuse me, Miss Emma, but Mr Stillwall is here to see you.'

Lizzie left to continue her planning.

'Good morning, Mr Stillwall. This is a surprise. How nice to see you. Is everything under control?'

'Sit down, Emma, please.'

'What is it? You look so serious! Is something wrong?'

'My dear, I fear that something is indeed wrong.' He hesitated.

'Please tell me, Mr Stillwall.'

'This morning I received a communication from a firm of solicitors – Messrs Gaunt, Murfot and Wilderspin. They seek an injunction to delay probate; they are contesting Lady Alston's will on behalf of a Mr Claude Loxton.'

'Loxton? I don't know the name. Who is he?'

'My dear, you will find this as difficult to believe as I do, but it appears he is Lady Alston's son.'

'But she only ever had one child, Juliet, you know, who –'

'That was what we all thought; but it is not the case. Mr Loxton has, it seems, documentary proof that she was his mother. He was . . .' Mr Stillwall was somewhat embarrassed. 'He was born outside the bonds of matrimony.'

'Illegitimate?'

'Just so. He was adopted very soon after his birth; his adoptive parents are now deceased. He contests the will on the grounds that Lady Alston was not of sound mind when she made it, and that she was unduly influenced to make it in your favour.'

'But surely he cannot succeed? Neither allegation is the truth.'

'As we know, my dear; but those are the grounds, and though he was never recognised by Lady Alston, and all ties between them were severed at birth, the law must take its course. As for the present, until the will is proved, one way or the other, all assets remain in Dr Minton's hands as executor. He is in fact temporarily the "owner" of the estate. When the matter comes to court –'

'To *court*? Will it go to court?'

'I fear so – the Queen's Bench. It's such a large estate.'

'I just can't believe I'm hearing this! It's not possible.'

'My dear, it's a dreadful shock, I know, and I'm so very sorry.' He took her hand and patted it in a fatherly way.

'And will we all have to clear out of this house? Where will we go? Will I have to dismiss Stratton and the others?'

'No, of course not.'

'But Mr Stillwall, what about our plans for the school and the house next door?'

'They will of necessity have to be held in abeyance, I'm afraid.'

'For how long – two or three weeks?'

'No, my dear, the law is slower than that, but it shouldn't take much longer than six months.'

'*Six months*! Oh, Mr Stillwall!' She burst into tears.

He had a lot more to tell her, but felt that she was in no state to hear it. There would be time – too much, probably. And they would have to engage a barrister.

'Lizzie, what *am* I going to do? It's awful!'

'Well, Emma dear, we know that the allegations are false. We know that Lady Alston was of sound mind. Dr Minton

405

will state that on oath, and he is impressive enough to persuade any jury.'

'Yes, of course. But as the executor, might he not appear to be biased?'

'But we all know that you yourself are entirely innocent. It sounds very much like a trumped-up case to me.'

'But if he is her *son* . . . Oh, Lizzie, I find that so dreadfully hard to believe.'

'She must have had a lover.'

'A lover who had to keep in the background. Oh, my goodness! That man at the funeral! Do you think . . .?'

'He looked a lovely, sad man, Emma; in fact –'

'Just the sort of man that Lady Alston . . .'

'Quite. But why weren't they in touch? After all, Lord Alston has been dead for years and years . . .'

'Perhaps he wasn't free. Perhaps he *still* isn't free.'

'You mean, his wife may be alive, and this Mr Loxton doesn't know who his real father was?'

'Well, Lizzie, this has nothing to do with us, and if Lady Alston and her lover wanted it kept a secret, then that's the way it must remain.'

Emma remembered what Lady Alston had said to her after the ball and they agreed that her comments now made sense.

'Meanwhile, what can we do?' Emma was attempting to be as practical as possible.

'When we both feel a little calmer, you must write to Eustace – what a welcome back to Plymouth for him! – and I'll contact Robert and my parents.'

'Lizzie, do feel free to go home.'

'And desert you? Emma, I'd never do that – especially not now! Remember what we said in front of the Albert Memorial that day back in 1894? Friends for life!'

Emma stifled a sob. 'But they must have some kind of proof. Lizzie, you do believe, don't you, that I never *ever* expected to inherit . . . just a little or some memento, but . . .'

'Don't go on, Emma, please. We all know the truth.'

In the difficult weeks that followed, both young women did their best to fill their days productively. Lizzie always had her piano to practise; Emma made new uniforms and casual garments for the three women servants, to cheer them a little, and she collected a few pupils for typing lessons. Time dragged. It was mainly Robert's strength that supported them. He suggested that they should continue to make plans and discuss details, and he did his best to keep them optimistic over the outcome of the case.

Emma lived for the half-term, when Eustace would return to London for a week. It was then that the four took heart; but the uncertainty hung over them.

The period between half-term and Christmas was the worst. Christmas and Emma's birthday made a welcome break; Emma joined the Newcombes, and together with Eustace they celebrated the season at West Hoe Terrace.

While there, Emma went up to Elliot Terrace – now unheated, rather damp, its contents swathed in dust sheets. Its appearance and atmosphere depressed her yet further. The house, like the one in Queen's Gate, was hers – yet it wasn't. The tension affected her health, and she suffered a bad attack of influenza in early January, when they returned to London.

'You are a very clever man, Mr Gaunt. You have my respect and admiration. I know you will do everything in your power.'

'Yes, Lady Cricklewood, you can be sure of that, and so will our barrister. I know just the man.'

'You know, of course, that there will be no dispute about costs. I am a wealthy woman, and a generous one, as you will find.'

'Thank you, thank you, Your Ladyship. I am sure we will win. We have the evidence. Solid evidence, and in writing.'

'In *her* writing, the devious little schemer. Oh yes, we'll finish her off – and dear Claude will benefit. Such a fine young man! Now *he* deserves the money.'

'And from what you've told me, you do too, having done so much for the departed over the years.'

'Well, yes, Mr Gaunt, I do. One thing's certain – *she* doesn't. Little fortune hunter, and sly with it.'

'I am a little concerned about the girl . . .?'

'Leave her to me. I shall school her well.'

1898

Chapter Thirty-Six

It was a typically cold, wet February day. The wind blew and the rain beat horizontally along the street market in the Caledonian Road, north London. It was not yet nine o'clock, and the reluctant stallholders were grumbling about the weather and the unprofitable day ahead of them, as they struggled to set out their wares.

Bertram Webber fastened the remaining buttons on his once smart winter overcoat and pushed his cart from his tiny back yard, four streets away. He had a sore throat and thought he might be starting a bout of flu, but there was the rent to pay.

Coughing and spluttering, he arrived at his pitch and struggled to hoist an old striped awning in position over his stall. It blew down twice before he succeeded. With aching back he lifted several cardboard boxes from the cart onto the stall. Opening one of them, he started to unpack his stock. He stripped the protective newspaper from a blue vase with a crudely painted Arcadian scene on it. He knew the thing like the back of his hand, and placed it, as usual, at the back of the stall, hoping that someone, some day, might be attracted to its bright glaze and not notice a deep crack.

Slowly he continued to unpack his miserable collection of china dogs, brass candlesticks and an assortment of plates. These always sold well, usually to middle-aged wives, who, Bertram assumed, threw them at their erring husbands with singular regularity. These he put right at the front of his stall.

'Mornin', Mr Webber!'

411

'Morning, Alfie. Thanks, here you are.'

He handed the cheerful ten-year-old a halfpenny taken in return for a pile of magazines which he used for wrapping and packing.

After collecting a tin mug of tea from a nearby refreshment stall, all he could do was wait for customers. They didn't come. In boredom he picked up a recent copy of a magazine renowned for society gossip. Skipping the theatre news and fashion notes, his eyes fell on:

> Miss Emma Cooper, who last year inherited the vast Alston estate amounting to over a million pounds, together with two properties and a collection of valuable works of art, is in danger of being disinherited. It appears that the late Lady Alston's will is being contested by a near relative. The case comes before the Queen's Bench on Tuesday 8 March. Solicitors for the plaintiff are Messrs Gaunt, Murfot and Wilderspin.

'So she did inherit.'

His pulse began to race as, he reread the paragraph. His thoughts flew back over the years, when he was on the brink of a successful career and had all but won Emma's heart.

'God! If only I hadn't . . . If only bloody Donkin hadn't interfered.'

He groaned and started to breathe heavily, crushing the magazine in his tense hands. His anger, self-pity and jealousy merged with a need for revenge. To vent his feeling, he grabbed the blue vase and flung it crashing to the ground.

The court was packed. Several members of the press were in evidence, with their nose for a juicy story; an artist from the *Illustrated London News* was present to sketch Mr Loxton and Emma.

It was established that the plaintiff was the illegitimate son of the late Lady Alston, his father unknown; and that the case rested on the allegation that Lady Alston had been unduly influenced and of unsound mind when the will was made.

Lady Cricklewood was called to the witness box. The plaintiff's barrister, Mr Twickell, questioned her.

412

'Lady Cricklewood, it is true, is it not, that you were a very close friend of the deceased?'

'Since our girlhood.'

'And it is the case that you supported Lady Alston at the time of her confinement with her second child, the plaintiff in this case?'

'It is.'

'You had to act with great discretion at the time, in assisting with the arrangements for the adoption?'

'That was so.'

'To turn to later years, you were a regular caller at Lady Alston's establishment during the time when Miss Emma Cooper was in her employ?'

'Indeed, yes.'

'Tell the court your opinion of Miss Cooper?'

'I had most strongly argued against her engagement. She was most unsuitable – not the sort of girl to be given so many advantages. She was of an undesirable background.'

'And her attitude to Lady Alston?'

'She fawned on her; she wormed her way into her affections, and abused her position by begging for favours.'

'Be more specific, if you can.'

'There were many examples of such behaviour. I saw her on one occasion go to Lady Alston's jewel case, remove a very important pearl necklace, and beg my friend to give it to her.'

'And did she?'

'Very unwisely, she did. Miss Cooper was seen wearing the necklace at a ball Lady Alston gave the day before her death. On another occasion I was just outside the drawing room and heard Miss Cooper say to Lady Alston, "When you make me rich – you *will* make me rich, will you not?" – and Lady Alston replied, "Yes, my dear, you know I will."'

A murmur ran through the court. Emma's heart pounded.

'Can you give me other examples, Lady Cricklewood?'

'On another occasion I was in Asprey's, and Miss Cooper was negotiating the sale of an antique bronze statuette. I heard her ask the salesman its value; she was told that it was worth one hundred pounds, and I saw her nod. The next day, when I visited Lady Alston and asked about the sale, she was surprised and said she knew nothing of it. I know

413

her mind was weak, then; she was evidently extremely forget-
ful, and was foolish enough to allow Miss Cooper to deal
with everything, including the salaries of her staff.'

'Miss Cooper paid the staff?'

'Indeed. And she was always appearing in new and expensive clothes – clothes completely unsuitable for a servant,
especially one of her background. One does wonder how she
managed to pay for them.'

'This is *awful*!' Emma whispered. 'I never sold that statue
– it was to be repaired, and Lady Alston . . .'

Mr Stillwall patted her hand.

'My dear, you will have a chance to correct all these
misunderstandings –'

'Silence in court!' called the judge, trying to interrupt Lady
Cricklewood, who was prattling on.

'She was most unsuitable, not used to the normal running
of a decent household. Oh yes, she was clever enough – but
in league with other grasping friends of hers, and –'

'Mr Twickell, could you keep the witness to the matter in
hand? Have you any other relevant questions?'

'No, my lord.'

'Thank you. Mr Cassingham?'

Mr Cassingham, counsel for the defence, cross-questioned.

'Lady Cricklewood, you and Lady Alston were close
friends, but close friends do not always completely agree
about everything.'

'Well, I dare say we didn't always . . . But I gave her good
advice, even if she seldom took it.'

'As in the matter of Miss Cooper's engagement; we have
heard. You can tell the court honestly that you never observed Miss Cooper being in the least helpful to Lady Alston?
You were never present when she treated her employer with
the least kindness and consideration?'

'Well, perhaps just now and again.'

'Just now and again. I see. You are yourself, Lady Cricklewood, a lady of substantial means.'

She nodded her head, and the judge told her to speak up.

'But no doubt would not object should Lady Alston have
chosen to acknowledge your friendship in, shall we say, a
financial sense?'

414

Lady Cricklewood could not deny it.

'I put it to you that your dislike of Miss Cooper is not due in any way to her behaviour, but arises entirely from the fact that you felt that Lady Alston should have repaid you for your assistance at the time of her son's birth, in fact, you felt you were entitled to a good proportion of that estate which was left to Miss Cooper?'

'That is *not* so.'

'I further put it to you that rather than see Miss Cooper benefit from Lady Alston's estate, you went to some lengths to discover Mr Loxton's whereabouts, to acquaint him of his mother's death, and to persuade him to contest her will.'

'That is a disgraceful allegation. I will not stand here to be insulted –'

'Thank you, Lady Alston.'

'But my lord, the insolence of this gentleman cannot go unanswered. I must –'

'Thank you, Lady Cricklewood, you may stand down.'

'Oh, but my lord, I must be allowed –'

'*Thank you*, Lady Cricklewood,' said the judge firmly.

The crowd in the courtroom muttered. Robert and Lizzie gripped each other's hands and smiled at each other. Lady Cricklewood swept majestically from the witness box and returned to her seat next to Loxton, who from time to time glanced at Emma. She thought he looked rather weak, and wondered just how many of his characteristics he had inherited from his mother.

'Call Miss Maisie Greenway.'

Maisie stood nervously in the box, her head bowed and her face hidden by a large hat.

'Speak up, Miss Greenway, so that we can all hear you,' the judge instructed.

'Miss Greenway, during the time you were Lady Alston's companion, did you reach any conclusions about her state of mind?' asked Mr Twickell.

'Oh, yes; I though it most unsound.'

She was encouraged to give examples.

'Well, for instance, when I did the flowers, Lady Alston would come round behind me and drain the water out of the vases; then, when the flowers faded, she would blame me for

415

not filling the vases in the first place. Then there were her clothes. She told me I should press her gowns with a hot iron, and when I did so and accidentally burned the silk and ruined one of them, she scolded me and said she would deduct the cost of the gown from my wages. She accused me of hiding things from her when I tidied her dressing table. Then there were four occasions when I had carefully dusted some pieces of porcelain and Chinese vases; I later saw her quite deliberately smash them, and then she accused me of breaking them. Nobody in their right mind would damage valuable antiques in such a way.'

'Miss Greenway, kindly tell the court what you found in the desk of your sitting room at Queen's Gate.'

'I found a notebook at the back of a drawer.'

Holding up a small black leather-bound book, Mr Twickell asked if it was the one she had found. She agreed.

'That's *my* book, Mr Stillwall,' Emma whispered.

'Miss Greenway, kindly take the book.'

An usher took it to her.

'Would you kindly open it and read what is written on the flyleaf.'

Miss Greenway hesitated.

'Inside the front cover,' Mr Twickell prompted.

'It has her name – that is, "Emma Coopper".'

'And what is written on the opening pages?'

'Well, there are some lists of pieces of clothing, and some notes about how much they cost –'

'Is this strictly relevant, Mr Twickell?' asked the judge.

'If I may have a moment, my lord. Miss Greenway, turn to the third page, if you please, and read what is written there.'

Maisie Greenway ruffled the pages, then read, '"I must do this, I must, I must. I will not rest until I do." Then it says, "Two weeks later", all underlined, and "I am so happy, I am now so very happy. Lady Alston has agreed. Now I can plan for the future."'

'Thank you, Miss Greenway; that will be all.'

Mr Cassingham briefly cross-questioned Maisie, who became more confident by the minute – though, when he asked how long she had been in Lady Alston's employ, she stammered a little as she had to admit that it had been but a few weeks.

'Call Bertram Webber!'

Emma turned pale and felt as if she were about to faint. Gripping Lizzie's hand, she gasped, 'Bertram? But I don't understand, how could *he* know . . .? Oh, Lizzie, *why*?'

Lizzie took smelling salts from her handbag and briefly put them to Emma's nose. 'Emma dear, don't worry. He can't possibly do you any harm, you'll see.' But secretly Lizzie was not convinced.

Bertram, in an old and shiny suit, took the oath.

Mr Twickell started his questioning. He established Bertram's West Country connection with Lady Alston.

'Mr Webber, how well did you know Miss Cooper at the time with which we are dealing?'

'Extremely well. Indeed, at one point I was about to propose marriage. But in the end I decided, with good reason, not to do so.'

'What was your reason?'

'On one occasion she came, uninvited, to my rooms – without a chaperon.'

A murmur of horror ran through the courtroom.

'I decided that such a young woman was not suitable as a fianceé – much less as a wife. Not long afterwards I had to leave Plymouth and return to my uncle, who needed me to work in the head office.'

'The head office of the bank?'

'Precisely so.'

'Mr Webber, you must have been very fond of Miss Cooper to be about to propose to her, was there any other reason why you changed your mind?'

'Well, I discovered she was dishonest. She proved untrustworthy in her financial transactions with Lady Alston. This was evident from her bank statement, which regularly increased, unbeknown to Lady Alston – as I soon discovered upon speaking to her Ladyship about the matter.'

'So Miss Cooper was guilty of embezzlement?'

'Yes, my lord.'

Emma could not believe what she was hearing. She put her hands over her ears and broke down.

Robert whispered to her, 'Emma, we know this is untrue. Please don't get so upset.'

417

'It's been such a shock, Robert, for that wretched Bertram suddenly to come out of the blue like that – blast him!' Lizzie replied. 'Emma dear, do you want to leave? I'm sure you could go outside for a bit.'

The tear-stained Emma said she must stay.

All the while, Lady Cricklewood looked self-satisfied and gave Claude Loxton smug, reassuring smiles.

'Thank you, Mr Webber.'

Smiling, Mr Twickell handed over to Mr Cassingham, who opened his cross-questioning with, 'Mr Webber, what was your position at the South Devon and Dorset Bank at the time in question?'

'I was a junior clerk.'

'A somewhat menial position.'

'But I was promoted to undermanager in November 1894.'

'Ah. And what is your present position at the bank?'

Bertram hesitated.

'I am no longer employed by the bank.'

'And your present employment?'

Bertram hesitated for even longer, then muttered an inaudible reply. The judge told him to speak up.

'I am a street trader in the Caledonian market.'

'A street trader?'

A ripple of laughter ran round the court.

'And from what incident did this strange metamorphosis result?'

Bertram did not reply. Once again, the judge prompted him. Finally, he stuttered, 'I – I have made a mistake, my lord. I no longer wish to participate in this trial.'

'It is rather too late for that, Mr Webber,' said Mr Cassingham. But Bertram was adamant.

'You have placed yourself in a serious position, Mr Webber,' the judge finally told him. 'It is a serious matter that you should have offered to give evidence in an important case, and then declined to do so. I will not enquire for what reason. But you must make amends for the time you have wasted in this court, and the trouble to which you have put both counsels. I commit you for contempt. Officers, remove this witness from the court.'

Bertram, extremely downcast and carefully avoiding Emma's eyes, was led away by two court officials.

418

Emma heaved a huge sigh of relief.

'Well,' said Robert, 'that's put Mr Webber in his place once more. I wish Eustace could have seen that!'

The court adjourned for a short recess.

Outside, in the corridors, Lizzie and Robert went up to Emma.

'I'm so confused; I can just see how they plan to twist the words in my little notebook.'

John Cassingham could not reassure her. 'But what did the entries in your notebook really signify?'

'I can't remember.' Emma's nerves were getting the better of her.

'You really must try, Miss Cooper. The words are certainly capable of being interpreted in a way which could damage our case.'

Emma thought desperately.

'Oh, just a moment – yes, I do remember. Some years ago I wanted to learn to typewrite, and Lady Alston was very much against it . . .'

She told him the story.

'But you did not date the notes?'

'I don't think so, Mr Cassingham.'

The court resumed.

Stratton gave his evidence with wonderful confidence; he had never seen any sign of Lady Alston's mind being weak, nor did he believe that Miss Cooper had ever attempted to influence her in the way suggested. This infuriated Lady Cricklewood, who very audibly remarked to her companion:

'How can this make any difference? No doubt that girl has made it worth his while.'

'Silence in court!' said the judge. But Lady Cricklewood would not be silenced. She stood up.

'I will *not* be silenced! This man is only a servant. What he says is quite untrue. How dare he imply that I am not speaking the truth?'

'Madam, you are in danger of being committed for contempt.'

The unfortunate Mr Twickell finally persuaded his client to sit down.

Emma was next to be called. Mr Twickell did his best to

force her to admit that the entries in her notebook referred to her attempts to persuade Lady Alston to name her in her will; but her obvious horror at the very idea, and her straightforward account of the truth, seemed to Lizzie and Robert to be completely convincing.

'One can never tell,' said Mr Cassingham afterwards. 'The fact that the judge has ordered another adjournment is not hopeful – he clearly feels that he needs time to consider the evidence. On the other hand, it *is* almost one o'clock; his honour may merely want a leisurely lunch.'

Robert and Lizzie took Emma to a nearby restaurant; she drank a brandy and water and was prevailed on to eat a little of a rather heavy meal.

At two thirty the court reassembled. The judge took his seat.

'I have carefully considered the evidence on both sides, and find that it is insufficiently strong to support the plaintiff's case. I therefore find for the defendant. The will remains valid, and I make an order to that effect.'

Chapter Thirty-Seven

Professor Rowe played 'Sheep in Pastures Safe Abiding' as the elegant congregation assembled. The church was abundantly decorated with yellow, gold and cream flowers – chrysanthemums, roses, dahlias, gladioli – adding to the splendour of the old building. The early September sunlight shone through the large stained-glass windows.

Mrs Townsend, wearing a rich shade of blue, produced a tiny lace-trimmed handkerchief and put it to her eyes as she spoke to the bridegroom sitting in the pew in front of her.

'My dearest son, I am so happy for you.'

'Thank you, Mother, but do try not to cry *too* much.'

Mrs Newcombe, in pale green, immediately opposite, smiled across the aisle, knowing full well that it wouldn't be long before she too would have to wipe her eyes.

'Are you sure everything's in order, Eustace?'

'Of course, Robert – and look, here's the ring!'

Joe and Robert's brother-in-law Archie were acting as ushers. With friends and relatives in place, there was little room left in the church for the interested public. A crowd had gathered near the north entrance to the church, taking a short break from their weekend shopping to see the beautiful and well-known bride arrive.

Cries of 'ooh' and 'ah' issued from them as the noon carillon from St Andrew's tower finished playing, and Lizzie, accompanied by her father, in commodore's full dress uniform, stepped down from the open landau drawn by two white horses.

'Nervous?'

'Not a bit, Papa – just happy and excited.'

'That's what I thought you'd say. You see, I know you so well that even on a day like this I can anticipate your reactions!'

'Papa, really!'

A few minutes before, Emma, with little Aimée, aged eight, and Clarence, aged six – Robert's small niece and nephew, who were acting as flower girl and pageboy – had arrived, and were in attendance in the porch. Emma was wearing silk taffeta in an unusual shade of peach, with a large matching hat trimmed with cream and peach roses, and carried a bouquet of the same flowers. The little flower girl's dress matched Emma's: she carried a basket of rose petals, which she would scatter as the bride and groom walked down the aisle after the ceremony. The pageboy wore black velvet breeches and a white silk shirt with a cravat.

'You look truly beautiful, Lizzie. How are you feeling?'

'Wonderful, thanks!'

Emma bent down and rearranged Lizzie's long, dramatic train, which had a wide border of flowers embroidered in gold thread, enhancing the very soft cream of the special silk. She wore a traditional garland of orange blossom on her head. Her bouquet was of cream and pale-peach roses. The whole ensemble added a glow to the rich colour of her shining hair, which was covered by a fine Honiton lace veil, a family heirloom from Caroline's grandmother.

'Ready, darling?'

'Yes, Papa.'

The Very Venerable Archdeacon Wilkinson, who had known Lizzie all her life, smiled warmly and gave Professor Rowe the signal. The congregation stood as the procession, led by the Archdeacon, started to make its way down the long aisle to the majestic Wedding March of Wagner.

At the altar steps the bride and her father were joined by the groom and the best man. Lizzie passed her bouquet and gloves to Emma, who helped her lift the veil to uncover her face.

'Dearly beloved . . .'

The ceremony over, there was an excited gathering in the vestry. Eustace and Emma stood back holding hands and looking on.

'It'll be our turn next.'

'I know, Eustace. The months will slip by. But I'm as happy today as I know I will be on our wedding day – aren't you?'

He looked quizzically at her. 'Well, almost, I suppose; of course I'm happy for Lizzie and Robert. Doesn't he look splendid?'

His tone was somewhat disconsolate. Robert did look splendid, his muscular frame shown off to full advantage in his elegant morning suit; even the way he moved expressed his vital energy.

'Very handsome – but no better than you will, when our turn comes.'

They queued up to kiss the bride and groom and to add their congratulations; then it was time for Robert and Lizzie to walk down the aisle as man and wife.

Outside, the bells were ringing, and the crowd had at least doubled in size. They cheered and waved as the guests left the church and entered the waiting carriages to take them up to West Hoe Terrace, where a huge marquee had been erected on the lawn.

It was a perfect setting for the reception. Mrs Newcombe's prayers had been answered. She knew how unreliable the weather could be; why, it might have been blowing a force-eight gale. Instead, the day was quite perfect, and the hundred and fifty guests were able to enjoy the garden and the magnificent view of the mouth of the Tamar and the whole sweep of the bay.

'Very proud of you, my dear, very proud. Clever young chap, that Robert of yours, eh, what? Openin' a school, eh?'

'Yes, Grandpapa, with our friends in London.'

'That friend of yours – she's rich, yes? *How* rich? Don't want you left in the lurch, especially when the family comes along. Wouldn't do – wouldn't do at all, y'know.'

'She's very, very rich, Grandpapa.'

'Inherited it, eh? Well, good, good. But your Robert – clever chap, too. Pity he's not in the service, though. But perhaps you and he can do something about that later on, eh, m'girl? A few cadets, hey?'

'Yes, Grandpapa.'

'Father, come and sit down over here.'

The Commodore guided the ancient retired admiral to a shady corner, while Lizzie and Robert went on to greet Lizzie's old school friends: Elsie, who was now the wife of a wealthy local businessman, Milly and Annie, both of whom were engaged to be married.

Aunts and uncles from both families filed past, along with a liberal smattering of high-ranking naval officers and their wives.

Aggie was sobbing her heart out.

'To think of it, my little Lizzie married! You take care of her, won't you, Mr Robert? She's very special, you know.'

'I know she is. You can trust me, Aggie.'

She gave him such a hearty kiss that she knocked her new smart hat sideways. Then it was Laura's turn.

'Lizzie, you do look lovely, and Emma too. What a beautiful service!'

The bride went on to greet her music teacher.

'Professor, thank you for your lovely music. It contributed so much to the service, and we'll never forget it, will we, darling?'

'No, dear professor – and we'll want you to come and give some special lessons when we have enough pupils. Will you promise to do that?'

'I'd like to very much. I always enjoy visiting London – so much good music, you know!'

At last they had greeted all their guests, and the master of ceremonies asked them to be seated for the wedding breakfast. The guests sat at large, round tables, while the long top table set out for the family, best man and bridesmaid, and the Archdeacon and his wife, stretched the length of one side of the marquee.

It was a truly elegant meal – one that befitted a grand occasion and matched the glorious weather and surroundings. Chilled consommé was followed by poached salmon and salads, then came grouse in a rich sauce with game chips and small potatoes and beans, lemon sorbet, and a savory of anchovy and french toast. For dessert, fruit salad and a charlotte russe, and finally a selection of cheeses, coffee and petit fours. The wines complemented the courses and were of a quality to match the beautifully prepared food.

'Darling, isn't it a simply wonderful atmosphere? What a lot of different people we know! There are our friends from Cambridge, my school friends, then all these naval types and your parents and your farming uncles and aunts! I was afraid they mightn't mix very well.'

'It's your papa's champagne that did it. We had to greet so many that by the time they all sat down they'd lost their inhibitions. Now look at old uncle Cedric over there – see how he's flirting with Annie Midgely.'

Robert was quite right – his elderly farming uncle was casting off years by the minute.

'Enjoying yourself, dearest? You're looking a bit sad.'

'Sorry, Eustace – no, I'm perfectly happy. I overheard Lizzie say what a mix of people there are here and how well they are getting on, and I was wondering how things'll work out on our big day.'

'I'll tell you: beautifully. But the speeches are about to start. I've got mine at the ready.'

'Good luck!'

'Ladies and gentlemen, pray silence for the father of the bride.'

Mrs Newcombe looked proudly up at her Peter as he rose to address the assembled company. As he opened his mouth to speak, the air was filled with squawking gulls having a fierce argument on the rocks a few yards away. He waited with feigned impatience for the birds to resolve their differences.

'Well now, what was I going to say before I was so rudely interrupted? Ah, yes – this is one of the proudest days of my life. Caroline and I, like most parents, have always been proud of our two children – with a very special pride. We've had the odd battle along the way, but we recognise in Lizzie an ardent determination; she has an inner strength and enthusiasm for life which will, I know, Robert, take quite a lot of coping with. 'We've coped – just about – and now it's your turn. I wish you luck, son-in-law!

'The toast is: the happy couple!'

Robert replied and Eustace read the telegrams. As he stood up, Lizzie and Emma exchanged glances. Thinking of the shy, stammering Eustace of several years ago they both knew they could take the credit for his transformation.

There were messages from Sarah, the Mistress and staff of Girton, Mr Stratton and all at Queen's Gate, the elder Coopers and Jim and Katy.

The cake, cut with a naval sword, was delicious. The bride and groom mingled with the guests, at times together, at others separately. Lizzie was enjoying wearing her gown and now had the loop inside the centre of the back of the train around her wrist, to prevent it being dragged over the hessian-covered grass or getting it caught on one of the many chairs. Still the sun shone through the pale-lemon and white striped marquee, which gently flapped in the breeze, causing the hanging baskets of flowers slightly to sway.

As the sun began to turn towards the west, it was time for Lizzie and Robert to change. Emma and Aggie joined the bride in her old bedroom.

'Now you be careful, my girl, don't you let him hurt you – you know what I mean.'

Lizzie smiled down at her old nurse. 'Yes, Aggie, I do know what you mean, but I love him very much!'

'Well, that's all that matters – you go on loving him, and don't work too hard. Miss Emma, you make sure she don't work too hard, eh?'

'Of course, Aggie. We always look after each other, you know.'

'And Aggie, you look after Mama, won't you?'

'You can rely on me and Laura – we does our best, especially when the master's away.'

By now Lizzie was dressed in pale blue – a lightweight woollen suit with matching hat trimmed with small blue flowers and feathers. She carried a Louis Vuitton handbag which was a present from Robert and matched their luggage.

'I expect the carriage will be down in the street by now. Go and look, Emma.'

Emma went to the landing on the first floor, which had a window overlooking the street side of the house.

'No, Lizzie, it's not there.'

'Oh, dear! It's getting late – we mustn't miss the train. Go and tell Joe, perhaps he can do something about it.'

Emma rushed back to the marquee to find Joe.

'Don't worry, Emma, everything's under control – wait and see. Go and tell Lizzie it'll be here soon.'

She did that, and shortly afterwards Lizzie made her reappearance, joined by Robert, who was now wearing a pale-grey suit.

Smiling proudly, he said, 'Well, you look simply gorgeous! I don't have long to wait now, do I?'

'It's a long train ride to Southampton, darling, and you're not thinking . . .'

Lizzie knew how passionate Robert was, and for a moment had a ghastly thought.

'I think I'll restrain myself on the train – if you can.'

By now they were surrounded by guests throwing rose petals and confetti. They were repeatedly kissed and hugged by their respective parents and closest relatives and friends.

'I know you're going to make our Robert a good wife, dear Lizzie. Do come and stay with us when you get back from your honeymoon, won't you? The hotel will be less busy come the end of September, and I'm sure the Duke and Duchess will want to met you at Burghley House.'

'I will, Mother, bless you – and thank you so much for Robert.'

She turned to Robert and said, 'Darling, we really must go. The train leaves in twenty minutes.'

She turned to re-enter the house through the drawing room, meaning to go out of the front door, where she expected the carriage to be waiting for them.

'No, Lizzie, not that way!'

'What do you mean? We *have* to go this way!'

'No, we don't – it's *this* way.'

Followed by the guests, all cheering and wishing them luck, he took his perplexed bride by the hand and guided her towards a gate that divided the far end of the garden from the rocky coastline. He then led the puzzled Lizzie towards a little boat. She attracted her father's attention.

'Papa, what is going on? I don't understand.'

'Well, we have a little surprise for you. You're not going on the train to Southampton.'

A rating saluted him smartly from the little boat.

'Step aboard, please, Mrs Townsend,' said her father mysteriously.

Lizzie was not best pleased.

'What, on *that*?'

'Yes, on that. I have a message from the Admiral of the Port. He presents his compliments to Mr and Mrs Townsend and informs them that his yacht is at their disposal. It will carry them across the channel to Rostoff, where they will, late tomorrow afternoon, join the express train for Nice.'

'The Admiral's yacht! All to ourselves! And to be waited on like the Admiral and his lady! Papa, Robert – why didn't you tell me? I thought we were going on the packet steamer to Le Havre!'

'No, Lizzie, it's their wedding present to you. Look, there she is, moored out in the sound!'

Her mother and Joe leaned over the wall with everyone else and waved goodbye as the couple boarded the little motorboat, and with all the efficiency of the Royal Navy the sailor steered it towards the impressive yacht, where, at long last, after the most exciting day of their lives, Lizzie and Robert would be quite alone on the calm September sea, heading towards France.

The sizeable cabin was lined throughout in highly polished mahogany. It had an impeccable double bed covered in a white linen bedspread embroidered with a large anchor. The fittings were of gleaming brass, and a narrow door led into a bathroom. At the other end of the cabin, towards the stern of the ships was another door through which was a day cabin complete with a dining table and chairs, a comfortable sofa and easy chairs. In one corner there was a small rolltop desk. All the portholes were furnished with white net curtains.

The yacht had both sails and an engine and plenty of deck area on which to walk, talk and sit enjoying the sea air. Lizzie found it quite familiar, having had several outings over the years with the Admiral, his wife and friends, and her family. However, she'd never seen the night cabin before, and now as they entered, following a rating who placed their luggage on a stand specially made for cases, she looked around in amazement. With great discretion, the rating asked them when they would like to have dinner.

'I'm not at all hungry, thank you. I honestly don't think we'll want dinner tonight, will we, Robert?'

'Madam, just ring if you would like some light food at any time this evening, or perhaps some coffee or drinks.' He left quickly and soundlessly.

'He called me madam! He called me madam!' she cried gleefully.

'Well, of course he did! You're a married woman now.' Laughing, Robert caught her in his arms.

As they enjoyed the first private kiss of their marriage, the anchor was weighed and they felt the gentle rocking of the yacht as she set sail for the open sea outside the breakwater.

'We don't want your nice new suit to get crumpled, do we?'

Robert, finding the first button of her jacket, undid it as he spoke, and soon was helping Lizzie out of it. Before he could release her from her blouse, she replied;

'And that new suit of yours – well, it might get rather creased, you know, and it is a very warm evening.'

'Very.'

They kissed – long, hard and passionately. He held her firmly and securely in his strong arms. Relieved of their outer clothes, soon blouse, shirt and his tie were scattered on the floor. Hurriedly Lizzie sat up to untie her corset and remove her chemise. Also naked to the waist, Robert laid her on the bed and sat looking down at her. The rays of the evening sun streamed through the portholes and made a lovely pattern of rich, pink shadows on her beautifully formed breasts, enhancing their shape and the colour of her alert nipples.

'You are so beautiful! So very, very beautiful.'

He found the fastening to her skirt and loosened it, along with her lace-trimmed petticoat and drawers. She slipped out of all the garments, leaving her with only her white silk stockings supported by garters. At this point she wanted to embrace and touch more of his body and found her way around his remaining clothes. He was soon taking considerable pleasure in removing her stockings, and within a few

429

minutes they were together on the bed, clothed only in the deepening red rays of the setting sun.

'We've waited so long for this moment. I'm glad we did. Oh, I know we've come near to it on several occasions, but to be with you now, and in such a setting, is so wonderful.'

All the while she was speaking, she was exploring his body, caressing his glorious torso, the prominent muscles of his strong thighs, stroking his rich brown wavy hair, while he softly ran his hands over her long, loose hair, her arms, her lower stomach. They were both passionately sexually aroused and yet relaxed in the knowledge that they were free to express their love in their own way, that they could take the full pleasure of each other's bodies. Robert realised that he had the benefit of being married to a wife who was uninhibited, not shy, modest or frightened.

With increasing excitement she caressed him, all the while enjoying the feeling that he with subtlety and a gentle touch gave her as he pressed his fingers deeper and deeper within her. They continually kissed and were reluctant to part their tongues; but from time to time when they did she would gently bite his shoulder. As they moved erotically against each other, she felt an intense excitement deep within her, and let out a little cry.

'You know what's happened?'

'Yes, of course.'

'Now for the real thing!'

He entered her. The sheer bliss of the feeling, the magic of the moment, their increasing passion and the quickening of their rhythmic movements carried them on to sensations new and exciting. Very quickly, in spite of Robert trying to pace himself, he climaxed, and their passion subsided.

After a while, she quietly said, 'That was wonderful, darling. Better than I expected it to be. But I felt I wanted just a bit more.'

'Oh, you did, did you, Mrs Townsend? Well, we'll have to see what we can do about it then, won't we? I must admit to more than just a certain amount of enjoyment, myself!'

His eyes gleamed and the warmth of his satisfaction and sense of humour gave Lizzie, then as always, that very special inner glow experienced only when the immense love of two people is fully reciprocated.

430

He turned to lie on his back, and she responded by turning over and lying on top of him, giving her the new experience of looking down on him while their bodies shared the close contact. She took his head in her hands and, opening his mouth with her tongue, lead him into another long kiss, and soon they had turned over and he had once more entered her. Their pleasure mounted more gradually, more slowly. Their pace quickened as her breathing deepened, until together jointly they experienced orgasm, which left them panting, hot and perspiring, but with utter satisfaction and contentment.

For a quite a while they lay side by side looking at each other, realising that they were at one in this area of their lives as in all others. There was no need to speak. Their eyes said everything. Robert took her in his arms, and with her head resting on his firm chest she soon fell asleep. Having enjoyed her body perfume and the scent of her hair, he too drifted off into the delicious sleep that accompanies contentment and blissful happiness.

'Just look at that blue!'

Lizzie awoke to the Mediterranean sky, seen through the slats of the louvred shutters. Rolling out of bed, she pulled on her negligée and rushed over to open them. She was greeted by dazzling light and the brilliant sun shining through the fronds of the palm trees, which lined the Promenade des Anglais.

'Darling, it's quite unbelievable! I thought we had bright sunshine in Plymouth, but it's nothing like this. No wonder so many painters come to the south of France!'

She surveyed the wide bay. Robert stood behind her, holding her gently around the waist.

'Haven't I brought my beautiful wife to a beautiful place?'

'Unbelievably beautiful – beautiful husband.'

And as she spoke she turned to embrace him with a lingering good-morning kiss.

The restaurant of the fashionable Negresco Hotel was buzzing with a mixture of languages spoken by wealthy tourists from all over the world. As they were shown to their table by the head waiter, they were struck by the smell of coffee, fresh croissants and brioches.

Grinning, Robert asked his wife, 'What would you like to do today? I've discovered that the hotel has its own stretch of private beach, so I think we should take advantage of it, to get over our journey – and other things.'

'Things?' Lizzie looked coyly over her huge, flat coffee cup. 'What *can* you mean, Mr Townsend?'

'I beg to inform Mrs Townsend that "things" are forming quite an important part of her *vacances*.'

'I do agree with you, Mr Townsend. I have a very daring bathing costume tucked away in my case. I think it may need airing. But I must buy a sun hat – my skin could suffer if I don't. And of course Mr Townsend will be swimming.'

'And so will Mrs Townsend.'

'Oh, Robert, no, I never swim! Besides –'

'No "besides"! I'm definitely going to teach you to swim – and that'll be something you can boast about for ever more. How many young women learn to swim on their honeymoon? How many, come to that, learn –'

'Robert, please!'

She took a second croissant, broke it and untidily filled it with unsalted French butter and apricot confiture.

'Isn't that delicious? Another new experience for you.'

Lizzie's mouth was too full to speak.

She had been in the sea before, many times, but was amazed at just how warm it was – quite different from the beaches of Devon or Cornwall. Soon she was relaxing in the heavenly water, enjoying the clear sky. By the end of the day she had swum four strokes.

After dinner she stood on the balcony, looking at the view. The bay faced south – exactly in the same direction as the one she'd known all her life. Here was far greater style and elegance, here the rich and famous mingled, many in this same hotel.

Their room was large, decoratively furnished in shades of blue and pink with no lack of gilding. The curtains were of very light cotton net with a wide border. They floated in the gentle breeze of the evening.

The adjoining bathroom was a sheer delight, with an enormous bath and gold-plated taps. The walls and floor were of the purest white marble.

Lizzie could not have appreciated this more. She felt she was in some sort of fairy tale.

'And the prince married the princess, and they lived happily ever after.'

'What did you say?'

Robert looked up from a map of the area he was studying to plan trips into the countryside.

'Oh, nothing, really.'

Chapter Thirty-Eight

For a moment or two they stood looking up at their house, the very house in Edwardes Square that the Newcombes had lived in the previous summer.

'Weren't we fortunate that it came up for sale? I love it so much, don't you?'

'Yes, darling, and we're going to be so very happy here, aren't we?'

With that Robert unlocked the door, and before Lizzie knew what was happening he had lifted her in his arms and carried her over the threshold. Her laughter was so infectious that he almost dropped her.

'Robert, it's so exciting!'

Hand in hand, they stood slightly awe-stricken at the sight of all their new furniture. The pieces blended beautifully with the easy proportions of the late-Georgian rooms, the long, slim windows giving plenty of light and showing to advantage the autumn tints just beginning to appear on the trees both in the square's communal garden and their own private patch at the back of the house.

'Welcome home, sir, madam!'

Their cook-general, engaged before they had left for their wedding, appeared from the basement kitchen.

'It's so good to see you – and you looking so well! Did you have a nice wedding and honeymoon?'

'Yes, Mrs Wilson, thank you. We'll show you the photographs when Mama sends them.'

'Sir, madam, I've got a nice swiss roll and some little sandwiches ready. I expect you'd like them right away? And a nice cup of English tea! Shall I bring it in here, or up to the drawing room?'

'Nice' was a word Mrs Wilson was very fond of using.

They were standing in the front room, which was to be their study and library.

'Up in the drawing room, I think, Mrs Wilson.'

'Oh, madam – before I forgets, you'll have a lovely surprise when you goes into the drawing room. You did say that was where you wanted it?'

'Emma's wedding present!'

Lizzie, even more excited, rushed upstairs, quickly followed by Robert. There it was: her first very own piano – a boudoir grand by her favourite maker, Bechstein. Black and shining, it seemed to smile up at Lizzie as she opened the lid to reveal the keyboard. She sat at the stool and rattled off some arpeggios. The sound was quite magical, the touch exactly right for her.

'Darling, I think we'll just have to drop in and see Emma this evening, to thank her again. It really is a superb instrument.'

They had furnished their house completely, with Robert's parents giving them enough money to buy all their bedroom and drawing-room furniture, while friends and relatives had given other presents which, when unpacked, would fill linen, glass and china cupboards. Lizzie's parents had given them a large canteen of heavy silver cutlery for twelve covers, which stood in the dining room, the cabinet itself a pleasing piece of furniture which matched sideboard, chairs and table. Joe's present had been a very fine desk which he had designed especially for their study, showing a strong influence of the new trends in architecture and furniture set by Lutyens and Mackintosh. This, along with most of their more important gifts, had arrived at number 18 a few days before they had left for Plymouth and their wedding.

All her life, Lizzie had hated rooms that felt cluttered and claustrophobic. She heartily disliked the heavily carved furniture, the numerous ornaments and the dark colours that were in vogue. Like Emma, she thoroughly approved of William Morris's designs, and had chosen several for the wallpapers and curtains in her home.

435

She couldn't wait to unpack their souvenirs: they had purchased from a small gallery a set of six charcoal sketches of ballet dancers by an artist called Degas and one quite large painting of a plate of apples by another artist, Cézanne. All the paintings were very modern, bright and colourful. The colours and the vivacity of the pictures would always remind them of their honeymoon. However, they expected that a great many people would not like or attempt to understand the pictures, which even to them looked rather unfinished. Still, they had only cost them a few francs.

'It was so beautiful, Emma – I can't describe the light! Palm trees everywhere.'

'Yes, Eustace says the light is quite remarkable once one is south of the Alps. Well, perhaps I'll see for myself, one of these days.'

'You know, I really cannot thank you enough for the piano. What a present, Emma darling!'

'You'll get pleasure from it all your life, Lizzie, and that's exactly how it should be.'

'Tell us, how are the new tenants settling in? Do they like living in Elliot Terrace?'

'Yes, Robert, they love it. And you know how concerned I was about taking all those paintings and the choicest pieces of furniture out of the house before they rented it? Well, they didn't mind at all. You see, they lost nearly everything in the fire in Cornwall, so they want to start collecting again, and now they have the space. They're devoted to Beauty, who is well and looking marvellous – I think she recognised me, and I know she's very happy with them.'

'That's good, I'd hate to think of that lovely mare not being well cared for. Now, what did they say about not having the piano?'

'They didn't mind at all, Lizzie. Neither they nor their children play; they completely understood when I explained that we'd taken it to put in our gymnasium here. The building has come on a little more since you've been away: the contractors are on time, and I must say that they're doing splendidly – in spite of that dreadful six months' delay. They're working so hard and there seems to be no reason why we shouldn't open the schools on time as we planned. Now, Robert, while you're back at Harrow, Lizzie and I can work on timetables, then over the Christmas holiday the four of us can finalise plans.'

'I didn't have a chance to tell you and Eustace, but at the wedding we spoke to Lucy. She's not at all happy at her school, so I'm glad to say she's very keen to join us for the start of our first term. Heavens! It's only seven months away!'

'That's excellent, Lizzie. I'm afraid I didn't talk to her properly – we were introduced, but that was all.'

'Darling, it's late, and I have to go to school tomorrow. We must go. And thank you again and again for being our chief bridesmaid, Emma – it was lovely.'

'My dear, I couldn't have enjoyed it more. And thank you again for that lovely cross and chain – a beautiful bridesmaid's present.'

Robert and Lizzie took a cab back to Edwardes Square to spend their first night in their new home.

Emma got up from her typing table and sorted out her copy for the entry in the seventh edition of *Hampton's Scholastic Directory for London and the Provinces*.

She reread the script to make sure there were no errors, and gave a little sigh of satisfaction as she clipped the batches of impeccable typing together. Having written Eustace a loving letter a little earlier, she placed that and his copy of the proposed advertisement in a large envelope and addressed it to his house in Plymouth.

1899

Chapter Thirty-Nine

'Don't our Charlie-boy look lovely? So smart and grown-up! To think he'll have a really good education! Why, soon his spelling'll be better than mine.'

'We've a lot to thank Emma for, love.'

'Yes, Jim, I know. Even that first fiver – our reward all them years ago – helped us such a lot when we was setting up home, didn't it? And now look at 'im there in his uniform.'

Charlie-boy was strutting around the kitchen in his grey Norfolk jacket and matching breeches and his smart pale-blue school cap with 'C.H.' on it.

'And then from September there'll be little Tabitha in 'er pink and white stripy blouse and grey skirt and her cape. We have to buy it up at Whiteley's, you know – just like our Charlie-boy's uniform.'

Katy and Jim were finishing their tea when there was a knock on their front door. Mrs Cook came down from her bedroom and answered.

'Emma! Lovely to see you, come in.'

'Thanks for everything, Emma,' said Jim as he gave her a friendly hug.

'Now, Emma, are you sure – quite sure?'

'Of course, Katy. It's the least I can do. You and Jim mean so much to me.'

'Well, look – what we'll do from now on is send you a big basket of fruit and a large bunch of flowers every week, to contribute something. After all, those school fees would be quite a burden for us.'

'I want the best for Charlie and Tabitha just as much as you. I'm going in to see Mama now, so I'll see you in the morning for a moment.'

'Let's drink to tomorrow,' suggested Robert, holding up his champagne flute.

'Tomorrow!' repeated Eustace, Lizzie, Lucy and Emma.

'And I have another toast,' said Emma. 'To Lucy – may she be happy with us!'

'Thank you all so much. I do feel very much at home, and I know I'm going to be happy working here in London with you. It really is wonderful to be joining you. Lizzie and I were such good friends at Girton, but I was afraid we'd hardly ever see one another again.'

'Our pupil count has risen steadily since the publication of the directory, but it leaped up after the item in the *Illustrated London News*,' Emma announced.

'The one that started "We hear that the heiress Miss Emma Cooper has invested part of the Alston fortune upon inaugurating two schools in Kensington . . ."' said Robert teasingly.

Emma blushed, as she always did when confronted with any gossip or publicity. 'Then,' she went on, 'we had two more enrolments after the piece in the church magazine, and a surprising ten after the article in the *Kensington Post*. Our total now is, for the boys' school, forty-one, and for the girls' school, thirty-eight.'

'Seventy-nine altogether. That's excellent, Emma,' replied Robert.

'Yes. I thought we might have had to struggle on with only thirty or forty. During the coming term we'll take some more advertising, and by September we should begin to flourish. Now, let's walk around the two schools and make quite certain everything's in place and ready for tomorrow, then I suggest you have an easy and relaxing afternoon. It'll be the last, for some time, apart from weekends.'

They went first to the gymnasium, its beautifully polished floor marked out for badminton, strong parallel bars along one wall, a collection of climbing ropes and vaulting horses. The high windows let in the spring sunshine, but had very thick black curtains on pulleys, so that the room could be

442

blacked out for lantern shows or performances. The stage could be hidden by the proscenium curtains. Lizzie looked round, proud of her brother's work. With the new electric lighting which had been installed, the room could make an almost professionally equipped theatre. But for now, on the stage stood a row of light oak chairs in the Mackintosh style, with high, tapering backs and plain, slim legs. There was a matching lectern on which was placed a large old family Bible that had belonged to Lady Alston.

They walked on through the large and small classrooms of both houses. There was a dormitory in each, for four pupils, should the time come when these would be needed; and in each house was a quiet room. It had been decided that on one day every week a priest and a rabbi should visit to give the Catholic and Jewish children their special instruction.

One of their real joys was the library, where, apart from the reference books, each of them could pick from the shelves a favourite childhood book – *Treasure Island, The Three Musketeers, Little Women, Jo's Boys, Alice in Wonderland, Little Lord Fauntleroy* . . .

After the others had left, Emma and Eustace were sitting, relaxed, in the drawing room. Suddenly she got up and made for the door.

'I must just go and check my list of –'

Eustace grabbed her by the hand.

'Don't, dearest! Please don't. I'm sure you've double-checked every possible list at least three times. Lizzie and Robert will be at home relaxing by now, so let's just stay as we are – no more work tonight.'

Slightly reluctantly she allowed herself to be guided back to the sofa and sit at his side. He put his arm round her and they kissed tenderly and gently.

'Would it be too much for you to begin to think about when we might be married? By tomorrow the schools will actually exist, and we agreed that –'

'Yes, we did agree that, didn't we?' replied Emma, smiling softly.

'I think we should p-perhaps see the schools running smoothly into their second term before the wedding, even if I am so very eager to have you as my wife. What do you think?'

'That would be fair to Lizzie, Robert and Lucy. Of course, it doesn't really make any difference whether we're married or not as far as the schools are concerned, and I think that I, like Lizzie, will continue to be Miss where the business is concerned – if you don't mind.'

'Whatever you say, Emma.'

'However, my dear, I do have a little idea. You know my birthday is –'

'January the first.'

'Precisely – January the first.'

'Oh, Emma, *yes*! Do let's be married on the first day of the new century.'

They kissed again.

'Do we keep this to ourselves or tell the others?'

'Secret for a while. Let's get the schools really under way first.'

The following morning pupils arrived in their smart uniforms, some on foot, some in carriages, some in cabs. Two fourteen-year-old boys turned up on bicycles from the other side of Hyde Park, and some younger children came with nannies wheeling younger brothers and sisters in bassinets. Proudest of all was Katy with Charlie-boy, who grinned more frequently and more happily than any other child in the school.

One small boy was sick immediately after finishing his rice pudding and milk at midday dinner, but otherwise the first school day passed almost without hitch. At three thirty the boys left, and were well out of the way by four o'clock when the girls were due to depart. Two groups had already used the gymnasium; Robert took the boys while Lizzie, donning her old cycling skirt, took the girls. Maths, history, French and German, English composition and grammar, geography, including a study of the large globe in the library, and auditions for the choir all added up to a full and rewarding first day of term in the new establishments.

As spring turned to summer, Robert built up a middle-school cricket eleven. He put out a challenge to the team he had been coaching the previous year at Harrow, and the boys travelled over to the huge public school on a Saturday in

June to beat the Harrow eleven by eighteen runs. Creswell House was jubilant. Emma had four fourteen-year-old girls who were interested in sewing; she enjoyed teaching them the rudiments of embroidery and dressmaking, and it was to this little group that she gave the task of arranging the huge bunch of flowers that arrived every Monday morning. Lucy worked hard in the mathematics classroom, and was quite appalled at the low standard of a group of children who had come from a school with a very poor reputation. Her kindness and patience won their shattered confidence (they had expected to be hit with a ruler every time they gave an incorrect answer).

Altogether the four teachers found it necessary to go in for a great deal of confidence-building, and they soon saw a marked difference in both boys and girls, who, instead of arriving at school every morning with bowed heads and looking glum, were now cheerful and greeted their teachers with big smiles. Physically, many of them were getting healthier. The regular sessions in the gymnasium were popular, though some of the girls were nervous and had to be treated gently, and for those who were terrified of climbing ropes or exercising on the parallel bars, Lizzie had a special session of musical drill which she took from the piano.

There were always essays to be marked, lessons to be set. One of Lizzie's greatest joys was teaching the tiniest boys and girls some of the lovely poems she had been prevented from teaching at Miss Creeber's Academy.

Eustace studied syllabi for the national and the civil-service entrance examinations. He was already consulting with two sets of parents who were especially keen for their sons to enter university, and weighing up the possibilities of their taking examinations that would give them exemption from the entrance examinations to Cambridge.

All four took groups of pupils on nature walks, outings to Richmond Park and Regent's Park Zoo; and at the end of the summer term they decided to give a reception for the parents of both schools, during which Lizzie and Eustace would give a short recital.

Three days later they broke up for the long summer holiday. That evening the five of them ate together in Emma's dining room. Their mood was jubilant. They had completed their first term.

Eustace took Emma's hand.

'We have something to tell you.'

Lizzie glanced at Robert with raised eyebrows.

'Tell all!' the happily married couple exclaimed in unison, while Lucy looked on with interest and amusement.

'Emma and I are going to be married on –'

'Yes?' the three of them interrupted together.

'We are going to be married on . . .' Eustace took a deep breath, 'The first of January – Emma's birthday, and the first day of the new century.'

'Wonderful! At last, at last!'

Chapter Forty

'Now, Sarah, have we thought of everything?'

'I think so, Emma. We'll just be calm and straightforward. They should be delighted. Is George coming?'

'Yes – and I don't damn well care any more. I now feel exactly the same way as you do!'

'Marvellous. That's really the spirit – at last!'

'But please, please, don't make me laugh.'

'Well, it'll be easy, provided we don't look at that gap where we pulled his tooth!'

'Oh, shut up, do! We must be at our most ladylike – not difficult for you and me, is it?'

'Of course not – we are ladies!'

'Mrs Cooper, I have the carriage ready for you.'

'Thank you, my man. Just a moment.'

She closed the front door on Toby and, changing from her smart voice, yelled, 'Will, George – are you ready? Em's sent the carriage.'

'Can't tie this bloody tie, Ma. Don't know why I've got to bother, anyway. We're only going to see me sisters, after all.'

'Now you be on your best behaviour, my son.'

'Quite right, Susan. George, let me see your nails. Are they clean?'

'Never dirty, Pa, never dirty – well, not after work.'

'Come on then, I'll lock up. Pity it's wet, I would have like to ride in the open carriage.'

'So that everyone could see you,' his wife murmured.

*

447

'Miss Emma, Mr and Mrs Cooper and Mr George Cooper are here.'

'Thank you, Stratton. Show them up, please. We'll have high tea in the dining room at five o'clock.'

The sisters giggled to each other.

Will nervously gripped the brim of his Sunday bowler and turned it in his hands. Stratton put out his hand for it. He hesitated, but eventually understood; his hand visibly shook as he gave the hat to the butler. Mrs Cooper looked up, awe-stricken, at the stucco ceiling and huge chandelier, while George at once threw himself untidily down into a large, comfortable armchair.

'My Gawd, my Gawd, I know I've been in 'ere before, but is all this really yours, Emma?'

'Well, if you ask *me*, I wouldn't want it as a gift.'

'No one *is* asking you, George!' said both sisters at once.

'Come on, Ma – sit down, dear.'

'Will here be all right?'

'Of course – and Pa?'

Will Cooper sat down heavily.

'Eustace'll be here in a minute; we'll not get down to real business till he comes.'

'What's it got to do with 'im? He's not family – we don't want 'im poking his nose into our affairs.'

'Pa, he is *going* to be family, and I want him here.'

'I still say it's none of his business.'

'Well, if that's how you feel, you can leave now, this minute!'

She frowned and pointed to the door. It was the first time Emma had spoken so sharply to her father. He grunted and settled himself more comfortably into his chair, his arms defiantly crossed.

'So what have you got to tell us, eh? I'm not wasting my Saturday afternoon for nothing – and neither is your brother here.'

'Quite right, Pa – I could be at the match.'

'We won't waste any more of your precious time than is absolutely necessary – especially yours, George, knowing how busy you always are.'

'Fair enough, fair enough, sweet sister.'

448

Sarah narrowed her eyes as she glared at him. 'Now –' She was interrupted by Eustace's entrance.

'Sorry I'm a bit late, Emma; hello, Sarah. Hatchard's lost the book I'd ordered. I have to have it for school next week. What a pretty blouse, Mrs Cooper – it suits you so well!'

'Thank you, Eustace. It's so nice when people notices what you've got on!'

Eustace settled himself next to Emma, knowing that everything he said, every little gesture he made, would be marked by his future father- and brother-in-law, who both regarded him with considerable suspicion.

'Now,' Sarah repeated, 'as I was about to say, we – Emma and I – have been very fortunate in life, and we feel we want to thank you for our education, along with everything else you've done for us over the years.'

'That's nice – isn't it, Will?'

'Um, yes. Good Christian attitude. Honour thy father and thy mother . . .'

The sisters looked at each other. Sarah, glancing down at her notes, took a breath to continue.

'But I don't want charity – no charity.'

'We're not giving you charity. It's not charity when you're family. However, may I go on?'

Her father nodded and folded his arms even more tightly.

'Ma, you've worked so very hard all these years – and so have you, Pa – and we want to make life a little easier for you.'

'Fair enough – what say you, George?'

'Seems sensible, Pa. What's in it for me?'

'We'll come to *you* later,' Emma replied briefly, taking Eustace's hand as she spoke.

'Ma, Pa – Emma and I together have purchased the cottage from the landlord, so from now on you'll have no rent to pay, and we'll cover all repairs and redecoration as necessary. So, Ma, think about what alterations you'd like – a better kitchen sink, a new range – anything like that we'll willingly provide.'

'Oh, dear girls, thank you, thank you!'

'Now, Pa, Emma and I want to put it to you that you might – you just might – be beginning to feel ready to retire from the business.'

'That's all very well – but how would we live?'

'Let's take this one step at a time, Pa. In theory, would you, if you could, *like* to retire?'

'Will, haven't you had enough of boots and shoes?'

'Business is business, Susan. But well, in theory, yes, I suppose so. But what –'

'Well, we've invested a sum of money that will give you and Ma a pension for life.'

'You can't do that.'

'We already have. It's ready and waiting to be sent to you on the first of every month.'

'Will, what generous daughters we have! You must surely be pleased! You know how bad you was last winter. Why, only this morning when it was foggy I heard you coughing again.'

He knew his wife was right.

'Pa, how can you refuse such an offer, don't be daft!'

'It's all very well for you, George. I don't want to be seen loafing about on money paid out by my daughters –'

'Always afraid of being seen, Pa?' asked Sarah shrewdly, and stared him out. He shifted uneasily in his seat, knowing full well what she was hinting at.

'Take our offer, for Ma's sake as much as your own,' Emma encouraged.

'Here, Pa, they've not said yet how much they'll be paying you.'

'With no rent to pay, we thought that twenty pounds a month would be reasonable.'

'It's a fortune! Oh, Will, please say yes. I could even afford to have a little kitchen maid to help with the housework. Oh, please, Will!'

He grunted and hesitated. 'But if I don't have the shop, what would I do with meself all day?'

'Well, I certainly don't want you under my feet all day long. But you could have an allotment, Will – that'd be nice, real nice. I likes fresh vegetables, spuds in particular.'

'Well, we've thought of that too.'

'Oh, you pair, you 'ave been busy, interfering with other people's lives.'

'Shut up, George!'

'Pa, Sarah and I went to see Mr Woodstock. We wondered if there was anything more you could do for the church, knowing what a devoted Christian you are.'

'What did he say?'

'More than we expected. We thought that perhaps he might be able to give you some little job like keeping the flowerbeds tidy. But, well, it's not been announced yet, but that old verger –'

'Mr Cross?'

'Yes, Mr Cross is retiring after Christmas, and the vicar wants to see you to talk about your having the job.'

'Me? Verger of St Matthew's? Me the verger?'

'How about that then, Will? Just fancy!'

'It's all meant, it's all meant. It's the work of the good Lord! Praise be!' Will Cooper lifted up both arms to heaven as he spoke.

Turning now directly to George, Sarah went on, 'George, when Pa retires, we assume that you'll be in sole charge of the business, and take all the profits. But for added security, Emma and I now own the lease of the shop, so you can work there rent-free. We also assume that you may want to employ someone to help you. Whether you want to train an apprentice or engage someone experienced is up to you, but – again to help you – we are willing to pay his wages for the first year, while you and he settle down to work together.

'Now, because we've purchased the lease, should you at any time want to settle down and get married we will open up, repair and redecorate the derelict flat above the shop, so that you can live there if you want to.'

'Didn't think you had it in you to be so generous to me. Be me own boss, eh? Not bad. I do have a lot to thank my little sisters for. Why are you doing this for me, eh? Little pretty sisters? That's what I want to know?'

'Because they are good and generous and bear no grudge against you – that's why,' said Eustace, giving George a steely stare. 'You be thankful. It's far more than you'll ever deserve from them, and you know it.'

'Oh, yeah? And what the 'ell do you know about it, stranger? It's got nothin' to do with you!'

'George, shut up, and don't speak to Eustace like that. We

451

all know that what he says is the truth. So *shut up* and be grateful.'

While Sarah was speaking, Emma gripped Eustace's hand and quietly asked him not to say any more.

'I had to stick up for the two of you,' he whispered. 'Don't worry, I only want to put him in his place.'

Mrs Cooper, horrified, sat silent looking at her husband, who knew precisely what the exchanges were really about. And she knew far more than he realised. The atmosphere was tense.

After collecting his thoughts, George came to the conclusion that he'd come out of the situation extremely well. After all, his sisters could have simply ignored him and done nothing for him.

'Well now, to be me own boss, yes, I likes that idea, and later on . . . yes, I might well want that upstairs flat too, you never know. And I will need help in the shop once Pa goes. Not bad, but what about a few hundred as well? You two could afford it, couldn't you?'

'Yes, we could – but no, not yet. When we see that you're a good boy we might think again,' Emma retorted.

'Yes. Just watch it, George. But that's been really easy for you since we've been out of the way, hasn't it?'

'Bitch!'

'Maybe, but a generous one, don't you think?' Sarah snapped back.

Mrs Cooper interrupted, 'Dear girls, thank you so much! What a lovely life we'll have! Your father verger, and me, well, quite the lady. Now I'll be able to concentrate on my knitting and sewing and making cakes. Lovely!'

Emma rang for Sybil and asked her to serve the high tea.

Chapter Forty-One

For six years, since the dramatic events of 1893, George had become more and more smug. He had got away with manslaughter and also almost killed his mother, but largely he had put this out of his mind, together with the unhappiness he had caused Sarah and Emma, which had so nearly ruined their lives. On the rare occasions when his thoughts of the day of the fire drifted back into his mind, it was only his moment of glory in the eyes of the neighbours that occurred to him – after all, he really had done what he could to save Aunty Tyrrell! He was greatly comforted by the fact that he had been the hero of the hour.

The awful shared secret between father and son was never mentioned, but both knew that if all was revealed, not only would George be charged with Aunty Tyrrell's death but the whole family would have to retreat to some dreary corner of the East End – and that would prematurely send Mrs Cooper to her grave. George was by now confident that his father would not denounce him. Will Cooper would never be able to face his customers and, more importantly, the vicar and congregation of St Matthew's if he took that step.

On returning home after the family meeting at Queen's Gate, his parents were jubilant, and George realised that life was going to get better and better for him too. He would now be his own boss and he was in a position to start looking for a lively wife.

But when he went to bed that night, Eustace's face came before his eyes. He remembered his future brother-in-law's expression – hard, steely and deeply penetrating. His words

453

stuck in his mind and would not go away. George could not go to sleep.

'Because they are good and generous and bear no grudge against you – that's why. You be thankful. It's far more than you deserve from them, *and you know it!*'

Eustace's statement gripped him time and time again. He tossed and turned in his bed. After about an hour he got up, crept downstairs and found the bottle of brandy that his mother kept for emergencies. He took several big swigs and went into the parlour, slumping into Will Cooper's exclusive armchair.

Still the words crowded his mind. Still, in spite of the brandy, they would not go away. Deep in thought and not looking at what he was doing, he put the brandy bottle down on a small table between the fireplace and the armchair. As he did so, he sent a little vase of dried lavender crashing to the floor. The sound made him jump and he bent over to pick up the fragments. He soon recognised it. It was white porclain and the gold lettering on it said, 'A present from Brighton for a dear friend.' The words struck him another blow. This souvenir had been given to his mother by Aunty Tyrrell, who had once been there on a day trip.

He gripped the arms of the chair so his knuckles turned white. Suddenly he relived the sight of Aunty Tyrrell at the window, and heard her agonised cries as her arms sunk into the flames.

'Dear God,' he muttered slowly to himself, 'what did I do, what *did* I do? I killed her, I killed her! I shouldn't be here. I should have been hanged years ago. Eustace was right. I've known all along, but wouldn't face up to it. I've been a fine fellow? Awful – bloody awful, wicked and sinful! Pa was right. I am wicked and sinful and the Devil has been in me all these years. Dear God, help me, please help me!'

For the first time since his dreadful wrongdoings, George Cooper burst into tears.

From the next morning, Mrs Cooper recognised a considerable change in her son. She put it down to his good fortune. He was kinder and more thoughtful towards her. In the past, when he had carried coals or washed the occasional pile of dishes, she knew that it was because he wanted something,

454

but now she began to feel that he wasn't simply being helpful for his own ends. She didn't say anything to Will, but quietly thanked God for the change in her son's attitude. Two days after the family meeting she saw him, on leaving the Havelock Arms, give a coin to a poor scrap of a boy. He might have been simply feeling generous, but when he smiled warmly at the child and patted him on the head she began to think otherwise.

On most days George spent most of his dinner hour in the church, sometimes just sitting, sometimes kneeling in prayer, asking forgiveness and trying to work out ways to atone for his sins. He came to the conclusion that he could never wipe his wrongdoings from his conscience, simply because he could unburden to no one except his father, and that would only raise old sores, so he had to rely on actions to show that he really had changed.

It was a cold day a week later. Blythe Road was wet. The fog permeated every crack of window and door. In a mistaken attempt to cheer up the gloomy atmosphere and the worried, apprehensive shoppers, a man creaked his barrel organ into action to accompany his small daughter, who yelled out in a thick cockney accent,

> 'The Boers have got my daddy,
>   My soldier dad,
> I don't like to hear my mammy sigh,
> I don't like to hear my mammy cry,
> I'm going in a big ship across the raging sea,
> I'm going to fight the Boers,
> And bring my daddy back to me!'

'Look at it, Boss – fog's that thick you can't see hand in front of your face. Grim, that's what I calls it. And look at 'im out there – don't know why 'ee's making his little girl sing that. After all, there's her dad right there beside her.'

Sam picked up another handful of nails and placed them between his lips. After hammering them expertly into the new sole of a boy's hobnailed boot, he went on, 'Yes, grim – as grim as the bloody war itself. Mind you, boss, I wouldn't say no to a bit of excitement, kill a few of them Boers and

455

see a bit of the world at the same time. If I was young and 'ealthy like you, I'd join up and go and give General Buller a hand to help relieve poor old Baden-Powell and his lot, locked in like they are at Mafeking.'

George was silent, listening to what his new assistant was saying. He had never thought about it before. Perhaps he should enlist. The war was awful. Could he do something to help alleviate the suffering, and play his part in restoring peace and happiness once more? He knew he could take bold action when needed, so maybe he was the right type for the front line.

'Sam, if I did – could you cope 'ere till I got back?'

'Yes, boss – if you'd let me bring in my youngest to learn the trade and help out.'

George decided he would see if he could join the army. He picked up the next pair of boots to be repaired and set to work with renewed vigour, promising himself that next day he'd walk over to the Princess Beatrice Barracks in Hammersmith Road to find out more.

Later that morning he went into the back of the shop to make himself a cup of tea. He packed his pipe with Embassy mixture and lit it, put his feet up on an old stool, and drifted off into dreams of battle in which he performed great feats of heroism.

''Scuse me, boss.'

'Eh? What? Yes, Sam?'

'Mary Ann's out there, wants to see you. All of a muck she is, in a dreadful state.'

George had had his eye on Mary Ann for some time. He liked her buxom figure, which in summer she did little to disguise as it bulged out over the top of her corsets. He liked her dark hair and her passionate look. She'd given him the glad eye once or twice, but he had done nothing about it, because he knew her husband, a huge man well over six foot tall, who worked as a ganger on the railway and drank heavily.

He went into the shop to find her in tears, her face smudged and dirty, her hands covered in mud.

'George, 'elp me, please! I don' know what to do.'

'What can I do for you then? You looks upset?'

456

'George, it's me husband.'

'What about 'im?'

'Dead – killed!'

She leaned over the counter, allowing her thin, worn-out shawl to reveal plenty of cleavage. She looked up at George. He was shocked at her news, but at the same time thought that just possibly she wasn't as upset as she pretended to be.

'Why don't you tell me how it happened?'

'It was a sleeper. He and his mates was unloading it from the wagon. One chap let go. He was crushed to death.'

'When?'

'Yesterday. Don' know what I've been doing since then – just walking around. Then me sister found me and she's making the arrangements for, you know . . .'

'The funeral?'

She nodded.

'So what do you want me for?' George had a sudden vision of being asked to be a bearer, and shuddered at the thought.

'Brown shoes. I only got brown shoes. Look, I tried to turn 'em black with the black lead what I uses for the grate, but see, it didn't work. I can't wear brown shoes to me old man's funeral, can I, George?'

She leaned nearer him as she spoke, and looked right into his eyes. She passed the down-at-heel shoes over the counter, and made sure she touched his hand as she did so.

'No, you can't wear brown shoes to yer old man's funeral. I'll dye 'em for you right away. Come in the back and get warm, and dry out your shawl and hair. I'll put on the oil stove.'

'Where will you live now?' he asked when he had settled her by the stove. 'You got a railway cottage, yes?'

'I'll be turned out. Glad we got no kids!'

'So – no home, eh?'

'No. I'll 'ave to get a job sewing shirts.'

'Maybe, maybe not. ''Ere you are. Don' touch 'em more than necessary till the morning. By then they'll be dry. I'll look in on you tomorrow dinner time, see if I can help in any way.'

'Thanks, George.' She lowered her eyes, smiled through her tear-stained face and left the shop.

'Poor bitch, boss! What a tragedy! What'll she do now? Mind you, I, didn't think she was as upset as all that.'

'No, neither did I. He had a nasty temper, 'orrible. I've seen him wallop her more than once outside the pub of a Saturday night, when she was trying to stop him spending all his money on drink.'

'Not a bad-looking woman. She'd need a lot of smartening up, mind – a lot. Full of fleas, that hair of hers, like as not, and her clothes – you could shoot peas through 'em.'

'Quite right, Sam, quite right. But she's 'ealthy.'

'Yes, like you, boss!' Sam paused. 'So it's the army for you, is it?'

'Yes, it's the army for me. I'll sort out poor Mary Ann, – make sure she's not on the streets, then do what I can to put them Boers in their place!'

'Goodbye, Your Highness. Yes, I'll look forward to that. Thank you so much.'

Sarah replaced the telephone on its hook and gave it to her maid to return to a nearby table.

'His Highness *again*, mademoiselle?'

'Yes, Lisette. He'll be calling this evening at eleven thirty.'

'I'll see that there's a cold chicken ready for him.'

'Thank you, Lisette. Has the morning post arrived?'

'Yes, mademoiselle.'

Lisette replaced Sarah's breakfast tray with a small silver salver on which was a smudgy, crumpled envelope. Her name and address were written in aggressive handwriting. She opened it and read:

3 Craven Cottages,
Hammersmith.
22 November 1899

Dear Sister Sarah,

When we had our family meeting and you and Em made arrangements for Ma and Pa, you said if I worked hard, that if ever I wanted to have a home of my own, you and she would repair the rooms up over the shop. Well, I have met the lady of my choice. So please, Sarah, can I keep you and Em to your promise?

458

For some time now I have known a lady who I like and who I know thinks well of me, but I have not been able to get to know her well as she is married. Well, was married until a few days ago when her husband (a bad man who drank a lot) was killed at work. She will be turned out of her little railway cottage, and it is for her I would like you to restore the rooms. She got no children. Then when the war is over I will marry her. If you and Em agree, I can go off to war, knowing that this lady won't be on the streets. I feel I must enlist as I want to do my bit in the struggle. I hope you understand, and thanking you in anticipation,

Your loving brother,
George

Sarah rolled over in her huge bed.
'George going off to war! never thought he had it in him! And wanting to look after a lady – it's quite extraordinary, what can she be like? I must telephone Emma.'
She slipped out of bed to reach for the telephone.
'Emma darling, is that you? Do hope I'm not disturbing any lessons.'
'No, Sarah, it's the midmorning break. I was about to telephone you!'
'Why – have you had one too?'
'From George? Yes. What does yours say?'
The letters were identical.
'Shall we do it for him, Emma?'
'Oh, I think so. Perhaps enlisting will be the making of him – and I must say the fact that he wants to care for his lady shows some unexpected chivalry, don't you think?'
'Yes, it does. He could turn out to be quite brave, you know. So let's help him all we can. Goodbye, sweetest – love to my brother-in-law to be!'
'Thank you, Sarah. It won't be long now!'
'You and George racing to the altar?'
'What a simply ghastly thought! But after the war, presumably. Another family wedding! Goodbye.'

'Now you're settled and comfortable, aren't you? And I've

got Sam, who's so good at his work, running the business. So I've come to a decision.'

'What is it, my son?'

'I'm going to enlist, Pa. I wants to do me bit for the war. I'm strong and healthy, and I'm proud of me country!'

'All that way away, George! Are you sure?'

'Yes, Ma, I'm sure. And I've got some other news for you too.'

George went on to tell his parents about his plans for Mary Ann.

'Well, you're doing the right thing by her. Between you, when the war's over, you'll make a good couple. You must bring her round for tea before you goes off to war.'

'Thanks, Ma! And Pa, while I'm away, if you can just look in on Sam and his little 'un that'll be joining him, and do the books for me . . .'

'Willingly, George, willingly.'

They heard Emma's voice calling them as she and Eustace opened the front door. They had come to discuss the wedding. Emma thought there might be difficulties with her father, and she was not wrong.

'I don't care what you say, I'm givin' you away *and* you'll be married in *our* church. I want none of yer airs and graces, my girl!'

'Well, Pa, I'm very sorry, but I live in the parish of St Mary Abbot's and have done for several years, so it'll have to be there.'

'Shan't give you away, then.'

'Will, how could you be so cruel? And when you think what your daughters have done for you!'

'If she's married up there to Kensington, I'll never be able to show my face in church again – *me* the verger, and my own daughter not married in my church!'

'Emma's quite right, you know, sir; she does live in that parish. Would the Reverend Woodstock come and assist our Reverend Glyn, do you think?'

Eustace was trying to be helpful in the delicate situation.

Will Cooper grunted.

'Pa, what if the Reverend Woodstock gave Eustace and our close friends communion – would you like that?'

460

'I suppose that would be somethin', but it just don't seem right to me.'

'Come outside, Emma, we'll talk in the kitchen while I gets the tea.'

Emma followed her mother into the newly redecorated kitchen.

'Look, Em, it's like this: yer Pa is afraid of going up to that big church and meeting your smart friends, for all the swanking he'll be doing about it to everyone. That's really why he wants you married down here, because he'll be on familiar ground, so to speak.'

'Of course you're right. But Ma, Eustace and I are keeping the wedding as quiet as possible. There'll be very few people in the church. If we didn't, it would be all over the *Illustrated London News* and other papers, and the pupils and their parents would fill the church. Besides, it's on a day when everyone will be celebrating – or doing their best to celebrate, when the news from the Transvaal gets worse daily. So we'll want to keep things quiet.'

'Come on, then, let's get back and see what he says. Will you bring the teapot?'

During their absence, Eustace had been trying to persuade his future father-in-law to change his mind.

'Sir, I'm sure no one in your parish will mind at all, and if the Reverend Woodstock –'

'No, I won't do it!'

'Very well, Pa, there is someone else who I know will be really delighted to give me away.'

'Who's that then, eh? That old sailor chap – 'im with the gold braid? I suppose he'd be grand enough for you!'

'I'm sure he'd be glad to, but I was thinking of someone else. So don't bother to come to my wedding, I'll not send a carriage for you.'

'Whaaat!' His anger and confusion were mounting.

'It'll be quite all right, we can do without you. Ma can come up and stay at Queen's Gate the night before, and you can stay here with George. Come on, Eustace, let's go! 'Bye, Ma, I'll see you again next week and we'll go through the arrangements!'

'Hang on, hang on! Who'll give you away?'

461

'Someone who loves me like a daughter: Dr Minton.'

'Oh, I know 'im, that nice old man with the bald head and red face! Yes, Will, you know him –'

Will Cooper folded his arms and took a deep breath. 'Right, Emma, I'll do it.'

'And so I should hope, Will. Whatever next!'

'And we'll arrange for Mr Woodstock to take the short communion service.'

Mrs Cooper was making mince pies in preparation for a family party on Christmas Day. The following day, George would be leaving home.

'Yes, Ma, I'll be joining number six battalion of the Princess Beatrice. I'm going to have a few weeks' training here, then it's off to the Veld.'

'Oh, George, I do admire you!' she said, scraping the bottom of the mincemeat jar. 'I dunno, somehow you've changed a lot in this week or two. It all goes back to the way you said sorry when you broke Aunty T's vase . . . Somethin' happened to you, hasn't it, my boy?'

'Yes, Ma, and I thanks the good Lord that it has.'

Mrs Cooper noted the tone of voice George had used when he said 'good Lord'. It had totally lost the mocking ring it usually had when he made reference to the One Above.

He got up.

'Ma, you've no mincemeat left – I'll go down the shop and get you another jar.'

'No! Don't bother, George . . .'

But George had already rushed out of the house and was making his way to Blythe Road and the grocer's shop.

It was bitterly cold and the road was thick with ice. George moved briskly, not having bothered to put on a muffler or overcoat. Suddenly he heard the nervous clatter of a horse's hooves coming up behind him. It was the milkman and his cart. For some reason his horse had taken fright and was attempting to bolt, but was slipping on the ice. The worried milkman was without success trying to gain control of the horse, but the more he slipped, the more anxious the animal became. Just as they drew level with George, he saw a

462

woman step off the path further down the road. The horse bolted on and George realised that unless the creature fell, the woman would be knocked down. He ran towards her and managed to pull her back onto the pavement, but then he slipped . . .

'Where am I?'

George opened his eyes to see a stranger looking down at him. As his eyes focused, he saw she was a nurse.

'You're in Hammersmith Hospital, Mr Cooper. You've had an accident, but you'll be fine.'

'What happened? I can't remember. How did I get here and . . .?'

'Don't worry, your parents know. They'll be along soon to see you.'

'Yes, I remember now, it was the horse. Is he all right?'

'Never mind about the horse! You were very brave. I'm afraid it's your arm . . . it's been hurt. Look, there's someone waiting to see you. She's been waiting ever since we brought you in – I think she wants to thank you.'

'Oh, did I help her?'

'Yes, you saved her life.'

'Nice of her to wait. Anyone would have done the same.'

'Nevertheless, she wants to see you. Shall I send her in?'

'Well, yes, I suppose so, thanks.'

George turned in his bed and made to arrange the top sheet with his left hand. A searing pain ran through it to the fingertips. Somehow he could not grip the sheet. He turned his head, expecting to see bandages, plaster or a sling, but it was his shoulder that was wrapped up. The awful truth dawned on him: his arm had been amputated.

Almost immediately the woman, who was wearing a heavy cloak with a hood, came up to his bed.

'George, George, I can't thank you enough! You saved my life.'

It was Katy.

It was the happiest party in the house since Lady Alston's death. Emma and Eustace, joined by Lizzie, Robert and Lucy, had also invited the Commodore and Mrs Newcombe

463

and Joe, who had spent Christmas in Edwardes Square with their daughter and son-in-law. After a wonderful dinner, they were moving back into the front drawing room to see in the new century and the wedding day.

'We are among the zeroists,' Eustace announced.

'But surely there can't be that many people who think that the new century doesn't begin until 1901, can there?' asked Robert.

'Quite a few, I think. I'm just wondering if the whole argument has sprung up because these are such dark days. The war will be over by next year this time, people say, and it'll be a more suitable time to celebrate.'

'There's a lot of truth in that. So many of the children's fathers who are in the army have been drafted to South Africa,' replied Lizzie.

'And of course the navy's involved in the transportation of thousands of troops.'

'Yes, Peter, and I'm so glad that you're safely on shore.'

'But we mustn't let this dreadful war mar Emma and Eustace's day, must we, everyone? Let's give them a musical tribute!' suggested Robert, and struck up 'For they are jolly good fellows!'

'Now, remember, when it's midnight Emma simply must disappear, for Eustace mustn't see her on her wedding day,' said Mrs Newcombe.

'No, *I'll* disappear.'

'How gallant of you, dearest.'

It was almost midnight.

'The end of the old century and the beginning of the new. To 1900!'

'To 1900! And "Should auld acquaintance be forgot . . ."'

Eustace kissed Emma lightly on her cheek and slipped away to spend his last night in his Earl's Court Road lodgings.

1900

Chapter Forty-Two

Emma had chosen silver-grey velvet for her wedding outfit. The coatee, cut off at the waistline and fastened up just below the bust with three silver buttons, was turned back to show white satin reveres and a white frilled blouse covered in Limerick lace. The skirt was plain but had a long train, and the pile of the velvet reflected the light of the candles which lit the church that was still ablaze with Christmas decorations. Sarah attended, in dark-pink velvet.

As Emma and the ecstatic Eustace exchanged vows, Robert turned around and looked lovingly at Lizzie. He noticed she was terribly pale.

'Are you feeling quite well, darling?'

She smiled weakly. 'Yes, I think so.'

But she had to sit down, and felt dreadful about doing so at such a beautiful moment for her dearest friend.

Katy and Jim, who were just behind them, exchanged knowing glances.

I've wanted to bring you here for years, dearest. It's been my dream, and now it's come true at last.'

They were on the balcony of the Palace Hotel, Lucerne, having just arrived. Deep snow covered the scene and sparkled in the winter sunshine, while the bright blue sky made the water of the lake take on a magical glow, reflecting the lakeside buildings which stood out against the mountain peaks beyond.

Eustace wrapped Emma's sable cloak more tightly around her, then went on, 'But I want to complete that dream very soon.'

'So do I.' Her short reply was full of warmth.

Momentarily, Eustace slipped back into their suite and reappeared with a small box.

'This is for you.'

He opened the box to reveal Lady Alston's engagement ring.

In sheer amazement she replied, 'But I don't understand! How did you get hold of that? I thought it was in the bank with all the rest of Lady Alston's jewellery.'

While she was speaking, he unfolded a piece of paper.

'Read this, dearest.'

It was a short note in Lady Alston's handwriting.

Dear Eustace,

As you know, it was because of this ring fate decreed that Emma and I should meet. I know one day you and she will marry, and when you have vowed to be together until death do you part, please give it to her with all my love, and in the knowledge that you both have my eternal blessing from beyond the grave.

Rosamund Alston.

He slipped it on the third finger of her right hand.

For a while words failed Emma. Momentarily, the feel of the ring took her back to that day in Kensington Gardens, all those years ago . . .

'Wasn't that typical of her? I'm sure she's watching over us, aren't you?'

He nodded.

Silently they left the balcony, the beautiful view of the lake and the mountains, and walked, arms entwined, into the bedroom.

Afterword

From the *Western Daily Mercury* and *The Times* on Friday 17 August 1900:

> *Birth.* TOWNSEND. On Wednesday August 15th. To Robert and Elizabeth (*née* Newcombe), at Queen Charlotte's Hospital, London, God's gift of a daughter, Alice Caroline.